Ireland
snapshots in time

Tellwell Talent
www.tellwell.ca

ISBN
978-1-77302-673-2 (Paperback)
978-1-77302-671-8 (eBook)

Ireland

snapshots in time

susan k. kehoe

acknowledgements

To family and friends who have given much time and encouragement for my first venture into authorship, I am truly grateful. My struggles with tenses, commas and the process of learning to put a story together has culminated in this creation. So, to Melody, Kathy, Clara, Allison, Roberta and Brenda – many thanks. I owe you more than you know.

To my editor Sahar and the design team at Tellwell, I really appreciate the work you have done turning my story into a more professional creation. For me the process has been a challenging one but extremely constructive. I find it very difficult to be objective about my own work, so kudos to you all.

To Ireland itself, it is an inspiration and the basis for these stories.

preface

In 2014, a friend asked me to accompany her on a bus trip
to Ireland. I happily accepted, having no idea of the impact
that trip would have. For twelve days, we traversed the
whole circle of this green lush yet distinctly rocky island
starting and ending in Dublin. The scenery was breath-
taking, and I took over 700 pictures. As a Canadian, the
concept of the history that could be tracked back to the
500s was mind boggling. I came home with a deep desire
to discover more about a country that had the ability to
overwhelm my senses. I was hooked.

This tiny island has somehow managed to maintain
a unique culture despite invaders, famines, and wars, a
culture that thrives to this day. I had many questions.
What does it mean to be Celtic and what impact did that
culture have on the people? Why had the change from
paganism to Christianity been such a relatively easy one?
Was there a historical basis for the myths, legends and

superstitions that permeated the culture? What caused the rift between the Protestants and the Catholics?

The Irish emigrated around the world and took their culture with them. The numbers of deaths from famine, wars and poverty is mind numbing. The talents in literature, music and business are astounding.

In order to put things in perspective, I chose to research the topics that interested me and to create short stories of ordinary people at various points in history, snapshots of village life and the extraordinary ability of these people to persevere under impossible conditions. The attached map shows our bus route and gives an approximation of where the stories took place on that magical green island.

The historical characters and places are real but my main characters are purely fictional.

Enjoy!

Susan Kehoe

Republic of Ireland

Portrush

LONDONDERRY

BELFAST

SLIGO

Castlebar

Clifden

DUBLIN
(Baile Átha Cliath)

LIMERICK
(LUIMNEACH)

Cashel

Waterford

Dingle

KILLARNEY

CORCAIGH
(CORK)

table of contents

the bus

Dublin, Ireland, Present day

Melissa and Pete were in the lineup for the bus. She felt a little jetlagged from the previous evening's Toronto to Dublin flight.

"Pete, I can't believe we're really here. This last week's been crazy trying to get ready for this trip, what with doing extra shifts because they were short staffed again at the hospital. Now we're here and I want to see everything. It really is as green as they say," she said getting glimpses of the countryside north of the Dublin airport.

"One of these days, you're going to learn to say no," he said.

The driver, a tall heavyset man with fading red hair, wore a blue shirt, navy blue vest and pants. He was checking off names on his clipboard. *Like Noah checking pairs onto the Ark.* Accents of all kinds – American, British and Irish – swirled around her but the American one

1

predominated. *A better comparison might be the tower of Babel*. Finally, it was their turn.

"Pete and Melissa Chandler," Pete said as the man checked their tickets. The name tag on his shirt read "John".

"Welcome" said John and ushered them aboard.

As they moved down the aisle they found seats and stashed their carry-ons.

"I still think we should have rented a car," Pete said.

"Listen, you old curmudgeon. We wouldn't even know what we were looking at, would we? And I don't want to spend all my time worrying about what side of the road we're supposed to be on," Melissa replied.

Having checked off the last name on his list, the bus driver got on. He was big enough to fill the stairwell and had a dour expression, looking with something akin to resignation at his passenger list. He completed the head count and as he started to speak the hubbub subsided.

"My name's John and I'm your driver-cum-tour guide for the trip around this blessed green island. Just a few rules – please leave your suitcases outside your room door by six a.m. We're on a tight schedule for seeing places. If we're booked for ten o'clock and we're late, then we don't get in – period. Be on time. There's a list on the bus every day with the seating arrangement. This changes daily, so check your seat numbers. That way everyone gets a chance at a good view. Now, we're off to Russborough House."

A middle-aged man at the front said to him in a loud voice: "I don't want to sit beside them on this trip. Can you fix your list?" he said, glaring at the Pakistani couple across from him.

"Oh Lord, just what we need, a bigot" Melissa muttered.

Pete just raised an eyebrow and grunted. Melissa watched John to see how he'd handle it.

She saw him lean over the man. "The seating arrangement is set for today, but I'll take that into consideration tomorrow."

Bigot man nodded. John went back to the driver's seat, acknowledging the Pakistanis with a brief nod.

Without further ado, John started the bus and with consummate skill, maneuvered the behemoth around the tight corners of the narrow streets, missing buildings by mere inches. Morning rush hour traffic was heavy but kept moving at speed unabated around the circles. Government buildings were ornate and columned while churches were large and Gothic. No time for photos, but the views were tantalizing.

"I'm glad I'm not driving in this traffic," Pete conceded.

After twenty minutes of bumper-to-bumper, they were passing through the suburbs with their rows of two-storey brick row houses with minute front gardens bursting with geraniums, roses and begonias and enclosed with waist high wrought iron fencing. Old and new seemed to blend seamlessly, with views of the river and bridges, some with wrought iron railings, some stone while others were very modern. *Lots of green space.* Melissa aimed her Nikon to capture colourful Georgian doorways and flanking stairs.

She looked at the couple in the adjacent seat. They were both elderly but the man seemed to be the caregiver for the frailer woman.

Having the aisle seat, Pete introduced both himself and Melissa.

The man replied with a broad Texan drawl: "I'm Brian and this is my wife, Mary. We're from Dallas."

The men talked and Melissa eavesdropped while continuing to gaze at the passing landscape. *So, Brian's an Army veteran and Mary's been a stay-at-home mum.*

She heard him say "She was born here. We met at the end of the war. We've been back many times, but she's not been well, so this might be our last trip."

Pete talked about his construction business back in Toronto.

Melissa looked at the woman and indeed she didn't look well. She appeared to be in her eighties and looked fragile, her hands tremulous, the skin so thin that the veins stood out like blue ropes. Her gray cheeks were sunken and Melissa had the impression that the woman lived in a state of perpetual pain camouflaged with a small, quiet smile. Melissa's nurse side kicked in. *She doesn't weigh more than ninety pounds soaking wet. I'd lay odds it's cancer.*

The landscape changed to lightly rolling fields with cattle, horses and sheep in neat meadows with either stone fences or clipped hedges.

John's voice broke the hum of conversations. "We're passing through some of the best grazing lands in Ireland. For those of you who are horseracing fans, this is where most of the big thoroughbred breeding farms are located, and a lot of the premier races like the Irish Derby are run at the Curragh Race Track to your right. You'll see some horses out on the training tracks. Also, if you look to the right on the far hill, you will see stone ruins. They say that was the first monastery built by St. Patrick around the year 546."

Melissa looked at Pete in amazement. "546! How do you deal with that kind of history? Canada's not even two hundred years old, at least not for Europeans."

"It is kind of mind blowing. I'm looking at the farm houses here. The old ones are stone or brick with thatched or slate roofs. They're probably at least three or four hundred years old too, if not older. I'm used to 2 x 4 framing on a concrete block foundation. I want to know how they did it, all hand built, hauling with horse and wagon" he said, starting to get interested. "Take a look at those stone fences, that takes skill and experience. Those things were built to last."

Melissa heaved a sigh of relief. It had been like pulling teeth to get him to take a trip during his busy season.

Andy, his older brother and partner in business, was dealing with it while Pete was away. The clincher was that old Barry, Pete's father, had specified before he had died, that his ashes be shipped to Ireland for burial in the family plot in Londonderry. That had happened a month ago. This was their opportunity to see the burial site in Northern Ireland and meet the family, if time permitted.

They arrived at Russborough House on time. As they exited through the side entrance of the bus, Melissa could see pushing and shoving at the front exit.

She nudged Pete. "Looks like that noisy bunch of Americans have tangled with Bigot Man..."

"Silly ass wants to piss off everybody," said Pete.

"Just to change the subject, did you see the toilet on the bus?"

"You mean the port-a-potty thing in the stairwell? That's a joke – you couldn't be any bigger than a leprechaun to fit in it. Don't know why they don't have it at the back like the buses back home." Melissa looked at several very large ladies descending the steep and narrow middle staircase. *That's a visual I don't even want to contemplate.* She smiled to herself.

Russborough House was a three-storey Palladian granite mansion with columned curved porches on both sides of the front entrance way, leading to the twin two storey wings. Sculptured stone lions greeted visitors at the foot of the staircase rising to the ornate front door. *What a contrast the plain outside is to this luxurious interior!* She lost Pete on the grand tour then found him in the library. Click: the picture caught him running his hands over the magnificent Cuban mahogany door molding, his blue eyes intent on the detail, black strands of wavy hair framing his face.

The tour guide's voice came over the ear phones. "It took ten years for the Francini brothers to complete the plaster work on the ceilings. They were considered the very best in Europe at the time. Every rose was handmade."

Pete, a stickler for fine detail was mesmerized with the craftsmanship. He disappeared again when they reached the mahogany staircase leading up to the private family quarters. She found him squatting to examine the monkey tail newel post at the bottom of the stairs.

"What are you doing?"

"Checking out how they did the join on this curve of wood."

"Beautifully done, isn't it?" said a voice behind them. They turned; it was the Pakistani gentleman and his wife.

"Sure is," said Pete. "I don't know any carpenters now who could achieve that with hand tools."

The two men went into deep discussion while the two wives walked together, delighting in the rich tapestries, four poster beds, formal dining room fully set out with china and silverware and the elaborate decor of a privileged era.

"The guide said most of the marble in the fireplaces is from Italy, but this one is from Galway," said Pete, indicating a highly polished mantelpiece of gray and light green stone.

Back on the bus, they got seated. John did the head count and came up two people short.

He glanced at his watch. The parking area was empty. He waited another few minutes: still nobody. He then strode over to the entrance and went in.

"There they are," said Melissa, as John ushered the bag laden couple towards the bus. They were part of the three noisy American couples.

"In the gift shop..." they said in unison.

The pair were greeted with hoots from their on-board companions. John was expressionless and promptly had the bus in motion.

"The Patels seem very nice. They're English. His wife Nafisa is a retired school teacher," said Melissa.

"Yeah," said Pete. "Bahir is a retired architect, so we had a grand chat about the building. Really interesting guy. He told me a whole pile of stuff I didn't know. I like him. He's worked all over the world, on everything from high rises and commercial buildings to private homes. I think I'm going to enjoy his company on this trip," he said settling in his seat.

Dinner that evening was at the Old Jameson Distillery, in the heart of Dublin. Melissa was enthralled with the original buildings.

John explained: "Barrels of whiskey were stored in these sheds. Teams of horses and wagons provided transportation from here to the wharf on the River Liffey from 1780 to 1920. It was shipped all over the world."

Melissa held her breath as John negotiated the bus through the tight fit. The travelers seemed to separate into groups, with the six noisy Americans, the Bigot and everyone else distancing themselves.

Click: the picture took in the bar area full of memorabilia, old barrels branded with the Jameson label and huge chandeliers made of whiskey bottles. There was a definite atmosphere of bygone times with dark beams and brick walls. They toured the plant with much of the original equipment still being actively used to make the world renowned distilled whiskey.

"I liked that scale model of the distillery across from the gift shop – all those miniature copper vats," said Pete.

While the group waited for their assigned meal time, they descended on the gift shop like a plague of locusts. Melissa bought some small sample bottles to take home. "Andy might like that for Christmas. No point in buying too much. We'd only have to lug it around."

They were taken to the upstairs dining area designed as a pub with a corner stage set up for the musicians and a tiny dance floor. Somehow, they ended up at the table with THEM.

"Where are you from?" asked Melissa.

"The four of us live in Seattle but Max and Ellie live in California," replied Joe. "We're here for a good time. Try the Irish coffee. It's really good," he said draining his cup in one long glug that made his Adam's apple bounce. He promptly ordered another, shouting down the table to his friends.

A trio was playing bass and guitar and the keyboard guy doubled on the bodhran for a few numbers. It was a mixed audience of several tours, the other group being young Germans who raised their mugs and sang along too.

"There are times that sounds like blue grass," said Pete leaning close so she could hear.

The meal was delicious and substantial. The first Irish coffee was on the house and the noise level escalated. Joe and company kept the server busy with the beverages which reappeared at an alarming rate. Melissa could see Grandpa Hardacre at the next table adjusting his hearing aid. *Bet he can't hear too well with all this background noise.* His grandson Todd, who was sitting beside him, was talking with Jane Cleveland and her daughter Becky.

"Todd and Becky look like kindred spirits," said Melissa. "They must both be in their twenties. I'm glad to see them together. Must be hard on a bus of old fogies."

"Who are you calling an old fogey?" said Pete, sucking in his belly and sitting up straighter, pouting his offended expression. She grinned and so did he.

After one set, two of the servers changed into traditional dress and joined the band. Click: the camera caught the blurred motion of the pair as they twirled and spun in intricate Gaelic step dances to ancient jigs and reels that set toes tapping. Flashes of blue light from other cameras and cell phones punctuated the darkness. It was all over too soon and the appreciative audience responded with a thunderous round of applause.

Melissa could see Todd and Becky talking to the band. "Someone said Becky was a violinist, so I'm not surprised she's interested in the music."

It was nearly midnight when they got back to the Alexander Hotel. "Oh Lord, we have to be up at six!"

Melissa phoned the main desk for a 5:45 wake-up call.

"We can head down to the early breakfast buffet and be on time for our 7:45 departure. Mel, I just realized that Brian and Mary didn't go tonight."

"I hope she makes it through the trip," replied Melissa, sinking gratefully into her chair. "I'm just going to go through my photos and make a list, or I'll never remember them all. Actually, some of these are quite good" she said scrolling through them.

The Alexander Hotel put on a beautiful breakfast buffet. The aroma assailed Melissa's nostrils before she even got into the dining room: bacon – then the mounds of food - sausages, eggs, black pudding as well as fruit, toast, granola and little bowls of homemade jams and marmalade. Once again, it was elegantly served with all the silverware and linen napkins. The servers in their white tops and black pants formally poured the tea and coffee. Faces were starting to be familiar.

As they boarded the bus, Pete checked the list. "We're in seats 23 and 24 today. Looks like THEY are all here, on time for a change and are seated up front."

Melissa noticed number of interesting things. The two ladies in 19 and 20 had been holding hands, (*I hope Bigot didn't see that*). The single lady in seat 3 had been all over the bus driver like poutine on fries and Brian was having difficulty getting Mary on the bus. John lent a hand and Mary tottered to her seat. The couple across from them in 39 and 40 seemed to be avoiding each other. The woman had the window seat and was already on her laptop playing a game, her body angled away from her hubby who was looking annoyed. *That body language isn't hard to read.*

She looked for Bigot man and saw that John had obligingly placed him beside THEM. The Patels obviously had not missed the significance of the placement and grinned at them over the seats from 7 and 8. Todd and Becky had switched seats and were sitting together while Grandpa Hardacre was sitting with Mrs. Cleveland.

At 7:45 sharp, John closed the doors, raised the deck to its running position and they were off to Waterford. The dual carriage way petered out as they moved onto the M9. The road seemed narrow as it had very little shoulder.

"I suppose they don't need shoulders if they don't have to leave room for snow removal," said Pete.

The crunch almost came when a commercial truck, the same width as the bus was passing in the opposite direction. Both vehicles slowed to a crawl. The bus pulled over into the shrubbery and Pete took a photo of the gap between them – a miserly six inches.

"You know, I am glad I'm not driving."

They passed tiny villages and saw the huge Tallagat soccer stadium. John's voice came over the air. "Soccer's very popular here. Each county is part of the GAA soccer association and each village has its local team and playing fields. You'll notice different coloured GAA flags as we go from county to county. Lots of rivalry. It's like the old Celtic days; one tribe against another."

Melissa watched the scenery unfold. *It seems every mile has a stone ruin.* The morning break was at a farm bed and breakfast just outside Kilkenny, past the river view of its medieval castle. The bus filled the lane from hedge to hedge. The crowd was a tight fit in the small tearoom but the food was abundant and all homemade.

Pete was still drooling as he wiped the crumbs from his mouth. "I can't remember the last time I had home baked scones and real cream."

Click: the picture captured the circle of passengers surrounding the young farmer and his family with the backdrop of the centuries old stucco farm house with its slate roof and ivy-covered walls.

"I'm fourth generation here and work it part time for cattle, sheep and horses. My full-time job is teaching at the University. Ireland is self-sufficient in dairy products and we ship a large quota of milk and butter to Britain and Europe."

Melissa found her way to Mary. "How are you feeling today?"

The rheumy blue eyes looked up at her. "Not too bad. I just don't have the stamina I used to and I get tired very easily. It's good to be home. I'm such a bother for poor Brian. He's been good to me and he tries so hard. It's our sixtieth anniversary on Friday."

"Mary, I'm a nurse so if you need help any time let me know. I wouldn't mind," she said quietly so no one else could hear.

A tiny smile crinkled the corner of Mary's mouth, she nodded and patted Melissa's hand.

Fully sated, most dozed the rest of the way to Waterford until John came to the city limits.

"Waterford was originally a Viking settlement just like Dublin. It was settled around 800 A.D.

On the pavement outside the Crystal factory there's a model of the Viking village on the banks of the River Suir. It's worth a look at."

They pulled in beneath the logo of the seahorse.

"Oh, look at that," said Melissa.

Click: the picture showed the glass blower working a glob of molten orange glass on the end of a blow pipe, the fiery maw of the furnace in the background. The glob seemed to take on a life of its own, writhing in the seething heat and transforming into the shape of a vase as he manipulated it with a wad of wet paper, put it into a mould, blew hard to expand it then severed it from the pipe with a pair of shears. As it cooled, the orange light died and the shape stayed.

Both of them stared intently as the glass cutters took the crystal bowls, vases or jugs and applied the saw to incise the designs. Click: the picture caught the intense concentration on the cutter's face as the blade cut into the glass, showering motes of crystal dust into the air.

The tour guide explained: "The apprenticeship in any department is five years. Each apprentice has to complete his signature bowl – proof he can do over two hundred different cuts with accuracy. Most of the routine pieces are produced in our Czechoslovakian factory but the custom pieces are made here. We do trophies and things like the Times Square crystal ball they drop in New York City on New Year's Eve. There are over six thousand pieces of crystal in that one."

"Look at the computerized setup" said Pete and they peered into the glass cabinet where a robotic saw arm was cutting a vase under jets of water. "In time, that will be a lost art too."

"It's hard to believe they can make a Viking ship and all the individual oars and spars out of glass," said Melissa looking at the two-foot model. "That harp with the strings in the lobby just blew my mind. I liked the carved horse too. I just can't imagine spending fifteen thousand euros for it. Seems a bit of an oxymoron to see a football trophy made of glass."

The 9/11 Memorial piece silenced everyone. Even THEY were quiet. Click: solemn faces deep in personal thought, eyes fixed on the shells of crystal ruins. Melissa noticed Bigot Man. *He's keeping well away from the Patels even in the lineups and seating for meals. I wonder why he has such an aversion to them. They're such nice people.*

After a quick lunch, they were on their way again heading to Cork. The land was now hilly and wooded and John regaled them with stories. "We had a highway man called William Crotty; he was an Irish version of Robin Hood. It took years for the British to capture him. He was finally betrayed by one of his closest friends. We've got whiskey runners and local saints. The Irish are a superstitious lot – fairies, ghosts and heroes. Many of these stories go back thousands of years."

"He seems to have a story for every town we go through. Is he making it up?"

"Who knows" replied Pete. "He's got the gift of the gab."

"Go in any pub along this route and ask for a John sandwich and you'll get the special of the day. They serve good food," John's voice continued.

"I bet they do" said Pete "There probably isn't a pub in the country this man doesn't know."

The young brunette in seat 3 bumped Pete as they got off the bus in Cork. She apologized, giving him the full batting-her-eye-lashes routine. Melissa watched in amusement; Pete hadn't seemed to pay much attention.

I do believe she's trying to hit on my husband. Let's see where it goes.

Lunch was a quick stop at a pub where John was obviously well known and welcome. He sat at the bar separately from the passengers despite the young lady's attentions. Melissa and Pete sat with the estranged couple who introduced themselves as Caroline and Derek.

"So, what brings you to Ireland?" asked Pete enjoying his Irish coffee and a hearty serving of Guinness beef stew.

"I'm doing some genealogy research on my family tree. Tomorrow, when we're in Cork, I'm going to the genealogy centre and see if I can locate my grandfather's grave. What about you?" said Derek.

"When we get to Londonderry, I'm going to visit my father's grave site and meet some relatives. Dad died this winter and the ashes were just shipped over. My cousin's in construction too and I want to check out how business is run here. We thought we'd see the sights first," replied Pete. "If it works out, we can always extend the trip a few days once the bus run's finished."

Melissa was finding Caroline very quiet. "Is it your first time here, too?"

Caroline nodded. "It's not my idea of a holiday. I'd rather be on the beach in the Caribbean."

"If he's off doing his research, why don't we go on the city tour? I think it's free time in the afternoon. I'd rather have some company in a strange place" said Melissa.

"Sure, anything to get away from his obsession with dead people."

Back on the bus, Caroline resumed her computer games and ignored the ancient landscape. Derek silently watched the scenery go by.

"They're not interested in the history or in each other, are they?" said Pete.

"I noticed," replied Melissa, surprised that even Pete had picked up on it. *He usually doesn't notice anything unless it's got a computer or a motor.*

By afternoon, the bus rolled into Cork, beside one of its many rivers. John came on the air again. "Cork was originally fourteen islands in the River Lee. Most of them are underground now and have been built over. That does cause occasional subsidence problems. Cork is still a very active port and there's a replica of a famine ship in the harbour. Thousands sailed from here to America during the potato famine of the 1840s. Many died at sea. This was also the last port of call for the Titanic."

A young local woman provided a guided walking tour of the downtown area and the poor people's Market in the city park.

"These headsets are really handy. At least you can hear properly," said Pete, putting his earphones on. "They must have bylaws to integrate the old and the new" he remarked pointing to a historic brick house wedged between modern shops.

Click: another frame of him, arm outstretched pointing to the small house surrounded by the glass walled modern shop fronts.

Click: a Catholic church hidden down a narrow side street. *They could have their church, but it couldn't be obvious.*

"She's walking too quickly for some people" said Melissa. "I wish she'd slow down a bit. Brian and Mary have stayed on the bus. This is too much for her. Oh, look at that fountain."

Click: the shot caught the guide explaining that the eight sculptured swans in the pool commemorated the city's eight-hundred-year history.

Click: pubs with signs for Murphy's Beer.

Click: parts of the original city wall still intact below street level.

The walking tour crossed the original stone Clarke bridge with views of St. Finbarr's church. *Another very active local saint.* Caroline walked with her, barely saying a word. They stopped at a pub and had a Murphy's.

Caroline's shoulders slumped as she started to speak. "We're from Boston. Derek works for an I.T. company as a programmer and I'm a clerk at our local grocery store. I never get to see him. He's always working on some project, often out of town and when he's home all he wants to do is research his family tree. I think I'd get more attention from him if I was a computer button."

"Is there anything so far that has interested you?"

"Not really. I never wanted to come here in the first place."

Melissa sighed for the woman. *How could she not enjoy the beauty here?* "So why did you come?"

Caroline shrugged. "Dunno, I thought we'd get some time together. He doesn't even know I'm here most of the time."

The bus pulled in to the River Lee Hotel. It was a newer hotel right on the river. Click: the picture captured a lovely view of the older shops across the river on the main road. The bus disgorged its occupants and their luggage, then John drove away.

"The parking area's not very big, is it? The drivers must stay somewhere else" said Pete.

"That's probably safer for him if that woman is an example of what he has to put up with. Must make it awkward. He's really very patient with everyone," replied Melissa.

"Maybe he doesn't mind…"

"Oh you…Typical man…"

Once again, they had a lavish supper dining with Derek, Caroline and the Patels. Derek had been really pleased. "I've found another branch of the family but I didn't find the location of the family burials." Caroline rolled her eyes.

The Patels were engaging and interesting. Melissa found the undercurrents from Derek and Caroline a bit depressing. Bigot man was down the end at another table. She was glad to get back to their room. She quickly checked her camera and got her list caught up.

"Well, Pete, we finally get a couple of hours to just relax together" Melissa said flopping down on the bed. "I think I'll just watch TV and get the weather for the next few days."

"I'm going to take a quick shower," he said as he disappeared into the bathroom.

She could hear the water running. It wasn't until a damp and naked body pounced on her that she realized she'd been asleep. "Peeete, you're all wet!"

Laughing, he peeled off her clothes and they rolled around on the bed to make love with abandon.

Later, with the darkness of the room broken only by street lights, they lay quietly nestled against each other. "It makes me realize that we don't make time for each other anymore, do we? With your schedule and my shift work we rarely get moments like this. Too busy, too tired. Now that the kids are at college, we need to resurrect us."

He didn't say anything, but she knew he was listening.

"I'm thinking of Caroline and Derek," she continued a few moments later. "They're barely aware of each other and there's an underlying resentment. I don't think he gets it at all. How would you even begin to heal that sort of rift? Then I look at Brian and Mary and after sixty years of marriage they still love each other. That's what I want for us."

She gently drew him to her and kissed him again, then drifted off to sleep.

"I forgot to ask you last night what the forecast was going to be," he said as they got up for another early start.

"Light rain in the morning but still around 21 degrees, clearing by afternoon. The news is still full of that shooting in Dublin. Some bigwig was robbed and killed in his apartment. They've got the shooter but are still looking for the driver of the getaway car, his sister, apparently."

They were in seats 29 and 30 this time. Melissa took the aisle seat so she could talk to Jane Cleveland.

"I brought Becky along because I didn't want to travel alone. This is the first time I've traveled anywhere since my husband died. I wasn't sure she would enjoy it, but she looks like she's having fun. It's worked out well that Todd and Stu are here. Stu wanted to come see his hometown and Todd's tagged along to make sure he's safe. Becky plays classical violin but you can see her getting into the Irish music. She had a blast at Jameson's. Todd's still at college and plays drums in a rock group."

"I'm enjoying the scenery," replied Melissa. "It's so green here and I'm loving all this history. It seems they were always at war with somebody but I guess it's the same everywhere else. All those ruins, all those lives..." *It's a haunted country with the ghosts of the past everywhere.*

The first stop of the day was Blarney Castle and woolen mills on the River Martin. A few went up the hill to kiss the Blarney stone but most attacked shopping with a vengeance. "I don't think I'm going to lay on my back to kiss something that thousands of other people have kissed. Yuck! You can go if you want to," said Melissa.

She remembered John relating the legend of the king of Blarney Castle who had three sons; the youngest one a poet. The poet was so popular that hundreds came to hear his poetry. The young man died accidentally and the king used the Blarney stone as a memorial to his son's eloquence.

"I think I will. I'll leave the shopping to you."

She watched him walk up the path.

Click: the photo showed Pete disappearing into the wooded area at the base of the ruined castle.

She toured the store. There were rows of sweaters, hand knit from the Aran Islands among many, plaids, tweeds, hats, yarns, shawls, knitting supplies and books. *This is knitters' paradise. I bet that in the old days the women living out on all the islands raised sheep and knitted for the whole family, shipping the remaining sweaters here. I wonder if it's true that a knitter's pattern is unique and was used as identification if their fisherman husbands died at sea?*

Later, still empty handed, she sat outside on the patio and had a coffee.

Click: the bus drivers of several coaches in the parking lot had gathered for a chat, veiled by the smoke from their cigarettes.

She saw Pete walking back down the path beside that woman, the flirt from the bus. Her hackles rose and her heart started to beat faster. *I've really been enjoying my time with Pete and I'm not going to let her spoil things. Calm down. She looks familiar somehow but I can't place her.*

She waved to them and put on a professional, polite smile. "Well, did you kiss the Blarney Stone? Not that you needed to."

"Yup, I did it. This is Erin O'Donnell. She's from Dublin," said Pete introducing the pert young woman who was giving Melissa the once over.

Melissa decided to keep her cool. "Hi Erin. I thought I detected an Irish accent. Have you done this tour before?"

"No, I've never had a chance to see my own country. There's a lot of family stuff going on at home and none of it good. So, I took off and I'm enjoying myself. These Americans are crazy. I've never seen people spend money like they do. Shouldn't complain – it's good for business. Just look at them and all their bags. That hat looks awful on that woman, wrong colour, looks like a cow patty."

"All this shopping doesn't make sense to me either," replied Melissa leaning into Pete and slipping her arm through his, "especially when I can go online and have them ship it. Ellie's going to have to buy another suitcase, just to get all that stuff home and pay the fee for the extra bag."

"I think I'm going to take a look inside before we get on that bus again," said Erin and sidled off with a grin on her face, provocatively swaying her hips.

Pete looked at her. "Do I detect the green-eyed dragon?"

"Who, me?"

A light rain had fallen, somehow intensifying the green of the countryside, as the bus climbed the steepening hills. "What did that sign say?" said Melissa, swivelling her head to read the bilingual sign.

"The Derrynasagarret Mountains or something," replied Pete.

By lunchtime, the rain had stopped. They had a delicious seafood lunch in a genuine old pub, O'Donnobhaine's, in the quaint village of Kenmare. *John said 'bh' is pronounced v – so that's O'Donnovaine's.* Most of the older homes were field stone with stone fences. Click:

the shot caught the stone garden walls with the vertically jagged top layer, enclosing the tiny garden full of flowers.

"Did you see Max and Ellie? They had a huge fight. I guess she's spent too much on all those gifts."

"They were pretty rowdy the other night too. Did you hear them? After supper, they were in the bar the whole evening and were pretty drunk. You must have fallen asleep, but they were noisy when they came back to the floor."

"I'm enjoying getting a full night's sleep. Not having night shifts is wonderful. Out of habit, she glanced at her watch. "Oh, Pete, we've got about an hour to spare. Let's see the stone circle," she said, her eyes catching the small sign on the street corner, the arrow indicating a narrow lane.

They followed the cobbled lane past the houses to a simple path that disappeared behind the trees to a field. A small wooden hut had a donation box and information on the historic stone circle. Click: the photo showed a forty feet wide circle of large slab boulders placed in their vertical position with a flat larger centre stone. To the north stood a hawthorn tree covered with ribbons. *It's primitive, so simple, yet somehow so powerful.* Click: ribbons blowing in the wind. *Memories, loves lost.*

"This looks like a mini Stonehenge."

Click: the photo showed the sign detailing the three-thousand years of history, starting with the stones having been brought from several miles away.

"Makes you wonder who built it and why? Druid rituals do you think?" said Pete.

"I don't know, but obviously it's still being used. Some of the ribbons on the tree are fairly new," replied Melissa. "I'll have to ask John when we get back." She felt a strange feeling as she walked about the stones, the same sort of feeling as walking in a cathedral. *I'm in a sacred space.*

New houses were being built on the other side of the lane. Click: she captured Pete looking at the double concrete block construction and the prefab insulation panels with the three men working on the roof. Four units were formed side by side.

"They're keeping to the traditional design but using more modern materials. Looks like they'll face the blocks with stone, then it'll look like all the rest" he said.

The afternoon bus run was uneventful. Melissa asked John about the fairy trees.

"They are considered sacred, a place for the fairies and little people," he explained. "Stillborn babies used to be buried there for the wee folk to take care of and also the dead from the famines or anyone who couldn't be buried in a consecrated church yard. They are most often hawthorn trees but can be other types of trees like the whitethorn. There's usually a water element, a lake or a river. Folks are very superstitious about these trees. If the road needs to be widened the locals won't cut them down. They say it's bad luck. The new road usually goes around it, or they hire foreigners to do the work."

Melissa scanned the travelers – Caroline was on her computer, Mary was dozing, her head resting on Brian's shoulder, Bigot Man was sitting alone, a sour expression on his face, and THEY, for once, were quiet. Joe was sound asleep with his mouth open. Ellie and Max were stiffly apart and the others were just quietly looking at the scenery. Todd and Becky were peering out taking photos, his body curved around her. The Patels looked cheerful and smiled at her. Jane and Stu were just sitting, quietly watching the land change.

They were in wild country now, a barren but beautiful scenery of boulders and peaks, a world of rock. *There's more rock here than in Ontario's Bancroft.* Trees were few and stunted on the upper slopes, but flourished in the valleys beside the creeks. Click: a shot was taken of horned sheep grazing the scant patches of grass between the boulders and clinging to the sixty-degree slopes.

"Not too many folks living out here, other than a few sheep farmers," said Pete.

The road snaked around curves and rockfalls, following the valleys. The bus pulled into a steep driveway, the stone farmhouse and barns hard to distinguish from the background rock.

John opened the doors. "We're stopping here to see how they use the border collies to herd sheep and there'll be a shearing demonstration in the barn after. They've got a nice little gift shop."

They were greeted by the farmer, his wife and their son with the dog then taken to the viewing area. Click: a panorama of boulder strewn paddocks in the valley before them was immortalised in her camera.

"There isn't a single farm or home in sight. This must be a lonely place in the winter" said Melissa.

"Look at the dog, Mel," said Pete.

Click: the young farmer looked typically Irish, with his tweed cap and rubber boots; the dog sat at his feet with its honey brown eyes riveted on his face, to the exclusion of all else.

"We have eight working dogs here on the farm. Kim is one of our pups and is eighteen months old. She is learning to herd the sheep and is doing very well. We'll be entering her in some sheep trials in August. I control her with hand signals and a whistle. We have twelve hundred sheep and a thousand acres here. The dogs are the only practical means of bringing the flock in – it's too rocky for ATV's. Unlike North America, there are no predators here. Wolves were exterminated hundreds of years ago."

He then made eye contact with the dog and swept his arm west. Kim took off on the run and in moments was a receding black and white dot.

"I can't see anything, can you? He must have good eyesight just to see what the dog's doing," said Melissa, staring across the valley.

Blasts from the whistle echoed. She still couldn't see the dog, but a growing white patch was moving towards them. Closer the patch came and she realized *it's a flock of sheep*. Finally, she could see Kim running from side to side, leaping boulders and keeping the stragglers tight to the flock. Another blast of the whistle and the dog dropped down. The flock stopped and a few rams turned to stare.

Click: a neat shot of one ram as it took a step forward to stamp its foot at the dog.

Click: Kim in the stealth position, her body low to the ground, her head down, showing the ruff on her neck and her eyes staring intently. The dog took a step forward and continued staring. The ram lost the staring contest, spun and returned to the flock.

Everyone watched the dog, as the farmer whistled and hand signalled. The dog cut four sheep from the flock and drove them up close to the viewing area where the farmer had the gate open and the quartet of woollies fled into the pen. He closed the gate and Kim grinned, sidling up to her master on dancing white feet, her tail wagging her whole being.

Melissa caught a glimpse of Bigot Man stooping over to gently pet the dog. *That's the first time in this whole trip*

I haven't seen a scowl on his face... Interesting. Maybe he's human, after all.

The young farmer escorted them up to the barn where the shearer was waiting. Everyone got seated in the bleachers. The farmer took the microphone.

"Welcome, welcome. We raise about fifteen hundred lambs a year here. The sheep you see here are all Scottish blackface. They're very tough and can stand the weather and the conditions. As you see, sheep are marked with coloured ink. Our mark is a red K on the shoulder and on the rump. That is unique to us, in case any of our flock gets mixed up with the neighbours'. Once a year, the whole flock is sheared and my wife processes some of the wool, does the carding and spinning for the sweaters you see here. The rest gets shipped, mainly to Britain. We'll show you how shearing is done and these lambs will get their vaccinations at the same time. We sell the lambs to both local markets and Europe and in November, we bring the breeding herd into the barns for the winter. I have to purchase hay as it isn't possible to grow it here."

Melissa watched the shearer grab one ram by its horns, flip it on its back between his knees and with the electric shears start cuts on the belly hair. Click: it caught the fleece peeling away in a mass and the rolling eyes of the bewildered ram. The man was fast and flipped the ram over, continuing his cut. It seemed only a couple of minutes later that a much smaller creature emerged from the fluff, received a needle, was sprayed with the red identification mark before being released.

"He made that look easy. Must be hard work with a whole flock to do," said Pete, looking at, the stocky, sweating man. "Wonder how many he could do in a day? That would be murder on your back."

"Yeah, don't imagine all of the sheep are that cooperative either," said Melissa.

She wandered to the gift shop which had a variety of knitted garments, skeins of hand spun wools, tanned fleece, lotions and soaps made from the wool's lanolin. She stood outside and once again felt the impact of the scenery. *What a tough, resilient people they are to make a living here. I wonder how many of the young people stay? Bus loads of tourists must be a welcome source of extra dollars. Good for them. They seem happy.*

Back on the bus they continued on through Killarney National Park. Red deer were spotted feeding beside the road.

"They're native to Ireland and are protected," John explained.

"They look a bit like our elk," said Pete, as the animals melted into the woodland shadows.

Click: the photo captured the hilly terrain and the fractured light of a dozen lakes.

"This area is grand for fishing, lots of places to hire a boat and fish for trout. Also a great spot for you golfers," said John as they passed a spot in the river with dozens of swans. "The reeds that you see in the shallows here are the best ones for making the thatching on the old-style cottages. They will last a lifetime. We are staying at the Plaza Hotel, and will be going out in the jaunting carts through the Park to Ross castle tomorrow morning."

"I'm so glad we're here for two nights. Maybe I can sleep in until seven. They sure put a lot into these trips," said Melissa with a sigh.

"Any regrets?"

"Oh no, I'm loving it, but once in a while I'd just like to put my feet up and do nothing."

After dinner, they rested on the bed, watched the news and shared a bottle of wine. "I'll get some more ice," said Pete and, ice bucket in hand, went down the hall to the ice machine.

Returning a few minutes later he said "Well, that was interesting. I just saw Joe slipping into Erin's room at the end of the hall. He winked when I saw him. That'll be dicey if his wife finds out."

"We've got enough drama on the bus. There's still a lot on the news about that shooting. They haven't found the sister yet. It wasn't a good photo of her, but it sorta looked like Erin. The hair was longer. You don't suppose..."

"You've got one hell of an imagination, Mel. Now hand me your glass," said Pete filling it and stuffing the bottle back into the tinkling ice cubes.

The next morning, Pete slipped down to the lobby early to send e-mails to Andy and to their sons, Sean and Brad.

It's nice now the boys are independent. I'm not rushing around taking them to hockey practice or ball games any more. Gives me more time.

They joined the rest of the group outside the hotel. "Just a couple of e-mails from work. Either everything is going fine or it's so bad they're not telling me. No problems with the boys."

"Just maybe they can handle it and are letting you have some down time," Melissa said.

Across the road, she could see half a dozen horse-drawn carts and their drivers waiting. The carts held about six people each. Warm woollen lap rugs covered their legs and padded the wooden benches against the cool, dewy morning air. Local rush hour traffic yielded to them and with the jingle of harness and clopping of hooves on the asphalt they were off down the main road, to exit into the coolness of the wooded Park. *It's like stepping back in time, what with the sound of hooves and wooden wheels on the gravel.* Click: a passing shot of a forestry hut sitting solitary at a cross roads. The thatched roof, white stuccoed walls and huge brick red chimneys echoed a time long past. She watched the view change over the bobbing rump and head of the horse. There was ancient tree growth, sometimes dense and misty vistas of the lakes with foggy islands that seemed to hover in the air amid quacks and bird calls. *This is mystical. I'm expecting fairies or the lady of the lake to emerge out of the mist and hover above the water.*

The driver pointed out the stone ruins of an old limestone kiln from a former copper mine and spoke about the birds.

"The most common bird is the gray crow. In the bays, you'll see many swans. We get a lot of migrating birds here. You might be lucky and see our ospreys – they have been repatriated. You'll see their nests – masses of twigs at the top of an open tree. We had a big storm in the spring and it took down a lot of old trees."

The ruined Ross castle loomed through the trees, still magnificent, the shining lake behind it. In the parking area outside the castle, John was waiting with the bus. They said goodbye to the horses and drivers and continued on foot to the castle. Click: the elderly driver, tweed cap and jacket, head-to-head with his old horse. *It's like a hundred years ago.*

"Oh Pete, this is gorgeous," she said looking at the castle's ruins, built on the bedrock, conforming to the shape of the boulder, with the lake spread before it. The fog's filmy fingers retreated with the sun and with minimal wind, the water was like a mirror. A few small fishing boats were out, the casters creating concentric circles to infinity as their lures touched the water. She caught up with Pete and click - snapped him with Bahir and Nafisa examining a set of rising stone steps and archway, a stairway to nowhere now.

"Hi, Mel, where did you go? I lost you."

"I was taking pictures of the lake. Incredible greens and blues, plays of light. It's magic."

Back on the bus, move three seats down and we're off. We've got this routine down pat. Melissa looked around and everyone was settling into their seats.

"Where did he say we were going?" she said looking at his map.

"The Dingle peninsula," replied Pete. "We're heading for the sea."

As they were leaving Killarney, John pointed out a large stone church with its ornate spires. In the church yard was a huge old pine. "It is said that two thousand famine victims were buried under that tree."

Melissa looked, trying to put the numbers into some kind of perspective. It looked so serene but there was darkness beneath the surface. *The losses here have been overwhelming.*

The bus was silent except for THEM who continued chattering. *I wonder why they came on this trip. They could just have easily stayed home, drunk themselves into a stupor every night and saved the airfare. I'm not sure they care where they are.*

The scenery was changing again to lower green rounded hills. She could catch glimpses of sunlight on water on the horizon. *The north Atlantic.* The bus came down the last valley and a vista opened before them. The hills flowed to the sea with long curves of open beach. Off shore, dark, hazy islands seemed to hang in the air, enticing yet elusive. The wide-open bay was quiet, with gentle waves slithering onto the cream coloured sand.

"This is Inch Beach, a very popular place in the summer and a good place for surfing," said John. "We have several Irish champions and it's impressive when the waves are up."

"Surfing! Now I'd never have thought of that here," said Pete. "The Atlantic would be cold. They must use wet suits."

They passed through the town of Dingle and John pulled off on the shoulder. "This is a quick fifteen-minute stop so you can see the stone beehive huts. A lot of these were built by monks between 800 and 1000 A.D. They only had stone to work with and they used the corbel method where each layer overhangs the layer beneath to come to a point at the top. Arches weren't known here until much later. There are no windows; just a hole for a doorway. It's a very primitive structure but an enduring one. Monastic communities gave up every comfort as part of their relationship with God. The huts out on Skellig Michael, those islands out there are even more isolated. These ones were used by the displaced poor during the 1845 famine."

As Melissa expected, Pete was off the bus and up the hill, before the photographers had even had their lenses adjusted. She stood beside the female half of THEM who were in a tight huddle. Click: she captured Mary snuggled into Brian's arm out of the wind, the long curve of the beach behind them and the distant dark mystical Skelligs on the horizon. As she turned she caught sight of Erin just behind Pete.

She overheard Joe's wife say "Keep an eye on that bitch, she's after anything in pants. I'm watching Joe." Then, as an aside, she said to Melissa "You might better look watch out for Pete."

"Do you really think Joe's been with her?" asked Ellie, wearing her cow patty hat.

"When he came back in the other night, I could smell perfume on his shirt and it's the same one she's wearing today. But I've got a plan, you'll see."

Melissa kept her mouth shut. *What is she up to?* Overhead, gulls mewed and coasted on the air currents of the light onshore breeze. She looked at the Skelligs,

trying to imagine the hardship and isolation, then got
back on the bus. Surprisingly, she noted Caroline was
talking with Bigot Man. She had a quick chat with Mary,
Brian and Stu. *Mary's looking even weaker.*

The usual group of stragglers finally made it back
but not within the fifteen-minute window. *He must build
these delays into his timetable.* The coastal road become a
winding one lane road with a cliff face to the right, inches
from the windows while the seaward side had a two-foot
high stone wall, the land dropping precipitously to the sea.
In a few places, the angle allowed rough pasture dotted
with sheep and the ruins of small stone houses, clinging
precariously to face the full fury of the Atlantic. *Where
did the people go?*

"This is spectacular" said Pete. "I've never seen anything like this. How could anyone survive and make a
living out here? No wonder they emigrated."

"Yes, and look at the first place they landed –
Newfoundland or Cape Breton. No wonder so many
settled there – just like home."

They spent the afternoon cruising the Blaskett Centre,
the museum celebrating the Blaskett Islands and their
former inhabitants.

"The islands produced a phenomenal number of
artists, poets and writers. The last remaining few were
brought back to the mainland in the 1950's, and nobody
lives there any more" said John. *Another lonely, windswept*

place. Melissa marveled at the hand-built boats made of tarred canvas over a wooden frame. Click: the sculpture of writer Tom O'Sullivan, his manuscript tucked inside his coat against a stiff wind that was tearing at his clothes, his body angled into the wind.

Completing the circle tour, John took them back to Dingle to Murphy's Pub for lunch.

"These lunches are wonderful, but they aren't doing my waistline any good," said Melissa, sampling a creamy fish chowder. "I heard there's a dolphin named Fungie that has come into the harbour every day for over twenty years. You can get boat rides out to see it." Low tide in the harbour showed the eight-foot drop with any moored boats riding on long vertical lines beside the docks.

Pete nodded but seemed preoccupied and was quiet for the ride back to Killarney.

Melissa helped Brian get Mary off the bus and her back was turned when a commotion started on the side-walk. Two men in suits and a uniformed policeman were talking to Erin. *What's going on?* There was a cruiser in the parking lot.

"I bloody well do mind," yelled Erin in the officer's face but he had her purse and rummaged through it to check her I.D.

"We've got her," he said to the two detectives. Click: the moment Erin was cuffed then locked in the back seat of the cruiser, anger and tension in her rigid resistance.

Melissa could hear Erin swear even with the windows rolled up, the distorted face raging behind the glass.

She looked at the other passengers who were all gaping and caught Joe's wife with a smirk on her face. *Now I know what she was up to. She recognized her, too, and called the cops.* Joe was open-mouthed but wasn't looking at his wife. Even John looked surprised and asked the officers what he should do with Erin's luggage. Word passed around immediately that Erin was the woman on the news, the getaway driver for the shooting in Dublin. *By suppertime, everyone in the U.S. is going to have an e-mail from here!*

They sat with Brian and Mary, the Patels, Jane and Becky, Stu and Todd. Erin was the topic of conversation.

"She was smart," said Todd. "She ditched the car, cut her hair and got a ticket for this bus, where no cop was gonna look for her. No one was going to check her at the hotels and she wouldn't need a passport to get on a ferry for Europe. Didn't they say a lot of money had been taken?"

"That's going to be a publicity nightmare for the bus company. I hope John doesn't get in trouble," said Bahir.

Brian cleared his throat, pinged his glass with his spoon to get their attention and stood up. "I would like to celebrate this moment with you all. Mary and I have been married sixty years today." He gently bent over and kissed her on the cheek. As pale as Mary was, Melissa thought she could see a faint blush on her cheeks. Every diner in the room, even strangers, applauded and raised their glasses.

Pete finished his meal quickly and moved his chair away from the table. "Mel, I've got to get an e-mail to Andy." Before she could reply, he had gone.

Something's going on. He's been off all day.

Melissa went back up to the room. *He's been gone over an hour.* She had her shower and rested on the bed watching the news full of the capture of the getaway driver in Killarney on a tourist bus. *Light rain tomorrow.* She was working on her photo list when Pete returned with a frown on his face.

"What's going on, Pete?"

"Problems with the business. I had an e-mail yesterday from Harrington, the accountant. There are some irregularities with one of the subcontractors who is Andy's good friend." He sat down on the bed, running his hand through his hair, looking tired.

"Pete, are you and Andy having problems? You haven't said anything before."

"This has been going on for a couple of months. Andy just wants to get the job done and he tends to cut corners on the quality of the work. One shoddy job and your reputation's in the toilet. We're known for quality of our houses."

"Pete, can't you put this aside for one week? If you can't trust your brother, then perhaps it's time you went out on your own."

"Believe me, I've thought about it. But it would be starting from scratch and with the boys in college, the money would be tight. We'd be competitors. Mel, I don't want to mess up my relationship with him. He's family. I don't think he's dishonest, but he's careless. He's a risk taker and he's got a hell of a temper. Sometimes he doesn't think things through and he's stubborn as hell. I want to talk to Braden while I'm here and see how he runs his business here in Ireland."

"If that's what you need to do then go ahead. I'm working, we won't starve. The boys can manage on their own. There's not much left on the mortgage. Do what's best for you." *How do I always get caught up in everyone else's problems?*

Melissa had trouble falling asleep as Pete tossed and turned. She checked the clock for the umpteenth time and it read two o'clock. She heard a siren somewhere close by but ignored it. A few minutes later there was a frantic knock on their door. Puzzled, they stumbled out of bed to find Brian in his pyjamas looking very distressed. "Mary..."

Melissa ran down the hall and into the room. Mary was laying on the bed, gray and still. Melissa felt for a pulse – none. "Brian – CPR? Did you call for an ambulance?"

"Yes" he croaked.

They slid the feather weight body to the floor. She gave two breaths and started chest compressions. The room receded to only her and Mary. *I know you're gone, love, but I must try for Brian.* She kept up the steady rhythm, focused on the rising and falling of the ribcage under her hands and sent love to that gentle spirit, *go to the light Mary, go to the light.* Within minutes, she heard the elevator doors open and the paramedics arrived. Quickly, they did their assessments. *Still no pulse.* Monitor hooked up - straight line, I.V. started. They took over from her and she stood there and watched Brian's world implode.

"Brian, get dressed and get your papers together. Go with them. Do you want us to come with you?"

Brian shook his head. Pete was standing in the doorway. She fled to him and burst into tears. "I've known them for four days – how can it hurt so much?"

They watched as the elevator doors closed, CPR still in progress and the hall was suddenly silent. Back in their room they sat on the bed and held each other. "It's silly, Pete but I feel I've lost a friend. She hung in until they'd got their sixty years together."

Six a.m. came all too quickly. Melissa was so tired she felt her insides sag. *I'm definitely the tortoise, not the hare, this morning.* Pete wasn't looking his best either. He gave her a gentle, silent hug. Melissa ate her breakfast but really didn't taste much of it.

"You guys were noisy last night" said Joe, passing behind them with a fully loaded plate.

"Mary went to the hospital..." said Melissa.

"Oh."

"I don't think you can complain about anyone being noisy. At least we weren't blind drunk like you lot. You don't give a damn about the racket you make when you come back to the floor every night" said Pete, looking decidedly menacing, his knuckles white around his utensils.

Lord, don't let him lose his temper here. Melissa placed her hand on his arm and said to him quietly: "you can't cure stupid. Let it go." *Pete complains about Andy's temper but he's from the same mold.*

Joe had enough sense to walk away.

On the bus, John got their attention. "Erin is no longer with us. She's in police custody in Dublin by now. I'm sorry to report that Mary passed away in hospital last night and Brian won't be back with us. He'll have funeral arrangements to make and will be heading back to Texas in a couple of days. He sends his thanks to everyone."

There was a low murmur. Melissa looked at the empty seats, then at the rain on the windows, like the world was crying too and she slept until the bus came into Adair. *It must be my mood. These lovely old thatched cottages just don't appeal to me this morning.* She went into the Trinitarian Monastery founded in 1230 and sat alone in the back pew. *I'm not religious but this seems the right place to be.* She sat quietly for fifteen minutes and gradually her mood shifted. *It feels like colour coming back into a sepia tone picture.* The heaviness slowly ebbed out of her and there was an acceptance. *If I were a mystic, I'd think that's Mary and she's at peace.*

Pete was waiting at the bus, a concerned look on his face. "Where'd you disappear to?"

"I just need some quiet, so I went in the church."

Back on the road, they stopped briefly at Bunratty Castle. Click: the blocky tower house sat across the river from the notorious pub called Durty Nelly's.

John proceeded with the story. "This tower was the home of the O'Brien clan in the 15th century. Later, it was owned by Admiral William Penn, William Penn's father. It fell into ruins, but has since been fully restored. Medieval banquets are very popular here. Durty Nelly's has quite a history too. Nelly was a very enterprising woman and owned the pub, providing liquid refreshment and other creature comforts to the menfolk in the castle and working the river trade that was very active here."

Melissa and Pete walked past Durty Nelly's and over the bridge, to get a better camera angle.

"These must be the ruins of the warehouses," said Pete, looking at the stone foundations along the river's edge. "They're well over a hundred feet long."

THEY were late getting back on the bus. *More shopping, more bags. Ellie's still wearing that awful hat.* She thought of Erin and wondered where she was. She pictured her in a cell being interrogated by police. *They're going to have quite a time with her... She's cocky and feisty. Wonder what her brother's like?*

Melissa noticed that Caroline was talking to Bigot Man again and realised that the two seem to be having ongoing conversations. *They talk more than Caroline and Derek do. I wonder what they have in common, other than being two lonely people?*

Jane came down the aisle to chat with her. "How are you doing? I know you were friendly with Mary. Must be difficult for Brian with her dying like that. There'll be lots of red tape. I wonder if he'll bury her here or back in Texas."

"I have no idea; he never said. I'm just tired today, didn't get more than a couple of hours of sleep last night. Thanks for asking," said Melissa.

The two elderly sisters were beside them this time and they were interesting jolly women; their casual chat passed the time.

John's voice came on again. "We're heading for the Cliffs of Moher and the Burren now. All this area is made of limestone slabs that have been polished by the glaciers and it is unique. To look at it, you wouldn't think much would grow here, but there are literally hundreds of different kinds of flowers including orchids growing in the cracks and lots of birds. The climate is quite mild but very windy. All the weather comes in from the Atlantic. It's a wild coast with cliffs and unpredictable currents – nasty place for shipping. Lots of wrecks along this coast, including some of the Spanish Armada. It is said that it was so barren that Oliver Cromwell didn't bother with it – no trees to hang a man, no water to drown him and not enough soil to bury him."

Melissa thought about Cromwell and his campaign of destruction. *That one man changed this whole country. He wiped out whole towns, destroyed all those churches and castles, and persecuted the Catholics. Changed the whole way of life here forever.*

Click: endless hills of long fragmented pavement broken by wild views of large waves endlessly breaking into wind-snatched shards of light against the rocks. No ships were in sight. The bus pulled into the Visitors Centre, buried in an ocean-fronted hill. They tugged on their raincoats and followed the pathway leading up to the viewing area, leaning into the wind.

"Look," said Pete, pointing to the step he was standing on. The pavement was a solid block of black rock full of thousands of white fossils. The stone retaining wall was chest high. Tiny Mrs. Foster was having trouble seeing over it and was on her tiptoes. Someone offered to lift her up but she declined. Click: ravens clustered on the wall, ignoring the tourists. It was a good flight deck for them, with an easy take off into the relentless air currents.

Melissa gasped when she saw the cliffs. The wind sucked the words right out of her mouth. Click: the cliffs ran in vertical folds down the coast, eventually disappearing into the low-lying fog. *Six hundred feet high, he said.* She could see caves and sea stacks where the waves were eroding the limestone. She heard a swoosh as someone's umbrella blew inside out. The flags on the pathway were snapping as they blew horizontally. Some brave souls were walking the cliff path, but Melissa opted to forego that as the rain finally drove them inside the Interpretive Centre.

"This is a really well-designed place," said Pete. "Most of it is underground. You can't even see it from the seaward side." Once again, they teamed up with Bahir and Nafisa for a video representation of the geology, and Grandpa Hardacre tagged along with them. The aerial photographs of the cliffs and coast were spectacular.

Stu spoke of ships going down, blown off course in storms. "Scuba divers found a Spanish wreck near Londonderry not so long ago. They salvaged a cannon and a lot of hardware. There's an exhibit in the Londonderry museum. Salvage conditions are limited in these waters."

"Are you from here, Stu?" Melissa asked.

"No, I'm a Galway lad. I'll be home tonight. I do have family here – my brother's boys, my nephews. Charlie's gone, but it will give Todd a chance to meet his cousins, and give me a chance to see what's left of my old neighbourhood."

"I suppose Todd's off with Becky?"

"That he is," he said with a smile and a merry twinkle in his clear blue eyes. "Nice girl. I want to hear her play a violin. Jane tells me the girl's got talent."

The ride from the Cliffs of Moher became less winding, as the road descended into a coastal region. Click: low tidal mud flats along the rivers and estuaries and small boats lying on their sides, awaiting the incoming tide.

John spoke of the Foynes airfield. "Flying boats from the U.S. landed there during World War II. Maureen O'Hara married a flying boat pilot when the war was over. Tomorrow, we'll be going to Cong, where she starred in The Quiet Man with John Wayne."

As they passed through the small fishing village of Doolin, Pete pointed out the small black fishing boats with white stripes just above the water line and red-brown sails.

"Those wee boats are called Doolin Hookers," said John, "hand crafted and still raced in these parts." Click: Melissa captured one slicing through the waves, its full sail heeling it on its side.

The overnight stop was at the Ardulean Hotel in Galway. Melissa heard grumbling from THEM, as it was an older building not located in the city core. *No shopping!* She saw a crowd of people greeting Stu and Todd before whisking them away in a private car.

"Stu's spending the night with his nephews. He'll be back tomorrow," said Melissa as they found their luggage and headed up to their room.

Ken and the Patels were on the elevator with them, and the tension was palpable. Ken's expression was one of distaste; he was off the elevator like a shot as soon as the doors opened. Bahir just shrugged.

The hotel had been added onto at different times, so the hallways were convoluted but the rooms were bright and clean.

"You really can't complain about the accommodation or the meals on this trip. We probably couldn't afford to book these types of places on our own. They're all four-star. The bus company must get group rates. The price of the trip is really very reasonable."

"If we were doing it on our own, we'd probably use bed and breakfasts," said Pete. "I'm going to touch base with the Chandler clan later. We'll be in Londonderry in two days. Are you sure you don't want to come with me?"

"No, I think I'll stay with the bus unless you really need me to come. I wouldn't mind some quiet time. The pace of this trip is tiring. You've never met these people before and Andy hinted they were a bit odd. Other than going to Barry's grave, I think your intention was to explore the business end of things here – maybe you need some private time."

Pete looked at her, his brow furrowed. "You're probably right. Now, you'll not run off with some slick talking young Irishman while I'm gone?" he added, his solemn look softening as laughter filled his eyes.

Melissa smiled as she swatted him on the arm.

The elderly sisters joined their table at supper time and introduced themselves as Margaret and Nell. Melissa found herself between Bigot Man and Caroline. The Patels, who were on the other side of Pete, chatted away as usual. *Oh, this could be interesting.* The sisters regaled them with tales of previous visits and were a mine of information on fairies, ghosts and haunted places, musical instruments and local folklore. They were even fluent in Gaelic.

"Where do you folks live?" Melissa asked.

"We've moved around a lot but right now we're living in Cape Breton."

"Are you Canadian?"

"No, we were born in Ireland but we're American citizens. We've lived all over the U.S. and Canada," replied Margaret. "Nell's a retired university professor. She taught some courses at St. Frances Xavier University in Cape Breton. I'm the talker; she's the writer. She plays the fiddle too. We're hoping at some point, she'll get a chance to play. It would be fun if she and Becky could jam together. We have a grand time."

Bigot Man was very quiet, seeming mainly to focus on Caroline.

Melissa introduced herself.

"I'm Ken," he replied.

"Are you from Boston, too?"

He nodded, hesitant to initiate conversation.

"Do you have any Irish connections?" said Melissa searching for a topic of conversation.

"My grandmother was from Belfast."

Melissa caught a momentary challenge in his voice. *It's almost as if he's defensive about that. Why?* "I don't think we actually stop in Belfast, do we? We only go into the Titanic museum."

"That O.K. It's the museum I want to see."

She could see an animated Derek talking to Pete. *He must have found more on his genealogy.* Caroline didn't say much of anything but Melissa noticed her frequent eye contact with Ken.

There's something between these two and I'm caught in the middle. Never mind. At least he's not fixated on the Patels.

Pete excused himself after dinner to make his phone calls. Melissa sat for a while talking to the others. She stayed with her group as they left the dining room and headed to their rooms. THEY went to the bar. Pete came back about half an hour later.

"Well, how did it go?" Melissa asked.

"Quite well, actually. I talked to Braden and he's going to pick me up as soon as the bus gets in. I'll stay overnight with him and his family and we'll go out to Dad's grave the next morning. Seems like a decent guy. I explained you weren't going this time and he was O.K. with that. He said you'd be welcome if you wanted to go."

"I think you've enough on your plate without me complicating things. It will give you a chance to see what they're like on their own turf." He gave her a big hug and they settled in for the night.

Another rainy day, but it's supposed to clear by noon. The bus was on the road again, this time to Cong. They followed the River Corrib north of Galway into a land of lakes and rivers.

"This is truly fishing country," said John. "The salmon and trout are stocked by the government and it's a huge tourist attraction for fly fishing. In the old days, the land-owners had fishing rights to the river frontage of their properties. Poachers would have been shot."

"Cong is our next stop. It's only claim to fame is the Quiet Man movie made there in 1951. Many of the locals were extras. You'll get an opportunity to take part in the re-enactments with a local tour guide."

This tour is fun. As a group, they walked up and down the streets, taking part in "scene shots" in front of the actual houses used in the film.

Click: Ellie and Max posed outside a single storey, white-washed "Dying Man" cottage with red trim and a black slate roof. The sidewalks were barely two feet wide.

Click: Max engaged in the fight scene with Joe, the rest of them egging them on.

Further up the street they stopped outside Pat Cohan's Bar, the pub used in the movie. Melissa and Pete walked ahead to a corner where there was relatively new statue of John Wayne, holding Maureen O'Hara in his arms, swinging her feet off the ground. Without any warning, Melissa found herself airborne as Pete picked her up and spun her around. She squealed with surprise and laughed. Cameras clicked.

"There, you're famous now," said Pete, grinning as he placed her back on the ground.

I haven't seen his playful side for ages. It's good to see him relax.

The tour continued along the streets to ruins of Cong Abbey. "This abbey and attached monastery were built in the 7th century. It was rebuilt several times but finally destroyed by the Normans in the 12th century," the tour guide explained. "There are some very old grave stones in the church yard."

Tour complete they returned to the bus. The country changed again as they left Lake Corrib and its 365 islands behind and the roadway rose into low rocky hills.

"These are the Maumturk mountains," said John. "This is one of the poorest areas we've been to so far. You'll notice long narrow strips of land going from the lake up the sides of the hills. Hardly any soil. These are poor beds. The farmers would dig two lines of sod and pile them in the middle and add seaweed. They only grew potatoes and it was one of the worst hit areas during the blight. Many thousands died."

Melissa looked at the melancholy scenery, beautiful and haunting in its own way. It flattened gently and she could see trenches in the ground with blocks of earth stacked in heaps.

"What you are seeing here are peat bogs. This is rotting vegetation that compressed over thousands of years. It can be dug with a peat spade and dried. It's an excellent fuel, burning clean with only a fine white ash. It has a distinctive aroma that you will notice when we're going through towns. Great place to store things because it's acidic. Farmers used to keep their butter in the bog. Archaeologists have found thousand-year-old bodies in the bogs that are well preserved; likely Druid sacrifices. The government is trying to conserve peat now because it is so slow to form."

The afternoon stop was at Kylemore Abbey, a Benedictine monastery on the grounds of Kylemore castle. Click: the crenellated castle sitting at the side of a long narrow lake between forested hills. *I don't think I have every seen anything quite so beautiful. It looks like a fairy tale palace in gray stone.* Pete was eager to check it out and soon he and Bahir were far ahead of them, eager to investigate the architecture.

Nafisa was checking out the map. "There are gardens down this way, and a small Gothic church down at the other end."

"The history is interesting," said Melissa. She read the sign which said it was built in the late 1800s by Dr. Henry but it changed hands several times before the Benedictine Nuns came over from Belgium after their nunnery was destroyed in World War I and they turned it into a girl's boarding school. "Some of them still live in the residence." *There is a richness to everything here. The building is impressive inside and the old wood mouldings around the fireplace and up the staircases are dark and mellow with age.*

"Do you realize the Irish nuns had been in Ypres since the 1600s? They supported King James and his dragoons who sided with the French after his defeat by the British in the Battle of the Boyne. The Dragoons retrieved the stolen Irish flag with the lyre design, and gave it to the nuns for safekeeping. They brought it back with them when they came here in 1920," said Nafisa, reading the poster beside the original flag now on the wall under glass. "That sounds like something out of romantic novel."

"It does get complicated, doesn't it? I tend to forget who fought who and which side they were on. All this religion stuff goes back so far" said Melissa.

Heading for the church, they walked down the path lined with ancient trees and small cascades of water tumbling down from the hills. Other than bird calls, its was quiet. Sunlight flickered through tremulous wind touched leaves weaving light patterns in the multiple shades of green. *Pictures don't do this justice.*

Click: the sign said Margaret Henry died suddenly while visiting Egypt with her husband Mitchell. In his grief for his beloved young wife, he had the church built in her memory.

It was a small Neogothic building with marble pillars made from the four marbles of Ireland (the Connaught Green, the Munster Rose, the Leinster Black and the Ulster Gray). Melissa lit a votive candle on the altar under the stained-glass window of the five graces. *This one's for you, Barry.* Melissa felt once again that quiet but insistent feeling of sacred space. *I'd be willing to bet this was built on an old pagan site. There's something here, a much larger presence.* Outside they checked out the cemetery of dead nuns.

"I don't think we're going to have time to look at the gardens," said Nafisa. "We should head back to the bus." A brief rain squall rolled through, driving them into the shelter of the main entrance along with many others, but in minutes it was gone, leaving the air cool and clear.

Across the parking lot, they could see Pete and Bashir talking to John.

At least we're not late.

Melissa was quite happy to slip into her seat. "It sure has been a full day," she said to Pete as he sat down.

"I can't get over the workmanship. The stone masons were so skilled. I've seen so much my brain's saturated. I'm glad you're taking a lot of pictures. I just won't remember all this." He relaxed into his seat with a contented sigh.

The bus was on its way back to Galway when John pulled over outside the Connemara Marble Company building. "Here folks, a quick stop. These people own a marble quarry outside Galway and make jewellery and carvings. The marble has a green tinge to it and looks a lot like jade."

Melissa watched the swarm descend again and followed them in. *This jewellery looks simple yet it isn't.* Small polished green oval earrings appealed to her and for a long time she looked at the Claddagh ring with its intertwined knots. She finally decided on the earrings. The owner explained the marbles and showed them samples of raw slabs and the process of polishing.

Melissa was glad to get back to the hotel. "Oh, lordy, my feet are tired. I'm beat."

Stu and Todd had returned and were full of smiles. Obviously, their trip had gone well.

"How did it go, Stu?" said Pete.

"We had a grand time. The nephews treated us like royalty and drove us around to my old street. I wouldn't have recognized the house where I was born. It's been converted into condos, but a lot of the upper part of the street was still there and the school I went to is now a shopping mall! They took us to a soccer practice so Todd could see it."

"The players are insane. It's so rough and no padding. Absolutely fearless, the whole lot of them. I think the old Celtic tribes all became soccer players" said Todd. "It makes Canadian football look like a bunch of sissies."

Melissa caught sight of Margaret and Nell sitting with Ken. There was a smile on his face which totally changed his appearance. *Those two just have the knack of making people laugh.* Beth and Jane were across the table. The conversation was lively. Even Caroline was smiling. *I'm glad to see her finally having a good time.* There was no sign of Derek.

THEY were reasonably quiet but Melissa noticed that the alcohol orders were still coming at a steady rate. *Don't they ever slow down on the booze?*

Their lovemaking was slow and gentle that night. Melissa felt the pleasure of his familiar body and later curled around him in contentment. She pushed the fallen black curl from his forehead and kissed him lightly. "Love you." *I haven't said that for ages.*

He murmured something and they drifted off to sleep.

Melissa lay there thinking about her life. *I'm forty-five years old. I've been a full-time nurse forever, I've been a full-time Mum to the boys and I've spent a lot of time as back up for Pete with his business and Andy. Where am I in this equation? If someone asked me what I want, I'm not even sure I could give them an answer. What do I want?*

Another day, another early start. The bus left the parking lot at 8:15. "We're on our way to Knock. Visions of Mary and St. John were seen here by the locals and a grand Shrine was built. The Pope visited a couple of years ago." The bus continued through small towns with impossible Gaelic names that Nell interpreted, through the rolling, green and gentle landscape.

Click: the old church sat in a stone walled yard. The Shrine to Mary and St. Joseph was attached.

Click: Melissa framed a double row of children in their school uniforms being shepherded by their teacher along the pavement. The little boys were in dark pants, white shirts with a red school tie, navy blue blazers and dark socks; the girls wore white blouses and the red ties with blue and green kilts and dark leggings. Some were very solemn, but others at the end of the line were smiling and jostling each other when the teacher wasn't looking. *Typical kids.*

Melissa and Pete went inside the Shrine. It was a lovely chapel, light and airy with flowing simple white marble statues of Mary and St. Joseph illuminated with natural light from the glass roof and full height glass windows in the east wall.

"It's neat the way this has been designed," said Pete. "The back wall of the shrine is the exterior wall of the old church. They've situated the altar below that original Gothic window aligning the cross and the altar."

"The artist has connected all the elements by curving the two arcs of angels between the statues, the cross and the window, and balancing it with the lamb on the altar," said Margaret behind them. "Very plain but beautifully done."

Melissa felt the serenity here and was glad of it. She took a few photos watching her fellow travelers walking the garden with the twelve stations of the cross. She noted that Derek and Caroline were walking far apart, Becky and Todd were together, and Margaret, Nell and Ken were a trio.

Back on board the bus, John told them "We're on our way to Castlebar to see the Museum of Country Life. It's well worth the visit. They've gone to a lot of trouble to accurately represent life as it was for most poor Irish even into the 20th century. People used whatever was available to them for clothing, or making a home. Life was very hard and a lot died young."

John's right. This place is fabulous. Melissa saw exhibits of handmade clothing, photos of gaunt, barefoot women hand harvesting the crops or working on the road construction along with the men carrying burlap bags of rocks. Click: everything was made of straw – furniture, horse collars, harness and roofing thatch.

Pete was looking at the exhibit on crime and punishment. "I can't believe this. It's a man trap used to catch poachers on the lord's estate! Those metal teeth look worse than a bear trap. Stealing a loaf of bread would get you whipped," he said looking at the cat o'nine tails with knotted strings.

"I never realized that the Raleigh bicycle was Irish," said Melissa. Click: the bicycle on the wall with its front wire rack was the original one used by the mailman to deliver letters out in the rural areas. "Bet he was fit."

They walked on to the next section displaying individual booths dedicated to the trades. Click: the tailor sitting in the light of the window, sewing a jacket with the old-fashioned treadle machine and putting the buttons on by hand. The bootmaker sat amid the wooden foot forms, his leather supplies and awls nailing hob nails to the soles of the boots, then finishing them by sewing the leather uppers to the soles on a sewing machine. The coopers were barrel making; the basket weavers were collecting willow wands to make panniers, baskets and fishing weirs. The weavers made the woolen and linen fabrics and the shop keeper sold a little bit of everything.

"Look, there's even a straw boat, coated with tar," said Melissa.

"They really were practical and clever, using whatever was at hand" said Pete, humbled by ingenuity born of necessity.

Back on the bus and as usual THEY were late.

"How can THEY be late again? It's ridiculous. Just to change the subject - did you see that exhibit on the travelling gypsies? The black and white breed of heavy horses we've seen are called the Irish cob" said Melissa.

She noticed that Caroline was preoccupied with her computer game and was totally ignoring Derek who was not looking well. His face looked drawn and there were shadows under his eyes. *I wonder if he's ill. He missed supper last night.* She noticed that he slept through Sligo, Donegal

and Ballyshannon and it wasn't until the bus stopped at
the Belleek Pottery factory that he roused himself and
got off the bus.

"I've seen some of their pottery in the specialty
catalogues at home. I often wondered why they were so
expensive. Looking at the girls making each piece now I
understand," she said.

Click: a young red head extruded the clay through a
machine that reminded Melissa of a spaghetti maker.
The long slender strand of clay came out and was cut in
lengths. The girl was delicately making a ceramic dish
with a basket weave bottom.

Click: the slender fingers taking six groups of four
strands each and placed them on the table then took other
four-strand groups, weaving them in and out forming an
interwoven mat which she trimmed to a circular shape.
Fascinated, Melissa watched her then take individual
strands and form a layer of angled spokes radiating six
inches, then a second layer with the spokes in the opposite
direction, forming a delicate mesh around the basket
weave bottom. A flat, braided piece was added to form
the lip around the outer edge of the plate.

The tour guide explained "The girls have to work
quickly before the clay dries. Later, small hand-painted
clay flowers will be added to that piece. Another one of
our staff makes the flowers. They are fired once, then

glazed and fired again. Any pieces that do not conform to our standards are destroyed."

"I'm not that interested in pottery but the workmanship is impeccable," said Pete. "I hope you're not going to order any of this stuff?" he said looking with a raised eyebrow at the price tags.

"There's a really nice mug over there, but I can order it at home on-line. They've had a mail order catalogue forever. I'd be afraid of it breaking on the way home. I think Joe is paying for his sins," she said looking over at THEM. Joe's wife was negotiating for the eight place settings of dinnerware.

"Oh my God, that's going to cost a fortune!"

"Hell hath no fury like a woman who's caught her husband in a compromising situation," said Melissa with a grin on her face. "It's called revenge."

Back on the bus, there was the usual confusion of stowing bags overhead or under the seats. The bus was starting to resemble Santa's sleigh. The landscape was changing to rolling farms and pastureland. Now they were in Northern Ireland. Click: a police station, looking grim with its high brick walls and barb wire. *A reminder of the Troubles.*

Someone asked John if it was safe to be in Northern Ireland. "The rifts are slowly healing. Catholics now have the same rights as Protestants. Jobs are open to everyone. That wasn't always the case. But it was a bitter and deadly civil war that tore families apart and spilled over into the rest of Ireland. For some, the memories are still fresh. There are places I won't go because of my Dublin accent but it is safe for tourists. You will note that the police here are armed. The ones in the Republic aren't. There's a tour tomorrow and your guide lived through those times. You'll find him interesting."

The bus crossed the wide flowing River Foyle into Londonderry – the famous walled city. They were spending two nights here and Pete was restless, looking for his cousin as they pulled into the parking lot of the City Hotel.

They were standing beside the bus as John unloaded luggage when a white SUV pulled in. The driver, a dark haired, middle-aged man got out and headed towards them. The family resemblance was uncanny. "That's Braden," said Pete. "I recognize him from Dad's photos."

Melissa watched the two men meet. Click: the moment of first contact – the firm handshake, the mutual assessments then the broad grins. *Those two look more like brothers than cousins.*

Introductions were made. Braden was the extrovert, his expression lively, his voice rich with the rapid rolling Irish accent. His laugh was infectious too. "Melissa, you are more than welcome to join us. My wife would love to meet you."

"Thank you, Braden. I think you two have a lot of ground to cover in a very short period of time. There'll be another time." Pete gave her a hug, snatched his suitcase from the growing pile and got into the SUV. She could see their heads turned in conversation then with a wave the two men were gone, leaving her bemused. *They're like flip sides of the same coin.*

The hotel room seemed very empty without Pete. Melissa looked out the window with a panoramic view of the tiny parking lot and the modern Peace bridge. She watched a BMW pull into the parking lot full of business men in their slick suits. They moved briskly into the hotel, with the air of power brokers. *Movers and shakers.*

After unpacking the necessities, she went down to the lobby and checked her e-mail. Her youngest son, Sean had sent her a long one all about his summer job and Brad was full of excitement over his job as a camp counsellor in Huntsville. She fired off a reply to both boys.

"Your dad has gone with his cousin Braden. They've hit it off right from the start. Londonderry looks interesting. I'm thoroughly enjoying myself. There's tons to see and so much history here. I've taken over five hundred pictures so far." With a touch of the send button, it was off into the ether.

In the dining room, she sat with the usual crowd: the Patels, Caroline and Derek, Margaret and Nell and Ken. *It seems strange to be alone. What's Pete's doing right now?* The salmon was delicious and so were the locally grown veggies. The wine was fruity and dessert a decadent chocolate concoction. Conversation was light. As usual, Margaret and Nell were recounting one of their escapades in a bubble of hilarity. *There isn't the usual angst tonight.* Ken sat between Nell and Caroline and looked comfortable talking to both women.

The power brokers sat at a nearby table and Melissa momentarily looked across to find one man, the dark haired one with the ruggedly handsome face, watching her. Melissa dropped her eyes and turned to Derek was quiet, eating his meal but not joining in the banter.

"Hi Derek. How have you been? I missed you the other night," said Melissa. "Are you feeling okay?"

Derek looked at her for a moment, fork in hand, eyed Caroline who was busy chatting and replied: "Not so good."

Melissa waited for him to elaborate but he wasn't forthcoming and went back to eating. *The subject is obviously closed. Hmm.*

After supper, she stopped in at the gift shop and looked at the jewellery display. She spotted a silver Celtic knot pendant. *That would make a real nice present for Pete's sister,* she thought, draping the chain around her neck and examining herself in the small mirror. Behind her, she glimpsed the same business man who had been watching her in the dining room. He was watching her again and for a millisecond their eyes met. Melissa looked away and proceeded to the cashier to pay for her purchase. *He's starting to make me feel uneasy.*

He was standing at the elevators in conversation with one of his companions. Melissa pressed the up button and waited.

"Excuse me," he said to his friend. "I was about to ask this lovely lady if she'd care to join us for a drink."

Melissa looked at him, stunned for a moment. *He looks just like the guy on the Boss commercial; ruggedly attractive and commanding.* "Thank you for the offer, but I think not," she said fingering her wedding ring. He saw the movement and smiled, totally unfazed.

"Lucky man" he said as the elevator doors closed, shutting him out of sight, leaving a faint hint of his cologne.

Back in her room, she took a deep breath, closed the door firmly so the latch engaged. *Well, that was interesting. The wife in me finds it a bit scary. The woman in me is intrigued. He was flirting and I enjoyed it. What could he possibly see in me when there's all the young stuff around? The last offer I had was from one of my ninety-five-year-old demented patients.* She looked at herself in the mirror and saw a slightly overweight middle-aged woman with thick brown hair and eyes. She examined the image – the short, back-swept haircut, no make up, a clean complexion and a ready smile. Running her hands over her waist and hips she thought, *I suppose I should lose a few pounds*.

She opened the curtains and looked at the night view. Click: the old clock tower with the illuminated clock faces silhouetted against the fading light. Click: the upright angled arms of the Peace bridge and its S-shaped floodlit road snaking across the Foyle to meld into the traffic circle in front of the hotel. The headlights of evening traffic were constant changing arcs of light in motion. She closed the curtains, settled into bed and watched the news.

Something woke her. She could hear voices through the wall behind her. *I can't hear what they're saying but they're angry. That's Caroline and Derek!* The shouting continued for another five minutes, then something heavy hit the wall, followed by silence. Melissa sat upright in the bed undecided. *I wonder if I should call the front desk. I hope he didn't hit her.* Muted voices continued for another few minutes, then silence prevailed. *Well she must be alright, both of them are talking.* It was a while before she could fall asleep and she was very aware of the empty space beside her.

The next morning was cloudy but without rain. Melissa saw that Caroline and Derek were both at breakfast but they were not speaking and were sitting at a small table by themselves. *They look o.k.*

At nine o'clock, a dapper older gentleman, impeccably dressed in a blue suit and striped tie, complete with umbrella, joined them on the bus and pointed out important landmarks as they drove by. John slowed the bus as they passed through neighbourhoods of brick row houses and the memorial to the people killed in the Bloody Sunday riot.

"This area is Bogside, a Catholic working-class housing estate. A crowd of protestors marched here for fairer voting rights. The British Army fired on the crowd killing fourteen. Most of the dead were teenage boys. Contrary to what the British said, they were not armed. The families wanted them exonerated, but the first Commission kept the status quo. That event resulted in outright civil war here eventually involved all of Ireland, not just the North."

Someone asked: "What started it all?

"It's a long and complicated history that goes back hundreds of years. In the 1700s and 1800s after Cromwell, the Catholic Irish were run off the land and it was given to Scottish and English Protestant settlers. There you get the loyalty to England. To have a vote required owning property. Although there were more Catholics than Protestants at the time, most of the landowners, police and civil servants were Protestant. Black Sunday created civil war here. It was brutal on both sides."

Why didn't I know that? I always thought it was a north versus south thing, not a civil war in Northern Ireland. I don't ever remember being taught that in school. The Catholics were always painted as the bad guys. Guess the winners wrote the history books. I feel I've been lied to.

"Is it safe for tourists?"

"It is now. Things are a lot better. The voting rules include everyone over 18 years of age with no requirements to own property. Jobs are open to everyone regardless of religion. Finally, in the 1990s, Britain initiated a second commission that established the blame on the British Army. Prime Minister David Blair made a formal apology to the Irish people on the steps of Parliament buildings. It has made a difference." There was passion in the man's voice.

I can't get my head around the violence, the loss of life. Here we are, decades later, and it's still here but to a lesser degree. There's still bickering between Catholics and Protestants. My uncle just hates the Irish Catholics and that's related to the IRA bombings in London years ago when he was a young man.

Click: a large mural on the end of a row of houses, depicting the haunting figure of a school girl and khaki clad soldiers. High on the upper left corner was a freshly painted butterfly. *Changes happening slowly.*

They left the bus at the Castle Gate and followed their guide up the stairs to the city wall to the twenty-foot-wide brick-paved Promenade.

"The town started with the building of a monastery by St. Colum Cille around 546 and the town and castle followed. Derry is the only city that still has the old walls intact. These arched gateways used to have wooden doors."

Click: a broad view of the Bogside estate with its red brick houses and chimneys and black slate roofs, punctuated with copper spires of stone churches.

Click: cannon on the promenade pointing out over the now sprawling city.

"Is it Derry or Londonderry?" someone asked.

"That's a bit controversial too. Originally it was Derry but with British occupation it was changed to Londonderry. In 1687, King James wanted Derry back but the locals were loyal to the Protestant King, William of Orange. The locals locked the city gates and declared "no surrender". The city was under siege for 105 days but William won. James fled to France, taking most of his followers with him."

That must be the flight of the Earls they talk about, Melissa thought. When the tour was over, he led them out the gates and down the street to the hotel. She shook his hand. "I have to thank you for giving me a much broader perspective on this. When I hear something about Ireland, I will perhaps be able to understand it more."

Their guide nodded with a sad smile on his face. "That's something the Irish people are still doing."

After lunch, the bus was on the road again to Portrush and the Giant's Causeway. The northern coastal road showed panoramas of cliffs, surf and perpendicular pastures with the now familiar blackface sheep. John stopped the bus for a photo shoot of the famous Dunluce Castle. "This beautiful old castle is literally falling into the sea. The story goes that the evening meal was being served when the front wall slid into the waves."

Click: a craggy promontory topped with the roofless stone walls and turrets on a backdrop of a curving beach and distant headlands; a never-ending battle of the sea clawing at the rock and stone.

Back on the bus, Caroline took the empty seat beside her. She was quiet. Derek had stayed at the hotel. *She doesn't have a mark on her that I can see. Thank goodness for that.* The road continued until darker rocks began to appear at the water's edge, the light reflecting on the flat tops.

John's voice again: "You can start to see the black basalt rocks in the water. They are octagonal posts that formed millions of years ago following volcanic activity. These formations run from here under the sea to Scotland. You can see multiple layers of coloured rock in the cliff faces. Pick up your headsets when you go in. There are different stations along the path with explanations of the geology. The centre itself has a lot of exhibits and photos if you aren't up to tackling the wind and there is a shuttle bus to get back. Be careful - the rocks are slippery even on a dry day."

Melissa and Caroline walked down the hill together. "You'd think someone had just laid them like patio stones. That shape is so regular."

"That looks like Devil's Butte out west, you know – strange encounters of the third kind," replied Caroline.

I know what she means. "I'm not that interested myself but my son is into this geology stuff so I promised him lots of pictures" said Melissa. Click: a sloping natural staircase of post tops from the mountain down to the beach, disappearing into the waves. Click: a solid wall of octagonal posts full of joints and cracks rising vertically thirty to forty feet into the hillside along the path, looking like a giant pipe organ.

"Are you ok, Caroline? It didn't sound so good last night."

Caroline looked at her. "Our marriage is over. We'll be getting a divorce when we get home. I'm glad I finally made up my mind. I'm just so tired of being ignored. He doesn't understand one bit."

Back at the centre, they looked at the exhibits and watched animated cartoons of the Irish legendary giant

Finn McCool who created the causeway during a fight
with a Scottish giant.

Margaret joined them. "That's a much more interesting
story than the cooling rates of various basaltic lavas."

They were back in Londonderry in time to spare and
Melissa headed to the Tower Museum. *Pete won't be back
until 4:30 anyway, so may as well have a look.* She watched
Caroline join Margaret, Nell and Ken who were on their
way to the cathedral. *No sign of Derek.*

This museum is interesting. She found the exhibit Stu
had mentioned where scuba divers had discovered the
wreck of a Spanish galleon from the Armada at Kinnagoe
Bay. There was a huge cannon and all kinds of relics – ship
parts, shoes, clothing and even a piece of lace. *Why did
the Armada come north after the battle? That was the long
way home and it's a wicked coast. It says here they lost thirty
ships in 1588. Some sailors must have got ashore. No wonder
so many Irish have black hair. Some of the horses must have
made it too - there's Spanish blood in the Connemara pony,
you can see it in the elegance of their heads.*

Another exhibit caught her eye; a recent archaeological
dig into a peat bog to recover a World War II spitfire. *Pete
would love that.* Click: the shiny Merlin engine with the
aerial picture of P8074 as the backdrop and a photo of
the pilot. *His leather flying helmet was recovered in pristine
condition along with most of the plane's fuselage and his rifle*

still in working order. It doesn't say if he was recovered now does it?

Click: pictures of the German U-boat command surrendering the submarine fleet to the British at the end of the war. The British scuttled all of them in Lough Foyle. *That's it. I've had enough for today.* She slowly walked down the hill to the hotel and flopped down on the bed.

Supper came and went and still no Pete. The business man smiled at her from across the room. She ignored him and went to check her e-mail. *Nothing. What's happening?* Going back to her room, she could feel the anxiety level rising as all kinds of thoughts tumbled through her mind. *Don't overreact.* The television was on but she really didn't take in the program.

It was seven o'clock when the door handle turned and Melissa jumped to her feet. Pete bounced in and flung his suitcase on the floor. He looked excited, a wide grin on his face and scooped her into his arms.

"Pete. I'm so glad you're back. I was starting to get worried. What's going on?" she said looking up into his blue eyes.

"Braden's down in the bar. Come down with me. He wants to meet you and he's got some important questions to ask."

Pete shepherded her to the elevator. She could feel the energy just vibrating from him. Braden was waiting for them in one of the booths, nursing a Guinness. They shook hands. Pete ordered a Guinness for himself and a whiskey for Melissa.

"You've had twenty-four hours together. How much trouble can two men get into or should I ask? What have you two been up to?"

"We've discovered we have a lot in common for starters," said Braden. "Both of us are builders; both of us like to handle the wood, the stone and appreciate the skills to work with them."

"Before you spin me a lovely Irish tale, remember, I live with blarney here," she said nudging Pete in the ribs and looked directly at Braden.

He let out a huge soft sigh. "Pete, you're right. I'll just get right down to it. I've landed a contract to restore an old estate. It's a plum, a chance of a lifetime. I'm going to need people with expertise, people who are good at what they do, and I want Pete to be part of it."

Melissa's jaw dropped. "You mean you want him to work with you here in Ireland?"

"Yes."

She looked at her husband. "Well, I've got no objections to that but it's not that simple. How long are you talking about?"

"Five years maybe. Well, as long as it takes to get it done."

"Pete, are you sure you really want to do this?" she said, seeing the eager face light up.

"Aye, I am. This feels like coming home somehow" said Pete.

Pete doesn't usually make rash decisions, but he seems set on this. "Braden, Pete's going to have to work out something with Andy and the business at home and get work permits. We'd have to do something with the house, and there's the kids to consider. Are you going to get flak for bringing in a foreign relative?"

"I don't know. That thought hadn't crossed my mind. I'll have to ask the rest of them tomorrow."

"The rest of them being?"

"My brother and two partners."

They ordered another round and spent an hour batting around ideas. *The hopes and dreams of two oddly idealist men. I think I have to run with this. Don't know if it's a good choice or not. It will be total upheaval for all of us. I need to stick with Pete. I don't want an ocean between us for any length of time. Marriages are too fragile for that. This bus trip proves that. On the positive side, this may force me to see what I want to do. Maybe I could sell photos to travel magazines instead of nursing.*

The men shook hands and Braden was on his way with a jaunty step. Pete watched him leave the building. "Mel, I hope I'm making the right decision. I'm not happy with what Andy's doing and I need to do something about it. Braden's offered me a good wage to be a project manager for him."

"I can see this is really important to you and I want to support you in any way I can, but I've got a lot of questions," she said looking up at his expectant face. "Part of me is thrilled, but the other part of me is terrified. I'm thinking of things like giving up my job and my pension, maybe selling the house. What will happen with the boys and our parents?"

He pulled up a chair and they sat looking at each other. *At least he's willing to listen to me.* "Has he given you a written proposal specifying salary and duties?"

"No, not yet. He was waiting to see how you'd react," said Pete. "I told him I'd get back to him after we'd had a chance to discuss it." He gently took her hands in his.

Melissa took a deep breath. "Now for the tough questions. Pete, we've always discussed business problems and batted around ideas. This isn't any different. I'm going to play devil's advocate. This is a really big deal and I want us to do the right thing."

Pete looked relieved and nodded. "You've always been a good sounding board. Fire away," he said.

"Number one, what's the advantage for him? He's hiring you, an outsider when there are, I'm sure, more experienced restoration people right here in Ireland. As meticulous as you are, you've never done restoration work before. Who are you displacing?"

Pete looked thoughtful, taking in what she was saying.

"Number two, do we know anything about his company? Is it solvent? Are there labour issues? Does it have a good reputation? Has he asked you to invest any money in it? You wouldn't be the first person to be conned by an Irishman's blarney."

He looked at her and chuckled gently, appreciation warming his tone. "You don't mince words do you? No, he hasn't asked for money. I'm going to get some information on the project too and see if it's as good as he says it is."

"Number three, what about our families? My Mum and Dad are getting on. Your Mum is alone now. Yes, we've got brothers and sisters but..."

"I'm sure Andy can step up to the plate on that one, Mel. He lives closer to her than we do and sees her regularly anyway."

"I'm concerned about Sean and Braden. They are good kids but without us there..."

"Well, there are all sorts of possibilities there, love. They could always go to college here. What else is on your mind?" he asked.

"What are we going to do with the house and all our stuff? Sell it, rent it, put our stuff in storage?"

"I think that's getting ahead of the game, Mel. Right now, I've got to get more information on the business end of it and make most of this opportunity."

Melissa looked up at him. *I'm starting to see him coming back down to earth, more like the Pete I know.* "Andy said they were strange. Whatever Andy's faults, he's no fool. I'm glad you've got the offer. It may be a phenomenal opportunity for us or not. I'm just expressing my concerns about the possible consequences and I'm asking you to research it thoroughly before you make your final decision," Melissa said quietly.

Pete gave her a hug. "Ah the sane voice of reason."

She smoothed the frown out of his forehead with her finger and smiled back.

The next morning, they were on the A6 heading for Belfast and the Titanic museum. *Pete seems preoccupied this morning. No small wonder... He's got a lot to think about, and so have I.*

"I sent an e-mail to Harrington this morning to do some investigative work on Braden's company. Hopefully he can dig up some contacts and any dirt. You're right. I need to do my homework before I make any major decisions. For now, let's just enjoy the rest of the trip."

"We were so busy with the new venture last night, it totally slipped my mind about Barry's ashes. I'm sorry about that. How did it go?" she said resting her hand on his knee.

"The Chandler family plot is in an old cemetery on the other side of the Foyle. The Church dates back to the 1700s and it's made of stone. Beautiful old place. The Chandlers go back forever. Their names are on one of the stained-glass windows. There's a remembrance wall, and they put up a plaque for him. Nicely done. I think Dad would have approved."

"When we come back, I'd like to go there," she said. "I was fond of Barry." She stared out the window to the serenity of the passing scenery, lush lowland pastures, rounded hills and glimpses of Lough Neagh. *I have a feeling serenity is going to be elusive for quite a while.*

The bus route bypassed Belfast and led them into the shipyards and the original drydock where Titanic was constructed. The museum was an ultramodern building sitting in an open space. "That looks like four ships' prows fused together," said Pete. Click: Pete craning his head to look up two hundred feet to the open sky at the level of the what would have been Titanic's main deck.

"It says the covering is 3,000 pieces of fitted aluminum, one for each of the workers who made her," said Melissa flipping through the pamphlet as they went in. "I guess we start at the top and work down."

The top floor revealed Belfast as it had been in 1907 including the slums, linen factories and the vast ship building yards. "Look, Pete. Here's how they made linen." Click: old photos of horses towing the barges along the river. Click: washing and processing the flax in the factory.

Click: the exhibit of fine linen tablecloths and napkins used on Titanic.

The next level down had real steel girders like the Titanic's framework, with the heat and the deafening noise of blast furnaces and riveters at work. "Pete, this is brutal. They got paid a penny a rivet..." The ship was enormous.

Level three showed the bare carcass of the ship being launched out of dry dock, ready to be fitted. Click: links of massive anchor chain piled in a day light window. "I think is really well done," said Pete as they toured the dining rooms, ball room, library and 1st class, 2nd class and 3rd class cabins, the bridge and engine rooms. Click: a first-class cabin with mahogany wainscoting, a four-poster bed and a writing desk. Click: 2nd class – bunk beds and a toilet and washbasin.

Third class just got crowded cots. Down one level to the maiden voyage to England then back to Cork. Down one more to the darkness with a visual of the sinking and the clicking of the recorded telegraph messages. Melissa felt a rush of anguish as the ship slipped below the sea in a froth of bubbles, the music silenced to the cries of the survivors in the life boats. The viewing room was dark now and completely silent. People paused here as Melissa did, as lives were extinguished.

Level 7 was the aftermath - body recovery and rescue of survivors. "I didn't know so many ended up in Halifax for burial," said Pete. "That life boat looks so small. I can't imagine it jammed with women and children," he added, looking at the recovered boat.

The ground floor was Robert Ballard's discovery of the Titanic. Click: the prow hung with streamers of seaweed that floated eerily in the dim light of the remotely operated vehicle, now a monument off-limits to treasure hunters. Pete found an interactive exhibit where all the wrecks around Ireland could be found. He played with the joystick and managed to uncover two Spanish wrecks, much to Melissa's amusement. *Sometimes, the kid shines through. It reminds me of Sean, my gamer.*

"Two hours wasn't nearly enough to see all of that," she said as they got back on the bus. Soon, they were out of Belfast and on their way to Cabra Castle Hotel. *A real castle.* The bus rolled onto the estate with its crenellated parapets and turrets to be greeted by an Irish wolf hound named Otto, a gentle giant well used to the crowds. A stylized wolf hound appeared on the coat of arms and the weathervane at the top turret on the main castle wall.

"Oh, Pete, I love it. They've turned the stables into extra rooms." Click: the view of the stone courtyard that had once housed horses, carriages and quarters for the serving staff.

"These walls are two feet thick. We won't be hearing THEM tonight," he replied.

We won't be hearing Caroline and Derek, either.

They wandered around the castle grounds before supper, taking in the manicured lawns, walled gardens, ivy covered stone walls and ancient cedars. Click: knobby trunks where the branches had been removed and the scars looked liked old men's faces.

"I see Ellie's out on the golf course," Melissa noted, as Ellie walked by pulling her golf bag, still wearing her cow-patty hat. *Every time I see Ellie in that hat, I think of Erin.* Click: the formal patio with white marble statues, set up for wedding receptions or formal affairs. Click: rose gardens in full bloom.

"Look at the woodwork" said Pete as they waited in the lounge area. Click: window wells two feet deep lined with richly carved mellow wood, leather furniture oozing comfort, ceiling to floor bookcases full of leather-bound books. Click: stone fireplaces with logs burning in old metal grates complete with hand forged andirons.

Islands of comfort and quiet.

Supper that night was a very formal affair in the main dining room. "I'd rather serve myself," said Pete, "rather than wait for this server to spoon it on everyone's plate. It will be cold by the time he gets to us." Another round of drinks encouraged high levels of conversations.

Melissa chatted with Nafisa and Bahir across from them. Margaret and Nell were keeping up the hilarity to her right. Caroline and Derek were sitting beside Pete to her left and both of them were silent. *Pete's thinking about the business. I can almost see the wheels spinning.* Stu, Todd, Becky and Jane were further down engaged in a lively discussion. Ken was sitting at the end quietly watching Caroline. *I wonder if they'll get together once Caroline's divorce goes through.*

After supper, they meandered their way through the winding passageways back to their room.

"Tomorrow's our last day, then we'll be on our way home," said Melissa. "I'm going to need a couple of days just to unwind. I can't believe how much we've done here."

"Yeah, I've been thinking about how to deal with Andy."

"How are you going to approach it?"

"Regardless of whether I take Branden's offer or not, I think I need to get out of the company and let him run it the way he wants. We've been butting heads for a while. Problem might be if he doesn't have the money to buy me out. I really like the idea of doing something different - that's why Branden's offer is so attractive. I'm going to talk to Bahir tomorrow, and see if he knows anyone in the restoration business."

The next morning, John drove them to Newgrange to see the passage tombs. "These megalithic tombs were built around 3,000 B.C. The interpretive centre shows how people of that time lived and how they built these monuments. Along this stretch of the Boyne there are three big tombs – Newgrange, Knowth and Dowth. Newgrange was excavated and rebuilt by archaeologists in the 60s and 70s. The tombs have been plundered and re-occupied over thousands of years."

My mind's preoccupied with Pete and his job. She looked at the dioramas of Celtic huts, made of poles and reed coverings, and village scenes with wicker coracles, hide clothing, shell necklaces and stone bowls. *I'm finding it hard to see these primitive hunter gatherers as being capable of building such a sophisticated and elegant tomb.*

Outside, they waited for the shuttle bus to take them to the site several miles away. Newgrange sat on the cusp of the hill overlooking the valley, a low, smoothly rounded hill edged with a white stone wall. Pete was very quiet. They passed small farms, some with smaller green mounds sitting undisturbed in the hay fields.

Nell pointed out "Those ones haven't been excavated."

Pete looked at the mound. "It must be over three hundred feet across. Imagine the time and manpower that must have taken."

"Did you see the diorama of them hauling those stones on sleds and rollers? Hundreds of men," she said. "The quarry is fifteen miles away. How did they get them here?"

The huge mound belied the limited space inside so only a small group could go in at one time. While they were waiting, she looked at the huge stones forming the base and the circles and spirals engraved on them. "I wonder what it all means? Do those symbols have a meaning or is it just a design? That one looks like a boat with oarsmen, with the sun behind it, just like the engravings on the pyramids in Egypt. They must have been sun worshippers too."

"Sounds like nobody knows the answer to that, Mel" said Pete.

Stone slabs lined the passage way that was barely shoulder width in places and Pete had to duck the low ceiling. The passage ended in a cruciform room of three large niches, a hollowed-out bowl in each one. Melissa gazed up at the ceiling seeing the now familiar corbelling, rising to a point about twenty-five feet up with a capstone.

The guide explained: "It is assumed that these bowls contained the bones of the high chief but that is an assumption. The site has been reoccupied over thousands of years and we only know that from other sites. This was also a place of ritual. On the winter solstice the sun shines through the roof box, illuminating the passageway all the way to the back. It is symbolic of fertility." She proceeded to turn out the lights leaving them in darkness and turned on an artificial sun recreating the effect. "It says a lot about their knowledge of the heavens and the seasons."

Melissa looked at the light coming down the passage and imagined the awe the ancients must have felt, having the sacred light enter and move toward them. *Lighting the way and promising a new spring.*

The mood on the bus was subdued. *The trip is winding down.*

John's voice came over the air again. "We're heading for Drogheda. Our last stop is the D Hotel on the Boyne River. There's a great view of the river and always a lot of swans. There's a walking tour this afternoon otherwise your time is your own. Our supper tonight is in the hotel's pub. There's usually good music, too."

"Pete, I'm exhausted. I think I'm going to have an afternoon nap. What about you?"

"I'm going to get on the internet and talk to Bahir. I've got lots of things to check into," he said as he carried their bags into their room. Melissa kicked off her shoes and was asleep before she knew it. He woke her at six.

"I don't believe it. I've slept away the whole afternoon. Any news?"

"The boys are fine. No word from Harrington yet. I spent some time with Bahir and he's given me some contacts in London who do restorations, old mansions and that sort of thing."

"I'm just going to freshen up then we'll go down for supper."

The pub was typical; brick walls and old beams, old beer posters, old photos and dim lighting. *As usual, the meal is excellent.* The beer flowed. Melissa was busy getting e-mail addresses from the people she liked. An elderly man carrying a violin case came in, followed shortly by two men, a younger man with a guitar and an middle-aged man with an accordion. A young girl with a flute joined them a few minutes later. The noise level escalated especially from THEM. *THEY are so loud I can't hear the music, thought Melissa frowning at the group behind who weren't even paying attention to the music.*

Pete slammed his chair back and glared at Joe. "Would you guys shut up? If you don't want to listen to the music go somewhere else."

"Are you going to make me?" Joe replied rising to meet him nose to nose with a sneer on his face.

"You're bloody right I will, you asshole" said Pete, his hands balled into fists, his teeth clenched and his chin jutting out.

Melissa was on her feet but John brushed passed her and put his hand on Pete's shoulder. She couldn't hear what John said but Pete took a deep breath and started to talk to him. *Thank God, he's managed to defuse him.* Pete sat down. Joe sat down. Some faces in the tour group were nodding. Others had been watching the musicians and missed it all together.

The music was mostly Gaelic folksongs. Margaret and
Nell, who knew all the words, sang along and translated
some of the lyrics for them. The whole group ended up
singing along and clapping in time. Nell spoke with the old
man and he nodded. To everyone's surprise, she pulled out
a violin case from under the table and joined them. The
two violins blended in complex harmonies. *Oh, she knows
the music! That's beautiful.* The lonely floating notes of the
flute echoed memories of a lover who never returned, the
ship lost at sea. *There's a sadness there in all of it.*

They played for about half an hour then took a beer
break. Nell walked over to Becky and handed her the
violin. For a moment, the girl looked stunned then took
the violin from Nell and ran her hands over the strings.
Nell said something in Gaelic to the musicians, who urged
her on. Becky stood before them quiet for a moment then
broke into a classical version of Danny Boy. *Her style is
so different but it's rich and flowing.* Click: Becky, her long
blonde hair framing her face, the violin tucked under her
chin, her long fingers moving over the strings and the
bow poised. She then played U2 numbers, movie themes,
then launched into Schindler's List. *I've got a CD of Itzak
Perlman playing that. It gives me goose bumps every time
I hear it.* After the last haunting notes faded, Melissa
glanced at Jane and saw the glistening stream of tears
on her face. *She got her wish.* Becky stopped and handed
the violin back to Nell. A loud round of applause went up

including the musicians. Becky walked back to her seat but paused to touch her mother's hand and a look passed between them. *They both got their wish.* Todd gave her a hug and a lingering kiss, to the applause of the table.

With some urging John got and sang a few well-known songs that everyone could sing along to. "His voice is pretty good" said Pete. The musicians played for another forty-five minutes, then the old fiddler put his violin in its case and waved goodnight to all.

He got an ovation too. "Well this holiday's over. We'll be home by three o'clock our time tomorrow. I've exchange email addresses with the Patels, Jane, Margaret and Nell," she said as they walked back to their room, leaving THEM in the pub. He nodded. She spotted Ken with his arm over Caroline's shoulder, heads close together momentarily. No sign of Derek.

"Sean will pick us up at Pearson airport. I'll be glad to sleep in my own bed and make my own coffee," said Pete as they looked out over the Boyne flowing silently past their window, flickering street lights illuminating the downstream current and a group of elegant swans.

The morning was uneventful, breakfast in dining room, bags out for the bus. "Thank you, John, for everything," said Melissa looking pointedly at Pete. *I never did*

ask Pete what John said to him last night. Pete slipped him an envelope with a substantial tip.

John nodded at them and soon they were at Dublin airport. *The usual lineups and security checks. Now the holiday's over I can't wait to get home. I've really enjoyed it but what an emotional rollercoaster this has been, one way or another.*

She read on her Kindle, dozed and inhaled her inflight meals. Soon the captain's voice came over the air: "We'll be arriving in Toronto in 30 minutes. Weather is clear and 22 degrees."

The plane touched down with a thud, the grinding of brakes and rushing air, then taxied slowly to their gate. Melissa let out a sigh of relief. *That's the part of flying I don't like – the going up and the coming down.* More lineups for security and the endless wait for the luggage carousel to spew out their suitcases.

Melissa spotted Sean waiting for them. At six feet four, he was heads above most of the waiting crowd. She waved and he grinned.

Sean enveloped her in a big hug and give his dad a hearty hand shake. "Good to have you back. Did you have a good time?"

"We sure did," said Pete as they walked across the roadway into the parking lot.

"Tell me Mum, what's it like being on a bus trip? I can't imagine it myself, being locked up with a bunch of strangers. Wasn't it boring?"

Melissa took one look at his earnest face. *Mary's death, Erin's arrest, Derek and Caroline's marriage breakup and our dilemma. I've witnessed history, got a feel for the Irish people. Boring!!* Both her and Pete burst into helpless, uncontrollable laughter.

"Sean, you've got to be kidding. More happened on that bus in twelve days than a year's worth of soap operas and the United Nations combined! We'll tell you all about it," said Melissa, wiping the tears from her eyes and walking between them over to the car park. *I've got a feeling this is just the beginning, for Pete and for me too.*

the book of kells

(or Leabhar Cheannis in Gaelic)

prologue

806 A.D. Island of Iona, Scotland.

They anchored the dragon-headed boat in the shallow waters of the beach in the stillness of the pre-dawn light as waves lapped quietly around them in the sheltered bay. Egill Forkbeard stood up to his full six-foot height and surveyed the low rocky island before him. The seasoned Viking chieftain with his flowing red hair, tattooed body, bronze helmet and fur cape remembered the rich haul of silver and coin from his raid two years earlier. "I want those gold books!" he said to Ketill, his son. Their soft leather boots made no noise on the rocky narrow path as they clambered up to the Abbey on the grassy knoll above.

Ignoring the locked gate, Egill boosted Lothar over the rocky curtain wall with ease and he scaled over the top. The others followed. Somewhere the bark of a dog was cut short. With brute force, Lothar hit the side door and a solid wedge of howling slashing men erupted into the

Abbey. Egill's shouts were drowned out in the deafening din of screams. The smell of blood, sweat, smoke and incense engulfed them.

"To the altar," he bellowed, easily hacking down two monks who tumbled from the dormitory in wide-eyed disbelief. Axes splintered the Sacristy door again and again until the wood gave way with the shriek of a dying soul. A broad grin spread over his blood-splattered face as he looked at the bags of coins, the silver chalices, and crosses. "They told me the books were gold. Where are they?" The ransacked Sacristy was empty. "No books," said Lothar hefting the bulging sack over his shoulder.

Enraged, Egill stormed out of the Sacristy, leading his men down the aisle and tossing a flaming brazier into the pews. He systematically searched every chamber in the stone building, killing as he went, leaving a scarlet tapestry of the dead and dying on the cold stone floor, eerily lit by the growing flames. *Still no books.* Without a further glance, he marshalled his men back to the boat laden with sacks. *There aren't even any women on this island to take as slaves!* The oarsmen moved the ship quickly off the beach and into deeper water and they rowed in fluid unison until the boat disappeared out into the bay beyond the rocky point. A pall of smoke hung over the Abbey as sounds faded to the crackling of fiery fingers in the Chapel. The Abbey stood black against the lightening east with flames flickering in the Chapel and smoke poured through its shattered windows.

A small knot of brown robed survivors gathered, numb with the devastation. "We've lost fifty- eight of our brethren. God help us" said the senior monk. The next day, after the stones had cooled, they entered the Chapel and together moved the stones of the altar, revealing a compartment containing a number of silk wrapped packages. Gently he peeled back the blue silk revealing the glittering gold covers of the precious manuscripts. "Praise be. No damage. But we can't protect them here any longer. We are defenseless against the Vikings. We need to go back to Ireland and start again," he said, thinking of the difficult journey in a small open boat across that wild and wind tossed Irish sea.

1007 A.D. O'Donnel's Hill, County Meath, Ireland

Tomorrow is the day I've been dreading; the day I hoped would never come. Tomorrow will be my tenth birthday and I will be leaving my home forever, destined for life as a monk in the Abbey of Kells. Lying on my bed against the stone wall with the evening light fading quickly through the narrow window, I could faintly hear my mother sobbing and the low growl of my father's voice. I am Aidan, the youngest son of Niall O'Donnel, a minor King of Meath.

My older brother Fearghus had kept me busy all afternoon mock fighting with wooden staves. I adored Fearghus. He was everything I wanted to be and wasn't. At eighteen he was tall, muscular and fit, looking every inch a soldier in his leather tunic, his auburn hair hanging loose under his helmet. I was a slighter build, much more like my mother. His final insult had been a hearty whack across my shoulder that left me flat in the dust.

"Aidan, I'm glad we're not using swords or I'd have taken your head off," he said extending his hand to help me back on my feet.

I grinned at him and shook off the dirt, my left shoulder still stinging. *As the youngest I knew my destiny was either the army or the church; the youngest never became king.*

"Even monks must be able to defend themselves. The Vikings still raid us," he said as we walked back to our tower house, his arm around my shoulder. "I'd not be wanting that life myself – no beer, no fighting and no women. I won't need Latin 'til they put it on pub signs. You'll do well as a monk. You can read and write which none of us can."

Our evening meal was in the great hall, with the long table set beside the huge stone fireplace. A blaze of

crackling glowing logs dimly lit the room and warded off
the chill of the evening air. Very little was said. Cianan
and Harkin, my other two brothers, argued over who had
the better hound and almost came to blows over it. *Any
excuse for a good fight.* Their wives just watched and shook
their heads while tending to their children.

My father had finished his venison, the juices still dripping down his beard. He raised his chalice after wiping his
chin on his sleeve. "I raise a toast and a prayer for Aidan.
You will be leaving this household to become a man of
God. You'll be sorely missed by all of us. Your journey will
not be easy but I have every confidence that you will do us
proud," he finished before draining his cup and everyone
did likewise. All the faces turned to me.

I stood and quietly raised my chalice in a salute to him,
praying I could keep the tremor from my voice. "I shall do
my best, sire to bring honour to the family name." With
that I sat down, not daring to look at Mother, who had
quiet tears streaming down her face. A hearty round of fist
thumping on the table was followed with cheers from the
men. Father looked solemn yet pleased, his eyes fixed on
me. *I knew his expectations. He wanted a scholar. Documents
brought to him had to read by someone else.*

Morning finally came. I had not slept well with shadows of dark creatures in my dreams. I heard the servants preparing the morning meal and the grooms in the stables readying the horses for our journey. My older brother Cianan was up, his sword strapped to his waist and his helmet close at hand. One of them always stayed home on guard duty as the threat of raiders was constant and usually involved the McCrory clan who lived on the next hill. He engulfed me in a rib-cracking hug. Looking down at me he said: "Safe trip, little brother. We didn't even have time to take you to the brothel, did we? You'll never know what you missed. One day we will meet again and you will be Brother Aidan."

I laughed. "You big lump. Look after Mother for me," I said lightly, knowing he would defend her to his death. By then father, Harkin and Fearghus were already mounted and fully armed, looking impatient to be on their way. The horses danced on the spot, restrained by strong hands. I quickly mounted my pony and looked back for the last time – Mother clutching Cianan's arm as she stood beside him on the step, the solid two-storey stone keep that had been my home, the jingle of harness and the baying of Harkin's hound chasing the chickens into a cackling chaos. With a final wave, I followed the others out the gate of the bailie, leaving the safety of those stout stone walls. My life was about to change.

We rode for over an hour and started to cross the Blackwater River at the ford when we heard the sound of combat – shouting and the metallic clash of swords. Instantly all four of us unsheathed our swords, raised our shields and pressed the horses forward. A riderless horse came careening down the road, its mane and tail flying.

"Don't recognize that one," called Fearghus. "Do you?"

"No," yelled Harkin. "Let's make sure this isn't a trap." He pulled off the road and up the hill disappearing into the trees. He returned moments later. "Wagon ahead; looks like a couple of merchants and one swordsman on foot with three raiders. Don't recognize the horses." The loose horse had slowed and was circling to follow us.

Riding four abreast we spurred the horses to a flat-out gallop, clods of dirt flying from their hooves. The wagon and fighting men came into view, then the air was torn by our combined scream of the O'Donnel war cry.

I saw that one moment when the combatants stood transfixed at the sight of our oncoming charge. The raiders spun, spurring their horses and fled down the road with Fearghus and Harkin close behind. The shouts and hoofbeats faded. The injured man stood firm, sword in hand, looking relieved that help had arrived. I jumped from my pony and helped the two merchants while father spoke with the warrior. The two men sized each other up and apparently were satisfied.

The stranger sat on the tailgate of the wagon while I bandaged his right shoulder with a strip of linen I had cut from my shirt. Blood from the open shoulder wound had stained the gold trimmed linen jacket down to the elbow. *I won't be needing my shirt anyway once I get to the Abbey.* "There, sir, that will get you to the Abbey, then the monks can do a proper job."

He rose, towering over me. He was dark-haired man of middle years with a well-trimmed beard and had the bearing of a noble man, a man used to authority. "I'm Diarmaid O'Brien, the Bishop's emissary," he said in a deep rich voice.

"I'm Naill O'Donnel," replied father. "You've had a rough welcome to Kells. Seems we're all heading to the Abbey. The merchants have calf hides and wine to deliver. You have Church business and I'm delivering my son. This attack is worrisome. The raiders are strangers to us, not the McCrory clan this time. It's unusual to attack a wagon when an experienced warrior such as yourself is present; that was very bold on their part."

"Aye. They were good swordsmen and well mounted. It takes a good man to unhorse me. No markings on clothing or shields to identify them. That's a concern I'll share with your Sheriff when I'm finished with the Abbot," replied O'Brien.

I caught his horse and led the animal to him. It was a fine looking chestnut stallion, well-fed with a gleaming coat. There was silver work on it's brow band and the saddle cloth bore the Bishop's insignia of the cross and the crown. It pranced nervously beside me, a sword slash having split the shiny hide on its flank. "He had reason to throw you, sir" I said, pointing out the wound.

O'Brien ran his good hand over the horse's rump and cursed. Taking the reins in his left hand and favouring his right arm, he mounted with relative ease and looked down at me. "Fortunately, it's just a surface wound. Entering the service of God, are you?"

"Yes, sir."

"It will be hard work – not as exciting as life on the outside."

"As my brother told me – no beer, no fighting and no women," I replied.

He laughed then winced from the pain of his injury.

We were crossing the ford when we were joined by Fearghus and Harkin leading two horses, dead riders lay face down across their saddles.

"Aye father, we got these two but the other one got away. They're not local," said Harkin, sporting a bloody cheek and several partial thickness cuts in his chest-protecting leather inar. "I'm wondering if these marauders are from Ulster or Connaught?"

Riding into Kells on the Navan Road, our strange procession created lots of attention, as people ran along side or were gawking out upper storey windows. The round stone tower of the Abbey loomed defiantly over the trees, marking our destination. We followed the high stone walls enclosing the Abbey lands until we came to the main gate. I dismounted and pulled the bell cord. The sound echoed.

I turned to father, unbuckled my sword, the one he had given me when I was seven and with two hands under the blade surrendered it to him. I hadn't had time to think about this moment. *I'm giving up my life and family to commit myself to something unknown. I'm scared but must not show it.* No words were spoken. He looked down from his horse with an infinite sadness in his eyes and his strong hands grasped the child sized blade. The gate creaked as the monk opened it and I turned away from my family.

The monk's eyes widened at the group before him. He recognized O'Brien immediately and summoned assistance for him. Two monks escorted him to the Infirmary. The merchants were sent to the stables to deliver their goods and I was taken aside to await my mentor. The gates closed behind me and I heard the departure of the horses as my family rode away, taking the dead to the Sheriff and no doubt, claiming the weapons and horses.

A middle-aged monk approached me. He was balding and slender in build. His clear blue eyes looked like they didn't miss much. "Aidan? I am Brother Connear. Follow me. We are going to the Chapel for afternoon prayers. We call it None or the Ninth Hour. We have prayers seven times a day and once through the night."

I followed him down the corridor, through a large set of wooden doors that swung silently on massive iron hinges. Monks in both black and brown cassocks were filing silently in, filling the pews. We sat at the back.

"We have a Rule of Silence here and don't speak unless it is necessary."

"Why is that?"

"Saint Benedict, the founder of our order, thought it broke communion with God" he replied.

The Abbot came in through a side door and took his position at the lectern. He was a stern upright man with forbidding face. *I don't think I'd want to cross him.* He began intoning the Invitatory: "God, come to my assistance; Lord, make haste to help me," then led us into a hymn, followed by psalms and a scripture reading. The voices of sixty men floated up filling the space and echoed off the stone, sound mingling with the light that filtered through the tall pointed stained-glass windows.

I listened intently. Father Peter, our local priest had been diligent in teaching me Latin but my knowledge was rudimentary and there was much here I didn't understand.

Thankfully the Lord's prayer was familiar - "Pater noster qui es in Caelis, sanctificatur nomen tuum..." *I have so much to learn.* From the corner of my eye I could see a small smile on Brother Connear's face.

After prayers, he took me to the dormitory, where there were rows of cots each with a plain gray blanket. Other than a wooden cross over each bed the room was bare – stone walls, stone floors and tall narrow windows. There wasn't much light except for a few candles. He offered me a brown hooded robe and I slipped into it. *It's coarse and scratchy.* He took my deer-hide boots and clothing and I found a simple pair of sandals that fit.

"Aidan, you are now a postulant – that's someone who joins us but hasn't taken vows. In about six months we'll decide if you fit into this community or not."

What would happen to me if they decided they didn't want me? I still couldn't go home. Father wouldn't allow it.

I was getting hungry. He said there were two meals a day held in the Refractory, one after Prime and one before Vespers. The Refractory was full of wooden bench seats, tables and hungry monks. The silence was overwhelming. They watched me with varying degrees of interest but no one spoke. It was a sea of faces, men of all ages from the very old to some even younger than me.

Brother Connear motioned me towards the front where there was a huge cast iron pot of soup and loaves of bread. He handed me a wooden bowl and spoon. It was a hearty soup full of vegetables and smelled good. I grabbed a chunk of bread and a piece of cheese and filled a pewter mug with red wine. *No meat? Guess not.*

"Every man has a job here. What can you do? Some work in the garden, raising our own vegetables and medicinal herbs; others have skills in the building trades."

"I can ride and hunt, and care for the horses and cattle. My brothers taught me to use the sword and the staff. I like to read and write. Father Peter was teaching me Latin, but I don't know enough yet."

"Perhaps the Scriptorium would be a good place to start," he said sopping up the dregs of the soup with his last crust of bread.

"Brother Connear, who is that angry man over there who keeps looking at me?"

He turned and looked across the rows of tables to the scowling dark-haired older man on the far side of the room. "That's Brother Senach." He paused for a moment. "Ah, of course, he's a McCrory. No love lost between your families I hear."

We sat in silence. *The family feuds continue even within these walls. I must watch my back.*

That night I slept on my cot. *I'm so lonely and it is so quiet. I never thought I'd miss my noisy brothers but I do. No one laughs here. It is strange to sleep in a room full of strangers.* As tired as I was, it was a long night and I had only just got to sleep when we were awoken for early prayers.

Following Prime and our morning prayers, Brother Connear took me to the stables. It was a low stone building with a thatched roof. I could see the rumps of six horses in their stalls including O'Brien's. *He's still here.* A monk was rubbing salve into the flank wound which the stallion didn't like much, flattening his ears and shifting his hooves. The far end of the stable was full of barrels, some containing calf skins, likely those the merchants had delivered yesterday.

"Aidan, the first step in making vellum is to fill a barrel with river water, add ten pounds of lime and wood ash and stir thoroughly. The rolled calf skin is put in the barrel with the hair side out and we stir it every day for a week."

"What does the lime do?" I asked, standing on my tiptoes to look into the barrel.

"It helps to loosen the hair so it's easier to scrape off. Here's a paddle for you. You do this row and I'll do the other. We'll get a block of wood for you to stand on. Don't get your hands wet – that stuff burns. I always leave a spare pail of water here just in case I get some on me."

Even standing on the wood block, I had trouble stirring the skins and was thoroughly glad when the bells rang for mid-morning prayer (Terce). As we made our way to chapel, I noticed another boy.

"Who's that?" I whispered.

"That's Mark. He works in the gardens and Infirmary with Brother Colum, making medicines from our herbs. Brother Colum has a lot of experience with battle wounds as he was in the army before he was ordained. He'll be taking good care of Diarmaid O'Brien."

I looked for Senach but did not see him.

Later in the scriptorium, Brother Connear took me to a carrel and set out an ink pot, a quill pen and a plain piece of vellum. He opened a small prayer book. "Aidan, I want you to copy this page."

I sat down and carefully penned my page while he sat beside me working on his own copy. "There I think I'm done."

"Now Aidan, stand and read the page to me just like the Abbot does in Chapel."

I took my page, stood up and read it through as I would have with Father Peter at home.

"Not bad, Aidan. Now I want you to translate this page into Gaelic like you were reading to your own brothers."

I got through most of it, but stumbled on a few words.

"Father Peter has certainly done a good job giving you the basics. We need to do more work on your writing. Some of these down strokes aren't straight and a few lines are crooked. The Latin will be a matter of practice. Have you cut quills before?"

"Only a few times. I'm not good at it yet."

He handed me a snowy white goose feather and placed it on the table. With a sharp knife, he cut off the tip. "If you don't trim enough, it won't hold ink; too much and it will make a blob that ruins your work." He demonstrated the angle he wanted. "When you've got the cut right, you trim off all the feather except three or four inches at the end of the vane."

An old man sat in a space where the light from two windows met. His snowy white hair cascaded down over his shoulders as he bent over his work, totally engrossed in his writing. There were pots of coloured inks all around him. Brother Connear followed my gaze and nodded but put a finger to his lips. Quietly we walked over and looked at his work. He was adding the coloured decoration to a very elaborate and complicated script like I'd never seen before on a beautifully finished white vellum. I gasped.

The old man paused and looked up at me. "Come boy. Behold the work of a master."

I stepped closer. Within the shape of the convoluted letter X, the first letter of the writing, were tiny angels, crosses, lions and Celtic knots as the X spread down the left margin of the page then curled upward enclosing a large P and I. I had never seen coloured inks before – bright yellow, green, blue and even pure gold. *It's beautiful. He's filling in the spaces one dot of colour at a time.*

He bowed his head and I knew I was dismissed. Brother Connear's hand on my shoulder brought me back to reality. Silently we walked from the scriptorium. "Who is he?"

"That is Brother Nuadu. He illustrates the precious manuscripts. He is the only one here with the skill to do the intricate Insular Scripts. One of those pages might take three or four months to complete."

"I've never seen coloured ink before. Where does it come from?"

"From different places all over the world. Traders bring them by ship from ports in the Mediterranean Sea, a month or more's sailing from here. The black ink we make ourselves from oak galls and iron. You'll get to make some later."

"What does the X, P and I mean?"

"That is called the Incantation of Christ. They are the first three letters of the Greek form of Christ's name. A Latin scholar would call that the Chi Rho."

It all seemed beyond my understanding. Perhaps when I learn more Latin it might make sense.

When we got back from Vespers, I found my little pile of quills hacked to pieces and scattered on the floor. I was so angry. "Who did this? Why?"

Brother Connear took one look at my face and became serious. "Aidan, I don't know who did this, but I can guess why. Pray for that soul."

Pray for that soul? I bet that soul was that man Senach. I don't want to pray for him; I'd like to take Fearghus' staff and knock him down with it. "Why would someone do that?" I asked.

He looked me straight in the eye. "Aidan, you are the son of a King. You have led a privileged life. You had parents who cared for you, with plenty of food, a roof over your head and clothing on your back. You have never been hungry. You have had an education; most here are illiterate. You have had a horse to ride. Many here may be jealous or resentful. You are an O'Donnel – to some that makes you the enemy. You are going to have to prove yourself – first to God then by your actions, to others. I'm not saying it's right but the best way to deal with this is to ignore it. We have a good supply of feathers and you need the practise anyway," he said.

Right.

Life settled into a routine now. In the mornings between prayers, we worked on the vellum; in the afternoons, it was writing and in the evenings, it was Latin – day in and day out. I am getting used to not having meat. *Is it a sin to think of a nice piece of venison?* I thought of Harkin with a carcass slung across his saddle after a successful hunt. There are times when I have trouble even remembering what his face looked like. There was no privacy here, no place to hide, so I held back my tears, not wanting others to see. The closest I could get to Mother was the Virgin Mary. I pause often before her statue in the chapel and sent a prayer. *There's never a day off and there is no laughter, no fun. God give me the strength and purpose to become the man I must become.*

Brother Connear took me to see the gardens. I found Mark pulling weeds in the herb bed and gathering some herbs for Brother Colum. I recognized sage, chamomile, comfrey, dill and mint. Mother used to grow those at home. Mark was not talkative but always had a smile on his face.

"He's childlike and rarely speaks," said Brother Connear. "He's a very gentle, caring soul. He was dropped off on our doorstep in a basket when he was a baby. We never knew his parents so the Abbot found a wet nurse in town and she raised him until he was old enough to come back to us."

The vegetable beds looked neat and thriving as several other monks were shovelling stable manure into the soil. Others were pulling vegetables for our next meal.

On our way to prayers, I could see the Abbey gates were open and merchants were bringing in fresh supplies. Some monks worked out in town, tending to the poor and the sick; others never left the property. News from the outside was gleaned, despite our Rule of Silence. Word filtered back that the O'Donnels and the McCrorys were fighting again. *I pray my family are safe.*

Diarmaid O'Brien was mounted and preparing to leave. He noticed me and rode over. I couldn't tell from his repaired tunic and the way he was using his arm that he had ever been wounded. The horse looked fine now, the scar just a faint hairless line on the otherwise glossy rump. "Goodbye, Aidan. There are dangers inside and outside these walls. Take care."

I nodded. "Has your shoulder healed?"

"Well enough to use a sword if I have to. Keep up the good work. They are pleased with your progress so far," he said and rode away.

What was I supposed to make of that warning? What danger was he talking about? Senach? Raiders? Any change of kingship would alter the balance of power at the Abbey. Had father sent me here for safety? I was more perplexed than ever and could not do anything about it.

Once a week, a group of younger monks practiced with their wooden staves for an hour with Brother Ennis, who had been a soldier. Some of them were out in the community carrying messages from one church to another for the Abbot. The staves were the only weapon they were allowed. I had been eyeing them enviously, as memories flooded back of hours battling with Fearghus. Brother Connear must have taken note.

"Would you wish to join them?" he asked. "You'd be the youngest. You're much smaller than they are. It would be a disadvantage."

"Maybe so, Brother Connear, but they didn't have to put up with my brother Fearghus. I'm surprised I don't still carry the bruises from our last meeting."

He grinned and spoke to Brother Ennis. The man cast a doubtful look but nodded. "Come Aidan. We don't use the leather inars here; no protection. You must rely on anticipating your opponent's moves and being quick on your feet. There's the pile of staves; choose one that suits your weight."

I went over to the pile stacked against the stone wall and tried one; it was too long and heavy. I selected a shorter one but the balance wasn't right. The third was ash and flexible which I preferred. Brother Ennis stood there, his feet spread apart. Fearghus' words rang in my head - *watch his eyes not his hands*. I stood still ready to move, my eyes fixed intently on him. The blow came quickly, I slipped sideways to the right so that it missed my left shoulder and thrust into his belly before he raised his staff again. I didn't hit hard enough to wind him. His face sharpened into a frown. We danced around each other striking back and forth - wood sounding on wood. I struck with all my might but was unable to knock the staff from his hand but did manage to get a good swing at his knees. He countered with a quick low move and I got a stinging hard slap in the left thigh that knocked me sideways onto the ground. He stopped. Getting to my feet, I noticed the other boys had stopped sparring and had gathered in a circle around us.

He grudgingly spoke. "You'll do. Your brothers have taught you well. You don't have the size or the weight to make a difference yet but that will come. You're good at keeping your eyes focussed and were varying the thrusts, so it was harder to anticipate your moves. Come to practice next week," he said, slapping me on the back.

I was pleased, too, and looked forward to next week, although my leg was throbbing. With no leather protection, I could see that I'd need to be more aware of the moves and be far more nimble on my feet. I looked at the other boys fixing their faces in my memory.

I seldom saw Senach at meals as we sat at opposite ends of the hall and he tended to sit near the front of the chapel, while I sat with a group of youngsters more my age. He was a stonemason and worked on the grounds repairing the buildings and walls. We rarely crossed paths which was probably a good thing. No further incidents had occurred with my quills and I was now proficient in cutting them. I wrote on a daily basis. Brother Connear still rigorously checked my work and I was making progress slowly. Just yesterday, as guardian of the keys, he had taken me to the Sacristy, unlocking the heavy wooden door with a large brass key and he unwrapped the books I had heard so much about.

The Book of Kells! If I had thought Brother Nuada's work was magnificent, it didn't compare to the thick books with embossed gold covers, containing page after page of scrolled writing and intricate illustrations of Christ, the disciples and Mary with the baby Jesus. *It is hard to believe this was made by men.* My own efforts now seemed childish. *This is the standard I must strive for.*

Brother Connear said: "These are the Gospels of Mathew, Mark, Luke and John written over two hundred years ago by St. Columba's monks on the Scottish island of Iona. The Vikings raided them in 806 and so many were killed that the whole surviving community fled here to keep the books safe. These books are unique and should last a thousand years if they are kept in a dry place."

"I now understand the standard of excellence you have been teaching me," I said. *That's why the quality of the vellum was so critical.* The hours of soaking, scraping and smoothing now made sense. It had to be smooth for the quality of the artwork to show and for the ink to sink in evenly. He carefully rewrapped the books and locked the door behind us, the keys jangling on his waist belt.

I sat on my bed that night and pictured Brother Nuadu sitting in the scriptorium, the tonsured head bowed in concentration over the page and that steady, steady hand on the quill. I had noticed the row of tiny pinholes in the vellum he used to keep his lines straight and marvelled at his dedication. The simplicity of the man was a sharp contrast to the glory of that page. He had given his whole life to God to do that work. I prayed for the opportunity to serve the Lord in this way. If I was going to be locked up in this place I wanted to create something beautiful. *My destiny lies with these books.*

We had just finished scraping a calf hide when there was a terrible cracking sound, a roar, then screams and shouts. Running out of the stables I could see a rising cloud of dust where the old barn had stood; one end had collapsed. I knew at least five monks had been working on roof repairs that morning.

Everyone joined in, even the Abbot, checking under broken boards, beams and hay looking for signs of the missing men. A shout went up and an unconscious brother was dragged from the hay pile. Brother Colum made a makeshift stretcher and the man was carried to the Infirmary. His moans meant at least he was alive. Mark and I continued wading through thigh high hay trying to avoid the razor sharp broken pieces of roof slate. *Some of these beams are ten inches thick. How could they come down like that?*

Another shout went up but then there was silence. The Abbot was there as the body was pulled out of the debris and gently moved to higher ground. I heard my name being called by Brother Connear. He was standing under a jumble of beams up to his waist in hay waving and calling for me to come over.

I extricated myself from the hole I was working in and ran over to him.

"There's someone under this mess. I can hear him calling but I can't see where he is. Aidan, you're the smallest. You can fit in this hole. Quiet everyone."

We all listened and a muffled voice called: "Help me, Lord, help me."

God help me. I got on my hands and knees and slithered in on my belly. The space between the two beams was tight. It was pitch black. I stopped and listened. I could hear him crying out to my left. I felt a small beam in front of me and had just enough room to wiggle over it. "Where are you? Keep talking," I yelled.

"Here, here! Oh God, help me!"

He's close. I felt a foot, then a knee but there was a huge beam across his body and my hands felt another one above it on an angle over my head. He was stuck beneath two cross beams, which had given him a breathing space. It had saved him from the tons of hay and the broken tiles but had wedged him in.

"I'm going back. We need to get horses to move these beams," I said and started to wiggle backwards.

"Don't leave me! I'm going to die."

"I have to get help to get you out." It took a while for me to worm my way out backwards. The air was full of dust and it was hard to breathe. Hands grabbed my ankles and hauled me into the daylight still coughing and sneezing. I looked into Brother Connear's face. "He's not far in, about ten feet to the left where you can see the ends of those beams, but there's another beam across his legs. We'll need the horses to move them."

While I had under the pile they had been busy and the horses were already harnessed, waiting. The men took over and carefully winched the two big beams out of the way, moving hay as they went. Then everyone started digging again with their hands. Finally, there was a hole and the face of Brother Senach appeared. More digging. Chains were wrapped around the big beam and the horses strained forward pulling the beam with them. Senach looked at me; I looked at him. I was too stunned to say or do anything. *Would I have gone down that hole if I had known it was him? Dunno. I guess you can't leave a man to die like that.* Meanwhile I was pleased to see that the other two brothers had been found with only minor cuts and bruises.

Brother Connear clapped me on the shoulder, raising dust. "Come lad, the Lord has been good to you. We owe him a prayer of thanks for those spared and a prayer for the one we lost."

I shook off some dust and the strands of hay from my cassock and followed him to Chapel.

After prayers, we went back to the calf hides. Having finally removed all the hair and being careful not to nick the hides, we stretched them on wooden frames to let them dry thoroughly.

"We need to check these rawhide thongs at least once a day as the skins stretch. We may have to tighten them."

"How many pages do we get out of one calf hide?" I asked.

"Usually five or six double pages. Once they are stretched we rub them with pumice stone to even out any rough spots and cut them to size. I save all the scraps from practice work."

Later, on the way to Vespers, I met Senach in the corridor as we were going to Chapel. He looked at me. There was no animosity in his face like before but not friendly either. *We would never be friends but I'd be happy with a truce. He's not a McCory anymore and I guess I'm not on O'Donnel.*

Several weeks later, I was in the Scriptorium labouring on another copy of the prayer book. I would sneak a look at Brother Nuada's work from time to time, being careful not to disturb him but wanting to see what he was doing. If he was aware of me, he didn't show it. Brother Connear approached. "Aidan, you will be going out tomorrow with Brothers Alby and Bairre to the oak forest near Navan. Our ink supply is running low and we need to collect oak galls. Autumn is a good time of year before the weather gets cold. You will stay overnight at the Priory then come back the next day."

My face lit up. *A chance to get out of here and see something different.*

Alby and Bairre were both eighteen and had taken their vows. I had met them before in my group with Brother Ennis. We spent two days in the forest looking for galls.

"Here Aidan," said Brother Alby pointing out a rough nut sized growth on one of the big oak's branches. He hitched up his cassock and shinnied up the tree to reach it. Sometimes the galls were low enough that we could use our staves to knock them down. I hadn't climbed a tree since I was little but it felt good to find a foothold in the bark and climb, getting a view of the woods and hillside, the tip of the Priory steeple just visible over the distant treetops. I must confess the Rule of Silence was broken on more than one occasion.

"So how do you make ink out of these?" I asked, holding up a black wizened nut.

"You grind them up into a powder then add water and old nails or other pieces of iron and it turns into ink," replied Bairre.

The brothers at the Prior made us very welcome and we seamlessly fit into their routine which was the same as the Abbey's but somehow less formal.

Alby and Bairre were good companions. They were both young and serious but still lively. It reminded me of my brothers. Our bulging sacks attested to our success. *Brother Connear will be pleased. I've enjoyed just being able to move around outside.* We moved steadily along the path until it crossed the Navan Road. The road was full of people, wagons and animals moving in both directions. A man driving a cart from Kells called out to us: "You'd better get back to the Abbey in a hurry. There's mischief afoot. I've heard they can't find the Books – they've been stolen."

What? We looked at each other. *How could the Books be gone? Only Brother Connear and the Abbot had keys.*

Brother Connear met us at the gate. "You've heard the news, I see."

"What happened?"

"When I went to the Sacristy the day you left, the door was closed but the books were gone."

"But only you and the Abbot have the keys!"

"Aye, so we thought. The Sheriff has been here. It was market day so the gates had been open. No one saw any strangers in the Chapel or any monks they didn't recognize. The Books had been there the previous week but when I went to get the chalice for morning prayers they were gone. I don't understand it."

"There must have been another key, and someone here used it" I said scanning my brethren. *One of these Brothers was a thief. They must have passed the Books to one of the merchants. It would have been easy to hide the Books in a wagon.*

"God help them. We've searched all the buildings. They're gone."

Our daily life went on as usual. I think all of us looked at each other and wondered who was the culprit. There was no other explanation. The Abbot's sermon was scathing and his threat of dire punishment by the Lord and the law left no doubt as to the outcome. Someone had been willing to risk his soul for gold.

Weeks went by and still nothing. Brother Connear told me the Sheriff had questioned all the merchants and none of them had seen or heard anything. No one was suddenly wealthy, either. It had rained for three days and finally stopped. I was bringing buckets of water back from the river for another batch of calf hides when a glimmer of blue caught my eye in a pile of rocks just outside the old cemetery wall. I'd walked past those rocks almost every day and never noticed anything before. I put the buckets down. I'd only seen that colour blue in one place, in the piece of silk wrapped around the Books. On my hands and knees, I carefully removed the rocks. My hands were trembling as I scooped the dirt aside. They were rolled up in a calf skin and the blue silk that had protected them from the rain. The covers were gone and so were some of the front and back pages where the covers had been torn off, but the bulk of them were there. The faces of the saints looked at me. I was speechless and sent a quick prayer of thanks to whatever angels had let me find them.

I yelled like a madman and people came running as I stood there holding the treasure of the Lord, cradling them in my arms, almost afraid to move. I don't think I will ever forget the look on Brother Connear's face when I handed them to him. A new lock was placed on the Sacristy door and the old keys destroyed. We never did discover who was responsible. At least he hadn't destroyed the books completely and for that I was thankful.

Over time my skills in writing improved, but I was never able to achieve the skill level of Brother Nuadu. He repaired some of the damaged pages. It was many years later as an older man that I eventually became keeper of the keys. The books remained safely locked away in the Sacristy. *I hope I will be able to preserve this legacy for the future faithful.*

epilogue

Trinity College, Dublin, present day

I am a tourist. Today, I waited outside the Trinity College Library for about an hour in the line up with a continuous stream of multinational people, for the opportunity to see what are considered to be one of Ireland's national treasures – four surviving folios of The Book of Kells. I had heard of them, but had never seen them before. These books are thought to have been written in the early 800s, likely on the Scottish Island of Iona at St. Columba's monastery until Viking raids forced the monks to seek a safer venue. The monks chose the Abbey at Kells in County Meath as a safe place to live and work. Some time in 1007, the Books were stolen and the gold covers removed. Parts of the books were found later and partially restored. They were added to over time but never finished. They represent an art form, a combination of Insular script and decorative artwork of Christian and

Celtic symbols, handwritten on calf vellum and made with inks ranging from gall ink (local) to coloured ones imported from distant and exotic places like the lapis lazuli blue from Afghanistan. The intricacy and style of writing is beyond description.

Over time, the Abbey of Kells became a parish church and the Books were still kept there until the time of Oliver Cromwell when once again they were at risk of destruction. They were given to Trinity College Library in Dublin where they remain to this day in a temperature and light controlled environment. As I looked at those pages, I watched the reactions of other people around me. The room was totally silent. The operative word was "awe". In our world where "instant" and "disposable" are the norms, I tried to imagine the world as it was in those times; the lives of the monks with their harsh and dedicated lifestyle, risking their lives often alone in a bleak and unforgiving landscape. I thought of the talent, the time and the belief needed to create those pages. I was told that one square inch on some pages could contain hundreds of pen strokes. It raised so many questions that I came home and started to research that era and the result was this piece of fiction and Aidan's journey, to recreate life as it was then. Ireland is full of the things the monks left behind, the ruins, myths, legends, huts and their writing. For the most part, the monks themselves were anonymous. Here we are, a thousand years later, proof that Brother Connear's prediction was a good one.

the equus diary

Milton, Ontario, Canada

Christie sat at her desk with her diary open, thinking about her day. She could hear her parents talking in the living room, their voices rising up the stairwell.

"Helen, you can't expect her to live at home forever. She's nineteen and she wants a better education. She can't get the courses around here" said her father.

"But Jack, I was hoping she'd get over this addiction to horses and get a real job, maybe work in your insurance office dealing with the horse insurance. I don't understand why she has to shovel horse manure and come home reeking of the stuff."

Oh Mum, I'll never be your little girl in pink fluffy dresses with bows in my hair. I'm happiest on the back of a horse, feeling the power beneath me, feeling the wind on my face when I ride.

"I've looked at the pamphlets she's been getting; some are in the States and there's one from Ireland too. All of them are for careers with thoroughbreds and they're all outside Canada. I knew when I got her that job in Milton that she wouldn't spend the rest of her life cleaning stalls and that she'd come to a decision. Well, luv, she's made it," replied her father.

"Jack, she's only nineteen and she'll be in a foreign country. How safe is that?"

Christie could hear the tremor in her mother's voice. *Oh, now she's starting to get teary. She's driving me crazy, treats me like I'm twelve years old. There are times I really want to get out of here.*

"Yes, she's nineteen but she's a sensible intelligent kid. Helen, we're just going to have to trust her."

Thank you, Dad, thought Christie. *I have made my decision and I want to work on a breeding farm not as general labour but as the manager. I need to take a course and get more experience to be good at it. The question is which one?*

Later that evening, Christie went downstairs. Her father had just finished reading the newspaper and her mum was in the kitchen. Christie glanced up at the photos on the mantel. One was of her at age five straddling a shaggy rotund pinto pony, with her riding helmet askew and an ear-to-ear grin (minus two front teeth). The smile said it all. *I fell in love with horses right then and there.* The other photo had been taken by her father at her first major horse show when she was thirteen. The thoroughbred mare was clearing a fence and the sunlight captured Christie's intently focused face, framed by blue sky and the wind-whipped mane of the soaring horse. *He got that shot right.*

Here goes. "Dad – can I talk to you about these courses?"

"Sure, Christie. What's on your mind?"

She sat down beside him on the sofa and laid out the pamphlets, plus the spreadsheet she had made up. "I think I've narrowed it down to three; the University of Kentucky programme, the Darley Flying Start and the Irish National Stud. The Kentucky one is a university programme and would take three years so the costs would be higher since I would be an international student. Room and board is extra. However, it's closer to home, so I could get a summer job here and I'd end up with a degree and probably could get a job easily in the U.S."

"What about the Darley one?" he said looking at the numbers on the spreadsheet.

"It's much the same as far as I can see," she replied.

"Now tell me about the Irish National Stud."

"The course in Ireland is only five months long and its very hands on. It's a practical course and costs about five thousand Euros; that includes room and board. The catch is that they only take twenty-four applicants. It has a fantastic reputation. There would be air fare and insurance to consider but I like that one best. I could always do a degree programme later. What do you think?"

"Well, considering your great grandfather was Irish, I'm probably a bit biased." He read over the INS pamphlet again. "How do you plan to pay for this?"

"I've saved $3,000 but that's not enough, so I was hoping I could get a loan from you and Mum," she said with a sigh. "Of course, I'll pay you back as soon as I start working."

Her mother came in from the kitchen and joined them. Christie went over the details again and sat there while her parents talked it over. *Oh please, say yes. I really want this.*

"Christie, your mother and I will have to look at our finances before we can fully commit, but I'm going to tentatively say yes. Talk to Jim at the stables tomorrow. It is very important for you to get a good letter of reference since the enrolment's so limited. See what he has to say about giving you a job here once you've qualified."

The next day Christie approached Jim, the barn manager at the stables.

"Christie, you have to be dead serious about doing this for a living. I've met grads from these programmes and I can tell you, it's not easy. The courses are excellent but it's a ton of work, both physically and mentally. You'll be doing barn chores same as here but you will also be responsible for seeing that a foal is safely delivered, and with a $100,000 baby there can be no mistakes. You must know what you're doing. One dead foal and you'd be out of a job. Reputation is everything with the owners," he said.

"I think the Irish one's my best option. It's more practical."

"Do you remember when you first came here, I was working with a young guy named Robert? Tall skinny kid, kind of quiet?"

"Vaguely, he helped during the first foaling I ever saw," she replied.

"Well, he's an INS grad. He's working in California now at one of the big breeding farms as their assistant barn manager and he's doing very well. The courses are all expensive. Have you discussed this with your parents?"

"I had that talk with them last night" Christie said. "They know I want a better career and I'm serious about furthering my education. They're going to figure out the finances as I'll need a loan to cover my tuition." *I'm not afraid of hard work and I'm eager to learn. Do I have what it takes to do this? Will it be enough?*

"I can certainly supply you with a reference for INS to get you started and with that kind of expertise behind you, there'd be a job here when you get back" he said.

She felt her excitement build and spent the rest of the day cleaning stalls and helping to feed the mares and foals. When she was leaving, Jim called her over and handed her an envelope. "There's your reference Christie, good luck with it."

She was so excited she sat in the car and read the reference. He had been honest about her skills and generous in his recommendations. Later, when she got home and took off her boots, her mother cornered her in the kitchen.

"Christie, my main concern is that you're very young to just take off to a foreign country all by yourself," her mother said looking at her doubtfully.

Christie felt her aggravation level rising. "Mum, what are you worried about? I've never been in trouble; I've never even had a speeding ticket. Going to Ireland isn't any different than me going to the University of Toronto. They do speak English there. I'd still be away from home, regardless of the distance, so what's the difference?" she said and before her mother could answer, stomped upstairs to have a shower.

After supper, her father gave her the good news. "Your mother and I can afford to loan you the tuition fees. You can repay it once you graduate."

She gave him a huge hug and bounded up the stairs to complete her application. *They're only accepting twenty-four students for the coming foaling year, starting in February.*

They'll be getting hundreds of applications from all over the world. I hope my credentials are good enough.

During the week Christie went out with her friends Shana and Megan after work at the local bar in Milton.

"When do you expect to hear from them?" asked Megan, passing the jug of beer to her.

"I have no idea. I guess it's too early to get a reply. My mother's driving me insane. I'm not going to sit in some stupid office pushing paper. She's got some antiquated idea that I should be a nice clean little secretary, settle down with some local yokel's son and have a bunch of kids. Not likely, any time soon!"

"Here are the guys," said Shana as a noisy foursome in toques and ski jackets came in out of the cold wind and snow to join them and watch the hockey game on the bar's big flat screen TV.

"I have no idea why I'm cheering for the Leafs, they never win. I think I'm going to become a Senators fan," she said, waving goodbye to the others as she maneuvered her way through the snow rutted parking lot and headed home.

Every evening on her way home she would stop at the mail box at the end of the lane to pick up the mail. *Nothing!* Canadian winter turned to spring. The snow drifts melted away, leaving muddy ruts and last year's dead leaves. The buds started to come out on the maples that lined the lane. She tried to put a positive spin on things and applied for her passport. At work, she looked for opportunities to take a more active role. Most of the staff were receptive to her questions, explaining what they were doing and why.

One spring morning she was getting ready to let the mares and foals out into the greening paddock and asked her co-worker "Diane, you've been here a long time. I want to make sure I'm doing things right. I've been around horses since I was a kid and I think I'm doing things right but I just want to double check that I'm doing it correctly. How do you teach a foal to lead?"

The mare and foal were standing at the stall door, waiting to go out. "You start first by introducing the foal to the halter. Go ahead and put the halter on this one," said Diane. Christie gently approached the foal and nudged it beside its mother. She calmly patted the curious baby and eased the nose band over its face, then fastened the buckle. Baby stood there bobbing its head up and down, then she clipped the lead line to the halter. "This one already knows the routine, but in the beginning, you'll need one of the longer lead lines and you loop it around its body and over its tail above the hocks. Now keep the lead in your right hand," said Diane.

"So now I have a come-a-long to move him forward without hurting his neck, right?" said Christie.

Diane nodded and snapped a short lead on the mare. "Make sure you don't catch the lead under the tail or you'll end up with a bucking bronco. This colt's three months old; the little ones need a bit more coaxing but generally they follow mum." With that they led the pair to the paddock and turned them loose.

"Thanks, Diane. I've got to learn as much as I can while I'm here," replied Christie.

Every day she found something new. On the blacksmith's next visit, she cross-tied the mare in the aisle and led the foal around.

"Mike, what exactly are you looking for?" she asked as he picked up the mare's left foreleg.

"Well, I'm looking at the legs to see if she has any swelling or heat that would indicate an injury. I'll run my hands down her legs to feel for that. I'm looking at how she is walking and moving. Is she limping? Is she standing square? These legs are fine. I also check the frog to make sure it isn't bruised. This hoof is long and needs trimming but the coronet band is parallel to the ground so her hoof's nice and square under her." Taking the nippers, he proceeded to trim off a thin crescent of hoof then filed the hoof smooth with the rasp. He proceeded to the other ones.

Christie kept the colt amused while Mike worked on the mare. She led the restless youngster in circles always keeping the mare in view and backed him up a few steps.

"She's done. Now it's his turn. Lead him over here beside her."

Christie led the colt over. It wobbled as Mike picked up a foreleg and tried to nip him. Christie snapped the lead to get his attention.

"Colts can be a handful. Distract him. If he gets too saucy, we could put a twitch on him but not at this stage. I don't want to make him head-shy. His feet are fine but I'm going to go through the whole process as he's got to learn some manners. Much easier to do now than when he weighs a thousand pounds." Mike felt the legs, examined the feet, ran the rasp over each one, looked at the angles, then straightened up and slapped him on the rump. "O.K. He's good to go." Christie untied the mare and led both animals back to their stall.

Over the summer, Christie and Diane separated the mares and foals in the noisy process of weaning the babies. Mares were taken to another farm out of earshot. *You feel so sad for them at first. They call incessantly for their mum but there's no answer. Heartbreaking, but with each day, they settle in a bit more. We watch them and keep on with routine, brushing, feeding and by the end of the week they've forgotten.*

"Here Christie, we're going to put the fillies out together today. We'll do the colts tomorrow."

"It's interesting to watch the herd behaviours. Look, they'll keep the pecking order by how dominant their mother was. Gypsy was boss mare in the paddock. Watch her filly; ears flat doing the ugly face, first to the water trough, first to the gate. They sort it out," said Diane.

Come September, the stables became even busier as the youngsters were prepared for the yearling sales. Christie marvelled at how cute fuzzy, gangly babies suddenly blossomed into glossy, elegant beasts 14 to 15 hands high. *I'm glad we did all that early work with the grooming and the automatic horse walker. It's paid off.* She helped Diane load and unload them on horse trailers to accustom them to enclosed spaces and noise.

"Diane, what do you think makes a person right for this job?" she asked one day.

"Well, love of horses first, but infinite patience and being calm with them. If you're upset about something, I guarantee it takes them ten seconds to figure it out and they can give you a hard time. They have to learn to trust you. If they are scared, talk to them, sing to them or do some Tellington Touch."

"What's that?"

"It's like a mini massage, using your fingers on their skin. They relax with that. I'll show you sometime."

October 20th

Christie opened the mailbox and as usual there wasn't anything for her. *I'm beginning to think INS has forgotten all about me.* She showered to get rid of the stable smell and threw her barn clothes in the wash. When she opened her e-mail, she found a message from INS.

"Dear Christine," she read under her breath, "we are pleased to offer you a position in our residential pro-gramme for the Thoroughbred Breeding course, starting in February. An information package covering everything you need to know about visas and insurance will follow by mail."

She let out a war whoop and yelled to Mum and Dad: "I got in, I got in!" and raced downstairs. Her mum started to cry. *This chick is so ready to fly! I'm so excited.* She came back upstairs and sent her acknowledgement to INS and then texted all her friends.

Later Dad put his arm around her and said: "You've set yourself a really high goal, girl. Do your best."

"I will, Dad, I will."

January 30th, Dublin

Christie was too revved up to sleep on the six-hour flight from Toronto and it was still dark when the plane landed. The glowing V of the runway lights guided them down. By the time she cleared customs and got her luggage, it was close to seven thirty. The student visa wasn't a problem; INS had made all the arrangements. Her passport was stamped and, walking through the gates, she could see of greenery around the airport through the glassed-in reception area, eager to embrace everything new.

A tall, aristocratic older man in tweeds was waiting in the arrival lounge, holding up an INS sign. "I'm glad to meet you all. My name is Thomas," he said when she introduced herself. Soon, five students had gathered; three young men and another girl. "Right, we're all here now so let's get on our way." He led them out to the parking lot to the INS van.

Dublin was a blur as they sped through but she had glimpses of four storey buildings with storefronts on either side of the river and ornate old bridges. It was Thomas who pointed out that Dublin had been settled by the Vikings in the 800s. *Wow, that's old*, thought Christie. She introduced herself to the girl beside her.

"Hi, I'm Jean and I'm from England." She looked to be in her early twenties with a clean scrubbed look and short ash blonde hair.

The men introduced themselves as Owen and Adam from Northern Ireland.

Rick shook her hand. "I'm from the States," he said with a twangy American accent.

"We'll be taking the M7 to Kildare" said Thomas, as they took the on ramp into heavy traffic.

Christie thought they were going to hit a car head on but realized it was right-hand driving here. *That's going to take a bit of getting used to.* Everything was neat, even on the highway medians. No garbage anywhere. Fields were small with either horse fencing or clipped hedges. The land flattened out to lightly rolling hills. *A lot like home but much greener for this time of year.* They passed the Curragh race track.

"You'll be spending some time there later in your course," said Thomas.

She could see horses in small groups with their riders putting them through their paces out on the gallops. The five students were curious and were soon chatting like they'd know each other for years. The trip to Tully took about an hour. Christie looked at the buildings. *This is impressive. It's old but it's just amazing – look at the land-scaping. Not a blade of grass out of place and all these ponds and flowers*. She could see barns, dark fencing, paddocks, cottages and well fed grazing horses.

Thomas parked at the back of the residence and they piled out of the van. "Here's the list," he said, pointing to the bulletin board. "Find your room, drop off your luggage, then come right back down to have your breakfast. The canteen is just around the corner here on the first floor. Here's the schedule for today. You've got an introductory tour at one o'clock with Mr. J. Good luck, everyone."

Christie found her name. *I've got a room on the second floor and I'm sharing with someone called Alana. I wonder who she is. I'll try and find her in the cafeteria.* She found her room and stashed her luggage beside the available twin bed. The bed beside the window was obviously Alana's, piled high with books and clothes. Quickly washing her face and hands, she checked herself in the mirror, pulling her brown hair back in a pony tail. *That'll do for now. I'm hungry.*

The canteen wasn't hard to find. The noise level led her there. She grabbed a tray and joined the lineup. *All kinds of food and plenty of it. I think I'll go for the bacon, eggs and a muffin this morning.* She quickly scanned the other students. *By the looks of it I'm probably one of the youngest. Not very many girls here, either.*

Jean was already seated and she headed over to her table, balancing her tray. She introduced herself to the others at the table and listened to the cacophony of accents; Irish ones, two guys speaking German, and a group speaking French. Everybody looked to be under thirty.

There's only eight girls here and sixteen guys. I like those odds. "Does anyone know who Alana is?" she asked and a lean, raven-haired girl was pointed out to her. Christie went over to the other table and introduced herself. *Ah, she's Irish, that lovely accent.* Christie answered a barrage of questions from the guys at the table. "No, I'm Canadian, not American" she said. Someone directed her to the community computer and she quickly sent an e-mail to her parents to let them know she had safely arrived. *It is such a relief to actually be here.*

After breakfast, she went back to the room, unpacked and talked to Alana. "What an opportunity! Have you seen the horses? I can't wait to get out there. It's my first time away and everything is so interesting."

The older girl grinned. "My home's not far from here. I'll show you around."

At one o'clock, they both went down to the lobby and met Mr. J. He was a slim, wiry individual full of enthusiasm and took them all on a tour of the foaling yard, the vet's office, lab, feed rooms, the stallion yards, the paddock areas and the public places – the museum and gardens. "We've got about 800 acres here. Public education is a big part of what we do, so there are tours going through; lots of school children. For them we start with the ponies."

Christie was mind boggled. *There's so much to see. I didn't realize the place was so big!* They had a quick supper then it was off for their first lecture by the vet on the reproductive system of the mare, complete with models and diagrams. She knew some of it but the muscles and ligaments had names, and there was an assignment due on Friday. By the end of the lecture her notes looked like chicken scratch. *Well, this has been one heck of a day.* She fell into bed and slept like the dead.

January 31st

Alana shook her awake at 6 a.m. Christie had even slept through the alarm. "Thanks, Alana. Good thing I'm low maintenance. I'm in the foaling yard this week." A quick shower and she was in her blue t-shirt, jeans and boots. She found her way to the Sun Chariot Broodmare yard. It was the classic set up with a quadrangle of box stalls, the black painted sliding doors opening into the yard. A gravel driveway divided the yard with the north exit going to the vet's office and the south one to the public area. There was even a fountain gracing the centre, surrounded by manicured lawn. *It's so tidy it doesn't look real.*

A tall blonde woman in barn clothes approached them. "Hello, I'm Beth. I'm looking for Donato, Christie, Jean

and Colin for my group." They converged around her like
satellite moons and she took them over to the stalls where
she introduced them to their group of mares. Christie was
amazed as Beth rhymed off their names, pedigrees, ages
and foaling histories.

"This is Flanagan's Girl," Beth said, running her hand
over the satiny hide of a very pregnant chestnut mare.
"This is her fourth foal. She's starting to bag up," she
said, looking at the udder, "so she's right on time. She's
had all her foals here with no problems. Big Bad Bob is
the sire of this baby. She's easy to work around and a
good-natured mum. I'm not anticipating any problems.
Pub Time is our second mare. She's a first timer, so we'll
keep a real close eye on her. She arrived yesterday and is
due to foal next week. She's bred to Worthadd and will be
re-bred on foal heat." Christie could see that Pub Time
was a glossy dark bay, elegant in her conformation and
aristocratic in her bearing.

A high-pitched whinny and a thump on the wall introduced them to the last mare. "This is a totally different
animal," said Beth. "She's a beautiful mare, well bred,
produces excellent foals and is a good mother. However,
she can be difficult and temperamental. For the time
being, make sure one of the staff is with you until she
gets used to you. This is Flight of Fancy." Beth slid the
stall door open, revealing a coal black vision with a coat
as shiny as patent leather, her ears flattened and wild

eyes. "She's owned by the McCormacks and is bred to Invincible Spirit. With a stud fee of 70,000 Euros, this will be one very important foal." The head tossing and pacing slowed as Beth continued to talk. "If you want any information on the horses, we do keep individual files on them in the main office."

That's good to know. I was beginning to think she was Wonder Woman, to remember all that stuff, thought Christie. *I guess I didn't really have any idea of the amount of money involved in owning horses like these.*

They toured the lab, fostering box for orphaned foals, the colostrum bank and met the vet. *I bet he doesn't get much sleep this time of the year. He's on call 24/7.* Christie could see several other groups working in the yard. They rechecked their mares then headed for breakfast.

Christie looked at Donato. *He's classic Italian – dark, stocky and muscular. His English is very good although he lapses into Italian if he gets stuck on a word.*

"I've worked on a thoroughbred farm just outside Rome for four years with my father and brother, who have been there much longer. My father wants me to specialize in stallion management once I graduate."

"My name's Colin" said the other young man. "My father has a training stable in Galway, so I've spent most of my life in barns. It's a four-hour drive from here on the west coast," he said, in his soft lilting voice, looking at

Christie. "Dad wants me to become more involved in the business so that we can expand our operation."

Christie looked him over. *He's tall and slim and kind of cute with that strawberry blonde hair and quirky little smile. This is one guy I'd really like to know.*

Jean explained that she had several years of stable management in England and remained just as pleasant as she had been in the van. Christie looked at them. *These are people I'm going to have to depend on.*

"Who is Sun Chariot?" Christie asked, thinking of the foaling yard.

It was Jean who explained it to her. "Sun Chariot was an Irish filly born and bred here, who won the Irish triple crown in the 1940's."

Christie looked around her. *I can see some interesting group dynamics already. The guys are competitive. Everyone's got an important agenda. But I'm noticing the really competitive ones are Amy, the Australian girl and Lisa, one of the Americans. They both look like models and oh man, the guys are paying attention.*

Late morning rounds began with more mare checks and grooming. Working along side Beth, Christie saw her opportunity. "Beth, I'd really like to work with Fancy. I've never had to deal with that kind of disposition." Beth nodded.

They had just started grooming the mare when Mr. J appeared at the stable door with the owners. Mr.

McCormack was in his late forties, expensively dressed in a classic silk suit and Italian leather shoes. Christie heard he was the C.E.O. of a computer company. He was obviously interested in his horse.

Mrs. McCormack was a tall, elegant and well-dressed woman who looked bored. The disdainful look on her face reminded Christie of the one her mother gave her when she came home from the stables smelling horsey. The woman could have been a model in her younger days, very thin with her black hair pulled back from the sculpted cheekbones in the severe style of a flamenco dancer. Introductions were made. The McCormacks didn't stay long, just checked the mare and left shortly after. Christie glimpsed their BMW leaving the back parking lot. The mare was now nervously pacing and tossing her head.

Christie started doing Tellington Tocuh soft circles on Fancy's neck with her finger tips. In a few minutes, the tension was easing and the black head came down, the ears going into neutral.

"What are you doing?" asked Beth.

"It's a relaxation technique I learned at home and most of the time it works. Fancy seemed agitated as soon as Mrs. McCormack came in. Don't they get along? She seemed O.K. with him. Can you work your side of her neck?" Soon Fancy finally stretched her neck down, then went back to eating her hay.

"Well, I'll be," said Beth. "It does work. I think it is more an issue between the McCormacks that the mare's picking up. There are divorce rumours. I don't think things are going too well at the moment. He's just spent another 70,000 Euros for the re-breed. It's not really any of our business unless it involves the horses. All we can do is look after her properly and give them top notch customer service."

Feeding, grooming and cleaning the stalls took up the rest of the morning. Christie's group kept a close eye on Flanagan's Girl who looked like she could drop the foal any time. They had a chance to look at two new foals across the yard, who had been born overnight. Christie's heart just melted when she saw them. *They're gorgeous and just plain cute – long legs, fuzzy brush cut manes and long whiskery velvet noses.*

The evening lecture was on disease control. The vet spoke of the measures required internationally. "Because diseases can spread from country to country with racing and breeding, controls are necessary. Each horse has an international passport for identification and it is part of any breeding contract that they have a negative Coggins test and have negative swabs and bloodwork for CEM and other diseases. The stallions are tested every year and so are any incoming mares. Some of the diseases can cause sterility so it is vitally important with the costs of blood stock and breeding fees, for these tests to be in place. Some of these horses are worth millions."

Back at the dorm, Christie could hear someone's radio playing down the hall. *Sounds like the same Top Ten we get at home, no different. Faces are starting to look familiar. Alana's on the night rotation, so I don't want to disturb her.* She spent some time talking to Jean, Jean-Philippe, and Rick in the lounge until nine o'clock. She tried out her rudimentary French on Jean-Philippe and he cracked up laughing. *Apparently French-French and Québec-French have some differences.* They watched the evening news and she sent Mum and Dad a more detailed e-mail of life in the dorm. *Somehow, home seems light years away. I'm too busy to miss them much. I'll have no problem sleeping tonight.*

February 1st

Flanagan's Girl foaled overnight and there was one copper coloured colt with a white blaze and two white socks, happily slurping his breakfast and bunting his head against the mare's belly for more; mum gently nuzzled his fuzzy bum, making small nickering noises to him.

Christie looked at them and said to no one in particular: "There's something profoundly satisfying in seeing all these lovely mares with healthy babies."

It was Colin who replied "Well it makes a beautiful picture – they're glowing with good health. Outside - good fences, lots of trees and grass. Idyllic...makes you feel good to be alive."

Pub Night was fine. Fancy was quiet, her udder just starting to fill. The mare ignored Christie. *I think that's a good sign – no fear, no anger.* Routine chores were done and they watched Doc doing his rounds. Later they were scheduled to see one of the stallions cover a mare. *This should be interesting. I've never seen horses breed before.*

The breeding shed was a separate round building just down the slope from Stallion Row. All the breeding staff were men who worked exclusively with the stallions. They brought in the teaser stallion, to test the mare's state of readiness. The mare was on one side of the shoulder height padded partition, whinnying and looking interested, hind end dancing and winking. Old Henry, the teaser stallion was led in on the other side of the partition. He pranced, snorted and screamed at her. She called back to him and stood looking ready. She didn't strike to drive him away when he nosed her neck. Old Henry was led away (*that must be frustrating*) and the mare's neck was padded. *I guess lovemaking can get rough.*

They heard Lord Shanakill long before he came in. He roared and sashayed through the doors, mostly on his hind legs, carefully controlled by his handler. His dark bay coat was gleaming. *He knows what he's here for and he's ready.* Christie felt stunned. *I don't think I've ever seen such raw strength and power. He's just plain savage. No wonder all the handlers are men.* The horse reared, biting the mare's neck and she bowed under his weight as he slipped into her like a heat seeking missile. The performance was over in a couple of minutes, followed by a Richter 5.0 shudder.

Christie was surprised. *That was brutal, more like rape* but found herself silently amused at the reactions of the others. Some of the guys were puffing out their chests with smirks on their faces. Lisa was staring intently at Paolo, the Brazilian guy. *I can see where this might be heading.* Christie noticed that Colin watching her; she smiled and turned away.

February 3ʳᵈ

Pub Night went into labour in the early evening and delivered a lovely bay filly. *It was beautiful to watch. Nature is amazing. How do you package a fifty-pound foal with three-foot-long legs inside the belly of a mare, then streamline it to a compact shape for delivery? That is a miracle.* Doc checked them both and gave his approval. Baby yoyoed to her feet and was up nursing within thirty minutes, licked clean by an attentive mum.

The evening lecture was on breeding and fertility, getting into more detail on the mare's cycle. She realized the pace was going to be relentless. *There is so much to cover in so little time. There's no time to slack off and I must get efficient with it.*

Christie watched the group dynamics. Protestants were rooming with Catholics, Germans with French. *I think these things will sort themselves out. None of us can afford to waste time and energy on politics. I don't want any distractions but these guys are very attractive, especially Colin. I'm not much of an attraction in comparison to Lisa. She seems to have it all - looks, brains and personality. Enough, I've got to study for a test tomorrow.*

February 5th

Fancy delivered a healthy dark bay filly with a tiny white star and one white front sock. *She's such a loving, protective mum and doesn't seem to find us a threat around her foal. I am glad Beth is here just in case things get dicey.*

As a group, they were all getting used to the routine and for the most part chores went seamlessly. *I feel like a sponge, absorbing things as I go. I like the expectation that things must always be done right. No slacking off, no excuses. This is totally about quality care for the animals and good service to the customers.*

Christie squeaked by on her first written test. *Well, it was tough but fair. Now I know what to expect and where my weaknesses are. I have the weekend off and will be starting my night shifts on Sunday.*

Some of them were going to the pub in Newbridge on Friday night. Colin told her that Newbridge was Droichead

Nua in Irish. Christie's attempts to pronounce it made
everyone laugh. He also informed her that she couldn't
possibly stay in Ireland without trying Murphy's beer.

Friday night found her looking in the mirror. *I hope
I look alright.* Alana helped her with her hair, braiding it
into a simple long braid down her back. The image in the
mirror looked back at her looking sleek in a simple white
camisole, black leggings and a blue and white top. Alana
suggested some light blush, mascara and lip gloss which
Christie thought was O.K. *I rarely use makeup.* She found
her leggings quite loose. *I seem to have lost some weight.
I suppose I shouldn't be surprised, what with the amount of
walking we do any given day. I know I don't compare to some
of the others like Lisa for looks but I think I look pretty good.*

Two taxis took them into town and headed for the pub
Alana had recommended. The eight students managed to
create space to sit together and for the first round Colin
placed a large glass of dark brown foamy beer in front of
her. "This is Murphy's."

She took her first sip. *It's strong and malty, quite different
from my usual Bud Light.*

"Don't let him lead you astray, luv," called a loud male
voice from the next table. "Hey mate, give the girl a real
beer, give her a Guinness." Lively banter and conversations ebbed back and forth.

Looking around, Christie could see the local girls
eyeing her companions. Paolo in particular looked exotic

with his dark Brazilian looks and megawatt smile. *He's able to make a girl feel very special when he zeroes in on her, like she's the only one in the world.* He was on the dance floor in no time and his Latin moves with Lisa were cause for comment.

The band was a trio of guitar, drums and keyboard. *They're playing a bit of everything – current hits, old hits I know and some Irish ones I don't,* thought Christie. The lead singer with his scruffy beard had a strong, smoky, resonant voice. She spent most of her time on the dance floor and lost track of her partners, some from the stable, some from town but quite often found herself in Colin's arms. *I really enjoyed dancing with him. He isn't the least bit pushy and he's a lot of fun. His touch sure excites me.*

February 8th

Two more mares foaled overnight. Beth was stepping back to let the students take a more active role, only directing as needed. Christie could feel her confidence improving. *The last foal presented with one leg forward and the other back.*

Doc gloved and intervened. "I'm going to reposition the foal by pushing it back and drawing the other leg forward. I need to cup the hoof to prevent it from tearing the lining of the vagina. Timing is essential here to keep the foal's airway clear." Two front hooves and a nose appeared, then the delivery went normally. Doc was watching intently. "A head twisted back is much more problematic. You have to recognize when there is a problem and call me as early as you can. In the old days, we would have lost both mare and foal for something like that."

The older foals were being moved with their mums during the day to the other barns to make room for new arrivals. *Quite a production line. Night duties include rounds on the mares and foals every couple of hours and preparing the feed for morning rounds. That's our introduction to feed formulations and it's individualized for each horse.*

"Does INS grow its hay?" Christie asked. Satoshi and Jean-Philippe were working with her.

"No, most of it is imported from Europe," said Kelly, the staffer. "We also buy alfalfa cubes, which the horses seem to do very well on. Some of the grain is local. Even though we have 800 acres, it isn't enough to feed all these horses."

I can't imagine they ever get two or three days without rain to dry hay. "When we open a bale of hay are we checking it for mold? Is that an issue?" she asked.

"Sure, always do that. The quality of the hay is important. Set that bale aside if you're doubtful. We'd be in touch with the suppliers if there was any amount of it."

"Is the other barn staffed at night?" asked Jean-Philippe.

"There is one staffer in the other barn who gets the rations ready. The mares and older foals don't need watching so much. We carry cell phones and will call each other if we need help" she replied. "As you see we have index cards for each horse with the type of mix and quantity listed. Each bucket is cleaned and the feed prepared and set out in order of the stalls. Stall number one has Pub Night's feed, etc. Her bucket is labelled number one. Some require vitamin additives; others don't."

"Night staff also watch the intensive care stall if we have a sick horse there. Doc bunks down in one of the cottages where he sleeps if he can. He's on his pager 24/7 for every foaling or if you think a horse needs attention. Having the vet here is a Godsend some nights."

"At what point are the horses allowed to go out to pasture? Back in Canada, it could be the end of April or even May," said Christie.

"Pasture's usually dry enough by the end of March, beginning of April. The calcium content from the limestone is quite high here, so the grazing is excellent for livestock, really good for their bones," said Kelly while gathering scoops of feed from various bags according to the index card for bucket number two. "Now each of you grab a pail, and fill it according to the index card for that stall.

The night passed quickly.

Fancy and baby are doing really well. The filly has lovely conformation and a sweet disposition. Christie stopped in to see them any chance she could. The foals were learning to wear their halters and Christie's previous experience was useful. *I'm glad Diane took the time to show me so much.*

Sleeping through the day hasn't been as much of a problem as I thought it might be. I'm so tired I just drop. It does screw up the meals a bit. The evening lectures this week are on the stallion – anatomy, physiology and breeding problems, including some of the sexually transmitted diseases.

I can see the group dynamics sorting themselves out. At least everyone's being civil. We are constantly working with different partners and I'm adjusting to that. It was a bit disconcerting at first, but not one of them has refused to answer my questions. Most of them have a lot more experience than I do.

She had a long e-mail from her parents wanting to know all sorts of things. *There's just too much to tell.* She replied and also got caught up with e-mails to some of her friends. *I miss my friends a lot but I'm not missing my parents or the house as much as I thought I would. Too darned busy here.*

It's great to work with people who think like I do, where smelly jeans are normal. I don't miss Mum nagging me. I love her dearly, but she's so narrow minded about a woman's role, the model housewife and the good little woman belonging to some church committee thing. I want to run a broodmare farm; all the other stuff can wait, if I want it at all.

INS was restarting the school programme for local childrens visits. It was part of public relations and teaching. INS had a small herd of Falabella ponies and there were all kinds of activities for the kids. *It's a great opportunity to start some education and it gets the foals and the kids used to each other.*

"Public relations are really important with both the children and the tourists. The extra income helps support this place, funds the museum and maintenance of the Japanese Gardens," Beth explained. Christie still had opportunities to view any breedings as outside mares were still coming in regularly. *The stallions represent some of the most potent bloodlines in the world. We watch a lot of the races on the telly. Everyone goes crazy if one of our two-year olds win. The more the babies win, the better chance of the studs being booked next year.*

Mr. J spent one evening discussing the history of the stables. "Colonel William Hall-Walker bought the property in the early 1900s. He believed in horoscopes and used them in his selection of horses. You'll notice that the stallion boxes have upper windows. The Colonel believed it gave them exposure to the "effects of the sun, the moon and the stars." As weird as that might sound, it worked for him. The sculpture at the foot of the stone steps commemorates that. When Colonel Hall-Walker retired in 1915, he donated the stables to the Irish government. Some of the INS horses have run under Royal colours."

Christie had an opportunity that afternoon to microchip a foal in the neck with a tool that looked like a pellet gun. *With that I.D. chip in place and a proper name, that foal will be eligible for a passport. The mares and foals go out every morning to the Kildare yard and it's fun to watch them galloping around and leaping in the air. They play tag, run back to mum for a drink, then conk out in the grass for a nap.*

February 20th

Christie was in her room studying when Donato yelled to go to the stable. "What's happening?"

"One of the mare's is in trouble and Doc's going to do a caesarian."

They flew out to the yard where a crowd was gathering outside the intensive care stall. Colin was standing there. "Doc's done an ultrasound; the foal's in breech position and it's a big one. Beth is prepping her now."

The mare was down, looking like a beached whale lying in the straw, with waves of contractions going through her. Doc was masked, in his scrubs and had already started the I.V. Beth had scrubbed too and was drawing up the anaesthetic which she handed to him.

"Time's critical here. In and out as quickly as possible to avoid anaesthetic effect on the foal" said Doc.

Beth opened the sterile instrument tray and with forceps and gauze painted the belly with iodine solution and draped it with sterile towels.

Christie felt a bit nauseated as the chestnut skin parted in a long red line, Doc's scalpel cutting through to the underlying muscle layers. She gulped then watched. *The uterus looks like a huge, white, pulsating egg.* Quickly, he sliced through the membranes and extracted the head of enormous colt. Beth quickly towelled the head dry to remove the mucus and slid the foal out onto the bedding, leaving Doc to remove the placenta and stitch up the mare.

Beth tossed another towel to Donato and they continued to dry the foal while she quickly clamped the umbilical cord, cut it with sterile scissors and dipped the end in iodine. "Christie, put on a pair of gloves and check that the placenta is intact. Any pieces left inside can cause bleeding," she said, sliding the liver-like mass away from the foal.

Christie checked the placenta. It was smooth and shiny and looked complete. She looked at Doc squatting beside the mare. There were beads of perspiration on his forehead as he took his time neatly suturing each layer back together. *I really admire his skill but I sure wouldn't want that responsibility.*

When he was finished Beth removed all the towels. They did an instrument count and it was correct. He checked the foal and the placenta. The foal was alert and looking around.

They took turns staying with the mare for the next few hours until she came out of the anaesthetic and got to her feet a bit wobbly. Kelly had now taken over from Beth and slipped the foal over to the mare. Everyone held their breath as the mare sniffed the foal from head to toe then started licking him. *I'm so glad she accepted him. But they do have surrogate mothers here, if she hadn't.*

The colt had been on his feet for a while and was hungry, nuzzling around for the teat. The moment he found it, his tail was in motion. *Just like a pump handle*, thought Christie. *I'm amazed. You'd never know she'd had surgery. She's acting like nothings happened. I'm so glad I've had a chance to see this. Thank God, Doc's on the premises. I'd better get some sleep. Tomorrow's going to be a busy day – Fancy and her foal are going home to McCormack's. Their stable's a couple of hours drive north west of here. I'm going to miss that mare.*

A white truck and horse trailer were parked in the yard and an older man was carefully loading Fancy into one side. Christie could see the foal was already loaded in the other.

"Aye, I know this mare. She gets a bit nasty when she's nervous. Once I get her loaded, she'll ride easy. She'll be fine as long as she knows the foal's O.K." he said. He walked her up the ramp and she followed him in. After securing her, he slipped out the front side door. Christie and Donato closed the tailgate and bolted it. Fancy responded with a hind foot kick that reverberated on the door. He grinned and signed off the papers with Beth.

"Here Eddy," Beth said, handing him the envelope. "All the paperwork's here; the passport, care documents and the DVD of the re-breeding."

With a wave, he said: "I'll be off then, a couple of hours and she'll be in her own stall." The truck pulled out and they were away.

It wasn't until lunch time that Mr. J signalled a group meeting in the canteen. He looked worried, which was unusual. "Listen up everyone." His demeanor and tone of voice reduced the noise level to silence.

"I just had a call from George McCormack – Fancy and her foal never arrived home. Something's happened. There is no sign of the truck or trailer so far on the route they should have taken. The police are now involved. This may be an abduction, but we don't know. There could be a lot of press coverage. I don't want any of you talking to the press or e-mailing anyone. Any enquiries should be directed to me. That's all I know for the moment. I'll keep you informed if anything changes." He abruptly turned and left.

Christie turned to Colin. "Where could she be? Is this something to do with the McCormacks' divorce?"

Colin replied: "Everyone knew she was going home today. It wasn't a secret. I wonder if it's an inside job.

McCormack must be going out of his mind. That foal's worth 70,000 Euros and the mare at least 200,000 since she's been re-bred. They're worth too much to just destroy."

Someone else chipped in "Unless you're an angry, soon-to-be ex-wife..."

Chores got done the rest of the day but Christie didn't remember much of it. *Please let them be safe. Would someone just kill them for the insurance money? I'll have to ask Dad about that later; being in the horse insurance business, he'd know.*

February 24th

"Beth, have you heard anything more?" Christie asked as she was forking manure into a wheelbarrow. *Surely if it was for the insurance, you'd need the bodies.*

"Nothing. It's disheartening. I'm really afraid they're both dead," she replied. "The police have all the border points monitored and everyone is looking for the truck."

About ten o'clock, Beth called her group together. "I've got news. Mr. J had a call from George McCormack. One of the traffic helicopters from Dublin did an air search and spotted a white truck and trailer up in a desolate part of the Wicklow mountains east of here on a back road. The police are on their way. The pilot didn't want to get too close in case he frightened the horses."

Christie's heart was thumping in her chest. *Please let them be alright.*

Around three o'clock Beth came around again, looking grim. "The news isn't good. It's his truck and trailer alright – doors wide open, no horses. Eddy's dead. His body was found beside the trailer. Some of his injuries could have been caused by a horse. There are hoofprints leading away from the trailer, up into the hills."

Christie was dumbfounded. "What the hell happened? Is this an abduction gone wrong? Eddy was fine when he left here – he knew Fancy and handled her well. He even talked about her being back in her own stall in a couple of hours!"

Speculation at the evening meal ran rampant. Their lecture that evening was on stable security.

I've never thought much about it, but under the circumstances, it's pertinent. Mr. J talked about security issues: the routines they followed, the positioning of security cameras, the locking of perimeter fences and exits, identification tags, personnel screening for employment and even their programme. They reviewed fire prevention and evacuation procedures. *Security isn't blatantly obvious. I guess I've never given it much thought, but with the value of the animals involved and the insurance liability, I can see the importance of this stuff.*

After the seminar, Mr. J called Beth, Colin, Jean, Donato and Christie aside and closed the door. "George

McCormack has asked for our help to find Fancy. It's still likely a case of abduction gone wrong. George went out with the helicopter pilot and they think they've sighted the mare. So far, there's no sign of the foal. He wants to get her off that mountain. You've worked with her the most. Would you be interested in going up there to get her out? Purely voluntary."

The chorus of "yes" was immediate.

"It's very wild country up there, rocky, steep, mostly wooded terrain. The going is rough. If we find her, she won't be easy to extricate. Dress for wet weather: rain-coats and good walking shoes. Rain and fog come in very quickly. I will pick you up at 6 a.m." They nodded.

After he'd gone, Beth made a list of everything they might need – lead line, spare halter, water bucket, grain, first aid kit, walkie-talkies, fluorescent vests, lengths of rope and packed lunches.

February 25th

Christie didn't sleep much, but neither did anyone else. They were waiting for Mr. J with all the gear in back packs. Beth said: "I packed a couple of bottles of mare's milk in case we need it."

Good thinking, thought Christie.

"George and I will be coming with you," said Mr. J and they all piled into the van.

The drive east to Laragh didn't take long. Christie looked at the scenery. *This should be beautiful and scenic but right now it is foreboding. The horses could really be in trouble. I wonder if the foal is even alive.* She could see the hills rising to 3,000 feet with sharp cliff faces and straight drops. Much of it was wooded with isolated small farms and some open fields but most of it was rugged terrain.

The gravel road was cordoned off with police tape. An officer escorted them in and Mr. J spoke with him. Christie could see the truck and trailer looking abandoned, the doors open, keys still in the ignition. She noticed the crime scene crew working the perimeter. Finger print dust covered the dash and steering wheel. The package of documents still lay on the passenger side of the front seat. The chalk line marked where Eddy's body had been. The reality of that hit Christie hard. *I can't believe he's dead. He seemed like a nice man. Is he an innocent victim, part of the plot or collateral damage? Why bring the horses here?*

George McCormack pulled in and parked behind the van. The officer released the truck to him. *It seems funny to see him in blue jeans, boots and an anorak. He looks gray with worry.* George indicated the hillside to the right of the road, where the pilot thought he'd seen Fancy. They divvied up the back packs and in single file headed up the road. The overnight rain had obliterated any tracks there might have been. About a mile down the road, it dead ended. *There are no fences so the mare could have easily moved off the road.* They climbed steadily for about an hour through fairly dense undergrowth, trees and rocks, when Donato spotted a pile of horse manure. *At least she's come this far.*

Colin whistled like he always did to bring the mares in. They stood still and listened. The distant reply was electrifying. Beth said: "Much higher and to the left." They continued to climb as the terrain became steeper and the trees were thinning out.

"Colin, whistle again," said Mr. J. He did. The whinny was closer but still higher and still to the left.

We've been climbing for nearly two hours. The going was treacherous with a lot of small loose rock called scree that slid under her boots. There were steep-sided gullies that could fill with rain. Christie saw a very faint path upward that reminded her of a deer run. She occasionally slipped on mossy stones and had to pause to get her breath. *The angle of ascent is definitely steeper. I'm not as fit as I thought.* George was behind her and she could hear his breathing getting more ragged. She kept her attention of the back of Beth's boots ten feet in front of her. *What fear drove the mare so far up?*

Mr. J shouted. "I can see movement up there," and all eyes followed his arm pointing to a flat knoll above. The pace picked up and they came to a small clearing. There was Fancy.

"Oh Lord, the mare's a mess." Christie could see her lead line was still attached to her halter and had snagged hard between two boulders, trapping her. The ground around her was bare, muddy and deeply churned where the horse had fought it. The skin under her halter was raw.

"I can't believe the leather held," said Beth. "There isn't a blade of grass or water in reach."

Christie looked at the prominent ribs, the torn, matted coat and the long linear wheal showing bright red across her left hind quarter. *Whip mark? Branches?* The mare just stood there quivering, snorting and rolling her eyes, the tips of her ears so alert they almost touched.

Beth took over. "Alright, we can't extricate her until she calms down. Donato get some water in the bucket. Jean, get the grain. Colin, Mr. J and Mr. McCormack, I want you to have a good hard look around and find the easiest way down this hill. Keep your eyes open for the foal. Christie, you and I are going to do that touch stuff on her and see if we can settle her down."

Everyone scattered to do their errands, while Beth and Christie quietly walked over to the mare. They started the small circles on her neck. Christie felt the tightness of the muscles beneath her fingers. Donato returned within a few minutes with the pail brimming full and quietly offered it to the horse; she drank it all. Jean put some grain and alfalfa cubes in the pail and Fancy inhaled them.

The men returned shortly. "We need a council of war," said George and they all sat down on the rocks, wolfing down their sandwiches. "Beth, the point is, there is no easy way down."

"Now that she's calmer," said Jean, "maybe we should just turn her loose and stay out of her way. She's likely going to go to the last place she saw the foal."

Mr. J thought for a few minutes. "There isn't a safe way and I don't want to have anybody hurt. George, you go down first. We'll spread out at 100-foot intervals. Beth, you'll be the last one. Stay at the top with her until we're all in position then turn her loose. Stay out of the horse's way just in case she falls."

George headed down and several minutes later disappeared from view. In turn, the others followed. Christie looked back just in time to see Beth unclip the lead line, and give the mare her head. She saw Fancy look down the slope, sniff the air and start down. The mare slid here and there and passed her. *She seems to know where she's going.* Christie grabbed branches to keep her balance and also slid on the rocks. At one small relatively flat spot, she saw the mare stop again, whinny and listen. The ears pricked. Christie heard nothing, but the mare turned more to the south and continued down the slope, stones sliding under her hooves. At one point, she was sliding on her hocks with her forelegs braced. *Sometimes I can't see her at all.* She used the walkie-talkie and called Donato ahead of her. "I can't see her now but I can hear her." He acknowledged.

Christie was having trouble getting herself down and prayed the rain would hold off. Her walkie-talkie squawked. "She's stopped at the stream, getting a quick drink. Hey, she just came to attention – she's heard something."

Christie heard Donato and someone else crashing through the woods. She followed the direction of the noise and saw the orange flash of a safety vest. Beth wasn't far behind her, now that the terrain wasn't as steep. Then there was a lot of noise and shouting. "They've found the foal!"

Both of them scrambled down as fast as they could and finally saw them gathered around Fancy. George and Mr. J were down on their knees with the foal's body between them. "I'd have missed her if Fancy hadn't been here," George said.

"Is she alive?" said Christie out of breath.

"Barely, by the look of it" said Beth. "This foal's been out here for three days with nothing to eat. It's not looking good." Beth took one look at Fancy's empty udder and rummaged through her backpack for the bottles of milk. George took off his jacket and covered the foal with it. Fancy stood with her nose on her baby, nickering.

"Colin, bring the truck and trailer as close as you can. The keys are still in it. We're going to have to carry the filly out, if there's any chance of her surviving at all. Call Doc and get him here. She needs IV fluids asap," said Mr. J, passing over his cell phone. "I can't get a signal up here." Colin nodded and disappeared downhill.

Beth cradled the foal in her arms and inserted her finger in the foal's mouth. "She's still got a bit of a suck reflex" and dribbled a few drops of milk on the foal's tongue. Christie and Jean found the foil blanket in the emergency kit and wrapped the foal in it. "That will preserve her body heat."

"Ah, the suck's a bit stronger and she's starting to take it." Fancy's nose was on Beth's shoulder. "Aye girl, we're doing our best."

It seemed like an eternity to Christie when a breathless Colin clambered up the hill, his T-shirt dark with sweat. He looked exhausted. "Doc's on his way. No cell reception down there either. The police relayed it on their car radio. The cop gave me this; he though we might be able to use it," he said giving Donato a small portable stretcher, all aluminum and lightweight.

Here I am in the middle of a crisis and I'm thinking how good he looks. I must be out of my mind.

They rolled the foal onto it wrapped in the blanket and strapped her in. Taking turns front and back, they began the agonizingly slow trip downhill. Fancy followed behind.

This would look funny if it wasn't so serious, thought Christie. She felt drained when she finished her turn and she said to Colin: "I hope you've prayed to all those Irish saints of yours. We could use some divine intervention." He merely nodded.

The angle of descent finally became bearable and they made better progress. George was leading the way, finding the shortest path down until they finally glimpsed the truck. "I've never been so glad to see a vehicle in my life" Christie said to no one in particular.

Doc was waiting for them at the trailer and walked right up the ramp, depositing the foal in the bed of straw. Fancy was right there and Donato loaded her without a problem. She immediately tackled the full hay net. Christie watched Doc get the IV going, despite the foal's severe dehydration.

"Will she make it, Doc?" asked George.

"Can't say at this point."

Christie returned the stretcher to the policeman who was quite interested in the proceedings. "Have you found out what happened yet?" she asked.

"Eddy's autopsy showed he'd been kicked in the shoulder by the horse, but it was the blow to the back of his head that killed him, blunt-force trauma – apparently not the horse. There were tire tracks from another vehicle, probably a SUV or truck, but not much else. We don't know why they came here – seems an odd place to abduct a horse. Truth is, we may never know," he said shrugging his shoulders.

Christie walked back to the others. Doc elected to sit on a bale of hay and ride in the back with the foal. *Oh, that's a total safety no-no.* The filly looked like she was sleeping and her breathing looked more regular. Jean and Christie went back with Beth in the van. The guys went with Mr. J in the truck, while George brought up the rear in his BMW. They left Doc's car behind, to pick up later. *It seems like a slow ride home as the sun's going down and the western sky's fading out to a pink.* They arrived back at INS going directly to the intensive care stall. Doc and the guys carried the filly in. Fancy walked off the trailer and followed her baby.

"She's had almost two litres of IV fluids," said Doc as the filly raised her head and touched noses with her mother.

George stood there looking at his horses. "I can't thank all of you enough. The courage of this horse is unbeliev-able. Eddy worked for me for fifteen years. I don't believe he would have put a whip to her. Whatever happened, I think she was defending herself when she ran and the foal followed her."

He turned to Mr. J. "I want them to stay here and recover. The filly's a long way from being out of the woods and Fancy might abort, but we'll have to wait and see. I will get to the bottom of this if it's the last thing I do." With a nod to Mr. J, he walked away looking very determined.

Once again, he's the C.E.O – in control, resourceful and powerful, thought Christie.

March 1ˢᵗ

Christie slipped away from her chores to check in on Fancy and the foal. She found Colin already there. "At least the foal's up nursing now."

"The mare's putting some weight back on, but she's not got the spunk she had before," Colin replied. "Rumour's going around that McCormack's donated her to INS for an interest in future foals."

"I suppose that would prevent his wife from getting her hands on them. Sounds like the divorce is getting very messy," replied Christie. "Well, at least Fancy hasn't aborted."

Beth joined them. "I think next week they'll be able to go out to pasture with the other mares and foals. Fresh grass would do both of them the world of good."

"Beth, what will happen to them if they don't fully recover?" said Christie.

"Even if the foal never races, with her bloodlines she'd still be a very valuable broodmare, and as you said Fancy's still pregnant. Give them time." replied Beth.

Pasture management and some stable tours were on that week's agenda. Christie had a feeling the abduction had impacted all the students and INS. *Somehow the atmosphere's different. There's an element of seriousness that wasn't here before. I think Fancy is a daily reminder of how badly things can go. Her hair's growing back, but she still looks scruffy. Colin's right, the fire's gone out of her. I don't think the police are any the wiser about who killed Eddy.*

Christie buried herself in her studies but spent her spare time brushing the mare. *I like seeing the motes of dust fly, getting into the rhythm of the brushing. Sometimes she stands with her head against my chest while I do circles on her ears. It's like we're both in the zone. Those moments are magic. Was it Churchill who said "What's good for the outside of a horse, is good for the inside of a man"?*

March 4th

Christie saw she was scheduled to do farrier rounds with Donato and Alaina. They watched him forge a miniature horse shoe for a colt with a slightly clubbed left front hoof. "This reminds me so much of Upper Canada pioneer village in Morrisburg back home," Christie said. The farrier just laughed and had Donato man the bellows for more heat as the metal glowed an orange-red.

He transferred the red-hot rod to the anvil and started hammering until it flattened, then placed it on the tip of the anvil and beat it into a circular shape. Quenching it in water produced a cloud of spitting steam.

"Most of the adult horseshoes are factory made. It's not often I have to make special ones. Bring the colt over here."

It took both Alana and Christie to keep the foal in one place. The farrier finally managed to check the fit and after re-heating he made a few adjustments, checked the angle of the hoof and set the shoe.

That afternoon, the whole class went on a tour of a local stud farm. "This one's not open to the public, but we have special permission to view it," said Mr. J.

Christie was dumbfounded with the property. "I thought that was an upscale bungalow but it's a stable for four stallions," she said to Colin. One of the stallion managers took them around. *The stable is immaculately clean with fresh shavings. The horses are sleek, healthy and well mannered except for one we have been warned not to touch. Look at the dapples on their coats. Look at the fencing and the grounds!*

Mr. J explained that the farm was owned by the Saudis. "They buy and keep the very best, both here and in the U.S."

This is a rich man's game, thought Christie. *This is the world I will be working in but will never be part of. A whole village could live on what is spent on feed and stabling here. I need to learn the skills to interact with these owners, just like Mr. J does. A few of those owners are down right obnoxious.*

Later that evening, Mr. J called Satoshi, their Japanese student, aside. Christie saw him leave Mr. J's office then go to his room and close the door. The expression of Satoshi's face was flat and controlled – totally unlike his usual demeanor.

"What's going on?" asked Jean. Christie shrugged.

The next morning, her day off, she noticed him entering the Japanese garden and followed him in. He was standing on the red bridge, looking at the reflections in the water. "Are you O.K?" she asked quietly.

"My brother was in a serious car accident. My father tells me the prognosis isn't good" he said.

"Will you have to go back home?"

"Not yet. My father will let me know what happens."

"It's so difficult when family things happen and we're so far away." *I wonder what I would do if I was in that situation. Guess I'd have to give up my year and go back home.*

He nodded and together they walked the winding Path of Life among the sculptured moss-covered Japanese maples and stone walkways, past the tea house. *A Japanese gardener created this beautiful garden nearly a hundred years ago. It was the very first Japanese garden in Ireland. The detailing is exquisite.* She realized that the walk had achieved its objective; both of them seemed much calmer. He nodded as she turned and quietly left him sitting on the stone bench.

Later, she was sitting with Colin in the lounge studying.

"Well, Christie, what are you going to do once you graduate? What are your plans?" he asked.

Looking at his gentle, handsome face, she thought for a few moments. "When I came here, I just wanted to get away from my mother and learn the horse business. Mum and Dad have been very good to me, don't get me wrong. Without their help, I wouldn't be here. I'm immensely grateful. But she's so narrow in her perspective, it's claustrophobic. She wants me to become like her. That's not who I am at all. She doesn't get the horse thing at all."

"And what do you want?" he said, gently taking her hand.

"I want to run a first-class broodmare establishment, just like Mr. J does here. This course is just a beginning. When I graduate I will have a job to go to in Milton and once I get a year or two under my belt, I'll start looking for an even better position, probably in the States."

"Is there any room in your agenda for a serious relationship?" he said gazing into her eyes.

She almost melted. "Maybe, but it would have to be someone who shares my passion for horses."

When the rest of the students retired to their rooms, he gently kissed her goodnight.

March 17th

Spending St. Patrick's Day in Ireland was special. *I think we make more of it than the Irish themselves do.* All the students wore whatever green they had and were silly, singing Irish songs all day long. *I'm not getting into the green beer tonight as I'm on night shift. The temperature is warming up and it's rained at least every other day. It's so green it almost hurts your eyes.*

She spent some of her days off on mini trips to local towns seeing the sights with Alana, Jean or whoever was free. *I could really live in this country.*

The evening lecture was on the foals and their growth and development. "I can't believe how much the babies have changed in six weeks," she said to Jean. "Look – their manes are longer, standing on end, their tails look like bottle brushes, they've doubled their size and some of them are starting to shed out."

"I love it, when they compete with each other in the paddock, galloping flat out. It's so inherent in their nature to be out in front," said Jean.

"I like that vertical leap they do with all four feet off the ground; it's like they've got a giant spring inside that just goes pop," replied Christie. "Fancy's foal is looking a lot better these days. She's not keeping up with the others yet but at least she's running around."

Christie was sitting on her bed later pondering on how the students were evolving too. *I'm thinking about what I was like six weeks ago and what I can do now. I know the right way to do things. The exposure to other students has been great and has helped my self-confidence. Beth keeps a close eye on us, but lets us handle situations. I don't need the level of supervision I used to.*

Satoshi came out of his room with a smile on his face, looking like his old self and announced to everyone in the lounge that his brother was off the critical list.

Thank God for that, thought Christie. *Now he won't have to go home. I'd miss his quiet and very analytical presence.*

She noticed Paolo and Lisa discreetly disappearing once in a while, but the rest of them seemed contented to be "good friends." *I really don't have time to get involved with anyone, although I must confess I really like having Colin near me. He arouses sensations in me I've never felt before.*

March 30th

Colin was looking at the roster. "We're doing that computerized breeding programme this week. That should be interesting. We really get to meet some interesting people, don't we?"

Mr. J introduced Equinome and the company rep. "This is Matt Foster and he's going to explain some new genetic information that could revolutionize pedigree tracking in the racing world."

Matt launched right into his spiel. "Recently, it has been discovered that there is a gene specific for muscle development in the Thoroughbred, located on the myostatin gene. This gene determines whether a horse will be a sprinter for short distances or a stayer for the longer ones. This is based on combinations of the C and T amino acids."

"So, you're saying that a blood test for the specific C and T proteins could determine which mare or stallion to use in a breeding programme?" asked Satoshi.

"Yes, that's exactly what this programme is about. Using your basic Mendellian format, a C and C cross of parents will produce a foal who will mature early and could race in two-year-old races less than a mile. The T by T cross of parents will produce a foal who will mature more slowly but have the endurance for the longer distances."

Christie could see Satoshi quickly filling in squares on his notes. "So, horses with C by T parents will all be crosses, or middle-distance runners?"

"Right again. It gets more complicated if both parents are themselves C by T crosses. Then the possibility for the offspring will be 25 percent C, 50 percent C by T, and 25 percent T. The foals' blood would have to be tested for the specifics. What is possible here is that once the genetics of each horse is identified, then the type can be predicted for any of its offspring. Can anyone suggest what the benefits of this might be?"

It was Colin who rose to that challenge. "It would enable you to select the right stallion and the foal would be tailor-made for the type of racing you wanted it to do. It would save an owner a lot of money if he knew the horse wasn't going to mature until it was three; that would save on training fees and the stress on a young horse's legs. My Dad sees a lot of young stock put down with leg injuries every year. However, you'd be missing some of those lucrative purses for the two-year-olds, and a horse out in the field an extra year isn't covering the cost of its room and board."

"That's true" said Matt. "On the other hand, it is more predictable than using racing results to select a pedigree. It also saves having to put down an injured young horse that cost thousands as a yearling just because his genetics dictate a longer period to maturity."

Christie didn't know her genetics well enough and it seemed rather baffling to her. *I wonder if I could do this at home as a separate business.* Later that evening she e-mailed Jim in Milton to see if he'd ever heard of the programme.

She got her answer a couple of days later. No, he hadn't known about the programme but was interested, and what was she intending to do when she graduated? Was she still interested in a job? She sent her reply. "Count me in. I want to start as soon as I get home." *Most of the others have jobs lined up; Amy will be working for the Australian stable who sponsored her; so is Satoshi in Japan; Paolo will be working on his father's farm in Brazil and Colin will be working for his father preparing youngsters for the track, but he's been making noises about broodmares lately.*

April 15th

The evening lectures had covered all the major body systems. Christie wondered if her brain could continue to absorb all this information. There were constant tests and mini exams. She realized final exams were in eight weeks. *Fancy's filly received her official name; it's Spirit of Flight. That's appropriate in more ways than one.*

The group went on a tour of the Galway area, taking in the training stable owned by Colin's father. It was clean and well-organized with a track and stalls for thirty horses in various stages of training. His dad was a big, hearty Irishman. *You couldn't mistake him for anything else – dark auburn hair, tweed cap and jacket and a big booming Irish voice. Colin seems so different from him.*

Colin introduced her to his father and his mother, who kindly provided lunch for the group. Christie was aware of the thorough inspection she was receiving. *Colin must have told them about me. He's got his Mum's colouring and build. I see where he gets that smile. What would it be like to have parents in the horse business?* The woman had made her feel comfortable.

On the way back to INS, Colin asked her "Would you ever consider working in Ireland?"

"I love it here, but I've got a job lined up in Milton. I have to pay back my parents and get some work experience before I can consider working somewhere else," she said. She didn't want to read too much into the question, but his arm was around her shoulders and it felt good.

Satoshi had been sitting in the lounge surrounded by racing forms and books. "I've been checking out the racing results from last year's stats and there does appear to be a definite correlation of the muscle type and race winners at different ages. I was a bit skeptical about that computer programme but it may be right on."

"You know Satoshi, I'm wondering if this is something I could do at home once I graduate. I was thinking I could start that as an independent business. It could be a really useful breeding tool for the owners and trainers," said Christie.

"It would certainly give a trainer another process for evaluating young stock. I can think of a dozen times me and my Dad have wondered why a colt wasn't working the way he should. This could explain it," said Colin.

May 9th

Christie had the opportunity to work in the stable's office, looking at breeding contracts, monthly client statements for the horse's board, feed, vet and farrier fees, breedings as well as the payroll, insurance and vehicle maintenance costs of running the stable. Individual horses had their care documented at the end of each shift. *I get to sit in on owner conferences to deal with any problems. It's giving me the opportunity to learn the one-on-one skills with the clients and learn how to present myself. Some of them are really demanding, intimidating, in fact.*

She attended several meetings involving lawyers with the owners to sign breeding contracts. *Mr. J made suggestions on how to deal with delinquent accounts in a tactful way.*

The evening lecture was on ethics. The ethicist presented situations and asked how they would respond. "Suppose your stable was having financial difficulties and you were cutting corners to make ends meet. Would you fix a race if the owner suggested it?"

"That's illegal," said Rick. "If you got caught doing that, you'd be in big trouble."

"It's not only illegal, it's unethical," replied the ethicist. "You've opened up a whole can of worms. If you do it once, you can be coerced into doing it again. Your reputation would be ruined and you could be out of business. Here's another situation. Would you race a two-year old you knew wasn't sound? Would you ask your vet to inject him, to mask the injury, knowing full well the leg could break? Bear in mind, you're putting the vet in an ethical dilemma by asking him to do it."

"You can't run a youngster if it's not fit to run," said Jean. "I don't think I could bear to be the cause of a horse being put down, let alone for money."

"But the owner insists," he said.

"Then the owner and I would have to disagree, and I'd have him put in writing that he is accepting responsibility for the consequences. If I lose him as a client, then so be it," she said. "He might be rich, but do I want a client like that?"

"If your financial situation is borderline, you might have to. It has to be made clear to everyone you deal with at the very beginning, whether it is in your business and or in your life, that you have standards and rules and that you are committed to them. That is the basis of the respect you need to run this kind of a business; even a rumour can destroy you. In the end, you will make your decisions and you will live with the consequences."

"Aye, and the one that loses is the horse," said Colin looking grim, "running his bloody heart out so lout can make a dollar, then be taken out behind the barn and shot."

Christie looked at the pale anger emanating from him. *That's happened to him.* She felt the chill that made the room go silent.

May 27ᵗʰ

The students went to the Curragh race track for the Athasi Stakes; a big race for three-year-old fillies. *It's so exciting!* Christie looked at the throngs filling the stands, absorbing the noise echoing around her. Standing at the rail, she watched as the fillies pranced out accompanied by the lead ponies, reacting to the crowds, the noise and the excitement.

"Oh Jean, don't they look magnificent; all that power! How do those jockeys have the strength to control them? This is different – the track's grass, and it's clockwise. At home, the track is dirt and they run counter clockwise."

The dancing, feisty horses were coaxed and chivied into the gates. There was a pause, the gates parted and seven fillies exploded in a mass of pounding hooves, straining muscles, flared nostrils and splashes of coloured silks. Christie watched as a bay filly rocketed into the lead, staying on the rail. Horses jostled for position, the big chestnut challenged moving closer inch by inch until its nose was even with the bay's hind quarters. The two front runners started to widen the gap from the others. Christie could hear their hooves and almost feel the ground tremble. She saw the jockeys pushing hard, their arms working the reins and going to the whip. In the stretch drive, the bay's jockey asked for more and the filly flattened, her neck and forelegs stretching, driving, crossing the finish line a nose ahead of her chestnut rival.

Christie screamed and cheered along with everyone else. The noise was deafening. "That was so exciting," she said hugging Jean. "I feel I rode every inch of that myself."

Jean was laughing. "She's one of ours – out of Big Bad Bob. Mr. J will be delighted."

June 28th

Other weekends, they watched the classic races on the telly in the dorm. They had a good laugh at the women's hats and made small bets with each other. "You know, it's so funny to see the owners up there in all their fancy top hats and tails when we've seen them here in blue jeans. Look at them, strutting around, talking about their horses to the commentator and discussing strategy with the jockey who's done it a thousand times" Christie said.

That night, Christie went out to the barn to see Fancy and Flight, who was almost old enough to wean. She heard Colin's step on the gravel and, when she turned, he took her face in his hands and kissed her, gently at first then, then she felt herself give in to him. She could feel the solid muscles under his cotton shirt, the heat and firmness of his body and realized as sensations mounted, *I want this.*

"Colin..."

He pulled her tightly to him and she felt his body close around her.

It's our last week and we've spent it touring the stud farms at Kildangan, Ballydoyle, Coolmore and Tinnakill. They're unbelievable. This country is amazing. I just love it.

Jean was on cloud nine. "I've had a job offer from George McCormack. He's keeping his horses and stable despite the divorce, and I accepted." Christie was thrilled for her.

Dad's arranged my flight home. We've all been studying like crazy. Exams are tomorrow, then it's all over. She talked to Alana. "I want to keep in touch with everyone. Give me your e-mail address. The thoroughbred business might be worldwide but it's a small circle of people really. You've been my family for five months and you've pulled me through a lot."

She sat on her bed seriously contemplating. *Could I have a future with Colin? I'm not Catholic; would his family accept me? They seemed friendly. I'd be lying if I said I didn't want him. I've had boyfriends before but I've never felt the way I do right now.*

Friday

She came out of the written exam feeling drained. *It covered everything; anatomy and physiology, stable management, the whole thing. That was tough. I think I did O.K. I'm pretty sure I passed my practicums. It's over.* She saw Satoshi packing his books with a grin on his face and smiled back.

Saturday

It was graduation. They were seated in the lecture hall all wearing their best clothes. Mr. J was standing at the podium with a huge grin on his face. "I'll break the suspense and congratulate all of you on passing your exams." A war whoop went up from Rick somewhere at the back and there was a babble of voices and a cheer.

"I made it," said Christie to Colin, who was sitting beside her.

"Did you have any doubts?" he asked, looking at her seriously.

"I was worried about it."

"You shouldn't have been; you know your stuff as well as I do," he gently chided her.

Mr. J called them up individually to receive their certificates. Christie looked down at it. *I can't believe it. I did it.*

After the class picture was taken, Christie found Beth and gave her a big hug. "Beth, you've been the perfect role model for me – your knowledge and common sense. You're always calm under fire." Both of them were getting teary-eyed.

She said goodbye to the office staff. "You've been a Godsend, everything from the paperwork to advice for the homesick and lovelorn. I'm going to miss you all." She quickly ran up to her room and e-mailed her parents the good news. *See you tomorrow.*

She walked out to the foaling yard and said goodbye patting Fancy's shiny, sleek black head for the last time and gave Flight a kiss on the nose. Colin was behind her and whispered. "Do I get one too?"

"That can be arranged" she said, holding his hand as they walked back to the dorm.

Sunday

She slept most of the flight home. *I can see Mum and Dad in arrivals. They looked the same.* "It feels good to be home. Neither of you have changed a bit." It was dark when they drove up the driveway. *The house looks the same too, except much smaller, somehow.* She looked at her bedroom as she threw her suitcases on the bed. Her childhood posters, the books in the bookcase, were just the way she'd left them. Fresh flowers were in a vase by the window.

"What do you think, Christie?" said her Mum.

"The flowers are lovely. Thanks Mum. But it's weird, this is like entering a shrine to the child I was and not the person I've become. Just think, I have a room all to myself again and it's going to be a whole lot quieter." *I need to get rid of all those posters too. That's no longer me.*

Her mother just looked at her. "Come downstairs and tell us all about it. Your father's putting on a pot of coffee."

They sat in the living room and talked for hours. Christie noticed a third picture on the mantle. It was the shot Colin had taken a couple of weeks ago when Christie had a quiet moment with Fancy. Girl and horse were head to head with the light coming through the stall door. *There's my life in three simple photos.*

"I'm going down to the stables in the morning and see what Jim's got lined up for me."

"So, you'll be in the office then?" asked her mother, looking hopeful.

"No, Mum, I might spend some time there but mostly I'll be out working with the horses, same as before. This time of year, we'll be getting them ready for the sales" she said. "That will always be part of the job Mum. I wouldn't want it any other way. Possibilities exist now that I can qualify in a few years' time for a really good job on a top-notch broodmare farm just about anywhere in the world, most probably in the States." *I hope a certain Irishman will be in my future too, but I don't know that yet.*

She met Shana at the bar on Friday night.

Shana gave her a huge hug and holding her at arm's length looked at her. "You're looking good, actually really good. How much weight have you lost? And you've got "that look." You've got a man in your life. Tell me all about him."

Christie laughed. "It's so good to see you. I've got so much to tell you I don't even know where to start. I don't suppose they have Murphy's or Guinness, here do they?" she said as they searched for a table and talked non-stop until closing time.

"Shana, I went to Ireland just to take that course. That's all I wanted. I thought I had my life all figured out. I never dreamed I'd find someone and fall in love. Now I'm thinking other things, like will his parents object because I'm not Catholic? Who knew? The whole world's turned upside down for me and now I'm not sure at all what's going to happen, except I really want him with me and we are three thousand miles apart. I'm not saying I want marriage and kids, but I care for him enough to consider that some time in the future."

"Wow, you've changed a lot in five months," said Shana.

At the end of the week, Christie opened her e-mail and there was one from Colin.

> "Greetings from rainy Galway. How far are you from Kentucky? Have discussed things with my Dad. He was a bit disappointed but realizes there may be better options for me in the U.S. Some old mate of his is working on a breeding farm there. No harm in applying is there? If that doesn't work out, I have other options. I can always visit or perhaps you could come here. I miss you. Mum sends her regards. Colin"

Christie sat down on her bed, her imagination soaring. *I can picture Colin working in Kentucky and me driving down to meet him. It makes me feel weak at the knees.* Thoughts popped into her head at the speed of light.

She thought about what he was willing to sacrifice, working for his father and started to think about her relationship with him. *When I first met Colin, I was attracted to him. I liked his looks and his personality. He's got strong opinions about some things and he's not easily swayed. He's very much his own man. He's got principles and ethics. Horses are his whole life and it's the same for me. What more could I ask for in a man?*

She sat for a long time thinking about their time together at INS. *I know the passion he arouses in me and my feelings for him. Will our relationship be a lasting one? Is there a future for us as a couple? I never expected this but now I'm thinking about what married life would be like with him, maybe even a family. Wow! I'm getting ahead of myself here. Before you know it, I'll be acting like my mother. Like that would ever happen!*

She looked at their graduation picture, at his proud smiling face and sent a mental image of herself to him. Later, she went downstairs and put on the coffee maker. Her mum had gone to her usual euchre game, so she called to her father "Dad, I'm making coffee, do you want one?"

"Sure," came the reply over the roar of the football game on television as the Argos scored a goal.

Walking into the living room carrying two mugs, Christie said "Dad, can I talk to you?"

He put the television on mute and looked at her expectantly. "What's on your mind, Christie?"

"I just got an e-mail from Colin. He's thinking about applying for a job in Kentucky instead of working at his father's stable. I think he's serious about me."

"Do you see a future for the two of you together?" he said, watching her closely over the rim of his coffee cup.

"My feelings tell me yes but until now I'd never put it together because of the distance between us," she replied. "I'd feel awful if he gave up his job and it didn't work out between us."

Her father sat there thinking. "Christie, only time will tell if your love will last. There's no way to predict what will happen. I can see that you care for him a lot. You've looked like a sad-eyed spaniel since you got back. Lots of people fall in love and just as quickly fall out of it. You'll have to take it one day at a time. If he gets a job in Kentucky, you'll be able to see him. I'd like to meet this young man. He's the only one you've met who has made you think of something other than horses. He must be quite a guy."

"Dad, I've never felt this way before about anyone. Right now, he's on my mind all the time."

"Look at your mother and I. We'll have our twenty-fifth anniversary this year. Yes, we've had our differences but the underlying feelings and respect haven't changed. The physical end of it is just as passionate as it ever was but in a different way, now that we're older."

Christie looked at him in stunned silence. *Mum, a passionate woman? I can't even imagine that! That just blows my mind. There's obviously a whole side of her I don't know about. What a concept.*

"Dad, he's Catholic. Would you and Mum have problems with that?"

"I don't think it would bother me too much but it might be a problem for her. She's so involved in her church committees. You'll have to talk to her about that. You realize of course that you would have the choice of staying Protestant but any children would likely be brought up Catholic?"

"The church doesn't play a big role in my life. It never has. I haven't thought that far ahead and what all that might mean. I didn't know it could get so complicated. Thanks, Dad," she said heading back up to her room. She sat down and thoughtfully sent a reply to Colin.

> E-mail to Colin:
> Hi love. I was surprised that you would consider leaving your family to work in the U.S. It would be just amazing to have you that close. At least I'd get to see you and I'm missing you badly. My friend Shauna says I'm love-sick and Dad just compared me to a sad-eyed spaniel. I have never had someone affect me the way that you do and I don't see that changing any time soon. With your qualifications, I don't think you'll have any problem getting a job on this side of the Atlantic. I want you here. Love, Christie.

If I follow Colonel Hall-Walker's theory, and the sun, the moon and the stars are in alignment, I'm betting I have a winner.

william crotty,
the irish highwayman

Waterford, Ireland, 1742

Crotty crept forward in the darkness and flattened himself against the stone wall bordering the English encampment. Deep shadow from the castle ruins provided good cover. The sentry had passed a few minutes before. He could hear the two officers in the small cottage to his right. Both men looked resplendent in their red and white uniforms, the brass buttons and leather boots polished to perfection and their long hair fashionably tied back in ponytails. Crotty grinned, mentally comparing their clothes to his own much used brown riding coat and baggy britches hanging on his slight, wiry frame and his mud-stained boots. Even his queue had come undone, tumbling his dark auburn hair onto his shoulders.

The Colonel's voice rose in anger, the table vibrating from his thumping fist. "Eight years we've been hunting him and nothing! It's like tracking a ghost."

The lieutenant nodded and pointed to the map. "We were in Kilmacthomas yesterday," he said noting the village west of Waterford. "He'd been there Sunday afternoon, playing a hurling game with the local lads, bold as can be. He then headed out, probably to Rathgormack. You can't get anything out of that rabble. They either hide him or send us on a wild goose chase, if they tell us anything at all. Half the time I can't understand a damn word they say, it's all in Gaelic – bloody Irish. Once he's in the Comeragh Hills, he's impossible to track. He knows every nook and crag up there."

The Colonel continued. "Friday, in Lemybrien, three men held up a coach of visitors going to the castle. No one was hurt but the Earl's none too pleased. They took jewellery from the ladies, money from the men and a case of whisky. Sounded like Stackpole and Cashmen; they're part of Crotty's lot. At least they didn't steal the horses. Ahearn's got men out looking for them now," he said.

"Sir, we need different tactics. Double the reward on them or bribe them. These peasants are as poor as dirt and would probably sell their mothers if the price was right."

"Well, you're right about changing tactics. We've got nothing to lose at this point," he replied.

Crotty melted back into the forest.

Hours later, Crotty scrambled to his vantage point high on a rocky slope, with a crescent of sheer walls falling below him several hundred feet to the narrow lough at the bottom, its clear blue waters reflecting the early morning sky. His hideaway was a narrow cave, high on the cliff face. *I can see the church spires of Waterford from here, over the trees. On a clear day like today, I can even see Lemybrien to the southwest. No sign of the redcoats yet. I'll head into the village for Harrigan's funeral.*

Nimble as a goat, he skittered down the scree to the woods and slipped into a small farm yard to collect his horse. *Paying the farmer a few pence to feed him is money well spent. It's close by if I need him. If anyone's nosing around he's just another non-descript bay horse with no markings. The farmer's been loyal to me for years.*

He pumped a bucket of water from the barn well, welcoming the opportunity to clean up and change his clothes. *The farmer's wife washes them for me and hides them in a burlap bag under the straw. Real handy if I can't get back to my wife for a few days.*

He rode to the edge of town and tied his gelding to a tree, surveying the road. It was a small village with an old Catholic church, an even more ancient pub, a few shops and about twenty thatched cottages. A clutch of grey figures were gathering in the church yard for the Gaelic service. He slipped through the back door of the pub, waiting for the all clear from the bartender. "I'll have a quick pint," he said, slapping down his coin.

"Have you heard, Crotty? They've doubled the reward on ya. Ahearn's caught Stackpole and Cashman too. They're heading for Waterford gaol. Poor buggers, it'll be hanging for them. Watch your back. I hear Norris got away," he said, his brawny arm manning the beer tap.

Crotty swore and downed his pint. "I'm over to the church. Molly Harrigan's gonna need something to get by, with five to feed and no husband now. T'anks," he said and slipped out the back again, using the alley as cover. He looked at the familiar faces around the grave. *No strangers. All of them have suffered at the hands of the English. I was ten when they killed my Da and Ma worked herself to death trying to feed us. Thank God, I was old enough to fend for myself. I've made them pay.*

Crotty mingled with the crowd, quietly acknowledged with a nod of a head or a strained smile. Over the gentle murmur of the Gaelic and Latin words came the wailing of the widow. He looked at her and the five children huddled around her skirts. Their raw grief was palpable. When the service was over, he approached the priest. "A word with you, Father."

The man turned to him and Crotty handed over enough coin to cover the funeral, the diggers and a few prayers. "Bless you Crotty. They've got nothing now but their faith. The Earl will have them out of their cottage by week's end if there's no man to work the land. God speed."

Crotty gently approached the widow. "Molly, here's a little something to feed them for a bit," he said, slipping a small purse into her hands. The woman looked forty but Crotty knew she was half that, barely older than himself. Her clothing was clean but threadbare. Her shawl covered hair already graying. She squeezed his hands as tears coursed down her cheeks; words were beyond her. The youngest barefoot child pulled on his coat tails, reminding him of his own son. Quickly he moved through the crowd, across the road and mounted his horse. *I need to see my wife and young Billy. I haven't seen them all week. I wonder if Davie is safe.*

Riding along the cart track in the hilly river valley, Crotty listened intently for sounds of travellers. The rumble of wagon wheels and voices caused him to hide his horse in the bushes until the farm wagon had passed, its two occupants unaware of him. Shortly after, he heard a drumming of hooves on the hard road, and once again Crotty hid his horse in the dense undergrowth. *A single horseman travelling fast – interesting.* He waited and checked his flintlock pistols, primed and ready in the holsters across his saddle. As the lathered bay came into view, he recognized the rider in his tricornered hat and black jacket. *It's Davie.*

"Ho Davie," he called, pulling back onto the road. The rider reined the tired, heaving horse to a halt in front of him.

"Crotty, I've just had the closest call of my life; they bloody near had me. Don't go to your wife. Ahearn's got soldiers going up there now."

Crotty looked at his friend, seeing torn and dirty clothing, the bruised face and bloody knuckles. *He's the closest thing I've had to family; we go back a long way. He's been with me since my parents died.* "Davie, we'd better head to the cave for a bit. They won't get anything out of my Jeanie."

Davie looked at his friend; despair settling over him. It had been a close call. The British brigade had cornered him and pinned him down. He'd landed a few punches but vividly recalled lying on his back with an English bayonet at his throat. Having tied his hands behind his back, they'd dragged him over to where Ahearn was sitting on his chestnut horse, smirking with satisfaction.

"Davie Norris, now you're in for it, me lad. We've got Stackpole and Cashmen. They'll swing on Tuesday. So will you unless you do something for me."

"And what would that be Sheriff?" asked Davie, spitting dirt out of his mouth.

"I want Crotty and you're going to give him to me."

Davie laughed. "Like hell."

"Not this time Davie. I've got your wife and three youngsters. Give me Crotty and they live and you get the reward. Refuse and they die. Your choice. What'll it be?"

Davie stood there agonizing. *He will kill them too, he's done it before. Traitors are killed by the local army. I'm damned either way.* "I'll give you Crotty. Where's my wife?"

"Never you mind. I've got her safe. What's your plan?"

"I'll get him up to the cave and tamper with his pistols. Just use a few men on foot and keep quiet. I'll signal when it's clear to get him."

Ahearn moved off and spoke with his men. Deep in the woods at the base of the mountain they untied him and let him ride off, the soldiers trailing him just out of sight. Davie knew full well this time he wouldn't be able to shake them, not if they had his family.

Crotty looked at his friend from time to time, puzzled by the unusual silence as they rode together. *I've never seen Davie look so defeated.* "They've got the others in Waterford, Davie."

"I know" he replied.

Leaving the horses in the farm field, they clambered up the scree, stopping briefly to get water. Crotty surveyed ahead and behind them; there was no movement. "Looks safe enough." The cave was a mere slit in the rocks, deep in shadow and easy to miss. *I found this place when I was just a boy.* The narrow passageway widened into a small cavern, a dry, safe haven.

Crotty looked at it now, his hazel eyes taking in the simple cots, a table, kegs for chairs, stores of gunpowder, food and a case of whiskey. "We've spent a lot of time up here over the years," he said. "It's been a hell of a day. I'm right tired out." Davie opened a whisky bottle and poured a couple of tumblers.

Rummaging in a box, they found some cheese, a loaf of stale bread and some apples. They sat at the table and finished the bottle and started on a second. Darkness fell and their candle threw eerie shadows on the ceiling crevices. They spoke of better days and the satisfaction of eluding the British army.

Crotty recalled starting his career on the road after his mother had died. She'd been the washerwoman on the Earl's estate. For a penny a day, she'd scrubbed clothes for the Earl's family, often working twelve hours. Crotty had seen the wealth and the waste. He'd stolen food from the kitchen when he could. Many of the servants fed their families on the left-over food, taking the scraps home each night. Used and discarded clothing had been coveted and resewn. Nothing thrown out had been wasted.

He'd met Davie there. Davie's father had worked the land on the estate. The boys had been inseparable, cleaning the stables and looking after the horses and the pack of hounds the Earl used for hunting. *I learned to be in the woods and hunt early on. I got to know the land. That's been a blessing in evading the troops.* Looking at Davie across the table, he said "You've been like an older brother and always been there for me over the years."

Tears started to well up in Davie's eyes and he quickly turned away to stretch out on the cot, not wanting Crotty to see his distress. "I'm done... Got to get some sleep," he said gruffly, pulling the blankets over him to ward off the cold night air. He heard Crotty settling onto his bed and waited. *Dear God, how can I do this to my friend? Ahearn will kill my family if I don't.*

Davie remained awake and waiting until Crotty's snores were deep and regular. He gently lifted the pistols from the table and placed a few drops of water in the flashpan, saturating the powder. As Davie stepped outside, he waved the candle across the doorway and disappeared into the night.

At first light six soldiers stormed the cave. Crotty pulled the triggers, but the pistols misfired. He went down in a flurry of fists and feet. They dragged him out the cave and shoved him down the hill with his hands tied behind his back and bayonets ready. Davie's body lay sprawled on the slope with a bayonet hole in his back. One soldier kicked the corpse, saying: "You can never trust a traitor."

Crotty sat on the straw strewn floor of the dank cell, the only light coming from a small window high in the stone wall. He ached from head to foot from the beating they'd given him, his cheeks swollen from the punches. *Damn, I think my nose is broken too.*

He sat there thinking about the day the British had killed his father. *They shot him for stealing a loaf of bread. He died right in front of us, my mother and me. They just laughed and kept on riding. My mother never got over it. She pined away for him. She struggled so hard to support us, getting a penny a day. I was only ten. She was just twenty-five when she died. I had no where to live and I vowed I'd get even with them and I have. It's taken them eight years to catch me. I've had a good run and helped as many as I could.*

Did Davie betray me? God rest his soul, they must have threatened his family for him to do that. They killed him anyway, no reward there for him. Would I have done any different if they had Jeanie and Billy?

The hammering outside had been going on for an hour; now it stopped. *The scaffold must be finished. They're going to hang me today. God give me the courage to face them. I'm bloody scared and I haven't said goodbye to Jeanie or Billy. I pray they can get away. God, I love them.* Images of his wife floated in front of his eyes: her cheeky flirty smile, the smile that made his heart melt. He remembered holding his son for the first time and vowing to himself he'd live long enough to see the boy grown. *That's one promise I'm breaking.* He felt his heart pounding wildly and his hands were sweaty and trembling.

Voices and the tramp of heavy boots out in the hall made him straighten up and he awkwardly clambered to his feet, straw clinging to his britches. The solid wooden door swung open with a creak of its iron hinges and the Sergeant entered with the priest. The Latin words washed over Crotty. He closed his eyes for a moment and silently prayed. When he finished his prayer, he opened his eyes and saw the sad eyes of the priest. "Go with God, my son." Crotty nodded and followed him out of the cell.

He blinked in the sunlight and was surprised to see Waterford's town square full of people, his people. Ahearn was standing on the scaffold platform, a parchment document in his hand. The Colonel and Lieutenant were astride their horses, a battalion of soldiers in their scarlet jackets at hand with their muskets ready.

Ahearn's expecting trouble. These are my people, not that they can retaliate openly against armed soldiers, he thought.

Stackpole and Cashmen were now climbing the wooden stairs. A musket barrel poked him in the back, nudging him forward and he walked ahead to join them.

They stood on the platform, their hands tied behind their backs and the black clad hangman placed a dangling noose around the neck of each man. Taking a deep breath and squaring his shoulders, Crotty felt a calm descend. *Damn, I'm not going to let them win even if they kill me.* Stackpole was snivelling and his wife and children were crying in the front row. Crotty scanned the crowd but couldn't see his wife and son. *Dear God, I hope she's safely away.*

Ahearn stood and read the parchment. "By the laws of Britain and the King, on this the 17th day of March, in the year 1742, these men have been found guilty of theft and highway robbery and are to be hanged, drawn and quartered and beheaded, with their heads placed on pikes in this square as a stern warning to those of you who break the law." Wails arose from the women as the crowd shouted and surged forward. The soldiers raised their muskets and the crowd fell back.

Ahearn stood in front of Crotty. "You are going to watch your men die."

Crotty stared at him. The hangman covered Stackman's face with the hood, tightened the rope and with a solid thunk the trap door opened and Stackman's legs thrashed and kicked for several minutes. Stackman's wife fainted, her children clustered around her.

A pale and visibly shaken Cashmen looked at Crotty as the hood was being placed over his head and the two men said goodbye with their eyes. The clang of the trap door and the dancing figure on the rope signalled it was his turn now.

The hangman approached with the hood but Crotty shook his head. "No, no hood. Ahearn, I've got one last thing to say to you."

Ahearn stepped forward and Crotty spit in his face. The trap door opened, the noose biting deeply into Crotty's neck. His last remembrance was the cheer of the crowd.

And so, the legend of William Crotty was born, the legend that grew over the years with the retelling. He became a folk hero in songs and poems. Some versions claim his wife and son escaped; others say she jumped from his lookout point, killing herself and their son. His story is a creation of his times: a harsh rocky geography, the poverty of a Gaelic Irish culture, a governing British hierarchy and the desperate, persevering courage of the local people. His hoard of buried treasure has never been found, if indeed it ever existed.

The Famine: One More Day

October, 1837

Pulling his collar up against the wind, Evan snugged down his cap and glanced at the darkened cottages. He looked at Henry's empty cottage beside his. *Only two months ago, eleven people lived in that house. Starvation's claimed every single one. Most of the other cottages are empty too. Just a few survivors with no money, no food and no heat. It feels like the eyes of dead houses are following me.*

He walked to the third house down and knocked on the door. The smell of death filled his nostrils. There was no answer. He slowly opened the door and glanced inside. He looked at the three bodies piled together in the corner. There was no life in them.

All these people are or were related to me. Today I buried the only woman I've ever loved. No casket, just a damned hole in the ground.

"Moira, I love you," he said to the wind and thought of her lying in his arms, taking her last breath.

"Evan," was all she'd said as stillness crept through her rags as life ebbed away.

We only had four years together. Was it only four? I remember the first time I saw her in the market; she took my breath away, she was so beautiful. Love at first sight. I've been a lucky man.

He looked at their acre of garden. *I could grow six tons of potatoes on that. It would feed us for the whole year. Our spring planting went well and the plants thrived. Then at the end of August the leaves turned black and the tubers rotted with a stink worse than pigs. It was the same everywhere in the county. I really tried to find work, but the mills were shutting down – too much competition from the British factories with their machines. The children died first. It broke our hearts. Now for the first time in my whole life, I'm alone.*

Old Peig, in the end cottage, is by herself too. She's not going to last more than another day. She was able to send her daughter and four children to Canada a couple of weeks ago. She lost her husband Jack this week. I'll check in on her; she's been good to all of us. Evan paused at her door and knocked. A frail voice answered and he entered. Peig lay on her bench, her wrinkled skin cold under the thin blanket. Grasping her bony hand, he sat beside her and they prayed together.

"Evan, it's my time to go. Jack will meet me on the other side. The Lord will take me tonight. There's three good potatoes left in the cupboard. You take 'em. Now off with you."

He stuffed the precious tubers in his pocket and said "Bless you Peig. You've been like a mother to me the last while. I'll never forget ya." He gave her hand a final squeeze and closed the door behind him as he left. *She'll be dead by morning – it's so bloody final.*

Walking back to his cottage, he thought about Baby James born in September to a starving Moira. He only lived a few hours and died before the priest could baptise him. Church rules forbade his burial in consecrated ground, so Evan had taken him to the rath, the faery hill fort. At dusk, he had buried the tiny bundle among the oaks and hawthorns near the sacred circle of the ancients. He prayed for the faeries or even the pagan gods to watch over his last child. *The Church doesn't believe in them but the old folks always said they were there.* "Please, I beg you. Watch my James. He didn't deserve this. None of them did." He hadn't expected an answer.

Tonight, the loneliness became a terror. *I can't stay in this cottage any longer – it's so empty. No Moira to hold me, no Tommy to tickle, no Ewart and no James. Love and laughter have seeped out of the walls, leaving a stark deep hole that's swallowing me. I'm being evicted tomorrow anyway. Haggerty wants our acre to pasture the Lord's cattle and this cottage is in the way. He wants us gone. Damn him and all those greedy buggers. I paid my rent in labour for the estate but now it's not enough. Other landlords ship their tenants to America to get rid of them but Haggerty's just gonna let us die. I'd like to kill the man. Rage may be the only thing keeping me alive.*

He walked out of the village and down the road, a burlap sack slung over his shoulder. *All I have is a tin pot, a spoon, mug, a shirt and three potatoes.*

The faery hill loomed larger with the dense forest cover making the night even darker. *I'm being watched,* the hair on the back of his neck stood on end and goose bumps came up on his chilled arms. He came to the old circle of stones; markers of a long-forgotten people. He found James' grave close to the faery tree, sat down and sobbed, crying for what he'd lost and what might have been. Moira's hair ribbon, tied to a branch on the hawthorn tree, fluttered in the night breeze, the only offering he'd had left. The faery tree was covered in ribbons; some old but many new.

Evan became aware of beings around him. He jumped to his feet but was too scared to move. At first, he couldn't see them but felt their presence. A faint phosphorescence coalesced into small human shapes three to four feet high. *Faeries? Ghosts?* The dozen beings encircled him and as they came closer became more solid. One female form moved forward to about six feet in front of him. She seemed to float silently above the ground, the grass unmoved beneath the hem of her gauzy dress. He stared in disbelief, mesmerized by the wings folded behind her. *She's as delicate as a butterfly, like an angel but smaller and her face is sharp.*

"I don't mean to intrude," he said to her. "I came to say goodbye to my son. His mother is dead now. I'm leaving this place forever. Please help me. Watch over him, there's no one else left," he begged, tears continuing to trickle down his face until his nose ran.

He thought he heard "we will" but it could have been the wind.

"Bless you," he said and fainted. When he awoke, he was cold, lying on the ground, alone. *It's time for me to go.* He gathered his bag and trudged down the path. Looking back through the trees for the last time, he saw a twinkling of lights in the circle. *They're still there.* The lights lit a tiny glow in the black hole that had been his heart.

Evan walked slowly onto the road. *I'm heading to Cork. Ships leave for America from there.* His stomach growled again, reminding him he hadn't eaten for a very long time. *Peig's given me a gift of three potatoes... They might get me through one more day.* The wind cut through his shirt and gnawed at his gaunt body. *I don't know how far I can get before I die. Lord give me one more day.*

He was about a mile down the deeply rutted road when his knees began to tremble. *I have to stop somewhere safe and get some sleep.* He chose an ancient pine with branches low enough to climb and clambered up about ten feet. Wedging himself into a fork of the branches, he ate a potato and fell asleep instantly.

It was the growling and snarling that awoke him at sunrise. *What's happening?* Parting the branches, he could clearly see a pack of feral dogs fighting over a large bone. *Oh Lord, they've found a body!* The two largest animals were on opposite ends of a human leg bone, their lips curled, showing fierce arrays of teeth. They were braced backwards with toes splayed for traction, ears flat and hackles up. There was a lot of head shaking and snarling, then one dog lost its grip and the winner trotted away dragging the bone, his head and tail high. Some of the dogs still had collars. *Someone's pet – owners are dead or can't feed them.* He retched but nothing came up. *I must remember to watch for them, especially in open areas. They'd tear me to pieces if they caught me.*

Evan waited for the dogs to move on and finally they went towards his village. He listened as their barking faded and descended the tree. Two curves in the road later, he found the source of the dogs' breakfast. A woman and two children had died in the ditch. The dogs had thoroughly dismembered what little had been left of them. *The smell is awful, but I might find something useful.*

I can't believe I'm scrounging on the dead. He found one penny and a rosary which he put in his sack. No food. He crossed a small stream taking a long, deep drink. *I can't see any fish or frogs here.* He washed his face and hands as best he could. The stubble on his face was becoming a skimpy beard.

Sitting on the bank, he ate another potato. *I've only got one left now. Dear God, let me find something else to eat. These weeds are probably safe. I've seen cattle eat those.* He picked a few but they were stringy and bitter.

The landscape looked peaceful. A few cattle grazed in rock-lined fields. Birds sang and a muted sun shone, but there were no people. A cottage came into view, the front door wide open, hanging on one hinge. He cautiously looked inside. *It's completely bare.* Behind the house was an overrun garden and an old apple tree. He rummaged through the weeds and found a dozen wizened apples which he put in his sack. The odour of decaying potatoes hung in the air.

Somewhere close, a dog barked. Evan looked for a high place but nothing was accessible, so he hid in the long grass behind the tree. A cart with two men, pulled by a thin horse, was coming along the path, the dog trailing behind. Evan listened to their conversation.

"It's a sin. Dead bodies all the way to Cork and it's no different in town either – crowds of starving people – no food anywhere for them and no place to put them."

"Aye," said the other man. "It's getting violent too. People breaking into shops to get a loaf of bread and murdering each other to steal it. The fever's started down the coast. They're dropping like flies."

"The ones sailing to America aren't much better off. Half of them will be dead before they get there. The British government's not doing a blessed thing except set up commissions. All this talk about work programmes and getting American corn. These poor souls will starve before we see one bag of maize on the docks," the first man said shaking his head. The cart moved along and out of sight.

Evan continued down the road, noting clouds starting to darken the horizon. *The wind's picking up too. I need to find shelter.* He tried to hurry but came across more bodies in the ditch. Once again, the dogs had preceded him. A rosary with a little tin cross was all he found this time. *That could have been Moira and the boys.*

To his right, he noticed the twinkling of tiny lights. *Faeries?* Curiosity got the better of him, so he climbed over the rock wall and followed the lights down to the river. Buried deep in the tall reeds was an overturned rowboat. The lights danced around it, then disappeared. Evan was at the end of his energy and drops of cold rain were starting to soak his jacket. He crawled under the boat only to confront a man curled up in the bow. Startled he called out "Hey, mister." No answer. Closer he went and reaching out, prodding the man – no response. *Newly dead he is. No smell yet.* Rain poured down, pounding on the hull above him. He collected a mug of rain water and sat there eating an apple.

I've got no money for boat fare. Sounds like Cork is full of people like me – no food, no work and getting worse. I don't know where I'm going. I've never been out of the village except to go to the estate market. All I've got is a couple of pennies and two rosaries. How am I going to survive?

He awoke with a start, staring up at the wooden slats above him, and thought for a moment he was already in a coffin. *No, it's the rowboat.* Clambering out from under-neath, he found the morning overcast and dry. *I thank the Lord and the faeries for another day.* He raised one side of the gunnel to get a good look at his companion. The man wore a faded tweed jacket, very tattered trousers and boots with holes in the soles. He removed the jacket with difficulty and checked the pockets – another penny and two flints. *Excellent! I'll be able to start a fire if I need to.* He tried the jacket on but it was too big. *Never mind, I might be able to sell or barter it.* He also took the ragged shirt and the boot laces.

As he walked away, he looked back at the boat. *If I could get it in the water, I might be able to get to Cork easier than walking. I've never been in one before. I could sell it in Cork and maybe have enough for boat fare.* He tried to shove the boat down the bank but it was too heavy. *I just don't have the strength to do it alone.* He found the oars in the reeds.

Starting to feel a bit more hopeful, he scavenged along the banks and found a handful of berries. *I don't know what kind they are. Hope they aren't poisonous.* He slowly chewed them, savouring the semi-sweet taste. The last of the oat and barley crop was still in the field. *There's nobody left to harvest it by the look of it.* He filled his cap with seed heads and found two river worn stones to grind them. About half a mile away, he could see the crown of a large oak towering over the other trees. *Maybe I can find some acorns.* He slowly worked his way through the scrub brush.

I think this used to be the O'Brien estate. There was a village around here, where is it? He was dumbfounded to find a rubble-filled clearing. *I don't believe it. The cottages have gone. There were over a hundred tenants here.*

He continued walking toward the oak, looking for signs of human activity. There were none. The oak was very old. Six people could have joined hands around it, the girth was so wide. Evan got down on his hands and knees and raked the leaves for acorns. After an hour, his pockets were full. Taking the old shirt from his sack, he ripped off the sleeves, tied each wrist into a knot and made makeshift bags, one for the grain, the other for the acorns. *I knew the laces would come in handy* he thought as he tied the bags closed. He sat and ate two apples. *Between the grain, the acorns and my last potato, I've got enough for a good feed today. Now to find a safe place to sleep.*

He started to gather small twigs to make a small fire. He was bent over still gathering when he heard a twig snap. Spinning around he saw a small child, a wide-eyed skinny little girl in a ragged shift who looked at him in terror and fled. "Wait! Don't go!" he cried out, but she vanished into the thick brush. *I haven't spoken to a living soul in two days. She must be Tommy's age.* The thought of Tommy brought the tears again. *Oh Lord, I miss them.*

Looking up, there were now two faces peeking out from behind a tree, a woman and the child. They ducked out of sight when he saw them, so he sat on the ground and waited.

"My name's Evan. I won't hurt you," he called out. The faces peered out again and slowly they moved away from the tree. Both were very thin and barefoot, their clothing threadbare, their hair long and matted.

"I found some acorns," he said, offering a handful.

The woman nodded and moved a little closer, the child hiding behind her.

"I used to live in the Barry estate up the road but my wife and boys died. I just buried her. The landlord was going to evict me, so I left. You're the first person I've talked to in two days. What happened to the O'Brien cottages – they're all gone. Did you live there?"

She nodded. "I'm Maureen and she's my daughter, Catherine. The rest of my family's gone too. My husband went to Midleton to get food but never came back. It seems like weeks ago. The landlord came with a big gang of men and smashed down our cottages. A few folk went to Cork, but I think most of them just died."

"I need to find a dry place to sleep. What's around here?" asked Evan.

"You can come back to our camp, it's not far," she said.

"I'd like that," he said picking up his sack and following them. They walked for about fifteen minutes, the woman in the lead and the child constantly turning to look at him as he brought up the rear. The brush was dense and the rocky ground slowly rose to a small knoll. His legs faltered and his steps became erratic. He paused, not sure he could continue.

"Not much further," she called. Somehow, he managed to put a foot in front of the other, again and again. The path was very faint, just bent blades of grass to show where it had been trodden. The fading light made it harder to see, then they disappeared. Evan stopped. *I can't see them at all.* Catherine appeared and beckoned him with a wave. He headed for where he'd seen her and there beneath the rocky overhang was a lean-to of boughs. It blended right in with the scenery. Maureen had brought reeds from the river and made deep mats for beds. *At least we're dry and out of the wind.* It was too dark to cook now so he brought out his apples and the last potato and shared them.

He awoke during the night to find the three of them curled up together like a litter of puppies. *I'm grateful for the warmth. I miss Moira and the boys, but it feels good to be with someone.* It was quiet outside except for the hooting of an owl and the rustling of small creatures. He fell back to sleep.

He awoke in the morning with a deep growling hunger. It was gray and overcast again. Maureen was outside grinding some of the grain between the rocks. "I've got my husband`s hammer to break the acorns open," she said and handed it to him.

He took his sleeve of acorns and started removing the shells, saving them for the fire. When he was done, he gathered the twigs and dried reeds he'd collected yesterday and managed to get a spark with the flints. Soon there was water boiling in his small tin pot. Catherine came back with an arm load of twigs. Moira added the oats and squatted there stirring it with a stick.

"How long do you think the acorns and grain are going to last?" he asked, knowing that the lean-to wouldn't be enough shelter for the coming winter months.

"Maybe two days," she replied.

"Then what do we do?"

"I don't know, Evan. My parents used to live in a fishing village just outside Cork. I don't know if they are still there. It's probably just as bad there. We can't stay here much longer. It's getting colder and we need clothes, shoes and a lot more food."

"I found a rowboat upriver, but I can't move it myself. Do you think both of us could turn it over and get it in the water? I've no experience with a boat, so it could be risky. If we could get to Cork, we might be able to find your parents and sell the boat for food."

Catherine walked out of the brush with her little arms full of more twigs. She smiled shyly at Evan and sat down beside her mother. The heat from the fire felt good and the smell of the gruel had his stomach rumbling again. The acorns were small and hard but tasty. They shared the spoon and took turns eating the gruel out of the pot. "We'd better not eat too much at once or we'll get sick," she said. They gathered acorns for the rest of the morning, filling the sleeves and later gathered more grain from the field. A driving rain forced them back to the lean-to.

The next morning, they bundled up their meager belongings then Evan lead them to the boat, avoiding the man's body which was now swollen and smelling badly. After several attempts, they were able to turn the boat over. "I don't see any holes in it." Gathering their scanty belongings, they climbed into the boat and pushed off into the river.

Evan found the oars awkward to handle and they went in circles a few times. Maureen and Catherine giggled, but the slow current of the Owenacurra River took them gently downstream as the land flattened. *I've never been this far from the estate before*. The grain fields were empty and the few cattle looked thinner. The whole landscape seemed devoid of humanity. Evan knew his strength was leaving him. *I'm too tired to row much and I don't feel well.*

They smelled the town long before they came to it. There were bodies along the riverbanks and quite a few floating in the water. When the town bridge came in view, Evan pulled the boat up beside the bank and they crawled out. It took their combined efforts to turn it over.

"Look" said Maureen, pointing to the bridge. There were dozens of people under it, many of them children. "They've nowhere else to go."

"I can't tell if they're dead or alive," said Ewen looking at the hollow faces, seeing many piled on top of each other. "I can see beggars on the street. They look like the walking dead. It's worse than I thought. There's no point in trying to find food here. We'd better eat some acorns and the apples. I think we are in for more rain shortly. I don't want to attract attention with a fire." He noted that Maureen looked flushed and the child listless.

A cold rain fell and continued all afternoon. He fell asleep filled with confused dreams of Moira, sunshine and his parents. When he awoke it was dusk and rain was still pounding on the boat. Looking at Maureen and Catherine, he could see the flesh melting from them. Catherine's breathing was very shallow. He looked at his own bony arms protruding from his sleeves. *They're not going to make it and neither am I*, he realized with a growing sense of the inevitable. *I know I don't have the strength to row any more and I just don't feel well.*

It was Maureen's moaning that awoke him later. He rolled over and looked at her out on the bank retching violently, clutching her belly. He crawled over to her and was horrified to feel the heat radiating from her skin. *Oh God, she's got the fever!* He crawled back to Catherine but the child lay motionless and cold. *Just like Tommy. She's gone.*

Evan lay there, his arms around the dead child. *I'm so weak. I haven't heard Maureen vomit for a while and she's not moving out there.* He closed his eyes and prayed for the end. *Lord take me now. I can't bear to lose anyone else.* It was just before dawn when a glow of faery lights gathered around the boat. They twinkled brilliantly for a few moments, then one by one went out.

the pub

October, Present day, the west coast of Ireland

Gripping the steering wheel, I eyeballed the single-file pedestrians on the narrow pavement. *There's barely six inches to spare between my mirror and oncoming traffic.* "Am I leaving enough room on your side?" I asked my friend Jane who was angling her camera out the passenger window. The car inched forward in the heavy traffic, giving her time to capture the pastel coloured shop fronts.

"You're O.K. Look at this main street, there's every conceivable colour. That plaque says 1673. Can you imagine? Lordy, look at those side streets undulating uphill like colourful serpents. They'd be a luge run in freezing rain." I could hear the steady click of her camera.

The small traffic circle gave me an opening to park at the harbour. Heaving a sigh of relief, I got out of the car breathing in the tang of sea air. Glancing up the street,

I saw what had attracted Jane's attention and took a
better look. The narrow street rose sharply with two
story houses either side. The brick layers matched the
inclines and it seemed every house had a coloured door
complete with brass door knocker and mail slot. Even
though it was October there were window boxes still full
of geraniums basking in the sunshine.

I joined Jane at the stone wall and we gazed at the
view across the harbour. "Fishing's obviously a going
concern," I said watching the commercial fishing trawl-
ers and sleeker small black boats with single stripes and
red-brown sails, negotiating the gap in the sea wall. Signs
advertised harbour tours on a daily schedule. "Why don't
we stay here tonight and go on a boat tour tomorrow?"
Across the sun-tipped waves, several miles out to sea,
were dark green islands, rugged, steep and mysterious, changing moment to moment in the cloud-broken
sunlight. *Makes me think of hovering seabirds, crashing
waves and monasteries. No wonder these places breed poets
and authors.*

"That sounds like a plan," she replied. "Let's find a
place to have lunch. I think you've had enough driving
for one day."

I nodded in wholehearted agreement, wondering if our
idea of self-driving in a country where traffic moves on
the wrong side of the road for us had been such a good
idea. *I've been so fixated on the road, I've been missing the*

*scenery – waves of green hills, tiny old houses, grazing sheep
in stony fields and roads winding like black ribbons.*

Just down from the traffic circle was a small pub sporting a squeaky, swinging sign – The Black Horse Inn. Irish
pubs have a reputation for good food, so in we went. The
yeasty aroma of beer and fresh baking was tantalising.
Pavlov would've had a field day here. The mahogany bar was
polished to a honey glow and behind it stood the barman.
He was a portly fellow with an infectious grin and his
crooked nose looked like he'd escorted more than a few
inebriates from his premises. I was willing to bet he was
more muscle than flab. You couldn't help but grin back.
"Come in ladies," he gestured. "We're serving lunch."

The mirrored shelving behind the bar contained a vast
assortment of amber filled bottles and reflected the layout
of the room. I could see tables and chairs in the front and
cubicles for four at the back. Half a dozen stools lined the
bar. "This probably looks like it did two hundred years
ago," I said and Jane laughed. "I bet these are the original
hand-hewn beams and wainscoting."

Jane chose a table close to the side wall and was examining the ancient advertisements. There was a flyer for
stud service from a fine-looking stallion, circa 1835 and
another for ladies' hats in 1874 from the milliners of the
time. "How old is this pub?" she asked the bar man. His
name was Patrick – of course.

"At least 1545, we think, though there've been a couple of fires and parts have been rebuilt. There's always been a pub here. Erin will be right with you," he said. We settled into comfortable chairs and then Erin came over. She was slim, young and clad in black jeans and a tee shirt sporting the black horse logo, which really set off her gorgeous wavy deep red hair and fair skin.

"Good morning. I see you're Canadian," she said, noting the maple leaf pins we both wore. "Here's the lunch menu. Most of the food is local – the beef, fish and veggies," she said in a quick, soft lilting accent. "The specials are poached salmon, shepherd's pie or Guinness beef stew with chips and salad. Would you like tea or coffee?"

I opted for the salmon while Jane selected the shepherd's pie and a large pot of tea. Erin returned with a bucketful of cutlery and formally set the table. *Oh no, which fork do I use this time? No matter where you eat here, the meals are properly presented.* The first bite of salmon was a revelation – sweet, deep and rich, so much more subtle than smoked or frozen. Jane was making purring noises with her shepherd's pie.

"Jane, can you put your finger on what's different in this pub? Something's missing," I said.

Jane looked around thoughtfully. "No television, at least in this part. Maybe it's around the back."

"You're right. Nobody's clustered around to get football or hockey scores."

"You know what else is different? There are children in here. That couple in the booth have their little girl and baby with them. You'd never see that in a bar at home."

Jane asked Patrick: "Is there any place in town to get a couple of rooms for the night?"

"I've got two upstairs," he said. "Erin can show them to you when you're finished your lunch."

Later Erin escorted us up the side stairs to the second floor. The front room overlooked the harbour with the changing sea and the bustle of the street. The low ceiling and thick walls seemed to give it substance and with the window it seemed light and airy. The simple wooden furniture appealed to me as did the homemade quilt.

Jane preferred the room at the back. "Look, that arched carriage way we saw opens into the old stable yard but they've turned them into apartments and ooh, an antique shop. I've got to check that out."

Somehow the curtain between past and present seemed veil thin and I half expected to see ancient travellers in period dress or a ghost or two in the hall; so, we stayed. Patrick assured us that the car would be safe in the harbour parking lot, so we retrieved our luggage. I wrote postcards, read through the stack of pamphlets we had accumulated and had a nap while Jane went out to rummage through treasurers in the antique shop. She returned later with mysterious bags, likely real mementos rather than plastic leprechauns.

Around five thirty, we went downstairs to check out the supper menu and to sample the atmosphere of a real Irish country pub. We were lucky to get a table by the front windows with the handmade bottle-bottom panes of glass giving a distorted view of the street. Supper was superb. "This lamb is so tender," I said, savouring the tasty medallions with small potatoes, fresh peas, carrots and parsnips garnished with sprigs of fresh mint.

"You were right. This salmon is really yummy," she replied. Dessert choices were either a to-die-for cheese-cake with a berry topping or a toffee torte. We sampled one of each and ordered Irish coffee. "Watch him make it," she said as he performed the ritual. First, he poured black coffee into a glass then added a shot of Potcheen.

"Potcheen used to be moonshine whisky, but it's legal now. There used to be thriving illegal business in these hills. No more though." He carefully poured cream over the back of spoon so that it floated on top of the coffee. He placed the two glasses on our table and with mock solemnity, said: "It's a sin to stir it, Slainte." The couples at the adjacent tables laughed.

Jane's first sip gave her a creamy moustache which she licked away. We giggled and clinked glasses. "That is one smooth and tasty drink."

The noise level rose steadily as time passed and more townsfolk came in. There was a steady hum of Irish conversations, the banging of pots in the kitchen and the click-click of snooker balls from the backroom pool table. A solitary, middle-aged man sat at the bar. *He's a regular. Patrick had that glass on the counter before he even had his bum on the stool.* He just sat there sipping his brew and minding his own business. A pod of young people crowded into a booth, laughing and jostling, all ordering beer. They were a culturally diverse group."

"I suppose that, with Ireland being part of the European Union, there'd be lots of foreign students attending the universities here. They wouldn't even need passports to travel around," said Jane.

An elderly man came in carrying a violin case and set up near the fireplace. He was bent and wiry but his wrinkled old face beamed from the warm reception of the crowd. "Charlie how are ya?"

"Good to see you."

Jane spoke with the couple at the next table and was informed that musicians came in most Fridays for a session and that Charlie was one of the best old-time fiddlers in the county. He was soon joined by a younger man with an acoustic guitar and a woman with a flute. There was no sheet music. Instruments were tuned, a few practice chords played and they were off – sweet strains of old melodies, lively jigs and reels, and sorrowful laments to dead heroes and lost loves. My feet were tapping, my hands were clapping. I loved it.

The couple with the young baby had it bouncing to the music on the young father's knee. Squeals of delight ensued. A lot of the music was in Gaelic but both of us sang along with the bits we knew. There were some lovely harmonies from a trio of Irish grannies at the back. The old man was good and they all deferred to his expertise.

A police car pulled up outside and an officer entered the pub. He called out: "Can I have your attention please?" The noise level died. "Old Reggie's wandered off again. Has anyone seen him? No? Well, keep your eye open for him, will you? And call us if you spot him. I'll be off, thanks," and departed with a wave.

What was that all about?

Once again, our neighbours enlightened us. "Reggie, poor old sod, hasn't been right in the head since his wife died. Won't go to the nursing home neither. Good thing the local coppers know him. Somebody usually finds him and takes him home."

A group of four sturdy, ruddy-faced men sat at another table. They were probably farmers since they talked about the price of cattle shipped to Europe, the local hay crop and something about silage I didn't catch. The accents were a bit tricky and they spoke very quickly.

Soccer was another hot topic. "Did you see the McRory lad get that goal? He's sharp. Can see him going professional." It seemed every small town we had passed through had a team and local field with competition right up to the county leagues. This obsession incited fierce rivalries in every male over the age of five.

Jane nudged me and brought my attention to the two couples at the bar. They were obviously good friends. One husband seemed to be spending an inordinate amount of time running his left hand up and down the back of his neighbour's wife, lingering on her bottom, while his right arm was firmly wrapped around his wife. He had no time to drink with both arms full, but the ladies didn't seem to mind. The other hubby drank steadily, seemingly oblivious to it all.

I had the view of a young couple in a dimly lit corner. She was a twenty-something brunette with long straight hair and a striking figure, displaying plenty of cleavage. Her male partner appeared totally mesmerized. At one point, his face flushed and a glazed expression appeared on his face. I could see her bare foot on his lap. I nudged Jane who pivoted to look. The girl had such a coy, innocent smile on her face. Her massage was obviously creating problems for him because they left about five minutes later amid knowing looks and laughter from the others, who'd probably seen her work her magic before. From what I could see, they managed to get as far as their car before melding into oneness in the shadows between the street lights.

It was amazing to watch the waitresses serving under crowded conditions. They wielded awkward trays of sudsy glasses up, over and around their clients with deft skill and remembered who had ordered the Guinness or the Murphy's. There was a constant banter back and forth that only comes with familiarity.

"Darling, come sit on my knee," offered a handsome young rogue with curly black hair and a wicked twinkle in his inviting blue eyes, at one of the booths.

"I'll not be sitting on your knee or anything else, Thomas Cochrane," came the rapid-fire response as she winked at the others and whipped her now empty tray back to the bar followed by laughter from the group.

The voices and accents were interesting. In these parts it was Gaelic, then English. The Gaelic influence showed not only in the language itself, which was evident on the road signs, but in the rhythms and cadences of speech even if it was English being spoken. It had a lyrical fluidity just like the music.

A crash of shattered glass and an angered curse broke the moment around the pool table where a knot of young men had been playing. That Irish accent had a sharp, menacing ring to it. Patrick emerged from the bar like a destroyer cleaving water. "What's up boys? We'll have none of that now," he declared in a voice that brooked no argument.

"He's a cheat," slurred the teenager, his scowling face as red as his hair.

"Liam, I think you've had enough for tonight," replied Patrick, the enforcer.

Liam slammed his way out the front door, leaving his pals to clean up the mess; the game continued as noise levels got back to normal. Around ten o'clock the placed started to empty out. The musicians wound down and packed up their gear. The gaggle of grannies departed down the main street followed by the young couple with the now sleeping baby draped over dad's shoulder. The good friends and loner remained at the bar when we finished our drinks and went upstairs to collapse into downy cocoons above the decreasing hubbub.

Our pub experience had been a treat. It had been a brief window into the lives of the locals and I thought how different a pub was from a bar at home. This was more than a pickup joint, it was the hub of a community, the nerve centre for the whole village. Everyone knew everyone else. It had given me some insights into the elusive threads in the tapestry of Irish life. The language and music drew me like a mystical siren call. I will never know why the loner sat at the bar estranged and remote as an island. What was his story? Did young Thomas ever get the girl? Did Old Reggie get home safe that night? I'll never know, unless of course I go back.

Even years later if I think back on that night, it is with pleasure and a fondness for the people we met. The memory of the room and the characters are crystal clear even now as indelible imprints.

What is it that makes the Irish such a memorable lot?

The Celtic Warrior: The Making of a Hero

The Kingdom of Munster, Ireland, 400 A.D.

Ruarc stopped scything the wheat as his wife Hilde came down the hill, carrying a bucket of water. He had stripped off his shirt long ago, showing a lean and muscular body, honed by hours of physical labour. The battle scars on his right arm and shoulder looked pale and hard as they ran through the double row of entwining blue wolf tattoos on his upper arms. He was soaked in sweat, his long red hair clinging in damp strands to his wet neck and shoulders.

"Here, Ruarc, take a drink. It's about time you and Barra had a break. You've both been working all morning to get this field done." Ruarc took a long draught, wiping his mouth on the back of his hand and watched her brother Barra as he completed the row rhythmically leaving a trail of falling wheat stems. Ruarc could hear the spirits of the grasses whispering.

"Thanks Hilde," he replied, smiling as she walked back to the huts, admiring the sway of her hips. *She's a good woman.* Tantalizing aromas of roasting meat and baking bread wafted down the hill, making his stomach growl. *My mother and aunt were grinding grain between the stones this morning. Our meal should be ready soon.*

Barra stopped beside him for a drink then passed the bucket to the gathering women. "How's the new scythe?"

"I'm really pleased with it," Ruarc replied, running his finger over the scalloped edge of the obsidian blade. "It's well worth the hide I traded for it. It's holding its edge well."

"It's too bad we don't have that kind of stone in these parts. I was told it can only be found in the far north, in the land of the giants. If we had an axe made of that we'd be able to take down that big oak in the meadow."

"Barra, we've done really well to get this place built so quickly," said Ruarc, looking at their village. Over the log palisade, he could see the conical thatched roofs of six round houses on mud and wattle walls and the framework of another one in progress. "We've cleared six fields so far. It should be a good harvest this year. The soil is rich and water plentiful. We've got everything we need here."

"Beacan has the boys digging more storage pits for the grain. They've been at it all week" said Barra, watching the group of boys, chest-deep in small round holes and the dirt flying out. "We've got enough clay to cap the pits. The pits were a good idea, much better than storing the loose grain in the huts. The clay seals out the moisture and grain stays dry. No more rats either. We will need to honour Lugh, God of the Harvest. He has been generous this year," said Barra.

"It looks like we should have enough wheat to make more beer too," said Ruarc with a grin. "Most of the barrels in our fogou are empty."

Just then three ravens landed on the tree to their right, cawing loudly. Both men immediately became alert and started looking around. "Oh, oh - that's a sure sign of trouble!" said Barra. The women and children, gathering and binding the wheat into sheaves behind them, stopped too.

"There's no wind, the sky's clear and none of the dogs are barking. I don't see anything, Barra. Do you?" said Ruarc, running his hand over the hilt of his sword strapped over his plaid trousers. He put his shirt back on, adjusting his belt.

"You never know around here," replied Barra. "You can never be without your sword. This little area where the four counties meet seems to be a hot spot. There are always cattle raids and skirmishes. I can't see the danger the ravens are predicting either."

They finished scything the last row then walked up the hill. The women and children followed them in. His aunt Aideen was turning the skewered carcass over the centre pit and waved at him. He returned the wave and walked toward his hut. He could see his wife's aunt squatting in front of the loom inside the house, her gnarled fingers moving the shuttle back and forth around the vertical threads weighted with stones, and pulling a strand of hand dyed wool through; the plaid grew day by day into a long piece of cloth. *It's like magic.* Ruarc could see his father, Ardal, with his limping gait, leading the horses to the corral. *He must have heard the ravens, too.*

Hilde pulled two loaves of bread from the small beehive oven by the fire pit as he stooped to enter. *She's quite capable of handling a spear or a sword too; she could just as easily have been a warrior. Thank the gods she chose to be my wife instead. I thank you, Goddesses of Plenty, for the good things you provide.* "Hilde, I still don't know what the ravens are warning about."

That words were barely out of his mouth when the distant sound of a horn blown three times turned all heads to the east. Above the hills, a small dark column of smoke was rising over the tree tops. *One blast for trouble, three blasts for raiders.*

"Raiders!" yelled Ardal who grabbed their bronze horn and three times blew a sharp reply. "That's Tearnach's village – now they know we got the signal and we've passed the warning on to the next village."

Eight young, able-bodied men scurried to gather their spears, shields, swords, daggers and helmets. Within minutes, they were mounted, their wives tossing sacks of food across the saddles. Ruarc looked down at his Hilde's face and said: "Help Ardal bring the cattle in. Take care of things." She blew him a kiss as he urged his horse forward and disappeared down the road after the others. *My father is our chief, the most experienced warrior. His battle injury may have stopped him from being a warrior for the king, but he is still a force to be reckoned with.*

They rode as fast as the narrow, pock-marked road would allow, up the hills, through the forest and across the streams. Half an hour of hard riding brought them to their neighbours' valley. Barra, raised his hand to bring them to a halt. The cleared fields lay deserted. Smoke and open flames could still be seen over the palisade. *No sign of life.* The lathered horses gulped the air, their red nostrils flared and their chests heaving. "Split up and we'll come in from all sides," he said and they moved among the trees, their spears on the ready and their shields up.

It would be so easy to fall into a trap here; raiders aren't fools, thought Ruarc. He circled the village until he was around the back, but saw no one. He could hear shouts from Barra and worked his way around to the front. *I don't believe it - the village is gone! The huts had burned down to the top of the mud walls.*

The thatch had been the first victim of the flames and was now was a deadly black blanket within each circle, pyramids of charred rafters smoking above. He could see bodies of men, women and children in the centre yard, slashed and trampled like discarded dolls. Tearnach, the man who had sounded the alarm lay face down, impaled by a spear through his back, the horn still clutched in his hand. The cattle and horses were gone and only frightened sheep remained outside, clustered in a bleating group. Anger mushroomed inside him. *There is no honour in killing people like this!*

Seeing the grim look on the faces of his companions, he yelled: "They've got a head start on us, but moving the cattle may slow them down. Maybe we can catch them before they reach the river."

"The river is the boundary between our Kingdoms, if only we can get there on time," replied Barra.

Ruarc pushed his horse as hard as he could, knowing he'd kill the beast if he went much further. *Goddess Epona, help me. Give my horse the strength to get me to the river.* It was easy to follow the raiders; the cattle and horses had left a wide swathe of trampled dirt. Ruarc knew the road well and soon they would be coming to Morrigan's Hill, a huge rocky, steep sided escarpment, the home of the witch Morrigan. The road curved up and around the base of the rock, then sloped down to the ford. *Livestock will never get around the hill by the eastern path. It might be shorter but it's too steep and narrow. I can get through on foot.*

He pulled his horse over when they came to the path, signalling his intention to the others. Barra nodded and continued on the road. Ruarc slowed his horse to a trot as the path between the trees became steeper. Higher he climbed, finally slowing to a walk. The path shrank to a crevice between two towering black walls of rock. Dismounting he proceeded on foot, leaving his horse with its feet splayed, the lathered chest heaving and head hanging. The path climbed higher narrowing to a ledge overlooking the river. He could see the raiders coming down the hill driving the cattle ahead of them but still on his side. *I must stop them from crossing.* He found a track barely a foot wide and slinging his shield over his back he started down. *If I slip here, I'm a dead man,* he thought, looking at the broken rocks below. It seemed to take forever but he finally slithered to the bottom, in time to hear the clash of swords and shouting. *Barra's caught up with them!*

He ran along the banks reaching the road just as the cattle came down the last slope. Bracing his shield in front of him he stood in the middle of the road with his back to the river and started pounding his spear in the dirt, screaming to scare them, screaming to fuel the rage inside, screaming to avenge the dead. The frightened herd split along the banks to avoid him. Several riders broke from the group fighting Barra and headed towards him with their weapons flashing in the light, trying to get through the cows and horses. He paused and let them advance. He saw a spear coming and felt it breeze by his head. He aimed at a rider caught between the livestock and drove his spear with full force catching the distracted man in the chest, knocking him from his horse. Ruarc sprinted forward slipping between cows, grabbed the reins and hauled himself into the saddle.

He barely had time to get his balance and draw his sword when he heard a roar and saw a red-headed giant riding straight for him swinging a bronze axe above his head, forcing his horse through the milling animals. Ruarc squeezed his knees to move his horse forward and raised the shield to protect his head. He concentrated on the giant's face – the flying mane of hair, the gaping screaming mouth, the burning eyes focused on his face and the battle craze overcame him too. The axe moved in slow motion towards him and bit deeply into his shield jarring his whole body. His horse swung to the left to avoid the other and he slashed his sword under and up cross the giant's belly. Penetrating the layers of protective leather, the blade emerged dripping scarlet. Spinning the horse, he got the giant in view again but trapped in the narrow gorge with the cattle between them. Cursing, the giant continued as is nothing had happened despite the expanding river of red on his trousers. The man seemed oblivious to his injuries and kept coming, wailing like a banshee. Raising his battle axe again, he came directly for him. Ruarc held his ground and roared back. The blow landed on his shield, nearly forcing him from the horse. The giant blocked his sword thrust, then shield to shield they shoved and pushed until the horses broke free. Ruarc circled in time to see the man slide from the saddle and land on the ground, the battle axe spinning in the air to bury itself in the dirt. There was silence for a moment, then unbelievably the giant struggled to his feet and drew his sword. "Fight!" he screamed, daring Ruarc to confront him.

Ruarc dismounted and strode toward him. *I must be on my feet to die a hero's death.* Face-to-face, they roared at each other. The giant was still lethal and continued a strong offence. Sword met sword and metal rang. They feinted and sprang apart over and over again. Ruarc looked for an advantage; the giant was two heads taller than him with a much longer reach but he was weakening from blood loss. This time he was slower to raise his shield and Ruarc saw his chance. Faking a belly blow, he momentarily paused as the giant's shield dropped and he side-stepped, slashing upward this time across the throat. The spray of bright red splattered all over him, and the man went down. There was no mistake now. Above a raven flew and cawed. *Right you are Morrigan, Queen of battle. The dead are yours.*

Breathless, he walked over to the giant's body, pleased he had sent the man to an honourable death. He knew the shame his father carried for not having died in battle. "Go to your glory," said Ruarc. Slowly, the sights and sounds beyond the dead man returned. He heard the quiet, no more shouting, no more clanging of swords, just the lowing of the cattle and whinnying of the horses. His breath slowed and the hill came back into focus as the battle craze ebbed away. He saw Barra and the others and knew it was over; revenge had been taken. He gathered the weapons, the shields and horses. *I am lucky to have survived this one.*

Barra rode to him. "Tis grand to see you in one piece, my friend. They took several girls from the village. We'll take them back with us." They rounded up the cattle and their horses, leaving three dead raiders where they lay. "It's not our habit to take the heads though some of our tribes do. He would have been a good trophy. Beacan has an arm wound and lost some teeth but otherwise we are good. We've captured two raiders; they belong to the King."

It was a sombre ride back with darkness coming. Ruarc left the party briefly to retrieve his own horse from the upper slope where he'd left it. The girls were tearful but silent and rode back with them, avoiding the two captured raiders, who rode stoically with their arms tied behind their backs, knowing their fate. The sun was starting to go down when they heard voices ahead of them. All swords came out again but Ruarc and Barra recognized the riders, they were from the village to the west of their own, neighbours who had answered the call just as they had. As the sun set, they camped in the cleared field of the burned-out village. They shared what little food they had, took water from the stream and bedded down under the trees. *A night raid is unlikely. No one here would challenge the spirits who roam the woods at night,* thought Ruarc.

He awoke to the quiet sobbing of the girls, who were going about the village gathering their dead. Ruarc knew from previous visits that these people had different customs from his own. He had met the older girl on other occasions. *I don't remember meeting the younger one. Their tribe is from Gaul and the accent is different but I can still understand it. Both girls are covered in dirt, their clothes torn and their faces stained with tears. I don't see any blood on them. I don't think they've been injured or raped.*

"As you know we are from the Eoghanachta tribe and we bury our dead. I know it is your custom to burn yours," said Ruarc. "We will help you then you must come back to our village. There is no one left for you here." All the men pitched in to gather the twenty-two bodies and stack them within the walls of the main hut. He felt the tears well up in his eyes as he carried the feather weight body of a young boy to the pile. *He's not much older than my son.* Remaining wood and straw were piled over them and using flints, they lit the pyre. All stood and silently watched the smoke rise, smelled the burning flesh and it was Barra who addressed the gods:

> "O mighty Gods of the underworld
> Accept the souls of your people
> To begin their new life in the Western Isles
> They have been avenged
> We will meet them again in a future life
> We have vanquished the raiders in battle
> We have recovered the cattle
> We have satisfied our honour, and allegiance
> to our King."

With the pyre still smouldering, the girls scavenged for anything useful; pots, the bronze family cauldron, the bronze horn. The others were herding the livestock together and starting the drive back toward their village. The ravens soared above them.

Ruarc and Barra rode ahead. "We've got plenty of room for these girls. Aideen might like a bit of female company in her hut, there's only twelve of them in it now and I'm sure they'd feel welcome," said Barra. "With the death of their kinsmen, these young girls have just become very wealthy as the livestock will be theirs. Won't be long before some young lad comes courting. Did you notice, they've already got their wheat in and the beehives haven't been damaged. We could go back later if we needed to, but I think our harvest is good enough to feed everyone."

"We haven't got enough winter fodder for all these cows though," said Ruarc. "I'll have to ask if they've got any other family."

They heard approaching horses and once again drew their swords. Through the trees, flashes of colour – blues, greens and yellows revealed a procession of richly-dressed warriors, big powerful men with hard faces riding magnificent horses. In their midst was middle-aged man in a flowing red cape, the golden torque around his neck, a figure exuding power and majesty.

"It's Conall Mor, King of Munster! Only the King can wear red," said Barra, looking at the red and gold and the superb metal work on the helmet, shield and sword. They rode forward to meet him, dismounted, and bowed their heads to him.

"Ardal told me about the raiders," said King Conall, looking down from his grey stallion at the people and animals before him. "What happened, Ruarc?"

Ruarc stepped forward. "Sire, five raiders attacked the village killing twenty-two people, all except these two young girls. They took them captive then set fire to the huts. After that, they drove off the cattle and horses. We caught up with them before they crossed the river and killed three including a giant with red hair. The other two are for your pleasure. We have taken their weapons and horses. The girls are coming back to our village for now. Our neighbours have come to help us move the herd."

"A giant with red hair? I know him, he's a Connaught man. He's dead?" asked the King.

"Yes, I killed him and left his body by the river at Morrigan's Hill. 'Tis his blood I wear," replied Ruarc, looking down at his splattered shirt. "His horse and shield are here," pointing to the big chestnut horse and the distinctive war shield across the saddle.

The King was momentarily silent then summoned a bearded elderly man, very plainly dressed in grey. The two conferred for a few minutes in quiet undertones, then the King sent two of his men down to the river. *That must be his Druid adviser,* thought Ruarc. *Even kings consult them. Despite the drab attire, the real power lays with the Priest, not the King.*

The King called the two girls over. They were so awe-struck, they didn't move until someone nudged them forward. "What is your name, child?"

"Nora, Sire, and this is Alyson," she said putting her arm around the younger girl.

"Do you have anyone else you can stay with?"

"No, Sire, all of them are dead," replied Nora, tears welling up in her eyes.

"Well then, you will stay with Ruarc and Barra. They will treat you well. I've known Ruarc's father for a long time. They are good, loyal people." The King looked at Ruarc. "Do all the cattle, horses and sheep belong to them?"

"Yes, Sire, a bull, twelve cows and calves, a ram and ten ewes with lambs, plus seven horses," Ruarc replied.

"The livestock belong to Nora and Alyson equally. The girls will be under the guardianship of your family until they marry. You both must return to me tomorrow. Under Brehon Law, we are entitled to compensation from Niall of the Nine Hostages, King of Connaught for this raid. You killed his warrior. You must tell your story to our lawyer. Keep their weapons and horses. Bring the captives to me."

The two men were led before him. They sat stone-faced on their horses. The King eyed them, then Ruarc overhead him say to his warrior beside him: "These men are Niall's knights; they're not just farmers. Bring them back to Caisil. They will be our prisoners until we are compensated. They will not get away with this destruction. My delegation leaves in two days time to present our charge and to demand reparation for this act of war." With that he turned and rode back the way they had come.

The two riders sent to scout the river passed them on the road with a shout and rode on to rejoin their companions and report to the King. Ruarc and Barra were far behind herding the animals, but thoroughly excited with the idea of going to the King's hill fort. "We'll get the herd home, and head out in the morning. I want to let Ardal know everything that's happened and spend the night with Hilde," said Ruarc. *This will be an adventure. I haven't been to Caisil for at least three years. Barra's grinning from ear to ear; he's as excited as I am.*

Everyone from the village, including the dogs, ran out to give them a noisy welcome. Ardal was there, leaning on his staff to support his twisted leg. Ruarc jumped from his horse and the pair embraced with hearty, bone-crushing hugs. Hilde, with young Egan in her arms, ran to him and he embraced her fiercely, savouring the smell of her and the heat of her body against his. His son pulled his hair and held his tiny arms out to him. He spun the happy, squealing child in the air then returned him to Hilde. The women and children clustered around their men and Ruarc watched as, predictably, Aideen went to the two girls, who had remained on their horses.

Ruarc called out for silence. "I want to thank our neighbours for coming. We will feed them and bring out the beer." A cheer went up. He then walked towards the two girls and everyone gathered around them. "This is Nora," said Ruarc, looking up into the brave face of the older girl. "This young lady here is Alyson," he said pointing to the shy ten-year-old. "They are the only survivors of Tearnach's village." A murmur arose from the crowd. "King Conall has appointed us as their guardians until they marry. By law, the livestock they bring with them belongs to them."

Aideen's voice broke in. "Ruarc, they would be welcome in my hut," she replied, her face wrinkled with concern as she offered her hand to Nora and the girl slowly took it.

Ruarc smiled. *That's what I was hoping she'd do. She hasn't been the same since her daughter married and left the village. There's only three women in that hut and a rambunctious bunch of men. Having the girls there will keep her busy.* He glanced at his father and saw the nod.

"Tomorrow, Barra and I must go to the King. He will officially demand compensation through his lawyer, for the death of Tearnach's people. We killed three raiders and have the rights to their horses and weapons. It is time for us to celebrate our victory. We all fought well. I'm keeping the chestnut horse; it's a better animal that my own. Let's get them to pasture, then we can gather round the fire, celebrate our victory and welcome the girls to our family."

Ruarc sat by the fire and watched as the evening progressed into the merriment of feasting, story telling, and singing songs. All eight men composed and sang their victory songs to the steady beat of the bodhran drum, a three-stringed harp and a flute. First Barra sang his song then the others. When his turn came, Ruarc stood in the centre of the hut and proudly sang his story of the red-haired giant:

> "The giant rode his chestnut horse
> Through the cattle with sheer force
> He swung his battle axe in the air
> His helmet framed with bright red hair
> He screamed and aimed his axe at me
> And struck with all his might
> My shield withstood the blow,
> And I survived to fight.
> Around again, we both did go
> My blade scored a belly wound
> That bled him, 'til he fell to ground
> True warrior, he stood again and
> Man-to-man, fought hand to hand
> I saw my chance and slashed up high
> His throat giving one last sigh
> He dared and I challenged

Tearnach's village is avenged. That is my tale."

Ardal sang some of the old songs, stories of ancient warriors in the family, their battles and sea voyages, ghosts and legends passed down to each generation. "Tis the songs that tell our story, that keep our ancestors alive in our hearts, that honour our fallen warriors" he said to the assembled crowd.

Barra's wife sang a song her mother had taught her. "She waited for her husband to return from battle but he never came home." It was a song of sadness and mourning and Ruarc saw the women with their arms around the two girls.

Replete with beef and homemade beer, Hilde and Ruarc slipped away to their hut and made love with a hunger fuelled with knowing he would be away. Lying beside her, his arm draped over her body, he could feel the rhythm of her breathing and the smooth curve of her warm breasts and belly. Little Egan murmured in his sleep and rolled over in his blanket at the head of the bed, a thumb firmly stuck in his mouth. Ruarc felt a contentment that never ceased to amaze him and drifted off to sleep.

He awoke early, and listened to the others snoring. The sleeping benches followed the curve of the walls and were filled with the inert blanketed bodies of eighteen men, women and children, all locked in their dreams. The fire had died down to embers and rising quietly he added a few more logs then slipped outside to relieve himself of last night's beer. Somewhere, a dog barked. Others were starting to leave the huts, too. The dawn was just starting to lighten the east. *I have much to do this day. I want clean clothing for my presentation to the King, and we will be taking two head of cattle for our annual tribute to him. I so much want to be part of his army, even if it means leaving my family for a while. I want more training, and a better sword. I'm glad I got the giant's horse, it's better than mine.* He thought fondly of his small, strong and shaggy pony who had served him well.

Walking down to the stream, he stripped off his clothes and leg wraps and jumped into the shallow pond, using his hands to scrub his whole body with the cold, clear flowing water. Goosebumps speckled his arms. He was dunking himself again when Barra joined him and promptly splashed him in the face and the fight was on. They tumbled, grappled and pulled each other under, until finally, Ruarc had to come up for air, spluttering and laughing. The row of wide-eyed children standing on the bank watching them were joined by bleary eyed villagers, curious about the ruckus that had awakened them. Dripping wet, they walked back to their huts together to find dry clothes. From the corner of his eye, he saw his parents and Hilde standing at the doorway, shaking their heads at their antics, and he grinned.

Ruarc and Barra left their neighbours at their village along the way and continued down the road towards the hill fort of Caisil. The road widened and settlements became more frequent. *It's more open here with fewer trees and more open fields with stone fences.* Many paths from other outlying areas joined the main road. "Looks like everyone is heading to Caisil," said Ruarc, looking at the crush of people on foot, on horseback or driving two wheeled carts drawn by a pony, loaded with hides and produce.

Barra led their bull and Ruarc, the cow. Ardal had decided to use the bull from Tearnach's village on their cows. *Two bulls would only fight.* On they rode, through two more valleys, as the hills opened up to a broad flat plain. All roads converged towards the distant hill where the grey stonework of the King's palisade and fortress glittered in the sunshine. They could see small companies of armed riders coming and going from cluster of huts at the foot of the wall. *People are everywhere – women and children in the fields, and men tending the cattle and horses.*

"I'm not used to the noise, all these people talking at once. It's overwhelming," said Ruarc. He could see street merchants with tables in front of their huts, selling bread, leather, harness, pottery and other wares. *Oh, the smell.* Raw sewage ran down the ruts in the road to an open cesspit at the bottom.

Barra found the man in charge of the cattle, and they released the bull and cow into the herd. The man knew Ardal, and commented: "He always did have an eye for livestock – good animals, the King will be pleased."

Tribute paid, Barra and Ruarc continued up to the west gate where they were stopped by the guards. "We have paid our tribute and are here at the request of King Conall." They were permitted through and escorted to the inner gate of the fort. Soldiers were milling around, coming and going. He could hear the blacksmith hammering a piece of metal somewhere close by. *The noise is constant.*

Their escort took them over to the corral and motioned them to tether their horses to the fence.

Barra commented "Look at these men - all of them are as big as your giant!"

Ruarc could see every man was two heads taller than himself and all of them more bulky in their multi-layered leather vests, cloaks held in place with metal brooches of intricate design. All wore their long swords, with elaborate scrolled metal work on the hilts.

"Wait here," said their escort, and spoke to another soldier, who sized them up and disappeared into a building of close fitted stones. He returned shortly after with a young warrior who was obviously a high-born son, from his bearing and the royal blue cloak.

"I am Murtagh, the youngest son of Conall Mor. Welcome, Ruarc, son of Ardal and Barra, son of Quinlan. Come, my father is expecting you." He turned and entered the house with the pair close behind him. The room seemed dark at first until their eyes adjusted to the dim light from the braziers along the tapestry and shield-covered walls.

There must be fifty people in here, thought Ruarc, glancing around at men, from commoners to knights, sitting on benches. They passed through a doorway into a smaller room again guarded by two enormous soldiers, and there, sitting on a carved wooden chair, was the King, with the Druid to his right and a woman on his left.

"Ruarc, Barra," said Conall. "This is Lady Geilis. She is our lawyer and will be presenting our claim for compensation to Niall, King of Connaught. Tell her your story. She will be leaving for Tara in the morning to present our case. You will accompany her."

I'm not surprised she's the royal lawyer. High born educated women often hold important positions. He could see she was younger than his mother but was not a young woman. Her dark hair was in two neat braids pulled back under a silver headband, embellished with an embossed hunting motif of wolves chasing a stag. She wore a plain dark green dress beneath a hip length fine leather bodice laced up the front, completed with a cloak trimmed in elaborate traditional Celtic patterns in silver thread. Her cloak pin was silver with green gem stones. She inspected them critically with clear blue eyes, motioning them to sit on the bench beside her.

"I am Lady Geilis, and I want you to tell me everything that happened," she said, her voice rich and authoritative.

Taking turns, the two young men recounted everything they could remember about the raid. From time to time, she interrupted them to clarify a detail. "Now I have the information I need. As you know, the King himself saw the aftermath of the destruction at Tearnach's village and I have confirmation from the two soldiers he sent to the river. I understand the two girls are now living with your family and the livestock has been recovered." Ruarc nodded. "Brehon law is very specific about the penalties for damages and applies to all Kingdoms in this land. This was more than a cattle raid. The killing of those villagers was a deliberate act of war. I shall be leaving in the morning to meet with my counterpart in Tara regarding this charge," she said. "The severity of the attack is unwarranted and must be settled immediately. So, you will be part of my escort?"

"Yes," replied Ruarc. "We are excited to see Tara."

She smiled and with a brief nod dismissed them.

They had the opportunity to explore the compound and, after feeding their horses, watched the blacksmith working on a large sword. The searing heat of the red-hot metal radiated outward as the man hammered the layers, heating, hammering, folding and hammering again until the metal finally melded into a double-edged blade. The man's muscular arms were formidable, and sweat ran in rivers beneath his leather apron as he rhythmically swung the heavy hammer. The walls were covered with horseshoes, hinges, horse bits and harness parts, spear heads, shield bosses, wagon wheels and plow shares. Two younger apprentices kept the forge fire fed, working the large bellows and making the simpler items. A barrel of cold water sat by the open door to quench the hot metal.

"How long does it take you to make one of these?" asked Barra.

"A couple of weeks to get the blade right, then another week or two to make the hilt, depending on how fancy it is and which metal I use. The gold ones are softer and easier to work, but you have to take a lot more care with the fancy work. I sometimes use a goldsmith, especially if it's for the King," replied the smith, wiping the sweat from his brow. "My father was a blacksmith and I started young, learning the trade from him. Been at it a long time. I put my mark on all my swords when I finish them," he said, handing Ruarc a finished sword. Just under the hilt was a tiny embossed diamond-shape containing a hammer.

He's as valuable to the King as a knight, maybe even more so, thought Ruarc. *There are many highly skilled artisans here, working for the King.*

They watched as two warriors in the courtyard started shoving and shouting. Others began gathering in a circle around them. The shouting was intensifying and both combatants drew their swords. Ruarc nudged a soldier beside him. "What's going on?"

"They might be the best of friends but they are always fighting each other, usually over a woman or a horse. They've been into the beer already. Pretty evenly matched, so it should be a good fight," the man replied before shouting and stamping his feet to urge them on. The noise became a pulsating throb echoing on the granite walls of the house and the hill behind them.

This fight is becoming deadly. It isn't a friendly sparing match. One man stripped off his leather vest, the rage and tension showing of his muscles and the whip cords in his neck. Ruarc watched closely to see how each man was using his sword, how they thrust and parried, side-stepped and used their shields. *I really don't see any difference in the way I've been trained by my father. They are just so much bigger and stronger than I am and if I want to become one of them, I'll have to move quicker, watch for openings, and keep out of range.*

The fight continued for about five minutes with neither man losing ground. The crowd was still shouting and stamping when the bare-chested man momentarily slipped as he stepped back and the next instant he lay dying with his opponent's sword through his chest. The winner raised his shield and shouted his victory to the world then became quiet, kneeling beside his fallen friend. They heard him say: "I'll meet you in the afterlife. We will live to fight again."

Ruarc and Barra looked at each other. "By the god Neit, they were friends. I hope it never comes to that for us."

They spent the evening sitting at the long tables, eating, drinking, watching and listening to all the activity around them. At the head table sat Conall with his queen, two daughters and three sons. Also at the head table were the Druid priest, the poet and the lawyer. Ruarc knew that by law, only certain classes of people could wear coloured clothing. *The King can wear all seven colours. As a warrior-farmer, I can only wear four.*

Barra had been speaking to the knight beside him, and the man burst out laughing. "You'll never be one of us, even if you're good warriors. You're both too small. Look at all of us!" he said draining his beer mug. "At least you get to go to Tara tomorrow with us."

Ruarc and Barra looked at each other, the disappointment showing clearly on their faces. Chanting voices could be heard approaching the room. Conversation and laughter died as twelve hooded figures in grey robes entered in single file, bearing standards topped with the skulls of horned bulls. They stopped in front of the head table. The Druid rose from his seat to join them. He stood in front of a large basin of water on the table, intoned a prayer, sprinkled the contents of a small leather bag into it and carefully watched the colours on its surface. He removed another leather pouch and emptied a pile of small bones onto the table. It was an eerie scene, the ghostly figures of the Druids, the flickering red light of the braziers casting sharp shadows over the attentive faces of the crowd, and the play of flickering light through the eye sockets of the cattle skulls.

By the Gods, they look like they're alive! thought Ruarc. He remembered years ago, a drought had brought the Druids to their compound to ritually slaughter a bull to appease the gods of the harvest, the hills and the weather. It had rained a few days later.

The Druid examined the bones minutely then turned to face the King. The chanting stopped. With measured steps, he approached him and said in a strong, clear voice: "There are dangers abroad on the road for your escort tomorrow. I see three ravens. There is danger lurking in the mist. Forces are at work in Connaught; forces that are hidden now, but will be revealed soon."

The King nodded. "I thank you for your warning, but our need is urgent. My warriors will be ready if challenged." The Priest bowed his head and walked out of the room, his acolytes padding quietly behind him.

"Just think," said Barra. "They study for twenty years to become a priest... Twenty years to memorize and learn all the secrets. I wouldn't have the patience."

For a few moments, there was silence in the crowd, then voices roared back to life. "Sounds like we could have a lively time tomorrow once we're in Connaught territory," said Barra casting an appreciative glance at the serving girl who was filling their mugs with mead. He smiled, she smiled back before coyly moving away, glancing back at him.

"I'd welcome a good fight right about now," replied Ruarc, still thinking about the red-headed giant, their mission in the morning and being too short to be in the King's guard.

The Poet was starting to sing as the musicians began playing again. Ruarc had met him before when he had visited their village as part of his circuit in the outlying communities. Poets and their student entourages were free to move anywhere, even to other Kingdoms. *The average freemen farmer like me is restricted to his village. Poets are welcome everywhere for news, the art of the story and poetry, the use of words, and maintaining the history of our race through myth and legend. They are our teachers.*

Briefly the man paused in front of him with a glance of recognition. "Ruarc, son of Ardal, it's been a while since I've seen you," he said, slapping him heartily on the shoulder.

"You should visit our village more often, Poet. I was just a boy the last time you came. My father would enjoy that. He still sings your poetry and songs," Ruarc replied, remembering the skill the Poet had to create beautiful flowing rhymes to please the gods.

Barra's seat beside him was empty. Looking around the room, Ruarc saw him disappearing outside with his arm around the girl's waist. Ruarc poured another mug of mead. It was sweet and heady, not at all like their home-made beer. He pondered how many hives would the King need to quench the thirst of all these men.

Barra returned to his seat a short time later, his black hair tussled and a satisfied smirk on his face. "She's willing, if you want," he said with a mischievous twinkle in his blue eyes.

"Not now," replied Ruarc, deeply disturbed at being inadequate to qualify as a King's warrior.

"That's not like you, my friend. You usually get to them first. Come, we've got a hard ride for the next four or five days. We can sleep in the hayloft out with the horses." A brooding Ruarc silently followed him.

The morning dawned gray and overcast. Quickly grabbing some fresh bread, they mounted their horses and joined the rear of the escort party of twenty knights.

Lady Geilis was speaking with the Priest. Ruarc overheard snippets of conversation between them, messages for his fellow Druids in Tara. The knight assisted her to mount her horse. Fastening her cloak around her, she nodded to the knight and they moved out at a brisk walk, through the gates, down the quiet street and onto the main road, taking the road to Connaught.

"There's no laughter this morning," noted Barra, looking at the bobbing heads of the riders and swaying rumps of the horses in front of them. Every man looked grim and armed for battle – swords, spears, shields. Other than the sound of hooves and the jingle of harness, the group was silent. They rode past small farms, fat cattle and gawking children. The plain became a series of low hills, with a winding tree-lined river valley. They passed the circle of standing stones and a grove of the sacred oaks. The Druids held their ceremonies there on the equinox. No one knew who had raised the stones –an unknown race lost in the mists of time. The priest's warning had been clear and every man was alert. The only calm person was Lady Geilis, looking regal on her dainty white mare. *Why wouldn't she look calm? She has twenty of the King's best surrounding her,* he thought.

Just ahead, the valley was split in two by a rocky outcrop, reminding him of Morrigan's Hill. The western fork was bathed in sunlight of the gods, the eastern fork in shadow. Ruarc had a feeling of apprehension as they entered the shade. Here it was cooler and he pulled his cloak tighter, feeling the hairs on the back of his neck stand on end. The spirits of the rocks called to them as the wind moaned. Sloane, the warrior they had sat beside the previous evening, moved his horse back to join them. Nothing was said, but Ruarc knew the man regarded them as weaker. *He probably doesn't want a weak spot at the rear.* A light mist was rising from the bog curling and twisting as if it was alive. The sound of the horses echoed off the rocky walls and was muted. There were no bird calls. The mist got thicker until it was hard to even see the riders immediately ahead of them. Then hell opened its gates.

There was one shout and bodies hurtled out of the bog around them. Horses reared and plunged, swords clashed, voices roared. Ruarc slashed and decapitated one attacker who had grabbed his reins. Barra disappeared into the mist. He heard a woman's scream. He felt hands pulling him from his horse and he hit the ground hard. A sudden blow to his head sent him spinning down, down into blackness and the sounds of battle faded.

Ruarc gradually came to. *I'm face down in the mud and I've got this weight on me. What happened?* There wasn't a sound about him. He tried to get up but something heavy was pinning him down. *Did my horse fall on me?*

He felt behind him and found folds of clothing and the shape of an arm. *By the Gods, I've got a dead man on me!* Squirming and pulling with his free hands, he managed to twist himself forward and turn on his side. What he saw defied belief. *It's Sloane.* The man's chest was full of puncture wounds. His helmet and sword were gone, probably stripped by the attackers. Finally managing to squirm out from underneath, Ruarc stood up, wiping the mud from his face. *My sword's gone, but I've got my knife.*

Still groggy, he stumbled about. The entire escort party lay before him, stripped of their weapons, some floating in the shallow bog, all contorted in their death poses. *The horses are gone. A couple are dead, but there's no sign of Lady Geilis or her white mare. They must have taken her. Where's Barra?* He walked around and looked but there was no sign of his friend.

As his head cleared, he realized he had to do something. *I'm the only one who knows what's happened and I'm the only one who can help.* He set off down the road following the tracks of the horses. *I don't know how long I was out but it must have been a couple of hours, since the sun's in the west.*

He jogged along at a steady pace, his mind going over and over. *I'm going to have to fight a different way here. That wasn't an open fight like I'm used to – that was a sneak attack. I'm not well armed; I've only got my knife. I need to steal a horse and a sword. I'll have to be very careful. By the gods, my head hurts*, he thought, running his fingers through the crust of blood in his tangled hair. There was a large lump and a sizeable gash but it seemed to have stopped bleeding.

He trotted along at a steady pace, following the road and listening to the woodland sounds. The light was fading, and he would have to keep going, despite his fear of the spirits and creatures who lived unseen in the night. *The raiding party will likely camp somewhere ahead.* He stopped at the stream and crouched down to drink the water, surprising a fox on the other side. The animal jumped straight up in the air and disappeared into the bushes only to stop a short distance away to watch him. *I need to be alert and cunning like you, Sir Fox.* The road continued on the other side and rose gently. He followed it.

He was losing the light now and still had not picked up any sounds. He found a few berries along the way, recognizing them as edible, but they didn't really sate his growling stomach. Night descended and he plodded on, keeping to the shadows of the heavy thicket. *Just a sliver of a crescent moon behind the clouds. That might be to my advantage – just enough to see by and hopefully they won't see me. I pray the wolves don't find me first.*

He was almost in a trance of walking and sleepiness when he heard a horse whinny ahead and ducked into the bushes. Keeping cover, he crept forward and could see the sparks of the firepit with the dark shapes of men around it. They had chosen an abandoned village to spend the night. The horses were tied to ropes strung between the trees. Ruarc noticed a smaller white rump among them, Lady Geilis' horse! *Where was she?*

From his vantage point, he looked for a sentry but didn't see one. *They wouldn't expect a survivor. They believe they killed everyone. Lucky for me, they don't have wolf-dogs or they would have scented me by now.* He crept from rock to rock, alert to every sound. Carefully, he circled the camp, always keeping to the shadows. *How many knights are there?* The men were eating and talking. There appeared to be about over twenty, including three men staying close to a small hut. *I'm guessing they've got her in there. Now to get a sword and two horses.*

Time dragged and gradually the fire burned down, the men wrapping themselves in their cloaks to settle on the ground around the dying embers. Cautiously, Ruarc kept track of each one, noting who came and went into the hut. A small two-wheeled wagon, loaded with his fallen comrades' weapons, had been unhitched near the horses and the two ponies tied beside it. He moved towards it on silent feet and nearly fell into the fogou. The mouth of the trench was inky black. *I hope there isn't anything or anybody in that hole.* He knew food and beer would have been kept here when the village was active and prayed something had been left behind. He felt his way along the rocky walls. It was about five feet high, four feet wide and tunnelled back into the hillside. His blind search revealed nothing; the fogou was empty.

Snores were coming from the men on the ground as he circled to the dozing horses who stood with heads lowered, ears relaxed and one hip down over the resting hoof. They were still saddled, ready for flight. He reached the wagon and looked at the array of swords, all from the escort party and too heavy for him. *Where's mine?* He spotted a familiar hilt, and realized with a pang that it was Barra's. He quietly moved it out from under the others and strapped it around his waist. It was very similar in size, weight and balance to his own, made by the same smithy in his village. *Ahh, it feels good to have a sword again. I felt naked without one.*

Voices came from the hut as two men came out. Ruarc backed away from the horses into the bushes, completely out of sight. The men relieved themselves, checked the horses then lay down with the others. Shortly they too were snoring, too. He checked if anyone had left their food sack on their saddles and sure enough, there were a couple. He scoffed down some bread and cheese. The rest he stashed beside the two horses at the end. The Lady's little white mare was too easy to see in this moonlight. There was one pony who looked like Barra's horse, but he wasn't certain.

He worked his way back to the hut, took a deep breath and staying in the shadows, slipped inside. There was one sleeping man inside by the fire and the Lady was bound to a bed frame. Ruarc crouched over the knight and in one quick motion slit his throat, clamping his hand over the man's mouth. There was a gurgle and spluttering then blood pooled around the head. The sound was enough to wake her and she was looked about to scream when a look of recognition came over her face. He raised a bloody finger to his lips and carefully cut through the ropes binding her hands and feet. He took the dagger from the man's belt and handed it to her. She slipped it in her belt. They crept out of the hut, into the woods. Ruarc motioned her over to the horses, stopping periodically to check the sleeping figures by the fire. They placed the food sacks over the saddles, untied the two horses and led them away from the others into the woods. *I pray they don't whinny.* Just over the hill, he gave her a leg up and they moved along the road at a slow walk into the darkness.

Ruarc turned his horse for home, but Lady Geilis said: "No, Ruarc, we are going on to Tara. I must warn King Niall. These men are planning to depose him, and their leader is his cousin's son, Lord Guaire. He has the lineage to qualify for the kingship. He plans to disfigure the King. As you know, a disfigured king must surrender his king-ship. They killed the villagers and our escort to gather arms and horses, hoping King Conall would retaliate and start a war, but he didn't. He sent me to negotiate instead. Conall and Niall have been on good terms for years. Lord Guaire wasn't planning to ambush Niall until they met at the horse fair this week. They were going to hold me captive until the damage was done. I know the way to Tara. We must go faster. They won't be far behind us."

"Lead the way, my Lady." Urging their horses forward at a sharp trot, they continued into Connaught's territory. Ruarc watched her with wonder. *What courage she has! She's as much a warrior as I. Her gown may be torn and dirty, but she still carries herself with dignity. I'm proud to serve her. Hilde would look like that.* He realized he hadn't thought of his wife for a while.

They slowed to a walk to pass settlements, not wanting to start dogs barking and alert the inhabitants. In the light of the half moon they trotted hard when it was safe to. He listened to the calls of the night creatures and prayed for the ghosts, fairies and spooks to leave them in peace. The night was a place where the forces of evil and darkness were free to roam and devour a mortal man. Ruarc shivered. *I've never been out in the darkness like this.*

The eastern sky started to turn pink. Ruarc began searching for a place for them to hide for the daylight hours. A wooden bridge crossed the stream just ahead and after watering the horses, Geilis pointed to an overgrown path leading off to the right.

"I remember the Poet telling an old tale. There used to be an forge along there." In single file they left the main road and followed the track up and over a few rises into the woods. From the top of the hill, there was a beautiful view as the low morning sun casting splashes of gold on the calm dark waters of the lough. They both made their salutations to the sun god. The old forge had three standing stone walls but the roof had fallen in. They tethered the horses out of sight from the road and hobbled them to let them graze on the small patch of grass between the trees. Climbing through the wreckage of the fallen roof, there was a deep shaded area in the back by the forge that was dry.

"How far is Tara from here?" asked Ruarc, sitting wearily on the floor with his back against the stones. He handed her one of the food bags and they chewed away on the bread and dried meat.

She slipped down on the floor across from him. "We've come farther than I thought. Another two nights and by the time the sun has reached it zenith we should be there. The next problem is that Tara sits in a wide open plain. There will be no cover once we are in view of the last bridge. She broke the bread in half and heartily chewed down the plain fare. "I hope King Niall rewards us with a nice beef dinner," she said looking at mold on the cheese. She picked it off and ate the cheese anyway.

Ruarc slept until bird calls awoke him. Startled he remembered where he was. Geilis' eyes were closed, and her breathing slow, the worry lines in her face soft in sleep. He gently got up and slipped outside. The horses were quiet, resting in the shade. The sun was low in the western sky. It was late afternoon. Creeping to the brow of the hill, he raised his head and peered down onto the road. He could see that it forked a short distance away by a copse of ancient trees. There were two mounted men at the fork but it was too far to hear their words. They were talking to a shepherd with a flock of black faced sheep. The man was shaking his head. The saddle cloths on their horses were the same as the one on his. Guaire's men had caught up with them. *They'll kill her if they catch us now.*

He slithered backwards and returned to the forge. He awoke her and assisted her to her feet. "We have company - two knights down at the fork in the road. I don't think the rest of the party can be far behind. Which fork takes us to Tara?"

"The right fork... But Lord Guaire's fortress is to the left. They may split up and send some of them home. The back group are slow with the wagon and horses."

"Is there any place out of sight here, where we can cross the river and get ahead of them?"

"Not really, it's very open. It might be best if we stayed put and waited until they've ridden by. I don't think they can make it home before dark. I'd expect them to camp another night. There's too many people on the road for us to move in daylight and I don't know who is loyal to the King."

He removed the hobbles from the horses but left them tied to a tree. *The trampled grass and fresh manure clearly mark our presence if anyone comes looking.* He stripped the saddle blankets from the horses so there were no nothing to identify them and stuffed them under his shirt. Geilis disappeared into the bushes. He was starting to get concerned when she hadn't returned but then she appeared through the trees clutching a sticky mess in her hands. "I found an old hive in the back field. The bees weren't too happy with me," she said passing him a handful of dripping honeycomb.

He grinned like a child and they spent the next few minutes licking the comb and their fingers until the honey was all gone. She wiped her hands and her dagger on her tattered gown. "I'll need a new dress when this is over."

Voices on the road wafted up to them and they scampered back to the horses, gently holding their noses to prevent them from whinnying. Leaving Geilis with them, Ruarc went back up to the ridge to watch the procession of soldiers. Each led a spare horse or two, some with dead riders, and the wagon followed filled with swords, shields and saddles. Four men had serious injuries from the battle. One was barely staying in the saddle. Bandages showed on heads, arms and legs. *There's seventeen men plus the two at the fork for nineteen and the one I killed, that's twenty. But there are nine men walking. From their clothes, they're not knights – they're slaves!* He remembered the men who had sprung from the bog, pulling him from his horse to strike his head. *They used slaves.* He confirmed the number by counting the horses that carried the Guaire's crest on their saddle blankets. He saw the two groups stop and talk briefly then the two knights moved onto the Tara Road and the rest of the group headed to Guaire's fort. He gave his findings to Geilis. "I'm amazed they used slaves in battle. I've never heard of it before," he said.

I could have killed a knight in a fair fight, but I was brought down by a slave, thought Ruarc in disgust. He thought about the desperation driving Lord Guaire, the planning and the measures he was willing to take to become King. *Killing the villagers and children to spark a border war; using slaves in the bog - there's nothing to stand in that man's way now except me.*

They spent the next two nights playing hide and seek with their followers. It had rained a few times, enough to wash out their tracks. Once they hid in a haystack and today it had been a small cave under an overhang. It was pitch black now and the air felt and smelt like rain. They both knew that somewhere between them and the bridge there were two knights.

"Once we get to the bridge, we'll have to run for the fort," said Geilis.

Ruarc was thankful she had ridden this road before. She spoke of three settlements they had to pass before they got to the bridge. They rode in silence expecting trouble at every curve in the road. A dog barked a few times from inside the first palisade but otherwise there was silence. The road became wider and flatter, rutted from frequent wagon traffic, obviously used by more people. There were fewer trees and less rock cover. They passed the second settlement in silence as a light rain started to fall. Soon they were soaked to the skin.

At least it's not cold, thought Ruarc.

Time passed and they rode by the third settlement. The rain was falling more heavily now. *Still no sign of the knights. Maybe they stayed in one of the settlements.* The dark of the eastern sky was starting to lighten to grey. Geilis suddenly reined in her horse, grabbed his arm and pointed. There was the bridge and two horses tethered beside it.

"They must have taken shelter under the bridge" said Ruarc. He looked at the river. It was wide and fast flowing. "Is there anywhere else to cross?" he whispered.

"Further downstream yes, but it would take too much time and we'd be in the open. People will be on this road soon."

He could dimly see flashes of torchlight on Tara with faint outlines of the walls, and settlements around it. *This is it. It's now or never; no choice but to cross the bridge.*

"Lady Geilis, I'm going to cut their horses loose. As soon as I do, you must make a run for the fort as fast as your horse can carry you and alert the King. Don't let anything or anyone stop you. By my honour, these two knights will not live to cross this bridge." He dismounted, handed her the reins and strode away, sword in his right hand and dagger in his left.

He moved over and approached the animals gently. The heads came up, ears pointing. Still no sign of the knights but then he saw a movement under the bridge as a large man started to climb up the bank. Slashing the reins with his sword, Ruarc screamed at the horses and they spun away in a panic. He raised his sword and hearing the stampede of hooves reverberating on the wooden bridge, knew that Geilis was on the move. *Neit, God of battle, be with me!*

The fight was on and they were evenly matched. The man was bigger, but Ruarc was quicker, angry and desperate; desperate to restore his tarnished pride and desperate to buy Geilis time. The grass was slippery in the rain and they struggled through the mud to the road and onto the bridge, slashing and feinting. The air was torn with the ring of metal and their defiant shouts.

It was a different fight without a shield, a more mobile fight, of slashing and moving, getting the timing right, anticipating, backing off, circling, looking for advantage. His opponent drew first blood as the sword tip caught Ruarc's left shoulder. He slashed in retaliation, slicing the man's cheek. Chest to chest, they bellowed and grunted, momentarily locked together. They shoved and pushed for what seemed an eternity, both tiring. Twisting away, his opponent slashed across him then raised his sword with both hands for a finishing blow.

Ruarc lunged forward, driving the sword through him, right up to the hilt. The impetus toppled both of them as they fell together into the mud. For a fleeting moment, he gasped for breath and rolled over onto his knees. His opponent lay sprawled before him, sword still clutched in his hand. Ruarc braced his foot on the man's chest and pulled his sword out. Limbs twitched but the broad chest did not rise. A cheer broke his concentration and when he turned, there arriving at the end of the bridge were a group of knights, Lady Geilis and villagers from the settlement.

It took all the strength he had left to walk to them. He noticed another dead man at their end of the bridge. It was the second knight. Staring down at the body he saw the hoof imprints and realized Geilis had ridden the man down. He raised his sword to salute her. *He would have got me from behind*. Slowly he stood beside her horse, looked at the dripping wet woman with her hair plastered flat on her head, then at the man on the horse beside her. His bearing was regal. *This must be King Niall. No fancy clothes this morning, just plain ones hastily thrown on and getting soaking wet, just like the rest of us*.

"Well done, Ruarc, son of Ardal. Let's get you both into the fort and you can tell me your tale," said the King. "Give the man your horse" he said to his knight, who dismounted and tossed Ruarc the reins. Pride got Ruarc into the saddle but blood was still flowing freely from his shoulder wound and his trousers were blood red too. He sheathed the sword and followed them through the streets and the main gate where throngs of people were gathering. *I'm not only tired, I feel light headed*.

Dismounting in the courtyard, he wobbled on his feet. His vision was starting to blur. There were people scurrying around him and he heard Lady Geilis beside him. "Ruarc, the doctor's here. Just a few more steps." Gentle hands guided him forward. He remembered an older, wise face peering at him, leading him to a bench where his legs gave out and he slipped into oblivion for a second time.

It was the pain that woke him, pain all over but mostly in his shoulder and belly. Opening his eyes, he blinked about in some confusion. An old woman was sitting beside his cot and gently put her hand on his right shoulder. "You are at Tara, young sir. You fought Guaire's knight and have many wounds but have survived." She offered him water and he took a few sips from the mug to clear away the bad taste in his mouth.

"How long have I been out?" he asked.

"They brought you in two days ago."

"Two days!" Recollections came crowding in. "Where is my Lady?"

"She is on her way back to Caisil with one of our escort parties. Let me find the physician and he can tell you more." She walked out the room and he could hear her shuffling steps going down the hall.

Every muscle in my body hurts. He tried sitting up but slumped back as pain across his middle pinned him to the bed. He tried moving his arms and found his left one bandaged in a sling. He could move his fingers but his shoulder was agony. *I can move both legs.* He saw his clothes neatly piled on the floor beside his cot and he was wearing someone's night shirt. *I've got bandages on my chest and belly. I don't remember being cut there but I must have been. The pain there is different. It's a deep burning. Any movement makes it worse. I've never felt so weak in all my life.* He felt cold and shivered, pulling the blanket up over him.

A short while later, he heard brisk footsteps and shuffling ones in the hall and an older man entered. *I saw him just before I passed out.*

"Well, young man, Nellie tells me you're awake and asking questions. I'm Shanahan, the King's physician. I have cleansed and stitched your shoulder wound. It was deep and bled a lot. It will take at least a month to heal but you should have full use of it. He sliced you from belly to chest, a much more difficult wound. The blood loss was severe. I have repaired what I could."

He opened Ruarc's shirt, checking the dressing around his chest and belly. "You've likely got some cracked ribs and that too will take time to heal. Each breath will hurt for quite a while. The only thing that saved your life was those two horse blankets you stuffed in your shirt. Nellie will be changing your bandages every day. I have made a special herbal ointment, which she will apply to both wounds to soothe and heal them."

He started his examination. "Painful?" he asked, as Ruarc winced under his touch. He nodded. "Then I will give you some Mandragora to ease it. You must only take small amounts; too much can drive a man mad. We need to get you eating a little to get your body humours balanced. Any questions?"

"Yes," said Ruarc. "What happened to Lady Geilis? Is the King safe? What's going to happen with Lord Guaire and when can I go home?"

Shanahan broke out laughing. "Whoa! First of all, that Lady is fine. Quite the woman, isn't she? More fire in her than I've seen in most men. She gave a full report to King Niall of the raid on Tearnach's village, the slaughter of your escort in the bog and being kidnapped by Lord Guaire's men. I have strict orders from her to get you well. She's on her way back to Munster with our escort party to inform King Conall of all the goings on. He's probably raising an army right now, preparing to invade. I doubt there'll be a war. Niall and Conall are sensible men and avoid unnecessary conflict between our kingdoms. As for Lord Guaire, Niall will deal with him now he's shown his true colours. Niall's two eldest sons Eoghan and Laeghaire are on their way there as we speak. They've got a sizeable force of experienced soldiers to deal with the traitor. They will make an effort to regain the horses and weapons taken from your people."

"And going home?"

"Not likely for a couple of months. Give your body a chance to heal. Once you're eating well and get your strength back we'll get you moving. You lost a tremendous amount of blood. You're lucky you're young and very fit. Those wounds would have killed a lesser man. Oh, and Lady Geilis will let your family know that you have survived when she gets back home. That's enough for now. Get some rest."

After giving Nellie instructions to burn some dry sage and the dosage for the Mandragora, Shanahan left. She gave Ruarc a small spoonful of the dark brown liquid, which puckered up his face, it tasted so vile and bitter. A few sips of water washed it down, and he drifted off into a turbulent sleep.

Nellie's voice came through the fog. "Get this down ya, lad," and the brown bitterness stung his tongue. The bog mists were swirling, and that fox scampered through, chased by shadows and the spectre of the knight with his slit throat. Ruarc awoke with a jolt and realized he'd been dreaming. The room was bright with sunshine and the sounds of people and horses came in from outside.

How long have I been here? Where am I? Tara, I'm in Tara. Moving carefully. he managed to sit on the side of the cot. *My arm's still in the sling but it doesn't hurt so much.* He took a deep breath and a dagger of pain shot through his left ribs. For a moment, it took his breath away. "Just like Shanahan said it would," he said to himself through clenched teeth and struggled to his feet, steadying himself against the wall. He broke out in a sweat.

I need to get outside. This is a prison! It was an awkward effort to get his trousers on with one hand. Barefoot, he moved to the door and looked down the hall. *I can hear voices but I can't see anyone.* Keeping his hand on the wall, he took tentative steps and shuffled forward. *At least I'm up.* The pain came in waves. He heard a sharp intake of breath and there was Nellie, looking horrified.

"Ruarc, you shouldn't be up yet!" she cried, running over to help him.

"Nellie – I must! I need to get outside."

Tut, tutting she helped him through the big doors. He felt the sunshine on his face and the breeze on his skin. It was like being cocooned in the arms of the sun god. Across the courtyard, three wooden statues of the gods were guarded by the Druids. The gray clad monks stood aside as he stumbled forward, the gods' savage radiating faces looming above him. "I come to offer thanks to the gods for sparing me" he said to a priest. He bowed his head and prayed for healing, strength and courage.

Please give me the courage to heal and become a warrior again. If I can't be a warrior, I am of no use to my family or Hilde. She needs a real man, not a cripple. I wouldn't be able to replace my father in my tribe if I am not a warrior. I will share his shame. He felt the muscles in his legs starting to tremble, so he sat down on the step.

He stayed there most of the day, just soaking up the sunshine. Nellie brought him a mug of mead and some fresh bread. Late afternoon, a rider came through the gates, shouting and clamouring for the King. People gathered round and he heard the word pass, Guaire had

been killed and all the inhabitants slaughtered. Eoghan
and Laeghaire were triumphantly on their way back.

*That is the price you pay for loyalty. I am loyal to Ardal
first; King Conall second. If I were a King's knight, I, too would
have to kill the traitors and their families. I've never killed
a woman or a child – I've never even had to kill a woman
warrior. What if I couldn't? As a King's knight, I would have
to.* Such thoughts left him in a sombre mood.

Struggling to his feet, he leaned against the wall and
heard the cheers of the villagers and thud of hooves long
before the war party reached the gates. With banners
flying, the two princes came through the gates, shouting
their victory and brandishing their swords. Dangling
from ropes around the necks of their horses were the
heads of the enemy, ghastly in death. Behind them came
their army. It had not been an easy fight, there were many
wounded and a dozen horses carried dead riders across
their saddles. *Shanahan and Nellie will be busy.* Within the
cheering there were the wails of the newly widowed as
wives searched and found their dead husbands. Next came
a large herd of horses including some he recognized – his
own chestnut, Lady Geilis' white mare, Sloan's white-
faced gelding and yes, Barra's bay. The wagon with their
weapons was the last to enter the yard.

The evening progressed as it would have done in his
village. The warriors including the princes sang their
songs. The heads of Guaire and his most important

knights were hung from branches of the large oak in the yard, near the statues. Ruarc sat on a bench on the fringe of the activities and watched. *How different it is to be an observer,* he thought. *I'm used to riding in victory. I've never paid attention to what else was going on. Those women have lost their husbands... Was Hilde like that when I didn't come home?* He drank and ate a little, but felt mostly tired and very sore. His shoulder and ribs throbbed. Nellie eventually found him and offered him the Mandragora. Despite its taste and the bizarre dreams that always came, he knew he'd get a good sleep.

"Nellie, do I go back to that room or are you full, what with your new arrivals?"

"You can go back there, but you'll have company."

It was all he could do to walk up the steps behind her. There were three other cots set up, and Shanahan was busy with the others. The man looked tired as he bandaged yet another wounded shoulder. The knight over by the window had his leg splinted and wrapped – *probably broken.* The third man had a head bandage and a hand and arm in a sling.

Ruarc carefully manoeuvred himself onto his bed. He was almost asleep when Shanahan awoke him. "Ruarc, let's have a look at your arm." Shanahan deftly slit the bandage. In the flickering candle light, Ruarc could see a long row of horsehair stitches across he upper arm just under the shoulder. The skin was purple and tight.

He'd been surprised there had only been a small stain of pink fluid on the bandage. Shanahan gently wiggled his fingers and moved the arm. Ruarc nearly passed out from the pain.

"Nellie, give me some of that ointment," he said smearing some along the suture line. "Ruarc, if you ever want to use a sword again, you must give this time to heal. I want you in that sling for at least another two weeks." He rebandaged the arm then turned his attention to the belly and chest wound. It was a diagonal slash from the right side of the belly right up and across the left ribs. The stitches were still holding but the bandage was wet. "The same goes here. Don't be so impatient. I don't want your guts falling out the first time you decide to get on a horse. Nellie, you can finish this for me. I still have a lot of men to see," he said before stomping out of the room.

Ruarc spent most of his time outside unless it was raining, but progress was slow. The weather was getting colder. *I can walk around the courtyard now, but it still takes effort and tires me. I've lost my stamina. Bending hurts. I have to be careful how much I eat otherwise I feel queasy. I pray to the gods every day to get me strong again. Today, I'm going to sort through the swords in the wagon and separate the ones that are ours. I should be able to do that with one hand.*

He was busy putting the swords in piles when two knights came over. They didn't look friendly. "All these weapons look alike to me. Stealing some of ours?" one said with a swaggering sneer.

"No, I'm not stealing any of yours. King Conall's blacksmith put his mark on the ones he made. I'm looking for his mark." He picked up a sword and showed him the hammer. "You can take that pile with you; they're not marked." *If I was healthy, I'd have fought him for that. Now I know what it's like for an ordinary man to deal with an arrogant knight.* The two knights picked up the swords and walked off. He found his own sword near the bottom and carried it back to his room in triumph. *Tomorrow I'll work on the spears and shields and gradually get it done. After that, I'll sort out the horses and saddles.* It made him feel useful to be busy and kept him outside where he could talk to the wind spirits. He often spoke with the Druids and made prayers to the gods.

Days blurred one into another. He rarely saw Shanahan. Nellie changed the bandages daily but now there was no drainage. Shanahan came in to see him and the others. The man ran his fingers over the shoulder scar. The bruising had gone and most of the swelling had subsided. Ruarc could move his arm, but the muscles felt tight and pulled, making him wince a little but he could do it. The belly wound had healed over too but it was tender when the physician touched it.

"Nellie, don't bandage these any more. They've healed quite well considering this young fool never says still. All right, Ruarc, leave the sling off. Be gentle with it. I know that word's not in your vocabulary. It still has to heal on the inside. Keep out of trouble if you can, no fighting or you'll undo everything.

"I'm not hungry most of the time and food doesn't want to stay down," said Ruarc.

"Yes, so I hear from Nellie. The innards take their own time. I don't think you need the Mandragora any more. If you need me, you know where to find me," he said and went over to the other men in the room.

The man with the head wound was not doing well. He had moaned a lot through the night and had not been out of bed. His wife and children had visited yesterday. Ruarc felt a great sorrow for them and it was a constant reminder of Hilde and Egan. Nellie was still burning sage every night for its healing powers. *I think I'll remember that smell for the rest of my life.*

Ruarc gently brushed his horse. He slid his left hand over the animal's shoulder, revelling in the smell and feel of muscle through the thickening coat. He braided the forelocks of the horses he could identify as Munster's.

The saddles were identifiable by their blankets and over the next two weeks he had stacked them in the stable.

Tara's busy today. Something's afoot. Riders had been coming and going all day.

That evening, in the great hall, King Niall rose and spoke to his assembly. "After much consultation with my lawyer and our Druid brethren, it has been decided the timing is right by the heavens that my eldest son Eoghan, will be leaving us soon to take over Guaire's fortress as his own."

A murmur rose through the gathering. "Some of you will be going with him. That corner of my kingdom needs a strong, loyal and trustworthy hand. I have also received news from Munster that an envoy will be coming this week to retrieve their animals, and weapons. Brehon Law demands compensation for the villagers killed in Guaire's raids, so twenty-two milch cows will also be sent. Guaire's head rots in the yard for the atrocities he and his followers did that day. Ruarc, you're going home. We owe you and Lady Geilis a debt of gratitude for preventing tragedy here," he said raising his chalice to a hundred voices.

Ruarc was stunned. *Home, Ardal, Hilde!* He stood and raised his mug to the King. "Sir, I propose a toast to your good health and continued reign. I have fought both against you and for you. I owe my recovery to your physician Shanahan, the prayers and skills of your Druids and to Nellie who has treated me like a mother would. I speak for Munster when I say that stability in the region under your son will be welcome and my home is just across the river." He raised his mug again to the assembly in a salute and sat down.

King Niall nodded with a smile on his face.

The next day, Ruarc saddled his horse. The muscles in his shoulder pulled as he tightened the girth and mounting was a painfully slow process. *By the gods, don't let my belly wound open up or Shanahan will have my hide.* He walked his horse around the yard, slowly using his knees and legs. *It feels amazingly good!* A grin spread across his face for the first time in a long time. The raising and outward motion of his left arm felt tight as he used the reins. *I've lost so much strength I'm like a newborn baby. I've still got a long way to go.* He savoured those moments, feeling the horse moving beneath him. *My body will be sore tomorrow, but my soul is flying.*

Every day, Ruarc rode his horse around the yard. He was very stiff and tired but it was a tonic. He was not wearing his sword yet. *I will not wear it, if I am unable to use it. I have a four-day ride ahead of me and I refuse to arrive home sitting in a wagon.* Lately his appetite was better and his eye was starting to wander to the comely maids around him. *I must have been very ill not be aroused by these young women. I pray I can be a man when I am with my wife.*

After his ride, he went to the statues and prayed with the young Druid there. Then he practised using his sword and getting the feel of its weight in his hand. His right arm worked well but the left was weaker, and he couldn't make a complete arc on a swing. *More practice, more practice.*

Later that afternoon, Ruarc heard the approaching horses. When the gates opened he saw the party of Connaught knights, escorting those of Munster. He saw the crest of Munster on the lead knight's horse and felt a joy explode in his chest. *These are my people!* Lady Geilis and the rest of the men looked splendid. To the rear of the procession were the two prisoners they had taken at the river. The prisoners took one look at the rotting heads of their former fellows swaying from the oak and blanched. Ruarc stood in the crowd, bareheaded and unarmed, and waited. King Niall, Eoghan and his lawyer came out in all their finery to meet her. There were the formal greetings then he could see her eyes searching for him. Momentarily they locked and she nodded.

He went over to the men of Munster who were unsaddling their horses. He was recognized and welcomed. He showed them where to water their horses, under the watchful eyes of Connaught's guards, each side respecting this surprisingly neutral occasion. Going back to his room, he put on his leather vest, noting the brown stained slit in it, then strapped on his sword for the first time. Taking his dagger, he trimmed his beard and hair. *I need to at least look presentable.* At the evening meal, Ruarc sat with the Munster contingent catching up with news from home. There were speeches and songs. Ruarc watched the two lawyers, heads bowed together discussing affairs of state. The Druid sat beside them, adding comments from time to time. He knew at some point he would be summoned.

It was much later that a page came over and told him: "The Lady wishes to see you now." He followed the lad over to the head table and bowed his head to her.

"Ruarc, I'm pleased to see you are recovering from your injuries. We leave for home at first light tomorrow."

"Our arms and horses are ready, my lady. I sorted them myself."

She nodded and dismissed him. He didn't get much sleep that night. *I am glad to go home but wonder if I can ride for four days.*

Dawn found him in the courtyard, saddling his horse along with the rest of the Munster men. He rode at the back along with the wagon load of weapons, the horse herd, and the milch cows, in his proper place behind the knights. Looking behind him as they went through the gates, he saw Nellie waving from his window. He returned the wave. He also saw some Connaught knights preparing to draw and quarter the two prisoners. *Soon enough, their heads will swing beside Guaire's.*

The journey home was very different from the night one coming in. *It seems to long ago.* They moved along at a brisk walk for hours and he put on many more miles trying to keep the herd together. They stopped at one village and camped overnight, buying bread, honey and dried meat from the villagers. *I am so stiff and my shoulder throbs. Eight hours in the saddle today.* He had no trouble sleeping. The next two days were a repetition as they crossed through woodlands and beautiful valleys with small scattered villages like his own.

On the fourth day, they came to the valley of the bog. Today it was clear, looking calm and benign. River reeds framed the shallow water that lay still awaiting the unwary. Ruarc broke into a sweat as they neared the battle site, remembering what it had looked like, but the bodies were gone; removed and buried he was told. Thin veils of mist clung to the valley walls, a light breeze sang softly, frogs croaked and ravens cawed. *How different from before.* Here the Connaught knights left them to return home; the boundary had been reached and the truce was over. *They treated me well*, thought Ruarc watching them go.

Now he was in more familiar territory. *I recognize these landmarks.* The road widened and Caisil came into view in the distance, a vision of stone in the foothills of the plain. *It's magnificent, even on a cold and cloudy day.* It took them the rest of the afternoon to reach it. Villagers along the way waved and cheered them on. Conall Mor rode out to meet them with young Murtagh at his side.

The King stopped and spoke with Lady Geilis, casting his eyes upon the column until they came to rest on the herd and on Ruarc at the very end. The King rode down the line, inspected the cows and looked pleased. "Well done, Ruarc, well done." He spun his horse and triumphantly lead the procession into the castle.

There was toasting and feasting in the great hall that evening. The poet was singing, the musicians were playing and mugs of mead were frequently refilled. Ruarc had eaten a good meal and was starting to relax his stiff arm when the King brought the hall to silence. "Ruarc, you have a tale to tell – the battle of the bog, the loss of our men, the abduction of Lady Geilis, and your triumph over Lord Guaire's man. Tell your story."

Ruarc was totally taken off guard. *I have no song made.* For a few moments he was silent, then very solemnly began. "I have no song prepared," he confessed. "But I'll tell you what happened." He stood before them in the centre of the hall and told his story as he remembered, eloquently describing the blinding fog, the grasping hands, of waking to find them all dead, with Barra and the lady missing. For over an hour, he mesmerized them, reliving the fights vividly as if they were happening again. His shirt was loose and he was sweating freely. The scars caught the torch light with their eerie red glow and seemed to do a macabre dance as he moved. He spoke of his terror of night rides, the unseen spirits and his shame of being taken down by slaves. He remembered the skill of Shanahan, Niall's generosity and the care given by Nellie. He spoke of his fear of not healing well enough to fight again. He spoke finally of the death of Lord Guaire, and the punishment to the knights, the heads swaying in the wind of the mighty oak in Tara's courtyard. When he was finished, he humbly stood before the King, his energy gone. "I owe my life to Lady Geilis, she is a truly brave woman and to the skills of Connaught's physician, Shanahan. I leave the poetry to your Poet." The knights pounded the tables with their mugs, a thundering ovation as Ruarc walked back to his seat. *I feel exonerated. I may not be tall enough to be a King's knight but this legend will live on.*

The next morning, he saddled both his horse and Barra's. He placed Barra's sword in the saddle scabbard. *In some ways, Barra was with me all the time. It was his sword that killed the last knight. My friend, I shall meet you again.* He was just about to mount his horse when Prince Murtagh appeared, accompanied by his two wolf dogs.

"Ruarc! Wait." He was carrying a woven basket and strode toward him. "You have served my father very bravely, as did Ardal before you. We need men like you in the villages, men of strength and loyalty, men who can raise strong and skilled children and inspire others. You may not be a poet, but you told your story like no other. May the gods be with you." He handed the basket to Ruarc who lifted the flap and there inside was a young wolf dog puppy.

Ruarc's jaw dropped. *A royal puppy! Only royalty is allowed to own one of these dogs! Men have been killed for stealing one or even causing injury to one.*

"They are fierce and loyal. He will get almost as big as a pony, like his parents here. He will protect you, keep the wolves from your sheep and sire his kind with your bitches. He is weaned from his mother and will eat just about anything," said Murtagh.

Ruarc smiled and tied the basket to the front of his saddle. "Prince Murtagh, my gratitude for this gift is beyond what I express to you. It is truly an honour." With that he turned the horses and headed for home.

The day was cold and overcast with the wind spirits whistling through the woods. He smiled, removing the warm furry pup from the basket to tuck him inside his shirt. A quick pink tongue washed his cheek. The pup occasionally awoke, two brown eyes peering up at him in curiosity through a mop of spiky grey hair. Several times he stopped and let the pup walk around. It stayed close behind him.

The ride was uneventful. The villages he passed became more familiar and he waved to people he recognized as he rode by. Much of the stiffness in his legs had gone, finally becoming used to activity again. When his valley opened up, through the bare trees, he saw the palisade and conical roofs of home. Wisps of smoke were weaving into the sky from each hut. He looked at it for a moment savouring the beauty of the spot and urged his horse forward. Barra's horse trotted alongside on the lead line. Dogs began to bark as he pulled in through the gate and a minute growl emanated from his shirt as a small wet nose and two bright eyes popped up. As he pulled to a halt in front of Ardal's hut, his family stumbled out.

Ardal stood there, a much-aged Ardal looking at his son. There were tears in the eyes of the old warrior which he blinked away. Ardal grasped his shoulders then the two embraced until a warm fuzzy body intervened. Ruarc handed the puppy to his father. "A gift from the King, for services rendered."

Ardal looked at the pup with amazement. Family clamoured around them. Ruarc turned to look for Hilde. She was right there beside him holding young Egan. Putting the child down, she buried herself in his arms. For a moment, Ruarc thought she would rebreak his ribs. *Oh, the strength of her.* For the longest moment, he realized

how much he had missed them, how much family mat-
tered. He felt his arousal in response to her. He grinned
and looked down at Egan, who was now standing on his
own, holding his leg.

"He's walking!"

Hilde nodded, grinning just as widely as him.

Everyone in the village clustered around. *I've been gone
over two months and they have changed so much.* Children
had grown. Alyson and Nora looked clean and happy
standing beside Aideen. Barra's wife, a lovely woman with
strawberry blonde wavy hair, came over. Ruarc removed
the sword from Barra's scabbard and offered it to her. As
she gazed down at the sword lying there in palms of his
hands, she wept. The whole group became quiet. Ruarc
handed her the reins to Barra's horse. "I believe he died in
battle but I couldn't find him in the bog. I used his sword
when mine was gone and I believe his spirit stood with
me as I fought Guaire's knight. Barra was a good warrior
and a good friend. I miss him badly."

"His body was found, Ruarc. He is buried near the
beehives," said Hilde quietly, resting her hand on his
shoulder. He knew that the death of her brother was a
great loss for her, too.

Ruarc heaved a sigh of relief. "It bothered me a lot that
I couldn't find him. I only assumed he was dead because
I recovered his sword; he would never have surrendered
it and lived."

One of the older dogs came over to check out the new pup who had been sitting at Ardal's feet. In response to the large sniffing dog, the pup snarled, showing small sharp teeth and stood with four feet firmly planted protecting Ardal. Everyone laughed. The older dog wandered off, undeterred, used to puppy behaviour.

The evening's festivities mirrored the previous night's in Caisil. He told his story and showed his scars. "I've had moments of bravery, I've had moments of fear. I'm not the same person I was when I left here. I lost my best friend. I won my battle but even now have not fully recovered my strength. I have learned a lot of things during my healing. I know I must be outside with the land and the trees. I found out that knights must do things by order of the King that I wouldn't want to do. I've had to rely on other people, which I have never liked doing and people have been kind to me, even those I would have considered enemies. I have come to respect some of them. King Niall was very fair. He had no knowledge of Guaire's treachery and dealt with it quickly when he found out. They are the same as us in many ways."

His father sat beside him smiling. "You're right, Ruarc. You've changed. Being wounded left you helpless and you learned from that. Injuries force a man to look at his talents and choose other paths. Sometimes those paths are better in the long run, than what he first had in mind. I think sometimes the gods play games with us."

Ruarc looked at him with surprise. *Perhaps my father is not as disappointed with his life as I thought he was. He has lived long enough to see his grandchildren and to pass his skills to all of us. Is it because I was injured that I have come to appreciate him more?*

That night, he lay with Hilde. Because of his wounds, their lovemaking was slower and gentler. He looked at her and buried his face in her long hair, savouring her scent. "Hilde, I didn't know how much I felt for you, until I almost lost everything. I was in a strange place with none of my own. I had lost Barra, my horse, my sword and my self respect. I had dreamed of being a King's knight but found that would never be. I worried so much that you wouldn't want me, if I couldn't be a knight. I wasn't even sure I'd recover from my wounds well enough to ever ride or use a sword. I'm not finished healing yet. Shanahan says it could take months. I've been so afraid I wouldn't be enough of a man for you."

"For a brave warrior and talented storyteller, sometimes you are a complete idiot," she replied with a throaty laugh, caressing his body until he responded. There wasn't time for talking after that. Under their bed curled up on blankets and snuggled up together for warmth was a future warrior and one happy puppy.

the quarry

Galway, Ireland, 1896

Alistair O'Flagherty reined his bay horse to the rim of the quarry where sixty-foot high tiers of green, variegated marble framed the fifty-acre site. He watched his crew cutting into the East face, creating huge unwieldy slabs and clouds of dust. The sheer scale dwarfed the men, including his son Michael who was helping load a slab onto the wagon. In the distance, he could see a familiar rider approaching. He waved and rode to meet his brother and partner, Brendan. *My, we look alike; red hair and moustaches, though mine's got some grey. Not hard to tell we're brothers.*

"Morning to ya, Brendan," said Alistair. "Why so gloomy?" he asked, noting the scowl on his brother's usually smiling face.

"Alistair, I'm in trouble. Let's go in the office."

"Come on, then," replied Alistair. They tied their horses to the fence and entered the small brick building. Brendan shut the door as Alistair shoved the work orders aside, and they sat down at the table.

For a few moments, there was silence as Brendan groped for words. "You know I like to play cards... Well, me luck's not been so good lately. I've lost a lot of money. I had a chance to cover me bets, and, well, I bet my partnership on the quarry..."

"You what?" exploded Alistair, rising from his chair, glaring at his brother.

Brendan sat with his head in his hands. "I lost."

"You bloody fool!" Alistair felt his face flush and his temples start to throb. "Who's holding the IOUs? How much?"

"Emerson Kelly for five hundred pounds," came the whispered reply.

"You must be stark raving mad after all the problems we've had with him. He's a liar and a thief. When do we have to pay? Did you put it writing?"

"Thirty days. I signed the IOUs and gave my word."

Alistair groaned. "Brendan, we only make two pounds a week each! We can't raise that kind of money. What about your cottage?" he said, scrambling for alternatives.

"It's already gone."

"I need MacPherson. He's a right canny lawyer and might find a way out of this mess. Will you come with me?" Brendan shook his head. Without a backward glance, Alistair flung open the door and strode to his horse, leaving Brendan sitting there. He rode down the ramp into the pit to Michael.

"Hey Dad, what's up?" said Michael, seeing the expression on his father's face.

"Michael, I've got to go to town to see MacPherson. We've got a big problem. I'll be back as soon as I can." He spun his horse and cantered up the slope.

It was late afternoon when Alistair returned home. *I've been the entire day with lawyers and accountants.* Opening the door, he was immediately surrounded by Millie his wife, his daughter Meagan and Michael.

"Whatever's wrong, Alistair?" implored Millie, worry deepening the wrinkles in her kindly face. Her fingers twisted the frills on her apron into knots.

"More than you can imagine," he said, as he poured a whiskey and dropped into his chair. He looked at their anxious faces. "Brendan's gambled away five hundred pounds to Emerson Kelly and has staked his share of our partnership. Kelly wants his money in thirty days or he becomes my partner. You know how I feel about Kelly. He's been a thorn in our side for years, just like his father. I detest the man."

He heard the sharp intake of breath from the others. "How are we going to cover that much money?" said Meagan.

"We'll have to raise it ourselves, find another partner or lose it. The accountants will be out to check the books in a couple of days and see what it's worth. MacPherson's not going to inform the owner just yet. We'll see what happens. We'll need a geologist's report on how much marble's left. Our lease with Lord White is good for another fifteen years."

"What about Brendan's cottage?" said Michael, a deep frown on his face.

"Brendan's already mortgaged that and lost the money, so I don't know what they'll do."

"Oh, poor Kate," cried Millie. "How will they even feed the children?"

"Not just poor Kate, Millie. What about us? We've all worked hard to get what we have. Lose the partnership and we lose everything too. It could mean our home here and the shop downstairs. I've been here since I was four-teen years old and at fifty-one I'm too old to get another trade. I won't work with Kelly. I was hoping Michael could take over from me later."

"I've got fifty pounds saved," said Michael. "Was saving it to marry Jenny. You can have it, if that'll help."

"Thanks lad, but even with what I've got, it's not enough. I'm gonna take the next few days to see if anyone will invest in us; maybe my cousins or the Flynns. They might be our competitors, but they're decent people and I could work with them. MacPherson may have some contacts too."

Tuesday and Wednesday were hectic. Alistair rode along the river road between verdant hills to neighbouring villages bordering Lough Corrib, visiting family and business acquaintances. Deep in thought, he concentrated hard on his choices, even to killing Kelly. *Dear God, what am I thinking! I've never deliberately hurt anyone, but it's tempting. Despicable swine! But if I did that, I'd be as bad as him.*

Returning late Wednesday, he stopped in at the shop. Millie and Meagan were assisting two ladies at the counter, making selections of jewellery from the many jade coloured stones. The display cases were full of rings, pendants, bracelets and small ornaments ranging from ashtrays and carved animals to inkwells. Watching them, he smiled for the first time that day. Meagan was eighteen, with glossy dark brown hair tied back in a ribbon. The high-necked pale green dress accented her slim figure and pale skin. The silver pendant she was wearing was one of theirs. *She's elegant and beautiful, a younger image of her mother.*

"Alistair, come talk to me when you're free," said Millie.

He nodded and went into the workshop out back, glancing at his three men working diligently at their benches. Thomas and Jeremy took raw stone, selected for colour and marbling and ground the surface on each piece to domed ovals or rounds of flawless high polish. William was their silversmith, working the malleable silver wire into intricate Celtic knots on rings, chains and pendants. All were skilled craftsmen. *They've worked for me for years. I hope I don't lose them. I couldn't replace them.*

Thomas brought over two work orders for his approval. Alistair initialled them, and sorted through the rock pile. Picking up a chunk of green marble with dark green veining, he remembered the geologist telling him they had been part of an ancient sea bed thousands of years ago. *So old.* "These will do nicely for that order, Thomas," he said handing them to him. *Must remember to ask Michael to bring another load of small pieces from the quarry. We haven't got much selection up here.*

Millie came in. "Mr. Kelly was here this morning."

"What did he want?"

"He said he was just looking around, then made a comment on how Meagan would be a nice addition to his family. Looked at her like a filly at a horse sale. I'm surprised he didn't check her teeth. I avoid him when I can.... Too smug for my liking," said Millie, a tone of indignation in her voice.

"Never mind him, Millie, I'll take care of him. Go out front and keep an eye on the customers. I'll be out in a few minutes. I want to talk to the men," he replied, feeling his teeth clench at the thought of Kelly anywhere near Meagan.

He was in the middle of explaining events to them when Meagan bolted in. "Dad, come quick" a look of total panic on her face.

Alistair charged out the door to find Arthur Conway, their young local police sergeant, standing at the counter looking grim and official in his dark blue uniform with the row of gleaming brass buttons.

"Arthur, what's going on?"

Arthur paused until the customers left the store. "I'm really sorry, Alistair but I've got bad news to tell you. We found Brendan this morning. He's dead. Ben Smith saw his horse wandering loose near the old pit and his body was down below. I need to ask you some questions, so can you come with me to the station?"

"Brendan's dead? How? What happened?" he blurted, remembering their last encounter.

"Alistair, I don't know why he died, except that he fell from the top of the quarry onto the rocks. It looks suspicious. There were two sets of horse tracks at the top and the ground was trampled. Don't know if he was pushed or whether he jumped."

"I don't believe it... He'd never jump, but who would want to push him? We're all so careful around the rim." Alistair was at a loss for words. He heard the gasps from Millie and Meagan behind him. He turned in confusion and looked at the women clinging to each other.

"I'd better go with him. Lock up the store," he said and followed Arthur in silence to the station three blocks away.

The station was busy and noisy with a quarrelsome thief being booked and a now somewhat sober drunk being released to his berating wife. Sergeant Conway ushered Alistair into a quieter room. "Have a seat Alistair. I've heard about your troubles with Brendan and I need to know where you've been since Monday, every minute of it." Paper, quill pen and ink well were on the ink-stained wooden table.

Alistair looked at Arthur and realized that Arthur the policeman was a very different man from the Arthur he knew off duty. There was an aura of authority in the young man he had not seen before. *Seems strange to have him look at me like I'm a criminal. Does he think I killed Brendan?*

As he wrote, he spoke about Brendan's confession on Monday, his visits to the lawyer, accountants, then to his trip to cousins and the Flynns. He wrote down times and the names of anyone he could remember who might have seen him, including the blacksmith at the four corners when he watered his horse and his quick stop at a pub for a meal and a pint. "I got back to the shop about fifteen minutes before you arrived," he said checking his pocket watch to the clock on the wall. As the ink dried, he passed the pages to Arthur, who quickly read over them.

"Alistair, one more question. What clothes were you wearing yesterday and today?"

"Same as now, brown jacket, boots, beige britches and bowler hat. I haven't had time to change. Why?"

"Do you ever wear blue?"

"No, my good suit is black."

"Alright. You realize I have to check everything you've written and I'm going to see Michael as well. I'm looking for motive right now and you two had the most to gain from that partnership agreement if he died."

Alistair arose in anger. "Are you suggesting I killed him?"

"Settle down, Alistair. That would be the most obvious motive at this point and it's why I need to clear you and know where you were. With him gone, his share of the partnership would go to you."

"Aye, but his debt does not die and I still have to pay it. Monday, I was bloody angry with him for the mess he'd created, but I never saw him after that and I can account for my time," he said pointing to the papers. "I don't believe he'd kill himself either but God knows he must have been desperate."

"I need to find out who was up there with him. I know you two were close. Can you identify his body for me? I warn you, the fall did a lot of damage. Might be easier for you rather than Kate. The coroner's already seen him."

Alistair nodded and followed him down the dim corridor to the morgue behind the station. A shape lay on the table covered with a sheet which Arthur removed, revealing the gray mottled and naked body. Alistair looked at the red hair, the open wound that had been a face and the bruising that stained the skin a deep purple. The left leg was a mass of twisted flesh punctured by jagged bones protruding through the skin just above the knee. A long scar showed bluish-white on the right forearm. *Brendan cut his arm on barb wire when he was but a lad.* There were fresh abrasions on both knuckles. *He's been in a fight.* He'd seen enough and nodded. "That's Brendan." Arthur replaced the sheet.

Alistair was unprepared for the implosion of feelings that flooded him. A lump rose in his throat and tears came to his eyes. Startled by his own reaction, he momentarily turned away, struggling to control the wave of nausea. *Deep breath, deep breath, I can't vomit here.* Moments later he regained some composure and said to Arthur: "If you're done with me, I'm going home. Millie and I will need to be with Kate to prepare the wake."

"The coroner is prepared to release the body for burial. Given the abrasions on his knuckles this looks like a fight, not a suicide" said Arthur.

"Thank God for that," said Alistair. "At least we can bury him in consecrated ground."

It was bedlam at Brendan's cottage the next day. Alistair noticed Kate's face was puffy from crying and the children clung to her, looking frightened. Millie gave each one a big hug, then bustled over to put the kettle on the fire for tea. The youngest nephew sat on his knee until Meagan took all the children outside to give Kate and Millie a chance to prepare the parlour. They turned the mirrors in the house to the wall and closed the curtains as was tradition.

Millie came over to him. "Alistair, Kate was telling me that Brendan left around nine yesterday morning but didn't tell her where he was going or who he was meeting. He just told her he'd figured a way out of the problem. The poor girl's so ashamed. She's been trying to stop him gambling for a couple of years."

"Does her family know about Brendan?"

"Yes. She said her brother Neal will be coming today, as soon as he can."

Three of the neighbourhood women came in to help prepare Brendan's body, to bathe him and dress him in his best suit, with the cross on his chest and the rosary in his hands. The carpenter was just putting the finishing touches to a wooden coffin, and sweeping up the sawdust. "It'll be a closed casket for him," he remarked.

Alistair knew the routine well as he'd helped at many a wake. *When they're done, I'll place him in the coffin and sit with him all night. He won't be alone until he's in the ground.* He heard Millie remind Kate to get the candles. A wagon pulled up with several crates of food and drinks.

A young lad from the tobacconist's shop came to the door handing Alistair a large pouch of tobacco and another of snuff. "Mr. O'Flagherty, me Dad said to give this to you."

"Tell him thank you very much," said Alistair. *Thank God for the neighbours. They always come through.* The high-pitched keening started as the women worked with Brendan's body. *It's an eerie sound, so sad and raw but that's how I feel too,* thought Alistair, picking out both Millie's and Meagan's voices among the others as the plaintive wailing permeated the walls and echoed in his head and his heart.

Later that night, Alistair sat alone in the flickering candlelight with Brendan, his silent companion. He took a pinch of snuff that calmed him. A few people came and went offering condolences. *Most will come tomorrow when Father Simon gives the blessing. Millie and Meagan have gone home, likely to cook. Hope she makes her colcannon. That always goes over well.* The hours passed slowly and Alistair had time to think. *Why didn't I see what was happening to him? How could I have missed it or did he hide it from me, knowing the reaction he'd get? I can't believe you're gone, little brother.*

Michael arrived early in the morning to take his turn sitting with Brendan. "It was after eleven before I got home Dad. I'm sure Arthur thinks I killed him. I can't prove where I was in the morning. I went down to the river, wracking my brains for a way out of the debt. Now that Brendan's dead, does that change the partnership agreement?"

"First of all, if Arthur thought you were guilty, you'd be sitting in gaol right now. He'll do what's right regardless of who you are. Brendan's death does affect the partnership. I hope he put something in his will like I have.

"Dad, do they think I killed him, so you would get his share?"

"Dunno," Alistair replied. "It would make more sense for us to kill Kelly, not Brendan." Both men became quiet.

All day people came and went, respectfully paying their condolences to Kate. Neal arrived and agreed to take his turn at the vigil that night. He also invited Kate to live with his family in their farmhouse as they had room to spare. *That's a blessing, there's no room to spare over the store,* thought Alistair. The mood was light-hearted at times. He heard reminiscences of amusing tales he had forgotten, like the time a five-year old Brendan had decided to ride Patrick's pig and it got loose. It had taken four of them to chase it back home through the peat bog. *We all got a beating for that one!* Piles of food disappeared, the smell of tobacco and a haze of smoke filled the kitchen and level of whiskey in the bottles dropped. Charlie Wallace was in the corner, playing his violin. *Brendan would have enjoyed this.*

"How long has Brendan been losing at cards?" asked Alistair to one of Brendan's friends when the opportunity arose.

The man looked a little guilty but replied: "No more than the rest of us at first, but things changed about two years ago when Kelly joined our card group. Brendan lost more when Kelly played. He's a pretty canny card player."

"Do you think he cheated?"

"No, I don't think so, but he could always persuade Brendan to play just one more hand, if you know what I mean, and if Brendan had a dram or two on board he was always willing. At the end, I don't think he could walk away from it."

Kelly again, always Kelly, manipulating to get the quarry.

It was Saturday. Brendan's body had been moved to the Church for the service and burial. Alistair look at the crowd. *Seems like half of Galway's here. Of course, he was well liked and had lived here all his life.* Kate, even paler than usual in mourning black and a veil, sat in the front pew with Neal, the children between them in a tight, forlorn little group. Alistair and family sat in the pew behind. The cousins and other relatives sat further back. The coffin was wreathed in flowers. Alistair caught a glimpse of Kelly in his blue suit, standing at the back with a smirk on his face. *He's got a nerve being here; he's trying to provoke me and succeeding at it.* Millie kept her face to the front.

The words of the service lulled him into more childhood memories; tough years through the famine, but mostly their escapades at school and later years sneaking into the pub, chasing the girls and working twelve hours a day at the quarry with their father. The rhythm of the hymns was punctuated with sobs from Kate and the oldest girl, gently hushed by Millie. When the service ended, Alistair, Michael and the quarry crew shouldered the casket out the main door to the dark hole in the grass beside the moss-covered rock wall in the churchyard. Neil led Kate and her brood along.

Alistair saw Arthur standing on the pavement with two other officers. Father Simon read the scriptures, gave a final blessing and the casket was gradually lowered into the ground, followed by handfuls of dirt and gentle

words. The crowd began to disperse. Alistair watched
Arthur approach Kelly and heard him say "Emerson Kelly,
I'm arresting you for the death of Brendan O'Flagherty."

A startled Kelly replied: "You can't arrest me for
murder; it was self- defence. He lured me out there, said
he had the money, then tried to push me over the edge.
We fought, he lost. You can't prove otherwise."

"That's something for a judge and jury to decide, Mr.
Kelly. Give me your jacket please." Puzzled, Kelly removed
his jacket and handed it to Arthur. The right pocket was
missing a button, the broken threads dangling. Arthur
quietly put his hand in his uniform pocket and opened
it revealing a single blue button. "This tells me that you
were there. Brendan had this button from your jacket
clenched in his fist when he died."

Alistair charged across the cemetery, confronting Kelly
face to face. "You... You killed him!" Enraged, he hit him
squarely in the jaw, knocking him to the pavement.

Arthur grabbed Alistair and held him back. "Stop
Alistair, stop!" He tightened his grip to the point where
Alistair felt the brass buttons digging into his back as
he strained forward. Then Michael was there, solidly
blocking his way. Gradually the rage ebbed and his ragged,
heaving breaths slowed. Arthur's grip slackened.

Michael released his arms. "Dad, he's not worth it. Let
Arthur deal with him."

Kelly got to his feet. "You'll pay for this," he said with a lopsided grin, rubbing his jaw.

I already have. I've lost my brother and now my dignity in front of all these people. A gent doesn't behave like that, he thought looking at his fellow parishioners. Some were tight-lipped and frowning; others quietly gave him a subtle nod of approval. He dusted off his suit, picked up his hat and went to Father Simon. "I must apologize to you Father, this wasn't the time or place to lose my temper."

Two weeks had passed since the funeral. MacPherson had notified him by messenger to bring Kate to the office for the reading of the will. They sat in the hall, Alistair's foot tapping with impatience as their wait dragged on. *Come on Mac. You know what's in it. You wrote the damned thing.*

Finally, MacPherson called them in. He was a tall, spare white-haired Scot with bushy side whiskers, a no-nonsense expression and an accent as broad as a Glasgow fog. He looked comfortable behind his walnut desk, framed by ceiling-to-floor bookcases of leather bound volumes. "Alistair, Kate, it's time." He slit the sealed envelope with a flourish and proceeded.

"I, Brendan Clancy O'Flagherty leave the cottage, its contents and all my possessions to my wife Katherine with the exception of the partnership agreement for the Galway Marble Quarry.

To my brother Alistair Kenna O'Flagherty I leave my share of the partnership agreement, on the condition that he pays my wife Katherine two pounds a week for the duration of the lease."

Alistair exhaled a sigh, not even aware that he'd been holding his breath. *The partnership is mine. We'll be paying Brendan's wages to Kate. It's gonna be tight.* He saw a tiny smile on Kate's face. "Relieved?" he asked.

"Oh Alistair, I am that. You said it would be alright. I'll have enough to look after the children and pay Neal some rent. There won't be much from the sale of the cottage, but we'll make a go of it."

It was trial day for Emerson Kelly. Alistair paced back and forth in the kitchen. *Should I go or not? I don't want to make a fool of myself again, like I did at the church.*

Michael bounded down the stairs, two at a time. "Morning, Dad," inhaling the aroma of the fresh cooked bacon Millie had left on the warmer.

"Michael, I'd like you to attend the trial for me, if you will. Can't trust myself when it comes to Kelly."

"Sure, I'll go, but you'll have to go to the quarry sometime. George will be finishing the big slab for the pillars at the Kylemore church. Mind you, he knows what he's doing."

"Right lad. First, I'll go to shipping office for the paperwork on the Londonderry shipment then I'll head to the quarry. I'll see you back home this afternoon and you can tell me all about it. I can't bear to think he'll find a way out of it and I don't want to hear all the gossip about Brendan."

"Dad, Arthur'll be a good witness. He's honest and thorough. Everyone at the church heard what Kelly said. He is responsible for Uncle Brendan's death. Speaking of Arthur, I think Meagan has taken a shine to him. She blushes every time his name is mentioned," he said with a grin as he stuffed slices of bacon between two slabs of bread and went out.

Meagan and Arthur? Maybe a policeman in the family wouldn't be a bad thing. Steady job.

Alistair walked down the cobbled streets of Galway, past the colourful shop fronts on Merchant Street and the ruins of the old Spanish Arch, to the quays and shipping office. The sun was a moving shimmer on the waves stretching to the horizon, broken by the shadows of passing ships and fishing boats. The Aran Islands showed as a distant blue smudge beyond Galway Bay. The rolling green hills and surf torn cliffs reminded him that life was going on for everyone else even if his world was upside down. He noticed familiar faces and acknowledged their greetings. *It will feel good to get back to normal.* The routine paperwork and casual banter from the shipping clerk calmed him and took his mind off the courthouse.

He had a quick pint at the Mariner's Pub then was on his way. At the quarry, off came his jacket, up went his shirt sleeves and he got dirty and dusty like the others. *It feels good to work.* The team finished the final cuts on the slab and it lay glistening in one solid piece. Carefully he eyed it looking for cracks and flaws. "I can't find a fault in it," he said to George and together they maneuvered it onto the wagon with the crane and chains. *Michael's right, George could take on more responsibility here and free up Michael to do some of Brendan's work.* Riding home at the end of the day, he felt the tension rising. Fearing the worst, he went straight upstairs only to be confronted by Millie.

"Alistair, look at you," she squealed, staring at his grimy clothes. "You'll not be sitting at my table like that! You're as bad as Michael. Off with you, get cleaned up." He bowed to a higher authority.

Across the dinner table, he looked at his son and said: "Well Michael, tell me what happened."

"Dad, you should have seen it. I was lucky to get a seat. The place was full and the coppers were turning them away. Judge McNaughton wouldn't put up with any nonsense in his court room. He banged his gavel and got the silence he wanted. Kelly was quiet, not cocky like he usually is. He didn't say two words the whole time. He just sat there with no expression on his face."

"Really?"

"Yes, and Arthur was a great witness. He'd done a thorough job and Kelly's lawyer, Middleton couldn't budge him or discredit him. Ben Smith confirmed he'd found Uncle Brendan's horse about ten in the morning and that was consistent with the coroner's time of death. Doc O'Connor said the fall and landing on the rocks caused his death, but there had been a fight. His knuckles were bruised and there was that blue button he found in Brendan's left hand that matched the ones on Kelly's jacket. Arthur confirmed Kelly's confession that all of us heard. Middleton couldn't deny that, but he said that Brendan had tried to kill Kelly over the debts and that it was self-defence. The jury will likely have a verdict tomorrow."

They did. Alistair and Michael were both seated in court when the jurors came back. The gavel banged and a hush descended. Turning to the jury, the Judge said: "Have you reached a verdict?"

"Yes, Your Honour," the jury foreman replied. "We find Emerson Kelly guilty in the death of Brendan O'Flagherty." Ripples coursed through the courthouse. Alistair's heart was pounding.

Kelly stood tall, straight and expressionless, staring at the Judge. "Emerson Kelly, you have been found guilty in the death of Brendan O'Flagherty. I hereby sentence you to fifteen years in prison." The gavel fell for the last time and there was an eruption of voices and the wailing of Kelly's wife. Kelly was marched away in shackles by two policemen. He looked at Alistair with such venom that it shook him.

It isn't over yet, he thought.

Alistair sorted through the newspapers and letters that had piled up. One in particular caught his attention.

> "I wish to offer my condolences on the death of your brother. I have dealt with Brendan for the last five years and found him both knowledgeable and personable. Your jewellery sells well here in Cork, particularly during the summer months with the influx of American tourists. I will be travelling to New York in the spring and wondered if you have a catalogue of your stock that I could take with me. I think there is a great opportunity to increase business using mail order. Looking forward to hearing from you. Yours truly,

Langford Doyle, Proprietor, Embassy
Hotel, Cork."

Alistair contemplated the letter. *Mail order... I 've never
even thought of doing sales that way. Go to them instead of
them coming to us.* He sat down that night and discussed
it with Michael who immediately saw the implications.

"Dad, if we could improve the profits of the shop, we
wouldn't need another partner. If we had mail orders
coming in, the business wouldn't be so seasonal. We
could manage it between us. I'd like to do some of Uncle
Brendan's job, handling the sales and putting together
this catalogue. We could use a picture of Meagan on the
cover, wearing our pendants and rings. Her looks could
sell anything."

"I'm taking fifty pounds to Kelly tomorrow at the
prison. It's our first instalment to show we'll honour
Brendan's debts. In the meantime, you start thinking
about this catalogue."

The prison was a cold dank and gray place. Alistair gave
his name to the warden and shivered. The prospect of ever
being confined in such a place would be soul destroying.
The guards checked him for contraband and he sat on one
side of the grill waiting. Kelly came in from the other side

in shackles, looking pale and tired. For a moment, Alistair almost felt sorry for him.

"What do you want?" Kelly asked, no emotion showing on his face.

"I've brought fifty pounds to start payment on those IOUs," said Alistair handing the money to him. "Do you want me to pay you or give it to Middleton?"

"Next time you can send Meagan. I want to see my daughter again. She's grown into a beautiful woman."

"What do you mean, your daughter?" he shouted, bristling, his fists clenched and his jaw jutting out.

Kelly laughed. "Why don't you ask Millie?" he said with a sneer and walked out.

No, Millie and Kelly? No, no, no! It can't be. A short time later he found himself at the church, the only refuge he could think of. He sat alone in that vast empty echoing space and on his knees before the saints, cried like a baby, his sobs reverberating. *Oh God, what do I do now?* He finally realized that Father Simon was sitting beside him speaking softly.

"I've never seen you like this Alistair. What's happened?"

"Kelly said Meagan is his daughter. I can't believe Millie's been unfaithful to me. I've loved her and Meagan. How could she? I trusted her... She's my wife. It's tearing my heart out."

"Wait, Alistair. Just because Kelly said it, doesn't mean it's true. Your fathers taught the pair of you to hate each other and carry on their feud. Kelly knows you well enough to hurt you in the deepest places. Don't be condemning Millie until you've spoken to her. I've known you both for years and I don't believe it. I'll send my housekeeper to bring her here."

Thirty minutes later, an out-of-breath Millie arrived. "Father, you wanted me?" she said and then saw Alistair in the front pew. Their eyes met and Alistair was the first to look away. She ran forward and grasped his arms. "Alistair, look at me. What's wrong?"

His eyes searched hers. *Was Kelly lying?* "Millie, Kelly tells me he's Meagan's father."

Millie gasped, her face crumpled and she burst into tears.

"So, it's true, is it?" he demanded.

"I knew one day I'd have to tell you. Nineteen years ago, when you were on a trip to Cork, Kelly came to the shop when I was closing up. The boys had gone home. I tried to fend him off. He was still angry that I'd married you and not him. He forced himself on me. I was too scared to tell you." She fell to her knees beside Father Simon, buried her face in her hands and wept, the priest's hands on her convulsing shoulders.

Alistair stood there totally numb. "The bastard raped you. Why didn't you tell me?" he said jerking her to her feet and shaking her.

"Alistair, if I had told you, you'd have killed him and they'd have hung you for it. So, I said nothing. I don't know if Meagan's yours or his and that's the truth. I got pregnant right after that."

He stood there, thoughts swirling through his mind. "It's a damn good thing he's in jail and I can't get at him, or I'd kill him now!" he said, pacing up and down the aisle releasing his pent-up rage. Father Simon quietly walked beside him.

Gradually the pacing slowed and Father Simon said to him: "Alistair, I think it's time for you to take Millie home. The pair of you have been together for a long time. You need to be gentle with each other. This must have been very difficult for Millie. She must love you very much to have protected you like that. She's been a good hard-working wife to you and a good mother to both your children. Work this through. Think about what you're saying."

It was a silent, awkward walk home. Alistair sat at the table. He missed the look Millie gave Michael and Meagan, the query on Michael's face and the shrug of Millie's shoulders. Allistair stared intently at Meagan, searching her features. *Her eyes are hazel like Millie's; Kelly's are blue. Her nose and chin look like Gramma's, not Kelly's;*

her hair is like his but that's Millie's colour too. I can't see features that shout Kelly.

He left the table not finishing his meal, leaving the colcannon congealing on the plate and slumped in his chair in the parlour. *Why did Kelly wait so long to spring this surprise? He's in prison and knows he can't ever have the quarry. Was this his final chance to destroy me?* A short time later, Michael quietly came in and Alistair heard the door close.

Michael pulled up a chair beside him. "Dad, talk to me."

"Michael, I don't have to tell you the past six weeks have been hell. First the partnership mess and Brendan's debts, then his death, then the court case and now...I'm overwhelmed."

"Can you tell me what's going on?"

Alistair looked at the young man before him. *He's not a child anymore, he's a man in his own right. He's never let me down.* "Michael, it's a long story. It started when I was just a young lad. My father and Kelly's both worked at the quarry. Both had high hopes of getting the foreman's job but Kelly senior was a heavy drinker and a mean one, too. When my father got the job, things were never right between them after that. They hated each other after a while and taught us to do the same."

"Dad, I never knew it went back that far."

"Kelly's a few years younger than me. We had lots of fights at school. I think his old man beat him, too. Some days, he'd come to school with bruises I hadn't given him. Mind you, we'd fight over anything – who could run the fastest, what colour the sky was, you name it.

The quarry lease was due to expire when my father inherited some money from an aunt in Dublin. He hadn't been expecting it, but she was a widow and didn't have any children and he was the nearest relative. He used the money to get the lease. Kelly senior was furious, got roaring drunk one night and got into a fight at the pub with a bunch of sailors. He got the worst of it and died from his injuries. His son's been getting even ever since."

Michael was listening intently. "So, he's always been trying to get the lease."

Alistair nodded. "Yes, he has. Michael, have I taught you to hate too?"

"Well, sort of but not the same. I was at school with his youngest boy, but we just avoided each other and now I'm working all the time, and don't associate with any of them, even at the pub."

"It's a terrible thing Michael. Everything that's happened is because me and Kelly kept up that fight. It's been going on all our lives and it's not ending well for us. All I wanted was to get ahead and earn enough for us to have a good life.

I thought I was a decent man; a man whose word was his honour and I'm proud of it. I've worked hard and tried to be fair to everyone. I feel guilty because I didn't see what was happening to Brendan. I might've been able to stop him before things got so bad. Now tonight I've had another shock. I don't seem to be in control any more. I'm just exhausted, I'm gonna go to bed." He poured himself a large glass of whiskey and downed it.

"If you don't want to talk about it now, we'll finish this discussion tomorrow then. Good night, Dad," said Michael and walked out.

He overheard Michael say to the women "Just let him be, he's trying to figure something out."

Alistair was laying in bed when Millie came in. She rolled over to him, but he turned away. He heard her stifle a cry, like a wounded kitten. *If I touch her it will be like seeing that rape all over again. All I want is quiet and a good sleep. I'll deal with it in the morning.* It was a long night and he didn't sleep much at all.

I keep seeing Kelly there forcing himself on her, like a rutting dog. I can't get that picture out of my head. His fists were clenched with a hatred that consumed him. He thought back to that summer when he had been on the road a lot, trying to remember Millie. *That was the summer she spent a lot of time with her sister, when I got back from Cork. That must have been right after it happened. Then she found out she was pregnant and she was sick most of the time. I don't think I bedded her for quite a while. After Meagan was born, she was slow to come to me. Now I know why.* He finally drifted off to sleep.

Alistair woke up as Millie got out of bed that morning. She quickly got dressed with her back to him.

"Millie, I..."

"Alistair O'Flagherty, don't talk to me. Last night you turned away from me like I was damaged goods! I never led him on. I didn't encourage him. I gave myself to you. I'm the one who's been living in fear of what would happen all these years, if you ever found out. You're treating me like a common whore. I hope you're proud of yourself!" She slammed the bedroom door as she went out.

Dear God, I've never seen her so angry. I didn't mean to insult her. I just can't deal with it right now. He quickly dressed and left the house, avoiding the pounding of pots and pans in the kitchen. He rode to the quarry and buried himself in the stack of paperwork on his desk. *I'm way behind here. Is it only six weeks ago that I sat here with Brendan? Seems like a lifetime.* The day went quickly. Later, he and Michael rode home together.

Dinner was a quiet affair with very little conversation. Both Millie and Meagan were subdued. When Alistair finished his meal, Michael directed him back to the parlour. "Come on Dad, we've got business to deal with."

In the parlour with the door closed Michael folded his arms and stared at him. "Well? Let's finish the discussion from last night. Then you can tell me what's going on between you and Mum."

Running his hands through his hair, Alistair pondered. "Over the years things have happened at the quarry that I think Kelly arranged; perfectly good equipment broke down, my foreman suddenly moved away, someone let the horses loose, things got stolen. You've seen it too. Then about two years ago that stopped. I found out that Kelly joined Brendan's card group about then and I think he gave up sabotaging the quarry and started to manipulate things so Brendan lost money and we know the outcome of that, don't we?"

"Something happened at the prison with you and Kelly. What was it?"

"Yes, there is something you need to know, something much more personal. I'm having trouble even talking about it. Kelly had his eye on your mum years ago, but then we started courting and got married. I don't think he's ever forgiven us for that, just like he's never forgiven me for having the lease on the quarry." Alistair paused and took a deep breath. "He told me he was Meagan's father."

"What? That's not possible," said Michael jumping up from his chair. "Mum would never have gone with him, never."

"Millie told me last night that when I was on a sales trip nineteen years ago, he raped her. Meagan was born the following year..."

Michael looked horrified. "The bastard, he raped her – he raped my mother. If I could get my hands on him,

I'd kill him myself. Dad, you can't possibly think is was her fault. You're the only man she's ever wanted. She worships you. I've seen how she looks at you when you're not watching. You only have to look at Meagan to see there isn't one single drop of Kelly's blood in her veins! It doesn't surprise me in the least that she didn't tell you. You'd have ended up in prison at the very least for killing him. Why was she mad at you this morning?"

"I couldn't bring myself to touch her. In my head, I kept seeing Kelly forcing her down and it sickened me."

"It wasn't her fault, Dad."

"Michael, I know that."

"Do you love her?" he asked, glaring at his father.

"Of course, I love her."

"Then bloody well tell her that, because right now she doesn't know if you do or not" said Michael wrenching open the parlour door.

Meagan came in first, almost hysterical, her face awash with tears. "Oh Dad, Mum just told me what happened." She threw her arms around his neck and said: "He's not my father. I'll never accept that. You're the only one I've ever known and I love you. You've looked out for me all my life. Don't let Kelly's jealousy destroy us. Please!

Millie stood silently in the doorway, waiting. Alistair looked over the top of Meagan's head and gently let his daughter go. Alistair opened his arms to her. "Millie, I love you. I'm just so angry. I would like to kill that man with my bare hands. But I can't undo what he's done. He's destroyed part of the absolute trust we had in each other. You've been hiding this secret all these years and he knew it. I hope he rots in Hell for that because trust is precious and he's never known it." He pulled them to him and held them tightly. The O'Flagherty's stood in that silence of uncertainty. They stood clasping each other, the bonds of love and faith as complex and interwoven as a Celtic knot and just as durable.

Family Tree

Dublin, April 27, 1847

James O'Connor trowelled another layer of mortar onto the line of bricks and started laying another course, setting the bricks down carefully and eyeing the string that ensured the wall was straight. He could hear his brother Frank and the other two men in the work crew laughing about some incident at the pub as they unloaded a pallet of bricks from Plunkett's horse-drawn wagon. The horses stood patiently at the curb.

This new row of houses is coming along well. It's my first job as a fully qualified bricklayer. I'm so pleased my apprenticeship is finished. I'm nineteen and I was worried they wouldn't hire me full time with famine all over the country and all the unemployed tradesmen coming into the city. Now I can seriously think about asking Emma to marry me. I'm going to have enough income to support her if I'm careful with my money.

As he continued to lay bricks and trim off the excess mortar he thought about some small but nagging incidents that had occurred recently. *Even though Frank and I look alike in our features, I don't know of two brothers who are more different. I'm tall and gangly; he's shorter and more compact. Of course, he's two years older but he's confident, quick and lively; always laughing and teasing. The women just love him. I'm the quiet, serious one. The last couple of weeks, Emma seems to be spending a lot of time talking to him when she's over at our house. The way she looks at him when she thinks I'm not looking isn't right either. I don't know what's going on. I hope she's not falling for him.*

That evening after supper, James opened the door and Emma came bouncing in, giving his Mum and two sisters a hug as she removed her bonnet. *As usual, she looks lovely*, he thought. His heart skipped a beat and he greeted her warmly. She looked into his eyes and gave him that gorgeous smile that lit up her face. He desperately wanted to take her into his arms and kiss her but knew full well that it wouldn't be considered appropriate by his parents or indeed Emma herself. *I've got to mind my manners and behave like a gentleman.*

Later when James was talking to his father, he noticed Emma and Frank slipping out the back door together. *I don't know what they are up to but I'm going to find out.* "I'm just going out for a smoke," he said to his father and went out the front door.

Something's going on. I thought it was my imagination at first but now I'm not sure. While I was thinking Emma loves me, she still responds to his teasing ways. I saw her whispering in his ear the other evening, like they had a secret and he had his arm around her. I don't want to be jealous of my own brother. He's got a girl of his own but I don't like him touching my Emma one bit. I even saw them talking on the street once.

I love her. I've known her all my life. We've grown up two houses apart on this very street. I was planning on talking to her father in a couple of months when I've got some money set aside. She's been my girl for two years now. I know Mum and Dad like her. Emma's welcome in our house any time and chums with my sisters. I've got to find out what's going on! He slipped into the dark, narrow alley between the houses, following the sound of their voices.

"Do you think he's caught on yet?" said Emma.

"No" replied Frank laughing. "I don't think he knows a thing. It's going to be a big surprise."

I can't believe it. My own brother taking up with Emma behind my back! And I wanted to marry her! James quickly went back inside the house to be engulfed in the uproar of his younger sisters doing the supper dishes with his mother and his father sitting by the fire telling stories. He sat quietly, his head a maelstrom of conflicting emotions, barely registering the others around him. Later, after Emma returned home and the others had gone to bed, James knew he had to make a decision.

He sat on his bed. *If I stay, I'd be seeing Frank ever day at work. That would be like rubbing salt in an open wound. It would drive me insane to see them as a couple with me living in the same house as them. Even if they had their own place, I'd be seeing them at family get-togethers when she should have been with me. What the hell am I going to do? I could move somewhere else in Dublin but I'd still see them. With the famine being as bad as it is, I'm lucky to have my job at Plunkett's brick yard. My chances of getting a job somewhere else in Ireland is zero with the unemployment as it is.*

Frank's the favourite son. Mum and Dad think the sun shines out of his arse. I'm not even sure they'd miss me much if I left. Maybe it would be best if I get out of Ireland all together. Right now, I feel like throttling the bastard. There's a ship in the harbour heading for Canada. I should be able to get work over there with my skills.

He gathered up his savings in a small leather pouch and threw his spare clothes, boots and shaving gear into his carpet bag. Slipping on his tweed jacket and cap, he carefully went downstairs avoiding the squeaky ones. Looking around the parlour for the last time, he saw the family Bible on the sideboard and on the spur of the moment, took it and put it in his bag. *That's the only part of them I can keep.* He opened the front door and was confronted by Frank having a quiet smoke on the front step.

"Where are you going?" asked Frank, clearly surprised to see him fully dressed, with bag in hand.

"None of your damn business, you scheming bastard, stealing Emma from me!" He dropped his bag and punched Frank in the jaw with every ounce of strength he had. Frank flailed backwards down the steps and smashed into the pavement. "Go on, get up!" James taunted him, but Frank didn't move. He didn't even look like he was breathing.

Oh my God – I've killed him... James grabbed his bag and ran into the darkness of the street, leaving the body untouched, an expanse of blood pooling around Frank's head. *I've got to slow down or someone will notice me.* He dropped back to a brisk walk, staying in the shadows of the shop fronts as he followed the River Liffey to the quays. Few people were out at that time of night; whores trolling for business outside the taverns, drunks weaving their way home and sailors returning to their ships. By morning, he was aboard the Dover Castle, a small leaky famine ship heading to Canada with a hold full of gaunt and ragged farm families.

One act of anger and my life's changed. I can never go back. I've killed my brother and they'll hang me. I didn't mean to kill him. I'm losing everything - my family, Emma and my job. Yesterday, I was on top of the world with a job and good prospects. Now I'm running for my life. I told the Captain my name was Connor Plunkett. That's who I am now. He leaned on the rail. *How could this have happened? My life's a disaster.*

The ship sailed on the morning tide. He heard the creaking of her timbers and the snap of canvas as scrambling sailors worked in the rigging to set the sails. She pulled away from the Liffey and he felt her motion change as the bow met the waves of the Irish Sea.

The O'Connor household was in quiet turmoil that morning, even the girls were silent. Frank, pale and bloody, sat on a kitchen chair while his mother washed the congealed blood from his hair.

"Da, I'm telling ya, I don't know what happened. I was having a smoke and he came out, mad as hell. He was all dressed, like he was going somewhere. Told me I was a bastard for stealing Emma from him, then knocked me out cold."

O'Connor senior looked at his son and then his wife. He stood there thinking. "He was preoccupied last night, ever so quiet after he came back in. Did ya notice?"

"Came back in? What do ya mean?" asked Frank, wincing as his mother scrubbed. "Emma and I went out back to talk about the party on Saturday. We were all excited about him getting hired at Plunkett's brick yard after three years apprenticing. Real feather in his cap to get hired with the job situation like it is."

"Oh no," wailed Mrs. O'Connor. "He must have seen you two go out together and took it the wrong way. Where is he?" she said looking at her husband in total dismay.

Present day, Toronto, Canada

Pauline sat at the computer, immersed in an ancestry discovery website, when her sister Becky got home from work. Pauline scratched her head. "You know Becky, I've hit a dead-end with Connor Plunkett. I've got him on the passenger list on the Dover Castle, sailing from Dublin in April 1947 and landing in Toronto in June. I've not had any problem with subsequent generations but I can't get anything more on him. Even my Irish researcher is stumped; nothing on the census, no background, nada."

"So now what?" Becky asked as Pauline handed her a cup of coffee.

"I don't know, I can't think of any way around it."

Pauline was reading the Toronto Star after supper and came across a feature article in the second section on the Irish famine refugees landing in Toronto. "Hey Becky, did you read this? Thirty-eight thousand Irish landed here in 1847 when Toronto only had a population of thirty thousand to begin with. Can you imagine the chaos? A lot were sick with cholera or typhus and died. How would you even begin to feed and house them all? The Church opened up Providence house and the Catholic community did the best they could. No wonder there were tensions with the locals, especially the Protestants."

Pauline looked at the neat charts on her wall, showing five generations since Connor Plunkett had arrived. "It's taken me ten years to fill in all those blanks. We've got some new contacts now out in Alberta."

"Yes, it's amazing when you see more and more coming to our annual clan gathering. We keep having to find bigger places to hold it," said Becky. "Grandpa Plunkett really is a mystery. All we have is that ad from the 1863 newspaper for his bricklaying business. We know he was skilled and literate but from all accounts he was very private, almost reclusive. There's just that one photo showing him with his wife and five children. You've got his death certificate from the archives too."

"But I've never been able to find an obituary or his grave. He's not buried with his wife or his sons." Pauline thought about her Aunt Bea, her Dad's youngest sister and the last of that generation. *We just cleared her house following her death from cancer. I was there the day all the cousins arrived with their trucks and U-hauls taking the furniture, the china and the pictures. I got the books.* She looked at the stack of boxes blocking half their hallway; papers, photo albums and books. *Well, that's going to take some time to sort through. Maybe Becky can give me a hand with it.*

A month passed before they had time to search through the boxes. "Here Becky, you start with that box and I'll tackle this one."

Becky was sitting in the recliner removing books carefully one at a time. "She's even saved her report cards from grade school. What a treasure! There's lots of photos, Pauline. Look at this one. Dad's in it too and he looks about ten," she chuckled, gently handing the black and white photo to Pauline.

"It's pretty dry and cracked, but I think I can repair the image on photoshop, one pixel at a time," she replied.

Soon the table was stacked with old photo albums and loose photos. "There must be ninety years worth of photos here. I don't think you're going to have any trouble keeping busy with this lot."

"Now, what's this?" Lying in the bottom of the box was a linen bag. Unwrapping it Becky gasped. "Pauline, it's a family Bible, and a really old one at that."

They placed the book gently on the table in better light and opened its thick black leather covers. Pauline scrutinized the spidery writing. "This goes back to 1780. There's all kinds of entries here – births, deaths, confirmations and they're in all in Dublin. Wait a minute – this says the "O'Connor Family Bible". That's weird. This was obviously very important to her but why would Aunt Bea have this Bible? Who were the O'Connors?"

"I'm surprised she didn't tell you about it. She knew you were doing the family tree."

"Dad must have known too. Is this some sort of family secret do you think? Let me see what the entries are for the mid-1800's. Look, the last entries are for Thomas O'Connor and his wife, Mary O'Connor, and their four children: Frank, James, Mary Elizabeth and Aileen. James' birth date is June 21, 1829. That's the same as Connor Plunkett's." A wave of excitement coursed through her. "Becky, I don't believe in coincidences. He must have changed his name when he left Ireland. That would explain everything."

"Could he do that? Just change his name like that?" asked Becky, looking puzzled.

"That would have been easy in those days – no passports. Paying the fare was the only requirement. There was no paper trail until much later" said Pauline. "Now I've got something to go by."

She hit the trail like a bloodhound on a scent. *That Bible's been an absolute treasure trove. I've worked on Frank O'Connor's line and come up with two sons. One lad stayed in Dublin but the other one went to Londonderry.* "Becky, I've found a man in Londonderry that I think could be Frank's great, great, great grandson Terence O'Connor. I'm going to write to him and see what happens."

<u>E-mail to Terence O'Connor:</u>

Dear Mr. O'Connor: My name is Pauline Alverson (nee Plunkett). I am trying to track the family tree of my grandfather Connor Plunkett five generations back. I recently came into possession of a family Bible belonging to him (we think). He arrived in Toronto, Canada in June 1847. This is an O'Connor family Bible and gives the last generation as Thomas and Mary O'Connor of Dublin with four children: Frank, James, Mary Elizabeth and Aileen. There is a strong possibility that James O'Connor and Connor Plunkett are the same person or it might be a coincidence that they both have a birth date of 21 June 1829. There are no records of Connor Plunkett prior to those dates. My research indicates you descend from Frank, James' brother. I hope this is not an intrusion, but would appreciate any information you may have and are willing to share. Yours truly, Pauline.

Three months went by and no response. *Oh well.* Pauline went online and let out a howl. "Becky, I've got a reply from Ireland!"

<u>E-mail from Terence O'Connor</u>
Hello Pauline: Your letter caused quite a
stir in our family. I am new to genealogy
so there are lots of gaps in my information.
Our family split in the 1880s when my great
grandfather left the Dublin Catholics and
married a Protestant girl in Londonderry.
I do know that his sister Aileen married a
riveter named Harry Hobson, who worked in
the Belfast shipyards. James disappeared in
1847, details unknown. I believe both Frank
and James were working in the Plunkett Brick
Yard at the time of his disappearance. That
might coincide with the name change. Have
attached a photo of Thomas and family from
1884. Would appreciate copies of the Bible
entries and any pics you might have of James/
Connor. Thanks. Terence.

Pauline and Becky sat at the table, sipping celebratory
glasses of wine. "Progress at last." She saved the attach-
ment photo and printed out the old sepia tone Terence
had sent. Placing the two photos side-by-side she gave it
to Becky. "The resemblance is there; similar build, height
and facial features; tall, slim, sandy coloured hair, bit hard
to tell with the beards." She scanned the Bible entries and
e-mailed everything back to Terence.

❖ ❖ ❖ ❖ ❖ ❖ ❖ ❖ ❖

Six months passed and there was no further com-
munication. "Maybe he's busy or isn't interested. After
all, not everyone's obsessed like you are. Or maybe it's a
Protestant-Catholic thing" said Becky.

"Becky, we're making all these plans for the family
reunion for August. Why don't we invite Terence and
his family?"

"Sure, why not?"

E-mail to Terence O'Connor
Hi Terence: We are in the throes of
organizing the family reunion for August.
So far, we have sixteen of the twenty-two
families confirmed. You and your family are
more than welcome to come. Some with be
camping; others will be at a local hotel. The
Alberta clan are coming for the first time.
We always discover a few more details when
everyone gets together. If you have any recent
photos of you and your family, I love to have
a copy. Am attaching one of myself and my
sister Becky with Mum and Dad taken about
ten years ago, just before Mum died. Pauline.

"I don't think we'll ever know why Connor Plunkett changed his name. Terence has given me Aileen Hobson's name in Belfast. She's the next person I'm going to track down" said Pauline, keen to tackle another ancestor.

E-mail from Terence:
Hello Pauline: Would love to come to the reunion some time but finances don't allow at the moment. Have attached some photos, recent ones of Maddie and I with the two boys and one from the 80s of Mum, Dad with my three brothers and I in Londonderry. Haven't had much time to do genealogy lately. The job and the house are eating up my time. Keep me posted on developments. Terence.

E-mail to Terence:
Hi Terence. Can appreciate the cost problem especially with a young family. I have a thought. Do you have access to Skype? If you are interested, it would be easy to set up a video conference call from the campground so you can participate long distance and meet some of your distant cousins. We usually have a Saturday evening barbecue and go over the year's discoveries. That would be early

Sunday morning with the time difference for
you. Let me know if that is feasible. Pauline.

The 2nd weekend in August found the Plunkett clan
firmly ensconced in Bayside Campground. Campers,
motor homes and tents filled the park. "We've even filled
the motel across the road" said Becky, laughing.

They'd spent the previous evening setting up the
gazebo full of family history charts pinned up on the
temporary walls and photos of different groups. She'd
marked the site numbers on the various families present.
New additions to the charts were on green Bristol boards
and families were bringing Pauline the updated list of
births and deaths as they came in. Relatives of all ages
were gathering and talking. The noise level was rising
as the meet and greet started, smiles and familiar faces.
The parents were setting up the camp sites but the kids
were heading to the lake, the plate glass jewel of this
morning now a froth of splashing, laughing youngsters
and high-spirited teens. Canoes and wind surfers now
dotted the lake.

The usual chaos, thought Pauline, keeping her eye
open for Alberta plates. A large truck pulled in, towing
a twenty-eight-foot Jayco. It pulled into the lot beside
Pauline's trailer and she went over to meet them. The

couple were in their early forties and with them was their son, a tall lanky teenager who looked about eighteen, with his ball cap on backwards and a sullen expression on his face.

There's something about him that looks familiar, she thought, looking at his strawberry blonde hair and slim build.

"We're the Kershaws. I'm Brad with my wife Dianne and this is our son Jason." The boy grunted and went back to texting, barely acknowledging her.

"I'm Pauline. I can't tell you where Becky is at the moment. I'm so glad you've come and got here safely. Welcome to the clan. Come on over as soon as you get set up," she replied and went over to talk to a cousin she hadn't seen in five years.

Later she got back to her campsite to find Brad and Dianne talking to Becky. Jason was sitting on the picnic table his back to everyone. Pauline took a deep breath and approached him. "Hi Jason."

He looked at her.

"I can see you're not too happy about being here," she said.

"Stupid waste of time. I don't care about who my grandparents were. They're dead so they don't count. Mum made me come; I could have been camping with my friends," he said in an aggrieved tone.

"Well, if you look around, there are a lot of girls your age here. That might make your holiday a bit more interesting. I'll introduce them to you. Come with me and we'll do it now," she said.

Reluctantly he got up and followed her down the road. Pauline headed for campsite 11 where a group of teens were hanging out. She was looking specifically for Amy and spotted the leggy blonde in cut off jeans and tight-fitting tank top.

Pauline called her "Amy, come on over, I want you to meet Jason."

The girl walked over to them, her eyes on Jason and her whole group of giggling female friends tagged along. Pauline glanced at him from the corner of her eye and noted with satisfaction that the sullen expression on his face had gone, erased by grin that changed his whole appearance.

"Hi Amy, I want to introduce you to Jason. His family is from Alberta, they've just arrived, never been to Ontario before or one of our reunions and I thought you girls could show him around."

"Hi Jason," said Amy, flicking her long hair and she saw the smile on his face as he suddenly had five girls all around him. His eyes remained on Amy.

"Brilliant," said Becky quietly, behind Pauline, surveying the scene. "I thought we might some problems there but I think Amy's got it under control. You know, when he smiles, he's the spitting image of Terence."

The highlight of the weekend was the Saturday night barbecue. Fully sated on pulled pork, chicken and hot dogs, plus potluck salads and mounds of buns and homemade pies, all brought their lawn chairs over to the gazebo.

"Welcome all of you. I'm so glad you were able to come. I have special news. As you all know, I've spent the last ten years trying to find out information on Connor Plunkett, our mutual grandfather who arrived from Ireland in 1847 on a famine ship. When my Aunt Becky died among her things we found an old Bible. We had a mystery on our hands as it wasn't a Plunkett family Bible but an O'Connor family Bible. It took a while but we were able to trace that family back to Dublin. One of the sons was a James O'Connor who very suddenly left his family and came to Canada using the name Connor Plunkett. We don't know why." The crowd was hushed, captivated by the new development.

Becky had the computer up and running and Pauline grinned as she saw Terence's face on the screen.

"I want all of you to welcome a new group to our family. Thanks to Skype, tonight we get to meet Terence who lives in Northern Ireland. He can trace his ancestry to James O'Connor's brother Frank O'Connor."

A couple of curious people went up and spoke with him.

Pauline cut in again. "There are many people who don't see the value of ancestry. However, I would like you all to look around and see that there is a common thread in our group. Tell me what you see." Everyone was looking around. "Take a look at the one photo we have of Connor Plunkett and what stands out is the shape of the face, the strawberry blonde hair, blue eyes and a slim build. Jason would please come up here?"

Jason looked perplexed but left the mixed group of teens at the back to stand there staring at the man who was half way around the world.

"Meet Terence," she said.

Jason looked at Terence on the monitor; Terence looked back.

"Terence, what do you see?" she asked.

"I see someone who could easily be mistaken for me, ten years ago. It's like looking in a mirror and seeing a younger me. This is uncanny," was the lilting Irish reply.

"He's right. We look like twins," replied Jason, a look of surprise on his face.

"Five or six generations have passed, and the gene pool has been diluted countless times yet the core genetics still show and Jason's not the only one. She called the names of other boys and girls who joined him around the monitor. When the commotion had died down, she thanked Terence for participating and the Skype session ended.

"I still don't know where Connor Plunkett is buried," she said.

"Could he have been buried under his real name?" someone asked.

"That's a good question, hadn't thought of that" replied Pauline. "Oh, another thing. As you all know I lost my daughter to MS about ten years ago. I've been tracking the death certificates for quite some time to see if anything shows up in the Plunkett line. So far there is no indication of a familial disease cause on either side. Lots of things like pneumonia, or accidents, death in child birth that sort of thing. I have James' alias Connor Plunkett's sister to follow through on. Terence gave me her married name so I should be able to track it. I appreciate all the updates you have provided. On a closing note, it might be a bit fanciful, but tonight Jason Kershaw, coming from James' line, met Terence O'Connor from Frank's line, so in a way two brothers who have been separated by one hundred and sixty-some odd years have just been reunited. Just a thought."

the last violin

City of Galway, Ireland, August 1651

Annie Morris lay in bed wide awake. Today she and her husband Dewain would be sending their two youngest children away forever. It was a decision that tore her heart out but she knew what was coming. Cromwell's army would lay siege to Galway and it would be slow death to all Catholics. Ten years earlier had been the same and thousands had died of starvation or the plague. Strahan and Fiona would be joining the Lynch's three sons on Captain Piera's ship to Spain, to freedom and safety.

Later that morning she stood on the wharf clasping her daughter tightly. She could feel the sobs wracking Fiona's body right through her coat. She blocked out the noises, the shouts of deck hands moving the last boxes, barrels and luggage up the gangplank, the sharp orders of the Spanish captain urging haste as he paced the deck and the weeping of other families saying their goodbyes.

Over Fiona's shoulder she looked at her youngest son not missing a detail. She saw a slim lad dressed in his good suit, a mop of unruly black curls framing the boy's serious face. *I know, deep in my heart, that I'm never going to see them again.*

Her husband Dewain was talking to him. "Strahan, take good care of your sister. Alden Lynch's family will be on board so you're in good company," he said. "You won't have any trouble finding a job in Spain. Good violinmakers are a rarity. Son, I'm so proud of you," he said pulling the lad to him in a fierce hug.

Annie watched as Captain Piera strode down the gang-plank, the gold braid on his tricornered hat and uniform glittering. She knew the pistol and gold hilted sword strapped to his waist were no ornaments. *Dewain's told me stories of him; skilled with a sword he is. He's fought and killed pirates defending his ship back and forth from Spain to Galway bringing us wine. He's a strong, arrogant man in his Spanish way with that trimmed goatee and dark skin.* His eyes were everywhere and missed nothing. She watched him usher the three young Lynch boys aboard, then the three Ffrenches. *This will likely be the last boat to escape before the blockade starts.*

Strahan grasped his father and squeezed him tightly. "The six violins you've given us should get us a good start. Your violins always sell well in Europe. Thanks, Da. I'm going to miss you all," he said choking out the words as he came and kissed her goodbye. Squaring his shoulders, Strahan gently disengaged Fiona from her father and guided her up the gangplank, the hem of her long skirt swishing against the railings.

Annie watched as Piera and Dewain shook hands then the captain returned to his ship. *T'was the Captain who brought him his first Italian violin twenty years ago. Dewain had been making the tin ones then. I remember him taking it apart to see how it was made and it took him years to master it but now he's got quite the reputation for his violins.* She watched as Strahan and Fiona turned to look back over the rail. Her last view of Fiona was the tear stained face and the rich dark auburn hair cascading over Annie's hand knitted Galway shawl. An officer shepherded them to the lower deck out of sight and away from the bustle of departure.

Swarthy, agile seamen unwound the hawsers from the dock cleats then hauled in the gangplank; others swarmed the yard arms barefoot, unfurling the sails. A team of straining sailors pulled in the anchor in unison, its massive clanking chain rising from the seafloor meshed with dripping seaweed. Slowly the creaking ship pulled away from the dock as the salty breeze gradually filled the flapping sails and the red and yellow Spanish flag fluttered. Gulls swooped and screamed, following the ship, leaving the crowd at dockside to disperse. Annie and Dewain quietly joined the Lynch family, all eyes fixed on the receding three-master as it majestically rose to meet the line of white capped waves where the calmer waters of Galway Bay met the Atlantic.

Arlen Lynch took Dewain aside, leaving their wives to commiserate their losses. Annie heard Arlen say: "God willing they'll reach Spain safely. Things can only get worse here. Galway's the last holdout. Cromwell's boys are entrenched at Limerick but we're next. I might be the richest of the fourteen tribes, but once those damned parliamentarians arrive, I'll lose my land and all of my possessions like every other Catholic. God help us all." She heard the anger and frustration in his words. "Some bloody English Protestant lord will be living in my house!"

Dewain replied: "Arlen, sending the children away is the hardest thing I've ever done. 'Tis like tearing my own flesh, but I see only starvation or worse ahead. Annie here won't leave, neither will Devlin and Myles, my other boys. We can only hope that Farrell can raise a force up in Connemara to back us."

Annie briefly glanced at Thomas Preston, the military governor of Galway astride his horse, supervising the loading of the mountain of supplies left by the ship for the waiting wagons, to supply the garrison protecting their twenty-seven acres of walled town. *Aye, and he's got two thousand soldiers to feed,* she thought. Preston looked harried, deep worry lines in his forehead and he shouted to his soldiers to keep the milling poor away from the food supply. She held Mrs. Lynch's hand for a moment then squeezed it. *Both of us are losing our children.*

"We've got good defences. The twelve cannons will keep them at bay," she heard Arlen say, "but Coote's advance party is already digging a siege line between Lough-a-thalia and Suckeen, just north of us. I'll see you at Church and the Council meeting on Tuesday," he said, assisting his wife into the carriage with its uniformed driver. The pair of matched greys moved off at a brisk pace, parting the crowd and moving toward Lynch's Castle, the stone three story tower house on Abbeygate Road.

Annie pictured the day the new cannons arrived. Dewain and Devlin had been fascinated, watching the massive twelve-foot-long cast iron barrels being hoisted through the air to be carefully loaded onto the waiting gun carts. Teams of eight horses had been needed to move them. *That was quite a sight. Kegs of gun powder and the cannon balls have been arriving for weeks. Another war – it scares me. We lost so much the last time.*

They walked side-by-side, jostled by the throngs on the busy streets. Locals were buying whatever they could as supplies in the shops dwindled and strangers were desperately looking for shelter. "Gossip has it," said Annie, "that Browne's mansion is now full of refugees. Hundreds of them broke in just to get out of the cold and the rain. The park's full too. It's such a shame. Those Limerick families once had lovely homes and now look at them – filthy, tattered clothing, sitting on boxes in makeshift tents or under the wagons with open fires and cooking pots. Their poor horses are so thin; there's nary a blade of grass to feed them anywhere within these walls." *That could be us soon enough. How are we going to feed all these people? There must be hundreds here.*

They arrived at a short street with a solid row of two storey stone houses. Their house was one of the middle ones. Inside, Devlin, their eldest son was unloading herring from two pails and gutting them on the kitchen table. "I managed to get fish from the Claddagh across the river. They're bringing in as much as they can before they're blockaded. I was lucky to get that. It's a good thing we know Ewan over there for the peat and the fish. He put some aside for me. The Brownes and Sweeneys were fighting down by the bridge for what was left. It's bedlam down there. Don't you be going out by yourself, Ma. I wasn't sure I was going to get home without someone slipping a knife between my ribs to steal my fish. So, you got Strahan and Fiona on their way?"

Annie nodded then slipped out of her coat. After adding another peat log on the fire, she put on her apron and stirred the pot of stew. Dewain hung his coat on the hook and changed into his working clothes. He took the glass from the coal oil lamp and wiped off the soot, trimmed the wick with a small pair of scissors and set it on the table.

Annie watched Dewain as he wandered out to his workshop, lit his lamp and glanced at his workbench. She knew he'd be looking at the stacks of twenty-year-old dried sycamore, pine and maple destined to become his violins; his planes, saws, wood clamps, sanders and bundles of horse hair for the bows hung neatly on the walls. *I wonder if we'll be alive for him to finish another one.* She watched him run his hand over the framework of the newest creation, feeling the smoothness of the ribs as he removed the clamps holding them to the back template. He then examined the form of the ribs and nodded, and she knew he'd spend the next hour looking for the right piece of wood to make the back. *As always, it takes forever for him to find a piece with just the right feel and graining.* With a sigh, she turned and stirred the stew again.

She set the table with six bowls then came back to reality. With a sharp intake of breath, she realized there were only four of them now and a tear trickled down her cheek. Wiping it away with her sleeve she caught Devlin watching her. "I'm going to miss them a lot."

He nodded and continued gutting the fish. "Ma, it will be easier to feed four of us." He stood there with shirt sleeves rolled up, the razor-sharp knife in one hand and his forearms sprinkled with sparkling small fish scales. "I think we've done all we can to prepare. We've double barred the doors and shuttered the windows. We've got a barrel of salted fish, one of beef, flour, potatoes, grain and that bushel of crab apples Myles managed to get. God willing, that will last us. I'm thankful we've got a walled garden. Our well and the peat pile should be safe." He then carried the two pails out to the workshop to add the silvery fish to the brine barrel. She could hear the low rumble of their voices.

Deep in thought she went out to the well to fill the pail. *As evening comes the town gets quiet. No barking. I think most of the dogs have been eaten. The stray cats have disappeared too. It wouldn't surprise me if they were trapping rats again.* The two men came back into the kitchen half an hour later to the rising aroma of the stew. Loops of blood sausage were drying over the fire place, shrinking and curing in the heat. She put her arms around Dewain and he held her close.

"It's so quiet in here without Fiona," she said. "It feels like she's still here – look, she left some ribbon behind. I'm going to miss her cheery laugh and her temper when the boys teased her too much. Myles should be back soon."

"He's probably up at the King's Arms enjoying his last pint."

"Don't say that, Dewain. We must get through this," she said looking up him, fingering the gold cross around her neck. "We've survived the last ten years."

"Look what happened in '42," he said lighting the lamp and closing the shutters on the window to the invasive eyes of the street. "We lost our house because we supported the King. If we can't hold out here, Cromwell and his damned Parliamentarians will take everything. The Protestant families will just be fined, but we'll lose everything again. We've paid a high price for our loyalty to King Charles. My family's been here for two hundred years. They've been judges, magistrates, sheriffs and mayors in this town and it comes down to this." The three of them sat down at the table. Dewain said the prayer and she served the thick stew in silence.

A hurried knock at the door brought Dewain to his feet. "Who is it?"

"Let me in Da," called a voice from outside.

"It's Myles" said Dewain as he lifted the drop bar for his son. Myles was out of breath, his chest heaving and he looked grim. "What is it, lad? What's happened?"

Myles dropped the bar behind him. "Plague's broken out in the refugee camp."

"Oh no," cried Annie. "It's only two years since the last one. We lost over 3,000 people that time and had to leave and let it run its course. We can't get away from here now..."

The three men stood looking at each other; they were very much alike, short and wiry with dark, curly hair and blue eyes. "Don't worry about supper for me, Ma. I ate at the pub. Everyone's locking their doors."

They all sat around the table, deep in thought. *Plague again. It could last for months. It wasn't just the poor, it was everyone.* The gruesome sight of the sick and dying vividly flooded back to her; the white faces with blackened noses and staring eyes, the begging black hands, the open sores on the neck and legs, the bloody vomit. *I shall never forget that fevered young woman, so thin she was, crying right out there on our front steps, begging for the Lord to take her, every movement an agony. We didn't dare open the door. It would have meant death for us. She was dead by morning. They took her body and just threw it on the wagon with the others and dumped their corpses in the bay.* "God help us," she said out loud and they sat in silent prayer. *I wonder sometimes if her ghost lingers here.*

Later Myles opened his violin case and on cue Dewain went to get his. Myles paused momentarily to tune it and slipping it under his chin, drew the bow into the slow lamenting strains of "Away".

Annie watched and listened to her son play. *He's good.* His eyes were closed and his body was flowing with the melody, the bow arm smooth and sure. It was a haunting old song, so old it went back generations, often played at funerals but always played for those leaving. *That's the right one for this night,* she thought. She watched Dewain caress the wood then he started to softly play a counter melody, later joining the tandem lament, the notes rising to a crescendo of grief as only a violin could emote then in unison they slipped into the melancholy long and fading finale.

Myles paused and put his fiddle down. "Da, I don't really feel much like playing tonight. I pray for those souls out there. There's not much hope for them. I didn't have it in me to down to the dock to see Strahan and Fiona off. I said my goodbyes last night. I doubt I'll ever see them again. Whatever happens, they're better out of it." He sat hunched over staring at the floor.

She knew her boy was hurting; he had lost his betrothed in the last plague. Most of the girl's family had died too. Until now, that house had sat empty two streets over. *'Tis likely filled with more victims tonight.* Dewain took up his violin again and played softly into the night.

It was a gray morning with low cloud and the promise of rain. *It's Sunday and we must get ready for church.* Annie was already heating water for bathing and a pot of oatmeal had been slowly cooking overnight. Dewain washed his face and hands. Devlin came in from the privy to clean up. Myles came downstairs to join them, his braces hanging loose below his open shirt. He unbarred the front door and looked outside. "The street's empty except for a few

stray dogs up by DeBurgo's shop. They won't last long..."
His voice trailed off as he locked the door again.

There was little conversation at the table that morning.
The four of them left the house and walked along Shop
Street and on further to Main Guard Street. Annie tried
not to look at a body lying in the gutter. It was a half naked
older woman, thin and gray haired with the characteristic
blackened hands. They kept to their side of the street to
avoid her. *From the rags, it looks like one of the park people.
If it isn't starvation, then it's the plague.*

She looked at the massive stone structure of St.
Nicholas' Church with it's triple roofed facade and sturdy
spire. *This has been here for over three hundred years. There's
no other like it in all of Ireland, I'm told.* She pulled her shawl
over her head and they entered through the massive oak
doors. Once inside they walked down the main aisle to
their usual pew, genuflecting before stepping in. Dewain
acknowledged the Lynchs and the Ffrenches in their own
private sections off the main apse. She sat there looking
at the towering tapered stained glass windows, the pale
morning sun peeping through the clouds backlighting
the glorious coloured panels. The marble statues of the
cherubs, saints and Mary glowed white. She silently
prayed for all who had left and those here who were
staying, whatever the outcome.

The mood was sombre as the altar servers led the procession down the main aisle carrying the heavy ornate

gold cross. Father Thomas followed looking splendid in his white cassock, the pectoral cross hanging around his neck on a thick gold chain. He was followed by two deacons and a retinue of altar boys. He genuflected before the altar, and walked behind it to face his congregation and began the opening prayer. She could sense that Dewain, beside her, was lost in thought through the drone of the Latin Scriptures. Looking at her men, she knew they had been through so much already. *What's ahead for us? I look at my friends and family and it's nothing but anger and desperation.*

Father Thomas stood before them, resolute and respected. His voice carried to the far reaches of the building as he went into the Psalm and raised his arms in supplication to the Lord: "Deliver me from mine enemies, O my God and defend me from them that rise up against me. Deliver me from them that work iniquity, and save me from bloody men..."

The voices of the congregation joined in unison from every corner of the church; the rich deep voices of the men, the gentler soprano of the women and higher pitched tones of the children. All were on their knees for the Liturgy then the Lord's prayer. The altar boys brought the Host to the altar and Father Thomas blessed them. "Lord, hear our prayers." They joined the other petitioners forming lines to receive communion. She received the bread, the body of Christ, then the blessing before returning to their pew. She prayed for the safety of Fiona and Strahan, for Dewain, Devlin and Myles. *O Blessed Virgin, give me a mother's strength to get through this. Let me be the glue that holds this family together.*

Communion completed, she watched Father Thomas wipe the chalice clean then carefully placing it on the altar he stood before them. "Dark days are ahead. Our enemies gather beyond our walls. We know that if this, our earthly house be destroyed, that we have a building of God not made of mortar forever inside us and eternal in heaven, for we walk by faith, not by sight. The Plague is back amongst us. Lord have mercy for the afflicted. May the spirit of the Lord be with all of you to keep you safe from harm. Amen." He left the altar and proceeded down the aisle to the main door of the church, blessing every member of his congregation.

The unexpected boom of a cannon from the waterfront tower and a rising cloud of smoke brought all conversation to a halt. Startled, all turned to the harbour in time to see a cannonball from the fort shattering the water in an erupting fountain. Two ships were sitting just out of range beyond the breakers. *Oh my God, the blockade...* She turned to Dewain and the boys and said: "It well and truly starts now."

She heard Father Thomas behind her say: "God have mercy on all of us." A clatter of hooves on the cobbles announced Commander Preston as the officer and two dragoons galloped down the street toward the tower, scattering parishioners to the safety of the steps. Families quickly regrouped and departed for home leaving Father Thomas and the deacons gravely keeping watch.

Being confined to the house made Annie restless. *I usually visit Amy Browne and Clare Blake, but it's not safe to go out, and we're all afraid of the plague. Dewain and Myles are working on their violins and Devlin's like a caged animal if he's inside long. He's out somewhere. I never know what he's doing now he's not working at the shop in town.* She picked up her mending, darning the holes in Devlin's sock and repairing a tear in his jacket sleeve. *There would have been a time when I'd just have thrown that out and bought a new one – no more. We haven't got the money to spare.* She mixed up flour and water for a batch of scones. She rolled the dough into balls then flattened them, added a little grease to the frying pan and set them over the fire. *I know we agreed to two meals a day from now on, but everyone's so upset.*

Dewain came in from the workshop, trailing sawdust even after stamping his feet on the mat. "Scones is it? Smells good" he said sniffing the air and poking one with his finger.

Annie smacked his arm with her wooden spoon. "They're not ready yet."

He grinned. "I'm going to the meeting at Lynch's. I need to find out what's going on and what we do from here on. I expect to see my cousin there as well." A rumble of cart wheels made him look out the window. He turned back looking distressed. "Dear God, Annie, there's a whole wagon load of bodies heading for the bay."

She stood beside him and watched the ghastly procession. "Those poor souls. They didn't stand a chance, did they? They've had precious little to eat since they got here and it's been so cold and wet. They're all crowded together; if one gets it then all the others do too." She cried, her heart going out to the people in the park. "At least we've got a roof over our heads and food put away."

He went upstairs to change his clothes and on the way down snatched a fresh scone, the hot bun burning his fingers as he tossed it from hand to hand until it was cool enough to eat. Stuffing it in his mouth and licking the crumbs from his fingers, he smiled and winked at her. "I think they're done. I'll be off."

Annie looked at the ships beyond the breakers. *Every time I look at them, I feel trapped.* She barred the door and removed the pan from the fire. She went out to the workshop where Myles was making a diagonal cut across a block of sycamore. "How's it going?" she asked.

He paused momentarily. "The graining is beautiful on this piece. Da's always had an eye for the right wood. It just takes time to get cut it right. A mistake now would ruin the whole thing."

"I'm going to make a fish stew," said Annie, prying the lid from the barrel and scooping out four small fish. She gathered four potatoes and an onion and went back to the kitchen, leaving him sawing carefully into the block.

It rained all afternoon, the skies leaden with a stiff, cold wind that chilled the air but Annie was reluctant to add more peat. She looked around her house. *If I had to leave now what would I take?* She went through each room in the house. *Oh, there's so many things, but we don't have a wagon, so we'd be carrying it. It's depressing and I hope it doesn't come to that.*

It was nearly dark when she heard Dewain at the door. She let him in and she could tell by the look on his face that the news wasn't good. Devlin was not far behind him coming from the direction of the harbour and bounded up the stairs.

"Well, Da, what did you learn up at Lynch's?" asked Myles once they were eating their meal.

"Terryland, Oranmore and Clare-Galway Castles have fallen. Clanricade and his men just left Terryland behind when they saw Coote's force arriving. They're coming here by boat. Can you imagine leaving a fully provisioned

castle for Coote to just walk in and take? It's disgraceful;
Canricade's a bloody traitor!" said Dewain, "He should
have burned the place to the ground."

"Any word from Duke of Lorraine?" Devlin asked.

"The French would help alright but they want to own
Galway. Right keen they are. We're willing to give trading
concessions but ownership of Galway – no, we turned it
down. They're no different from the Marquis of Ormande
last winter, he wanted the same thing – ownership and we
refused then. We spent the afternoon arguing over on our
terms of surrender. No help to be had from Farrell either.
He can't get enough men together to come here. His lads
have been fighting Cromwell for eight years. They're tired
and sick and most of them have gone home if Cromwell's
left them a home to go to."

Annie listened in silence, clearing the bowls
and heating water to wash the dishes. "Did you see
your cousin?"

"That I did. Joseph closed up his shop here now that
the blockade's on so he's heading back to his Spiddal
house. Well, Devlin, what were you up to today?"

"I went over to the Claddagh's village to see Ewan.
His clan's got more freedom to move outside these walls
than we do. Some of the fisherman are taking their hooker
boats up the coast to fish and will move at night. With
the boats being black and small, they'll keep out of range
of the ships and there's nothing faster than a hooker in a

good wind. Big risk though. I warned him about the plague but he already knew. So far it hasn't happened over there yet. You know what they're like about letting strangers into their village; they're a kingdom unto themselves."

"You get in there easy enough. Rescuing Ewan like you did must make the difference" said Dewain.

Annie thought back to the time when Devlin found Ewan caught in a man trap when the boy was poaching on the Earl's property. *He freed him and carried him to the village on his back. That was a near thing. Lucky, they both weren't shot. They've been close ever since.*

"It's true. They're fine people in their own way. They're Catholics but they're not royalists so I don't think Coote will bother with their village much. The only good news is that the O'Flaghertys have held off Coote's party north of here so the western roads are still open to us if we want to leave."

Annie paused. *That's a glimmer of hope then.*

Monday was wash day. Annie heated the water and had her washboard and bar soap ready. *Good wind today and it's dry, so I can hang clothes out, much easier that stringing the clothesline in the house. As usual, Devlin's out.* She could hear the low murmur of Dewain and Myles talking in the workshop. *They must be putting the back pieces together, I*

can smell the glue. It took her all morning to scrub their shirts, socks, britches sand her skirts. *I'm thankful Devlin got me a good supply of brown soap.* By the end of the wash her hands were chapped and red from scrubbing.

She was pegging the clothes on the line, when she saw her immediate neighbours, Amy and Clare, doing the same thing. *Everybody washes on Monday.* Over the stone walls they engaged in lively conversation. "I'm so glad to see you both. I've wanted to visit but I'm so afraid of the sickness. Is everyone on the block well?"

"We're alright but I haven't seen Aileen down the end for three days now. Did you know that Coote is letting in more Limerick refugees? He knows full well we can't feed them. It's a cheap and dirty way to get rid of people!" replied Amy. "I wish you two would come over for a visit. I'd love the company even if we only say some prayers and get our sewing done."

"I'll have to check to my husband about it," said Clare. "Being locked inside with my men all the time will drive me mad. All they do is argue, plot and plan and have no power to do anything. I wish we'd had enough money to get on that boat, too."

"I'll be seeing you," said Annie as the three of them went back inside their houses. It was later the next day when she saw people running and heard a commotion on the street. "Dewain, come, come! Something's happening!"

He unbarred the door and they stepped out. At the last house in the row a crowd had gathered and the sergeant was trying to force the door. "That's Aileen's house," she said, feeling the dread rise inside her. Repeated blows to the door forced the lock. The sergeant cautiously went inside. He was gone no more than a minute and came out shaking his head.

"They're all dead... The plague."

A collective groan went through the crowd. "Oh my God, there were eight of them... The children, too?" She went back into the house and sat down heavily at the kitchen table her mind a jumble of images of the family she knew so well. "We won't even be able to bury them," her voice husky. She sat there and sobbed until she could cry no more. Later that day, the death cart stopped at the end of the road and she watched the bodies being removed.

Dewain stood beside her with his hand on her shoulder. "By dark, there won't be one piece of furniture or clothing in that house. It will be stripped clean."

The following weeks brought more losses. "Annie, I despair of even going to church. There are more dead in this town than there are living. They're using soldiers to move the bodies now and they can't keep up with it," said Dewain. "The plague is at the fort too."

"The last time we were in church, there were so many empty pews. I wasn't sure if people had died or if they were too scared to leave their homes," she replied. "God forgive me, but I don't want to go out any more. I don't want to see those bare corpses stripped of their dignity, robbed of even their wretched clothes, lying in the gutter, waiting for the death wagon." She broke into tears and fled upstairs to their room.

She came back down in time so prepare the evening meal, her eye lids still red and swollen. She could hear Dewain puttering in the workshop. Myles was quietly playing his violin. "What have you been doing?" she asked.

He put the bow down, resting the violin on his knee. "Da's been shaping the back and I found a good piece of ebony for the scroll and neck. Piera brought us that years ago, so it's well aged but it's beastly hard to work. Even with a good gouge, it's taking its own sweet time to shape. Da's right, you really can't rush it," he said resuming his playing. "I'm learning to have his patience."

Dewain came back in and sat at the head of the table. "I think this would be a good time to say some prayers, especially for Aileen and her family." They bowed their heads and gave thanks for what they had and for having been spared so far. The meal was eaten slowly and in silence.

We're all losing weight. I can see the marks on their belts where they've tightened up a notch and my skirt is loose. Our food supply is dwindling. We may have to cut back even more. Where is Devlin?

It was well after dark when Devlin got home.

"Where have you been today, lad?" asked Dewain.

"Up at the fort. Spies have reported back - Limerick's fallen. They've surrendered, but Ireton's ignoring the Terms of Surrender and doing as he pleases. They've destroyed churches, dug up graves and started evicting people. They've even killed priests. Anyone who has supported the King will be losing their property."

"Now it will be us," said Dewain running his hand through his hair in despair. "Limerick's siege was lengthy and cost Ireton dearly in men and supplies. I heard he's caught the plague, but they'll will send someone else against us. I don't think they will honour our terms either."

It was late November and the sun was rarely out. Annie sat near the window mending clothes. *We all keep busy. Dewain's violin is coming along nicely. He's finished the back and glued it to the ribs. It'll be the belly next. Myles finally got the scroll done. I think he's drilling the holes for the tuning pegs. Council's still arguing on the terms of the surrender. They've turned down Coote's offer. 'Twas the same one they gave Limerick. I don't think we can hold out much longer.*

She looked across the street. Two more families had died but the houses were now full of families of rank and the clergy escaping Limerick. A fully loaded wagon of bodies passed down the road toward the harbour. *The*

soldiers driving that team doesn't look much better than the
dead they're taking to the bay. When will it end?

Distant cannon fire brought everyone out onto their front steps. "We've got a sea battle going on here; some-one's trying to run the blockade!" cried Myles pointing to approaching sails of two merchant ships beyond the Aran Islands. "The wind's not in their favour" he said putting a dampened finger to the wind.

The pursuing English frigates were firing warning shots. Over the next twenty minutes, the crowd stood still, mesmerized by the drama as the slower merchant ships fought the wind but were inexorably drawn within firing range.

"They're driving them onto Aran Island... They're not going to make it!" cried Dewain. A collective groan went up from the street as one of the merchant ships struck the far rocky shoreline and continued fire from the frigates hit the second ship, which slowly started to sink. The sails and masts toppled and disappeared as the waves consumed them leaving silent, endless waves. People quietly went back inside their houses. Looking at her neighbours, Annie couldn't help but notice how thin and haggard everyone was. *My God, I barely recognize Amy. They must be running out of food and I've none to spare.*

"Tomorrow's tides will be washing the bodies and the driftwood ashore here. That'll be fuel and clothing for somebody" remarked Dewain.

Later in the week, Devlin went out as usual but Myles, who usually stayed home. also left shortly after. *I don't know where he's gone. Not like him to go anywhere. Those two are so different. It seems strange with just Dewain and me.* She swept up the trailing of sawdust and dumped them on the fire which flared into sparks of light. She went out to the workshop where Dewain was hunched over the workbench, slowly gouging out the shape of the violin's belly reducing the thickness of the wood. She could see the curve slowly emerging from the block. She swept up all the shavings and placed them in a bucket. *I'll save that for this evening. The peat pile is down by half already.*

It's getting colder, just above freezing, brrr. She shivered and pulled her shawl around her and just sat by the window. *I just don't feel like doing much today.* She got out her knitting and quietly worked on a sweater for Dewain. *I've got enough wool for two more.*

It was late afternoon when the sound of sustained musket fire had everyone out on their doorsteps. "It's coming from the north, from the fort," said Dewain. The gunfire became sporadic then stopped after fifteen minutes. "No cannon fire, that's odd," he said. The rest of the afternoon was quiet.

Annie was pacing. "Dewain, it's getting dark and the boys aren't home yet. I'm getting worried. What's happened? Devlin's always up to something but Myles isn't like that. Where are they?"

"I don't know, Annie. Neither of them said anything to me this morning." He went back to the workshop but emerged a short time later. "I can't work on that violin now. I can't get the boys out of my mind." Together they sat at the kitchen table, silently prayed and waited.

Voices outside their door jolted both of them. Dewain flung the door open and it was the sergeant half carrying, half dragging a wounded Devlin up the stairs. The boy could barely stand and was covered in mud. The dirty bandage on his left thigh was black with blood and his shirt and britches shredded. They sat him down on a chair and Annie clung to him.

"What happened?" demanded Dewain, turning to the sergeant.

"A group of the young lads cooked up a scheme with O'Leary to bring in a hundred head of cattle. O'Leary had been gathering them quiet-like and about eighty of the boys went out to bring them back to town. They went cross-country and almost made it back. They were within half a mile of our walls when Coote's snipers saw them and opened fire. The cattle stampeded and got away. He got caught in the stampede after he'd been shot," he said with a nod towards Devlin. The man paused, "We only got twenty boys back."

Annie gasped "Myles?"

The sergeant lowered his eyes and shook his head. "He didn't make it back. There are a lot of bodies out there but we can't get to them without being fired on. I'd better be going," he said looking at a grim Dewain.

Together they stripped Devlin's bloody shirt. Annie ran upstairs grabbing clean clothes, clean rags and a couple of blankets. Dewain threw more peat on the fire and moved the lamp to the table.

"Let's get a good look at him," he said as Annie started washing the mud and dried blood from her son's face revealing a jagged cut on his left temple, a severely swollen left eye and cheek. Devlin was silent except for an occasional groan when she touched a sore spot. Dewain poured a large glass of whiskey and put it in Devlin's hand. He barely had the strength to sip it.

"What do you see, Annie?" asked Dewain as he scrubbed away the mud on Devlin's chest and arms. The water in the pail was dark brown and murky already.

"Mostly hoof prints, bad bruises, a lot of small cuts all over his back," she replied. "He's black and blue all over. Bring me another pail of water, will you?"

Dewain brought in a fresh pail and heaved it on the stove. He went upstairs and dragged the straw mattress down from the boys' room and put it on the floor.

Together they helped Devlin stand and half-carried him to the mattress. *He sounds like a wounded animal any time he moves.* Annie took her scissors and cut the seams of his britches, tossing them aside then cut the bandage.

Oh Lord, there's a gaping hole the size of my fist in his thigh where the musket ball's blown it away. Gently she removed the mud and soaked off the wad of cloth someone had stuck in the hole. Devlin cried out then grabbed his ribs, drawing up his knees, his face contorted in agony. Dewain held his head up and placed the glass of whiskey to his lips. As the raspy, uneven breathing started to settle, Devlin took another sip.

Annie hurried to her cupboard and found a bag of comfrey. Taking a cupful, she stirred in a small amount of hot water until it was a gooey green mass. Gently she applied it to the open wound, covered it with clean cloth and bound it with linen strips. "He's exhausted, let him rest now," she said applying the last of the comfrey to the gash on his forehead. "I'll leave that one open, it's not deep."

The two of them sat there through the night in a silent vigil. Annie prayed. *Please, dear Lord, save my son. He's the only one I've got left now. Myles is somewhere out on that field and I can't bring him home. I can't even give him a proper burial.* Totally numb, she rested her head on the table and dozed off.

Daylight brought little relief. "Dewain, he's running a fever," she said, her hand gently on his forehead. She checked the bandage; it was pink-tinged and wet. Tucking the blankets over him, she put more peat on the fire and stirred the oatmeal. "I need to change this soon and I don't have much comfrey left, nor any willow. He's going to need something for the pain. We don't even have much whiskey. I'll have to visit my friends and find some. I won't be gone long. If he wakes up give him some gravy from the stew."

Annie left the house with Dewain sitting quietly beside his son, watching every move. She hurried down to Shop Street, oblivious to the stares of the strangers, past the closed stores to a tiny stone house tucked away in a back street near the Spanish gate. She rapped sharply on the door.

"Who is it?" came a growl from inside.

"It's Annie Morris."

She could hear the chain jingle and the door opened a crack. The shrunken, wizened face of Ken O'Connor looked back at her. "What do you want, Annie?"

"Devlin was shot in the cattle raid. I need some herbs if Millie has any to spare," she said.

"Millie's gone, died a month ago and my boy died in the raid," said Ken.

"I'm so sorry Mr. O'Connor, I didn't know. Myles died out there too, somewhere on that field. I'll go and see if Mrs. Martin can help me. God help us all," said Annie.

Before closing the door, he said: "Don't be wasting your time. She's gone too – plague wiped out her whole family." Then he disappeared into the gloomy room, leaving her on the doorstep.

What am I going to do now? I don't know anybody else. A wild thought entered her mind… The Claddagh. *Dare I go there? Devlin could die if I don't.* With a resolute step, she passed the soldiers and walked under the arch of the Spanish gate. The dock area was deserted. The closer she got to the bridge, the more she could feel her resolution fading as she put one foot in front of the other but finally crossed it. *I can see all the thatched roofed cottages of the village but I don't know where Ewan lives.*

Two men were mending fishing nets beside their upturned boat on the pebbly beach. As she continued on the pathway, one stood up and walked toward her. He was thin and wiry with a few days stubble on his chin and tweed hat firmly pulled down against the wind. Two very clear blue eyes peered out of his weather-beaten face and looked her all over. "What would you be wanting over here, Missus?" he said, blocking her way.

Annie was shaking so badly she could hardly speak. "I need to find Ewan," she said as firmly as she could muster. *I don't even know Ewan's last name.*

"And what you be wanting him for?"

"I'm Devlin Morris' mother. Devlin was shot in the cattle raid and I need some herbs to help him mend. There's no one left in Galway to help me. I thought Ewan might know..." Her voice trailed off as her courage almost deserted her.

"Padraigh," he yelled to the other man, "go get Carrick. Missus, we're being especially careful with the plague and all." The other man walked down the muddy lane into the maze of cottages.

They waited silently. Annie looked at Galway for the first time from the outer shore. The view around the bay showed the surrounding wooded hills clothed in the winter drab of gray, the rocky shores darkly forbidding. *I never knew those stone walls were so tall and so thick.* She watched the soldiers beside their cannons on the ramparts, the barrels aimed at the blockade ships slowly cruising the bay. *Those ships seem much closer here. Oh God, I can see things floating on the tide. They must be plague bodies. The gulls are feeding on them.*

Hearing footsteps on the shingle she turned to see Padraigh returning with a nondescript man maybe the same age as Dewain, dressed in tweed, a man who would have passed unnoticed in a crowd. He approached her. "I'm Carrick O'Shaughnessy, King in these parts and Ewan is my son. Who are you and why are you here?" he asked, his Gaelic accent thick. She noticed the Claddagh ring on his finger; the other men wore them too.

He listened carefully to every word, watching every gesture she made. "And you came over here to help Devlin?" She nodded her head. "Where's your husband, does he know you're here?"

"God no! He's at home with Devlin. He'd never have let me come," she said rolling her eyes in horror. "There'll be the devil to pay when I get home."

The corners of Carrick's mouth twitched in a ghost of a smile. "Well, Missus Morris, I think my wife can help you. Devlin saved our son Ewan. Maybe God's given us the opportunity to help yours." He turned toward the cottages and beckoned her to follow.

The cottage was small, clean and cozy. *It's good to get into the warm.* The older woman, in the corner chair knitting and the girl cutting up potatoes, both stopped and looked at her with surprise. "Boann, this here is Devlin's mother, Annie. He's been shot and she needs herbs to heal the wound," he said and walked out.

What do I say to this woman? thought Annie.

"It's seldom we get visitors. What is it you need, then?" asked Boann, appraising her.

"I'll be needing more comfrey and any willow bark if you have it, anything to heal the wound and keep him comfortable," she said. "I don't know much about herbs and there's no one left in Galway to ask, so I'm here. I was hoping someone would know these things." The daughter was standing there with her mouth gaping, looking aghast.

The old woman went to her cupboard, rummaged through several cloth bags and brought one to the table. "Fenella, go out back and bring me some willow bark. It's in the wooden box and while you're at it, bring the honey jar." The girl disappeared into the back room.

"Your Devlin and my boy Ewan are as close as brothers," she said. "They hunt and fish together. Only the Lord knows the mischief they get into. Neither of them mind taking a risk."

"I never know where Devlin is. He doesn't say. He comes here often, then?" said Annie intrigued.

"That he does. Mind you sometimes I think it's more than Ewan that brings him back" with a quick glance over her shoulder as Fenella came back in the room.

I'm more concerned with keeping him alive than which pretty girl he's chasing. Annie watched as Boann quickly wrapped up the comfrey and the pieces of willow bark in linen, along with a chunk of honey comb in paper and a small bottle of clear liquid.

"Get him to chew on a sliver or two of the bark; it'll ease the pain. A small dab of honey around the edges of the wound - works better than the comfrey sometimes. Hide this in your pocket, it's precious," she said putting a small bottle in Annie's hand. "It's sacred water from St. Brigid's well. Put a couple of drops on his lips every morning and pray to the Lady. I'd give you some poisin but you'd never get a bottle of moonshine past the soldiers at the gate."

Annie was trembling with emotion, the tears welling up in her eyes. "Bless you, Boann O'Shaughnessy, you're a good woman. I lost my son Myles out on that field yesterday. I don't intend to lose the only one I've got left." Annie threw her arms around the startled woman and hugged her. Then she quietly slipped a few small coins into Boann's hands. "I wish it was more." The two women looked into each other's face. *She knows what it is like to nearly lose a son,* she thought as she opened the door and hurried along the stony path back to the bridge. The men nodded to her as she passed by, momentarily pausing their net mending to watch her cross the bridge out of their territory.

The soldier stopped her as she walked through the Spanish gate. "What would ya be wanting with the Claddagh, Missus Morris?" he said eyeing her with curiosity.

"Just some herbs to keep the infection out of Devlin's wound" she said showing him the bundle of comfrey. She felt the little bottle in her pocket bumping against her thigh. She knew this man, he was one of the Ffrenches. *I'd lie if I had to. God forgive me. This soldier knows Devlin. For that matter, it's a small place and we all know each other.*

"You'd best be on your way then, but I'll go with you. You can't trust the streets. Charlie, look after the gate. I'm taking Missus Morris home."

Dewain flung the door open when she knocked. "Annie where have you been? It's been hours!" he said grabbing her by the shoulders. The soldier slipped away.

Annie's eyes went straight to Devlin who was looking very pale, lying on the mattress, propped up on pillows. She put her bags on the table and took the bottle from her pocket. *Confession time...*

Taking a deep breath, she faced him. "Dewain, I'm alright. It's been a difficult day. I went to Millie O'Connor's but Ken told me she was dead. He lost his son yesterday too. Then I found out Mrs. Martin had died. There was nobody left in town to go to, so I went to the Claddaghs."

"You did what?" said Dewain. "Good God woman, you were by yourself!" There was an angry edge to his voice. "I wouldn't have let you go alone! What sort of man would I be to let you go there alone? What will people think?"

"What choice did I have? I need to heal this wound and who'd have taken care of him if you'd come with me? Besides, this was a woman thing and I did fine with Ewan's mother. I probably wouldn't have got the medicines if you'd been with me" she said her eyes never leaving her son's purple swollen face.

"Ma, you went to the Claddaghs?" a hoarsely whispered query from Devlin.

Kneeling beside her son she said: "That I did. Boann O'Shaughnessy is a kind and generous woman." She uncorked the bottle and put a few drops on a spoon. She placed it gently on his dried lips, like she was giving him absolution. He licked it, a question in his eyes. *At least he can open the left one now, the swellings down a bit.*

"It's sacred water from St. Brigid's well. I'm to give it to you once a day and pray."

"I'm surprised she parted with it; 'tis a treasure to her. She's wise in the old ways" he said, lying on the mattress in such a weak state that Annie was scared. *Just saying the words has exhausted him.*

She placed a sliver of willow into his mouth. "Now you chew on that. She said it would help the pain. I'll change the bandage." Her eye caught sight of a pile of bloody bandages on the floor.

"Who took them off?"

"The surgeon from the fort was here and sewed together what he could. There's still a fist sized hole. He thinks he's got broken ribs too. Father Thomas just left."

Annie pulled back the blankets and looked at the fresh bandage, then covered him back up. "I'll leave it 'til morning. I'll be getting supper then..." Dewain followed her into the workshop as she took a small piece of beef from the brine barrel and a handful of potatoes.

"Annie, he didn't know Myles was dead. It's hit him hard and he's blaming himself for taking him along. Father Thomas talked to him and gave him the blessing. He told Father that God could forgive him, but it would be much harder to forgive himself."

Annie coaxed Devlin to take a few mouthfuls of stew but he rolled over to drift into a fitful sleep.

Dewain finally broke the quiet. "Annie, I've made up my mind. As soon as Devlin's well enough to travel, we're going to leave here. It's a hard decision. I've never even been out of Galway."

"And where will we be going?"

"Over to Spiddal, to my cousin's house to start with, then we'll see." Dewain took out his violin. The lone violin sounded mournfully like a lost soul. She could see his eyes on Myles' violin hanging on the wall. He played most of the evening, playing to the son he'd lost and the wounded one lying at his feet. First, she washed the bowls then the soiled bandages and hung them to dry. Then she sat and listened.

Annie woke up early with Dewain still asleep. She realized a whole week had gone by. *It's been the same every day:*

tend Devlin's wound, try and get him to eat and watch my husband working in silence on his last violin. I don't think any of us knew how much Myles did here... He was the quietest of the lot, and yet he took a lot of space. I miss him. I've spent a lot of time praying to St. Brigid, bless her. The wound is healing well but Devlin's spirit is unsettled. Myles is preying heavily on his mind.

Coming down the stairs, she saw the empty mattress and for a moment her heart raced but there he was, sitting at the table. Somehow, he'd gotten his shirt on and wrapped himself in a blanket. How he'd managed to get to the chair she couldn't imagine. She opened the shutters and daylight revealed her son to her. *The bruises are fading to yellow now. He's nothing but skin and bones and he looks like a wild man with a week's worth of hair on his face.*

"I'm glad to see you're up," she said adding peat and a couple of pieces of wood to the fire.

"I can't believe how weak I am, Ma." he said. "I can't even get my britches on."

"That's alright. After you get some oatmeal into you, I'll change the bandage, then we'll get you dressed. Are your ribs still hurting?"

"I still get a pain in my right side if I take a deep breath or move the wrong way. But it's not as bad as it was. I chewed some willow; it helps."

"Boann told me you were a frequent visitor in their house, not just to see Ewan either. Is it Fenella then?" she asked trying to distract him from Myles.

There was a pause and he looked at her. "Aye, Ma. I'm right fond of the girl. Me and Ewan go back nearly ten years so she's been like a little sister. But she's not a little girl any more; she's becoming a beautiful woman. I think she has feelings for me," he said spooning in some oatmeal. Annie gave him two drops of St. Brigid's water.

"She certainly looked very upset when I told them you'd been shot."

"Being an outsider, I'm not sure the Claddagh will let us marry. That would be up to Carrick. Other than hunting and fishing, I've got no skills to support her. Depends on how this leg heals."

"When you were little, you used to help your father in the tinsmith shop. He could teach you again. His violin making days may be done if we have to move. We've burned some of his wood to keep the fire going. Spiddal's just across the bay, so if you were living in the village, you'd only be a boat ride away. It's up to you to get yourself better and find a way, if that's what you want," she said. "Now let me look at your leg."

The wound's clean, the edges pink and shiny. There's still that big hole in the middle leaking but it's clean. Moving around hasn't made it bleed. "I'm surprised it didn't break bones" she said.

"I'm surprised the bloody cows didn't kill me."

"If you're feeling up to it, perhaps you could shave. The water's still hot. You look like one of the beggars on the street," she said, smearing a small amount of honey on the edges of the wound and snipping out the surgeon's horsehair stitches. The wound held. She filled the hole with comfrey and rewrapped the leg. "It's a whole lot easier to do this with you sitting up. Now let's get your britches on."

It was awkward but once she got the britches over his ankles and pulled half way up to his knees, she helped him stand and he did the rest himself. "Your father's going be so pleased to see you up," she said pulling his socks and shoes on. She placed the straight razor and mirror on the table.

"Who's taking my name in vain?" said a voice from above as Dewain came to the head of the stairs. "Oh good, you're up. Your mother's right, I am pleased, very pleased. We thought we'd lose you too, for the first few days."

Dewain opened the door and looked outside. "There are a couple of ships down at the dock flying English flags. Maybe the blockade's over and supplies will get in. Two English dragoons are coming up the street. Look, the horses are pushing the crowds apart. They're heading to the fort," he said closing the door.

March had come with a warming of the winds, more frequent sunshine and the landscape turning into waves of pale green. Annie hung out the washing. *I'm thankful it's warmer. There's hardly any peat left. Amy and Clare aren't saying much. They look awful. Seems like the plague is over. Haven't seen the death cart for a week now.*

Dewain returned from another council meeting. "Ludlow will be arriving this week and it will be Clanricade doing the formal surrender discussions. Preston's making arrangements to leave on the next available boat along with a few hundred of our soldiers. If he doesn't get out now, they'll hang him. Some of the clergy want to go too. Colonel Peter Stubber landed yesterday with two platoons of soldiers. He's going to be the new military governor. He's moved into the High Street house."

"What about the Lynches?" said Devlin sitting with his crutch propped up against the table, several nicks showing from his botched shaving job.

"They hoping to keep their property and pay a fine of one third its market value. I'm doubting it will be that easy."

"When will we be leaving?" asked Annie. "I've been through my things and I know what I want to take. Will we have a wagon or are we carrying it ourselves?"

"Devlin, do you think Ewan can get us to Spiddal in one of their boats?" asked Dewain.

"I don't know Da. I can try to get a message to him."

"I've almost got that violin finished. I finished the purfling and f-holes on the belly last night. I've signed it and glued the belly on. Just have to varnish it now. I'd like to take some of the best wood with me and my tools. I can start up again somewhere else or go back to making tin ones. As soon as we can, we'll go."

Annie looked out the window. The English presence was more obvious with soldiers out on the street. Dewain and Devlin had left together earlier. *They've gone to the Spanish gate to see if they can get a message to Ewan.* She started packing her clothes into a sea-chest. She took Myles' violin from the wall and gently looked at it. *It's the best one he ever made.* The wood was stained a mellow deep mahogany with chestnut highlights, smooth as silk to the touch. *I can see through the f-holes – yes, there's the Morris signature inside. My heart aches for my gentle son.* With great care, she placed it and the bow between her dresses in the trunk. *That should protect it from any rough handling.*

There was a knock at the door. "Who is it?" she called out.

"Annie, it's me, Amy. Please open the door."

Annie pulled up the bar. Amy was looking distraught. "Come in, come in. What's happened Amy?" she cried, clasping her arm and drawing her into the room.

"Oh Annie. Harry's just got back from the church. The soldiers have smashed the statues and are stabling their horses in there... In our beautiful church! And they're burning all the Bibles and records." Amy burst into tears.

Annie couldn't believe it. "Our church a stable? Where's Father Thomas?"

"Harry says they've got him in the prison cells up at the fort."

"Remember what Father said, Amy... The Lord is in our hearts, not in the building... But it's criminal to do that to a church." They both quietly stood and said a prayer for their pastor.

Amy dried her eyes on her sleeve and looked at the half-packed trunk. "So, you'll be leaving, then."

"Aye, but I don't know when yet. Dewain and Devlin have gone to send a message to Ewan. We're hoping to go to Spiddal by boat, if they can get hold of him. I've got some things I'm not taking. Do you want to go through these clothes? I've lost so much weight they don't fit any more, but they're a bit fancy, too. I don't think I'm going to need fancy for a long time. They're good quality and you could take them in or use the material."

Amy took half a dozen and gave Annie a big hug. "I'm wishing you luck. We've been friends for a long time. I'll be missing you. I must get back home. There's no leaving for us. We'll have to tough it out," she said as she opened the door and was gone.

Annie barred the door again and felt her shoulders slump. *Father Thomas in prison and horses in the church, how can it get worse?* She took some fish from the nearly empty barrel and wearily went about making a stew.

Within the hour Dewain and Devlin returned. Dewain helped a badly limping Devlin wobble up the steps with his handmade cane. Annie passed on Amy's news. "Well, I can see that no matter what document we draw up they're not going to abide by any conditions and will do as they please! The first week in April should see an official surrender."

"Did you find Ewan?" Annie asked.

"That we did. With the blockade over, the Claddagh are out fishing. Fresh fish will be a good thing for those with money to buy it. I've sent a letter to my cousin. Ewan will get one of his boys to deliver it to Spiddal. He'll bring a boat over on Friday if the weather's favourable. We'll pack up and I'll see if I can get a horse and cart to take it down to the dock." He looked at the bare wall. "Where's the violin?"

"I packed it in with my clothes. Do you want me to get your clothes ready too? I'll be needing a box to put my dishes in and another one for the linens."

He nodded. "I'll just put another coat of varnish on the violin then I'll find you some," and quietly went into the workshop.

Devlin was just sitting. He looked gray with exhaustion. Annie opened the cupboard and handed him a piece of willow which he took and silently started chewing. "Do I need to change the bandage?"

"Later Ma, not now. It's wet but it can wait. Just a walk to the dock and I'm as weak as a babe," he said and lay down on the mattress. It seemed he nodded off almost as soon as his head hit the pillow.

It was later that evening as darkness fell they heard voices from the street. Dewain looked out. "I don't believe it. The soldiers are rounding up women and children refugees from the park. They're heading for the docks. There must be over a hundred of them. There were two ships tied up on the quay this morning. What in the world would they be wanting with them? Those poor souls have nothing."

Devlin was awake by then and Annie changed the bandage. *The hole's a lot smaller but it's still leaking fluid. Thank the Lord and Boann, there's no infection.*

They quietly had their supper. "I wonder what tomorrow will bring" said Annie.

"I've no idea. I'll bring the other trunk down and you can sort Devlin's things. Myles' clothes will fit either one of us. We can't take everything. We'll give what's left to the neighbours."

Dewain brought out two crates from the workshop. "I'm going up the street to make arrangements for the wagon and then I've got some business to attend to," he said, closing the door behind him.

Devlin was sorting through his clothes. Annie choked back tears while folding Myles' shirts. "I still can't believe he's gone," she said in a whisper.

"Neither can I" said Devlin. "I lost my musket out there. Good thing we've got Da's. We'll need that for hunting once we get across the bay."

They spent the morning deciding what to take and stacked the rest against the wall. She packed blankets and quilts into the crate, but took the crucifixes and put them in the trunk with her dresses.

That's a sturdier trunk, waterproof too. I've done this in my mind for months but now it's so hard to part with things. I'll be needing my pot, the dishes and mugs, cutlery, the oil lamps and the candles.

It was mid-afternoon before Dewain returned. He looked tired and despondent.

"Well Da, did you get the wagon arranged?"

"I did. Old James is coming early Friday and we'll load everything up. I've spent the rest of my day across the street with the Limerick lot. I've sold them the house. Didn't get anywhere near what it's worth, but it's enough to pay Ewan to take us over to Spiddal and some left over," he said. He looked at the open trunks and the piles of oddities stacked along the living room wall. "You've been busy I see. I've got to finish the last crate for the two violins. Once I've done that and got the sawdust out of the way, I've still got to put the final coat of varnish on."

"Dewain, did you find out what's going on with the refugees?" asked Annie.

"That's another tale. The ships in the harbour are owned by some of Stubber's friends, plantation owners in the West Indies. They're taking these people to sell them as slaves – can you believe it? Slaves... It's an abomination. There's a rumour too that they're rounding up the clergy and shipping them as well."

Annie was appalled. *Slaves. Imagine surviving the siege of Limerick, losing their homes, then the plague in Galway only to be transported to be field labour. It defies belief. Every time I think nothing worse could possibly happen, it does.*

Annie fried some blood sausage and potatoes for the evening meal. There was little to say. After supper Dewain played his violin and Devlin sat quietly at the table, seemingly a thousand miles away. More voices were suddenly heard on the street.

"They've got another batch rounded up, just like last night," said Dewain, shaking his head and closing the shutters. "Thank God we're leaving or it would be us next."

❖ ❖ ❖ ❖ ❖ ❖ ❖ ❖ ❖

Friday morning came soon enough and at daybreak, Dewain was on the step looking at the sky. "No cloud this morning and the wind's light from the south. We're good to go." The slow clopping of hooves on the cobblestones announced the arrival of Old James and his horse drawn wagon.

Annie felt sorry for the bony beast, a shadow of its former self, the harness loose and dirty. She watched them load the two trunks and the six wooden crates with help from Harry next door. She looked at the rooms, bare except for the furniture. *This has been my home for ten years. I don't know where we'll live in Spiddal but it has to be safer than here. A new start but I'm leaving a lot behind. This is where I've raised Fiona and Strahan, Devlin and Myles. Both memories and ghosts are here.*

Devlin was sitting on the back of the wagon, looking disgusted. "I'm not much damned use to anyone."

"You can make sure nobody steals anything while we're getting things loaded," Dewain retorted.

Annie carried out a burlap sack loaded with the remnants of flour, onions, potatoes and sausage. In her pocket was the precious vial of St. Brigid's water. *There's a little bit left for him.* She hugged Clara and Amy. "There's clothes and a bit of fish left in the barrel. We can't take the furniture. Help yourselves," she said and climbed up on the wagon seat beside the driver. Dewain swung up beside

her. With a cluck and shake of the reins, Old James urged
the horse forward and the wagon lurched on.

She looked at the street for the last time, the houses
she'd known all her life, the boarded-up stores and the
rooms above with familiar thin faces watching them.
She saw the armed soldiers standing there eyeing them
and she was afraid. Turning she looked back and saw
the neighbours streaming in and out of her house carrying clothes and chairs. The sentries at the Spanish gate
stopped the wagon. Annie's heart was in her mouth.
Dewain bargained with them and reluctantly handed
over the fee they demanded. She watched the expression
on Devlin's face. *'Tis a good thing he's not well enough to
fight or he'd be right into one now.*

The soldiers motioned them on, the sentry pocketing
the coins, smirking and sniggering with muskets ready.
She overheard one say: "Good riddance, get these damn
Papists out of here" and spit on the cobbles.

Dewain slid off the wagon seat and helped Annie down,
muttering something under his breath, his face red with
anger. Annie pretended not to have heard it and couldn't
look at either of them.

Dewain and Old James unloaded the boxes and stacked
them on the dock. The musket was wrapped in a blanket
out of sight. Dewain slipped him some coin and they
shook hands. She watched the wagon slowly disappear

through the gate back up the street then sat on the crates and waited.

"I can see a hooker coming our way" said Devlin. "That must be Ewan." The brown sailed boat looked tiny, cutting through the waves from the Claddagh's village. "I hope he's got room for all this."

There was a commotion at the far end of the pier where the two ships were quietly at anchor, riding the early morning swells. A troupe of soldiers were prodding and shoving a group of men up the gangplank.

Dewain stood up, staring. "Look, they've got the deacons and Father Thomas in chains. I see a couple of the priests from across the street too. They're shipping them with the slaves!"

Devlin swore. Startled Annie, looked in horror at the figure of Father Thomas. *It's hard to believe it's him. The cassock's filthy; there's blood on it too. They've chained his hands and his feet. I can see the bruises all over him from here. He's so weak he can barely walk, all hunched over. What have they done to him?*

She heard Devlin call out. The small black boat was closer now and she could see the two men. *The younger one must be Ewan.* She recognized the other man as Padraigh. Looking back at the three-master, there was no sign of the priests on deck and the soldiers where heading back to the fort. Ewan took down the sail, bringing the boat alongside the dock with practised ease. Devlin looked pleased to see his friend and tied off the boat to the nearest cleat. She watched the men carefully load their belongings into the boat, with Ewan watching the weight and placement of each crate. Finally, they were done.

Ewan offered her his hand. "Now Mrs Morris, it's your turn. Don't be afraid, I've got you" he said, gently holding her as she stepped down. The boat rocked and she froze. "First time on a boat, I'm thinking. Keep your feet apart and wait for the wave to settle. That's it. Now sit right here in front of the mast while I get these men of yours on board."

Annie watched him. Dewain was not much better than she'd been but was soon sitting beside her. Ewan said to Devlin: "Your turn, mate." *He knows better than to offer his friend a hand.* Devlin was awkward as he climbed down into the gently rocking boat, tossing his cane onto the deck. Padraigh raised the sail and Ewan pushed the boat away from the dock.

Annie watched Galway slowly recede as they went into open water. *Thank God, he's not going too far out.* She clung to Dewain and braced her legs against the rolling of the boat. As the wind filled the sail she felt the boat start to slice through the water. *The sides of the boat are only a foot or so above the waves. I hope we don't sink.* She watched the Claddagh's village glide by. The heavily wooded hills sprinkled with new shades of green rose higher and higher. The shoreline was rocky with tiny pebbled beaches, the smoke of hidden houses rising into a blue sky. Small docks and fishing boats at anchor dotted the coves. Red cliffs jutted forth from the headlands and sea torn caves foaming with white water warned of dangerous currents.

Ewan called and pointed out into the Atlantic. "The boat with the white sail out there is my father's. Good day for the fleet to be out." They had been sailing for over an hour, when she could see a break in the trees and the outline of buildings. The wind was light and steady keeping the sail full. White water curled and boiled as they cut through the waves. *I've never been so scared*. The town came closer. Now she could see the individual buildings – shops, cottages, the spire of a church and the stone turret of a big house. *No walls, how strange*.

A knot of people had gathered on the dock. "Dewain, is that your cousin?" she asked.

"Looks like it. Good, my letter did reach him then."

Ewan eased the sail down and came in close to the dock tossing the rope to willing hands. He was the first one out and came to her end of the boat. He slipped down beside her and helped her to her feet. "You did well, Missus," he said supporting her elbow as she climbed back onto dry land.

Padraigh and Ewan quickly off loaded the boxes. Annie took Ewan by the hand and looked up at his windburned young face. "I've much to thank you for Ewan. You've been a good friend to all of us and saved us from whatever hell is happening in Galway. Tell your mother that the medicines worked. He's not fully recovered yet but he will, if he wants a chance with a certain young woman in your village."

Ewan threw back his head and laughed. "He's a right stubborn cuss when he wants something bad enough."

Dewain had been talking to his family but now broke away and shook Ewan's hand. "My cousin will be taking us in until we can find our own place. I'm immensely grateful to you and your family for all the help you've given us." He pressed two coins into Ewan's hand.

Ewan's look changed to surprise. "I wouldn't have charged you that much, Mr. Morris."

"You've earned it getting us out of there," said Dewain, closing the lad's fingers over the coins. "Annie, we'll give Devlin a few minutes to say goodbye. Come and meet my family." He led her over and started the introductions.

Annie was shy at first but cousin Joseph and his two sons seemed genuinely friendly. She glanced over at Devlin but he was in deep conversation with Ewan. Ewan untied the boat, jumped in and with a final wave pulled away. Devlin hesitated for a moment then limped towards them. The younger boy brought the pony cart and they loaded the trunks and boxes.

"Be careful with that box," said Dewain. "My violins are in that one."

"We just live up the street off the main road," said Joseph. "It's a five-minute walk. Will you be alright with that, Devlin?"

"Aye, if I take my time, I'll be fine," he said and together they walked along the main street with its pubs and small shops towards the two-storey house up a side road set in a stone fenced yard. She could see the spire of a small church over the next block of houses.

Annie couldn't believe it. *Everyone looks so clean and healthy, so normal. Children are playing in the streets. Everyone's going about their business. You'd never know there was a war on.* As they entered the house, cousin Joseph said "Welcome to our home. We've prepared rooms for you upstairs."

His wife Catherine was a cheerful, plump, middle-aged woman bustling around in her domain. "My Lord, Annie, what a terrible time you've been through. Come in, come in. We've got a meal laid on for you. You look like you need a good feed." The smell of fresh baked bread and a rich beef aroma filled the whole house. The boys were carrying their boxes upstairs.

Annie looked down at their hands, Catherine's chubby soft white ones encasing her own bony, callused, chapped ones. *I must look like a refugee.* "Here Catherine, this is the last of the food we had," and handed her the burlap sack.

Catherine took her offering and passed it to one of the two girls who were obviously her daughters. "Morna, take this to the kitchen. Noreen's got the water on so you can freshen up, Annie."

Joseph was busy uncorking the whiskey bottle. Devlin and Dewain were standing there in their threadbare clothing looking as stunned as she felt. *No shutters, no bars on the doors. It's all so bright and clean.*

Later, as they all sat down for the meal, Joseph lead the prayer of thanks for bountiful food on the table. *I'll give a hearty Amen to that.* Annie looked around at the noisy chattering crowd to see Devlin engaged in a lively conversation with his two girl cousins. *I haven't seen him smile like that in a long time.* Joseph and Dewain were talking about Joseph's local shop that sold household goods. The boys, Ross and Owen, sat either side of her and were full of questions about Galway.

After the meal, it was Dewain who unpacked his violin and strains of happy music filled the house. *Ah, just listen to it, those jigs make me want to dance, not that sad, dreary music he's played since Strahan and Fiona left. We're safe.*

Present day, Spiddal

Michael O'Connor pulled the car into the hotel parking lot. "That didn't take long did it? From Dublin to here in less than six hours," he said, looking at Ailanna beside him.

"Michael, look at the view," she said gazing at the expanse of water, numerous coves and tiny pebble beaches as far as the eye could see. The hazy smudge of the Aran Islands lay further out. "The play of colour in those blues is stunning in this light. I'd like to paint that. I'm so glad you decided to come. You can do your own exploring while I'm taking my Gaelic course for the next two weeks. I've come here for the last five years. I don't want to lose the language. Most of my family are fluent but they're getting on and the younger ones don't bother." She looked at him, loving the young man with the dark tousled hair, blue eyes, beguiling smile and a lithe wiry body.

"My mother wants me to hunt down family history while I'm here. Gran's mother was a Morris. There's a story of a Morris being a violin maker back in the mid 1600s, in Galway, she thinks, and somehow there's a Claddagh connection. Granny Gran's got a Claddagh ring. It's been passed down for generations. It'll not be easy to trace. All the parish records were burned during the siege."

"Well, I can ask my Gaeltach friends if any one's heard of them or at least they might know where you could find out. Where are we going to eat tonight?"

"We can try one of the pubs. It's Saturday night and I've got my violin in the car."

The pub was lively. After a hearty meal of fresh salmon and Guinness, they sat back and listened to the music. "I know some of the songs but not all of them; I'll have a chat with the musicians when they take a break; see if I can join them," he said.

Ailanna happily chatted with the people at the next table. Her fluent Gaelic soon had others joining in. "Tell me, Michael, how are you going to go about finding your ancestors?" she asked.

"I think I'll start with the oldest church in town and see if there are any records; births, burials. Other options might be the local genealogy society or even the town hall for land records. Maybe you could ask your friends if they have any Morris roots," he said admiring her dark brown curly hair and brown eyes. *I get lost every time I look in her eyes.*

The musicians paused for a short break and Michael took the opportunity to speak with them. Ailanna smiled to herself as he gave the thumbs up sign and went to the car for his violin. She sat back and watched him with the others. He played the tunes he knew, fitting in seamlessly with the two local men and sat out the ones he didn't. His attention was fully on the music. The bodhran drum and button accordion rhythms kept the pace lively. *If I stick with him, I can see I'm going to play second fiddle to a fiddle. My passion's language and his is music.*

When the session finished, Michael waved her over. "Ailanna, could you please explain to Mr. Flynn what I'm looking for? As you know well, my Gaelic's limited to road signs at the moment."

She introduced herself and explained Michael's mission to the eighty plus gentleman sitting there cradling his violin on his knee. The man nodded, thought for a few moments, then gave a rapid set of instructions totally unintelligible to Michael. Ailanna grabbed a pen from her purse and frantically scribbled the information on a napkin. Michael, meanwhile, ordered a round for everyone.

"There you are," she said triumphantly, handing him the napkin. "I'll rewrite my scribble when we get back to the hotel. He does remember the mention of a Morris violin, but it was years ago when he was a boy. He suggests the museum as they have some old instruments and a Morris used to own a house four streets over, but it's only a ruin now."

He gave her a hug. "My Lord, I'd never have got that information myself. You're worth your weight in gold!"

The next day Ailanna was off to her class by 8:30 and Michael walked down the side road to the ruins. *There's little but the foundation left and it's badly overgrown.* He took some photos and walked back to the main street looking for either the museum or the town hall. He found the museum first. There were old black and white photos of an earlier Spiddal, the women in long skirts and shawls, the men in tweeds and practical leather boots. *There are views of thatched cottages, the picture's dated 1895 but the cottages were over 300 years old then.* There were pictures of pubs, the butcher shop and hooker boats. A handcrafted curragh boat, wooden and tin tools completed the collection but at the far end was a glass cabinet containing several violins, a tin flute and an old lyre.

A voice came over his shoulder. "May I help you with anything?"

He turned to see an older woman. "I'm trying to track down one of my ancestors. He was a Morris and he made violins. Would you know anything about that?"

She pondered the question for a few moments, her eyebrows knotted in thought. "There were Morrises here but it was early on, maybe late 1600s, early 1700s. I'd have to look it up, but I think they ran the general store. Are you in town long?"

"Two weeks while my friend is on her Gaeltacht course, then I'm back to work in Dublin. We're staying at the hotel, so I can leave you my name and number. I'd be grateful if you could tell me anything at all about the Morrises. My mother's done the genealogy bit and has run out of leads. How old is the violin you have on display?"

"That one was made in the early 1800s in Dublin, so it'd not be the right one for your man. It will take me some time. We've got a lot of old things in storage."

Michael filled out an information card and handed it to her. "What does your middle initial C stand for?" she asked.

"Oh, that's Carrick. That's a family name too somewhere down the line."

"You might have better luck in Galway. Carrick was one of the old Claddagh names way back when. If the man you're looking for made violins, he'd have been more likely over there to get the wood he'd need by trading with the French and Spanish."

"I never even thought of that angle. Thanks so much," he said. His next stop was the old Catholic church, a small stone building on the back street. He walked around the graveyard looking at the stones and in the back corner found ones so old the names and dates had worn away. He ran his hands over one small stone, black with age topped with what might have been an angel carrying something that could have been a musical instrument. With his eyes closed, he ran his fingers over the surface searching for shapes. *It doesn't feel like a harp. A violin? I'll have to come back on Sunday and ask the priest.*

After a pub lunch, he headed to the genealogy centre and spent the afternoon comparing his mother's chart to the information they had. Back at the hotel, he spread out the stack of paper he had collected and scratched his head.

Ailanna came bouncing in around 4:30. "Well, how did your day go?" she said giving him a hug.

"I've been to the old church, the museum and the genealogy centre. Morrises did exist here but the details are sketchy. On Sunday, I'll be going to church to see the priest. That is the original church. The lady at the museum suggested a violin-maker would have been in Galway, since he'd need foreign woods and he could only get that from the trading ships. I may have to go into Galway. How was your day?"

"Just grand. We spent the day going over some of some old books and poems. Life was really hard in those days. By the way, Julia Spencer does have ancestors who were Morrises. She's going to look up her family tree and see what she can find out for you."

The next day was gray and it poured rain. He decided to spend the morning compiling the information he had gathered so far. He got out his laptop and typed away. *I'm getting a vague picture here of a family who ran the general store but were gone by the mid 1700s. The Morrises were one of the fourteen tribes of Galway, with Spiddal as their rural seat. Many records up to 1650 were destroyed in the siege. Where did they go? The last ancestor on Ma's chart is Henry Carrick Morris, living in Moycullen, up north of here in the peat bogs. I must get my name from him.*

The ringing of the phone startled Michael out of his pondering. "Hello?"

"Mr. O'Connor?" asked a vaguely familiar female voice.

"Yes, this is Michael."

"This is Mrs. Finnigan from the museum. I've found something you're going to be interested in. Can you come down? I'm here 'til 4:30."

"I'm on my way," he said, her excitement coming through the phone lines. Snatching his umbrella and his camera, he almost ran out the door and was buffeted by the wind as he headed along main street. Within ten minutes he opened the museum doors and launched himself inside, dripping wet.

"Wipe your feet on the mat. We do try to keep these old wooden floors in good condition. You can hang your coat and umbrella on the hook," she said primly.

I'd better do as I'm told. "What did you find?" he said as she offered him a seat at the long oak table. She reappeared from her office carrying a small wooden box no bigger than two feet square and four inches deep. She placed it carefully on the table. She donned a pair of cotton gloves and handed him a pair.

Gently opening the lid, she slid the box over to him and he peered inside. The box was stained and dusty, but whatever was inside was wrapped in a gossamer fine woven cloth of undyed wool with hand sewn binding. The violin lay in pieces, the ribs broken but the belly, back and scrolled neck undamaged. What drew his attention was a small square of delicate paper glued to the lower portion of the back. His fingers trembled as he repositioned the box. The spidery handwriting had faded but it clearly read: "D. Morris, Galway, 1652."

"This has been tucked away in storage because it was broken. Someone cared, look how it was wrapped. That's home spun, woven wool." she said. "The index card is so old I can barely read it. I remember when I was a small child, my father used to take me to estate auctions. A lot of the old cottages were empty in those days, sickness and such..."

"Is there a local newspaper here?" Michael asked.

"Yes, why?"

"Because, my dear Mrs. Finnigan, this could be the oldest violin ever made in Ireland and broken as it is, it's newsworthy."

She scurried to her office and he heard her talking on the phone. He very gently picked up the neck. *It's ebony, I'm sure of it.* After taking pictures from every angle including close-ups of the label, he turned the back over. *Oh, look at the graining – it's tiger striped and the colour's out of this world. What kind of wood is this and what varnish did he use?* Very gently he placed it back in the box. He sat there mesmerized, willing the pieces to speak to him.

Within twenty minutes, people started arriving. First it was the mayor, then a reporter. Michael sat back and watched. Mrs. Finnigan artistically arranged the pieces on the woolen cloth and photographs were taken. She stood beside the table protecting her now prized exhibit. The reporter interviewed him and took his picture standing beside the violin. "If anyone local has any knowledge of the Morris clan, they can reach me at my e-mail address," Michael said, giving him the information. *All this publicity could make my search a lot easier. Won't Ma be excited!*

"You're going to need a special display case for that. A conservator might be able to repair it."

"You're right, I hadn't even thought that far ahead. This is a bit overwhelming. Just think, it's been sitting in storage and we didn't know what we had," she said. "I think I need to talk to the Mayor. It might be a good idea for us to re-catalogue the whole lot. Who knows what else is down there? There must be hundreds of items on the shelves" she said.

"I'll be going now, but please keep in touch if anything else comes up," he said.

The rest of the week was like being in the eye of a hurricane. *The story from the local paper has gone national. I've even had an e-mail from a music professor in Edinburgh. He thinks there's a connection to a violin in the Barcelona music museum. Mrs Finnigan has had more people through*

the museum this week than all of last month. I'm starting to
get people sending me their family tree. I'll pass all that to Ma.

Sunday found Michael and Ailanna sitting in the back
pew of the small stone church. It was a traditional service
and after all the week's excitement, it seemed a breath
of calm to sit and listen to the sermon. After the service
when the last of the parishioners had left, Michael introduced himself to the priest.

"I'm Michael O'Connor and I'm looking for records
on the Morris family. I wonder if any of them are buried
here," he said. "It's a D. Morris I'm particularly interested
in finding."

"Ah, so you're the one in the news. I was thinking
you might come here, so I started going through some
of the old parish registers. There are Morrises buried
here – going back to Joseph and Catherine Morris from
that time period. Joseph died in 1667 and Catherine in
1673. That's the large stone in the back corner. You'll not
see much as the stones have eroded," he said leading them
to where Michael had been looking earlier in the week.

"What about that smaller one beside it?"

"Would probably be related but I don't know yet"
Father replied.

"You've been very quiet tonight," said Ailanna as they sat savouring the beef pot pie in the hotel's restaurant. "What are you thinking?"

"This is becoming a much bigger project than I anticipated. I think I need to talk to Ma and get some professional researchers involved. Finding that violin was pure luck. Tracking back 350 years isn't going to be feasible with my work schedule once I'm back in Dublin, especially as this story seems to have taken on a life of its own."

"Well, if there is a Claddagh connection and if it started with D. Morris, then the only explanation is that he had a son who married a Claddagh girl and the male line continued to the time of your Henry Carrick Morris in Moycullen," she said sipping her wine.

He looked at her for a moment over the foam of his Guinness. "You've thought this through more than I have. I've got caught up in the details. Ailanna, I can't explain the feeling I got when I picked up that violin. A lot of emotion went into the making of it and I almost felt it trying to speak to me. I'm very interested in what the museum will do with it. I doubt it can be repaired. Do you think there's room for one more person in your Gaelic class next year? Seems to me if I want to see more of you, then I need to learn the language."

"I think that could be arranged. Anyway, let's leave the research to the pros and let's enjoy our holiday. We haven't been to Galway or the Aran Islands yet. It's time to play tourist and just enjoy the sights. I think you'd get more out of this part of Ireland if you knew the language."

Six months later, Michael received another piece of the puzzle. He immediately phoned Ailanna. "I got an e-mail today from the Scottish professor. The violin in the Barcelona Museum was signed by an S. Morris, dated 1653. That would tie in with what the researcher found with that Dewain Morris family. It's too bad they only list the wife as "daughter of …." Their youngest son Strahan was born in Galway but there's no mention of Strahan or the daughter Fiona after the siege."

"Maybe they sent them to Spain. A lot of the rich left before the siege. 1653 means Strahan got to Spain and made that violin. If your theory's right, then it was either Devlin or Myles who would have married the Claddagh girl" she said. "It's too bad you can't date the Claddagh ring your Gran's got."

"A couple of other things have come up too. Mrs. Finnigan from the museum sent a picture of the new violin display. They've done a really clever job of mounting the parts on three plexiglass shelves with the pieces suspended above each other. They did get the ribs repaired. You can see the label and all the graining. They also found a box of tools – gouges, clamps and horse hair. Don't know if it's Dewain's or not but it looks fabulous. I'll e-mail it to you. Are you doing anything Friday night? I'm going the pub for a session."

"I'd love to come," she said, wondering if there were music genes or merely phantoms of the past.

Friday, he found her waiting for him at the pub and she'd managed to get a table. She waved him over. "Traffic was better than usual and I got here early," she said. "What's going on? You've got a grin like the Cheshire Cat."

"I had a call from Mum. She's been flooded with genealogy stuff for the last six months but some really significant information has come in and she's over the moon. I'm going over to see her tomorrow. Do you want to come with me?"

"Sure, I don't have anything planned tomorrow except for grocery shopping. I'll stay over and we'll go together. It's been a while since we've seen her. What's she found?"

Michael grabbed his beer and took a satisfying sip. "Ahh, that hits the spot. So, you're staying over are you?" he said with a mocking leer, slipping his arm around her and giving her a quick kiss.

"She heard back from the priest in Spiddal. That old grave stone with the angel was for Annie Morris, Dewain's wife. She died in 1878. He didn't find any record of Dewain being buried there."

"Do you notice that when you get more information, inevitably it just leads to another question? Like where is Dewain buried?" she said.

Michael paused. "Well, we know Joseph and his wife died before Annie. Maybe Dewain went back to Galway to live with his son. Who knows?" he said. The rest of the evening was spent chatting and sharing the music.

Michael awoke early with the pleasant sensation of Ailanna's body snuggled up against him.

She's so beautiful. Looks like an angel sleeping like that. I'm one lucky man. I'm going to propose soon. I'm just waiting for the right moment. I've got a Claddagh ring for her that matches the one Gran gave me.

He carefully slipped out of bed and padded barefoot to the bathroom. When he came out he was shocked to see her sitting at the side of the bed, the night table drawer open, and the blue velvet box in her hand. He sat down beside her. She looked at him with a guilty expression on her face.

"I was looking for a Kleenex..."

"I was waiting for a special evening to ask you, but you've found me out. So, now it is." He slipped Gran's ring on his left ring finger. "Ailanna, a chuisle mo chroisie (Gaelic for sweetheart), I'm asking you to be my wife," he said, taking her ring out the box, gently offering it to her. He was suddenly lost for words and he held his breath.

There was a long moment of silence when both of them gazed at each other. She took her ring and placed it on her finger, looking at the old silver one on his hand, the interlocking silver hearts turned towards his heart. "Oh Michael, the answer is yes."

He exhaled and hugged her in a moment of pure joy.

They were late getting to his mother's house.

Mrs. O'Connor took one look at them when she opened the door and knew. "Alright you two, what have you been up to?"

They both held up their rings and grabbed her for a group hug. She held them at arm's length and looked at them, bright tears in her eyes. "I'm so pleased for you. Here I am, crying like an old fool. Michael, I wish your father was still alive. He'd have been just delighted. Ailanna, have you told your mother yet?"

Ailanna's face was just glowing. "He just proposed this morning. I tried to get her earlier but it went to voice mail. I'll try again now," she said rummaging in her purse for her phone.

"I'll put on the kettle for tea while you're making your call," said Mrs. O'Connor headed for the kitchen.

Michael looked around the living room in amazement. There were stacks of paper everywhere.

"I can't believe you've got all this mail. You said you had some new information. I didn't realize just how much you had. Where are you at with it now?"

"I've got a lot of new leads, mostly generated by that newspaper article on the violin. People are sending me stuff every day. I haven't even been through half of it yet but the most informative ones are these. There's a connection to the Lynch family."

"Weren't they one of the Tribes of Galway?" asked Michael.

"You're right. They were a very influential family of merchants. They were titled and owned castles and mansions and were quite prominent during the siege of Galway, contemporaries of Dewain Morris. They were eventually stripped of their property after Galway fell to the Cromwellians and they ended up with property north of Lake Corrib near Lake Mask. Listen to this," she said picking up a letter. "This is from a man named Peter Kelly."

My family tree includes members of the Lynch family who owned Lynch Castle in Galway at the time of the siege. It was rumoured that some of the Lynch sons were sent to Spain to escape the blockade. Narratives handed down through the generations describe correspondence between the Spanish Lynchs and the Irish ones, mentioning a marriage of the youngest son to a Galway girl whose father made violins. That would have been back in the late 1600s. There is no correspondence surviving in my family's possession now, as far as I know. I've never tried to track the Lynchs back to that time.

"That could tie in with Dewain's son Strahan and the daughter Fiona and with the violin in the Barcelona museum, too."

"There's more information on Henry Carrick Morris too," said his Mum going through another pile of papers. "Ah, here it is. This is from a Ewan Browne. He's head of the genealogy society in Moycullen."

Henry Carrick Morris of Moycullen was an ancestor on my mother's side of the family. From conversations I had over the years with my mother and my grandmother, I have learned he was a local innkeeper and is buried at the St. James cemetery in Moycullen. I remember hearing as a child, he came from a long line of Morris men who worked the peat bogs and supplied both Galway and the

Claddagh village over a period of a hundred
years. The Carrick in his name goes back
to an early Claddagh king whose daughter
married a Morris. It was unusual at the time
for a Claddagh woman to marry outside the
clan. Henry had a brother whose middle
name was Devlin, and that name too occurs
frequently in the family. There is a very strong
musical talent in our family. Don't know if
this information is helpful, but it might point
you in the right direction. Good luck.

"Mum, if he's right about the names, it looks like it
was Devlin Morris who married the Claddagh girl," said
Michael. "We still don't know what happened to Miles.
There's no trace of him after the siege."

Turning to Ailanna, he said "When we do down to
Spiddall for our Gaelic course next summer, I'm going
to start in the Claddagh village and work my way up to
Moycullen. I'll check every church and cemetery for signs
of Dewain and Devlin Morris or any of the Morris clan.
There must be a record somewhere of the Carrick who
was king at the time of the siege. Once I have his last
name it will be much easier to search for relatives. The
hunt is on. It might be a good idea for me to talk to Ewan
Browne in person."

"Maybe Moycullen would be a good place for a traditional Claddagh wedding in the county where all this began," suggested his mother, looking at her son and future daughter-in-law.

Ailaan laughed. "If there's one thing I know about Michael, he'll have his violin in the back of the car. That's tradition too."